SEAN BYRNE

PATRICK *and the* HOLY GRAIL

By the same author:

The Tragic History of Esoteric Christianity (non-fiction)

Gnosis! (fiction)

Poems for the Path (verse)

~~www.seanbyrne.net~~

SEAN BYRNE

PATRICK *and the* HOLY GRAIL

PUBLISHED BY AGE-OLD BOOKS, NORTHERN IRELAND

ISBN: 978-0-9540255-4-0

Cover design by Ray Lipscombe

www.seanbyrne.net

Contents

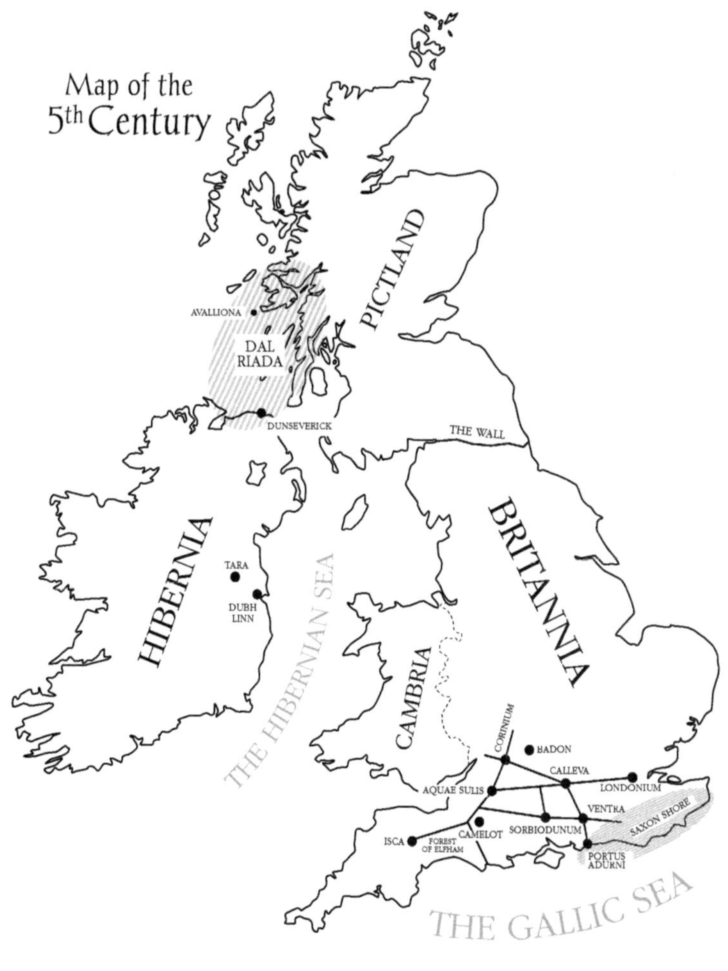

Map of the 5th Century
PICTLAND
AVALLIONA
DAL RIADA
DUNSEVERICK
THE WALL
HIBERNIA
TARA
DUBH LINN
THE HIBERNIAN SEA
BRITANNIA
CAMBRIA
CORINIUM
BADON
CALLEVA
LONDONIUM
AQUAE SULIS
VENTRA
SAXON SHORE
CAMELOT
SORBIODUNUM
ISCA
FOREST OF ELFHAM
PORTUS ADURNI
THE GALLIC SEA

'IN DREAMS BEGINS RESPONSIBILITY'

(W.B.YEATS)

AUTHOR'S FOREWORD

The following story is set in approximately the 5th century AD and is based on historical characters and facts. The most pertinent of these facts was the Roman's hatred of the Druids.

In Britannia, for centuries after their arrival there, the Romans steadfastly oppressed and persecuted this ancient Brotherhood. For the Druids had magical power over the people, and the Romans deeply resented that power. The Roman's policy in Britannia therefore was the one they had long and successfully used in Gaul: to eliminate the Druids altogether as a force in society.

Thus, as Roman civilization, with its towns and cities, its gods and laws, and most of all its 'creature comforts' expanded in Britannia, the Druids, and all their ancient, mysterious ways, contracted.

The Roman way of life however was always confined more or less to the lowlands. In the western hills and northern highlands a remnant of the old ways inevitably survived.

It was a totally different situation in nearby Hibernia! There the Romans never went and the Druids remained very powerful. They had long regarded Rome as a many-headed beast and were therefore very glad when the beast finally left their doorstep, which occurred in the 5th century AD. However, with the withdrawal of the imperial army, Britannia itself became a kind of wasteland. Then out of the wasteland a new and very different species of beast arose for the Druids, one that in time became for them even more powerful than Rome.

This 'beast' too had many heads, but only one name, and that was Jesus Christ.

PROLOGUE

What a weird county! The sky pure black and a rainbow in it!

He gazed, and the more he gazed, the more iridescent the rainbow became. Then from it something separated and fell towards him. Strangely, he was not afraid.

At first the thing spun rapidly, but as it drew closer the spinning slowed. He could see then that it was a flat, white, rectangular stone. Soon it came to a standstill directly above him and he saw a spiral neatly incised on its base. He reached out, but the moment he touched the stone it fell on him and he awoke shouting 'Helios! Helios!'

Patrick sat up, rubbed his eyes and looked around. He was relieved to find himself still in his little shepherd's hut on the hillside. After dreamily muttering 'Helios' a few more times he eventually asked himself, 'But what can it all mean?'

Patrick got up, pulled on his tattered trews and tunic and opened the door of his hut. It was a fine summer's morning.

The sun was rising above the green foothills to the east of Slemish Mountain on which he tended his master's sheep.

Patrick was a young slave. A few years previously he had been abducted by a Hibernian pirate from his Christian home in Cambria and with many others taken to Hibernia and sold as a slave. A Druid named Miliuc bought him.

Miliuc was a lonely but kindly old man who liked Patrick and treated him as his own son. He taught him the language of the natives, and instructed him in the ancient customs and ways of the countryside and its various tribes and clans.

Miliuc lived in a small but comfortable wattle house - comfortable, that is, compared to Patrick's ramshackle hut - near the bottom of Slemish Mountain which he owned. And although Patrick had nothing to report after counting the sheep this day, in the evening he made his way down the mountainside to Miliuc's house, for he felt compelled to tell his master of his strange dream.

Patrick found Miliuc fishing on a mossy bank of the broad, black river that flowed rapidly passed his house. He was in the throes of landing a fish. It was a mighty struggle, for Miliuc's small, stooped body seemed no match for the fish!

It must be a very big one, Patrick thought.

Patrick approached stealthily. He had witnessed similar scenes before and knew that the golden rule was silence. But this tussle seemed much more fraught than usual. For Miliuc was puffing, sweating and yes, even cursing! Patrick got ready to rescue Miliuc, for he feared he was in grave danger of being pulled into the river by the fish! But just as this seemed about to happen the fishing line snapped and Miliuc fell back in a heap onto the grass.

'Master!' Patrick cried, running.

Stooping over the old man he asked, 'Are you hurt?'

Miliuc smiled at the sight of Patrick. Then he sighed heavily.

'It was Finnius', he said sorrowfully, raising himself. 'I'm certain of it.'

'Finnius?' Patrick queried, putting his hand under Miliuc's arm.

'I've seen him up at the weir several times,' Miliuc informed. 'He's one of the biggest salmon in the whole river! Oh, but I'll get him yet!'

'You nearly had him, master.'

When Miliuc was steady on his feet he irritably examined the broken line swinging at the end of his old oaken rod.

'Damn this stuff!' he growled. 'MacManus the cobbler sold it to me. He said I could take a bloody whale with it! Whale me backside!'

'You need bear gut, master,' Patrick ventured. 'The Romans use it.'

'Mmmm.......What brings you here, boy? Not bad news, I hope?'

Patrick was suddenly embarrassed. He could not tell his dream under these circumstances.

'N.....no, master,' he stuttered. 'No bad news. But.....but I was thinking....I thought you should know.........'

'Know what boy?'

'That.....that......'

'Bah!' Miliuc declared. 'I understand, boy. You were lonely. That's it, isn't it? Be honest now. You just wanted a wee bit of company. A week on your own up there can be a long time.' He put his arm around Patrick. 'Come up to my house, lad. I'll make you a nice meal. How's that? On an evening like this those damn sheep can look after themselves, eh?'

A cake of sweetbread was baking on an iron pan suspended over the open fire in Miliuc's smoky little house. Immediately upon entering the house Miliuc took a knife from his belt and plunged it deep into the cake. After a moment he withdrew the knife and examined it carefully.

'Done,' he proudly announced.

Then he deftly removed the cake from the pan with a wooden spatula and placed it piping hot on the table opposite Patrick who sat hungrily watching. Miliuc then cut a big slice of the cake with his knife, covered it with thick yellow butter, and together with a beaker of sweet mead placed it directly in front of Patrick.

'Eat, boy!' he commanded.

Patrick greedily devoured his unexpected meal. Nothing ever tasted better than Miliuc's bread!

Miliuc sat on a stool by the fire and studied Patrick. When Patrick finished eating Miliuc said, 'You do have something on your mind, boy. I can see it.'

Patrick drained his beaker and after wiping his mouth enthusiastically declared, 'I had a dream, master!'

Miliuc laughed. 'What! Another one! By the gods, but aren't you the quare one for the dreaming, eh? Anyway, out with it.'

Patrick told Miliuc every detail of his dream. And as Miliuc listened, a look of astonishment came over his old, wrinkled face. For the boy was describing in detail none other than the Stone of Destiny, one of the *Four Treasures of Hibernia*! No ordinary person ever saw these *Treasures*, only Druids and kings in initiation ceremonies. But if seen in a dream it meant the dreamer had a very special destiny. This boy, Miliuc concluded, whom he had bought for a pittance in the slave market, might be useful in more ways than one.

'Helios, you say?' he questioned Patrick.

'Yes, master,' Patrick replied. 'That's what I kept on saying. What does it mean?'

'Helios is Greek, boy. The name of the sun god.'

'Mother says Jesus is the sun god.'

'Huh. Does she now?'

Miliuc jumped up and fetched his staff.

'Kneel down, boy, quickly!' he commanded.

Patrick obediently knelt down. Miliuc then stretched his staff over Patrick and uttered a long incantation. When he finished he touched Patrick's head with the staff and said, 'Tell me every dream you have from now on, boy. Leave nothing out. You understand? Nothing.'

'Yes, master. I will,' Patrick said.

Before getting into bed every night in his lonely little hut on the mountainside Patrick usually prayed to Jesus, as his mother had taught him at home in Cambria; but this particular night he prayed long and hard to Helios, the god of the sun.

CHAPTER ONE

THE WASTELAND

Merlin couldn't sleep. Something was eating him. He got up, left his little hut in the Forest of Elfham where he lived alone with his big white cat, Ariel, and his faithful donkey, Caliban, and rambled about all night in the forest. Every so often he stopped and listened intensely to the trees or touched them with his fingertips, always sniffing the fingers afterwards.

It was midsummer, and the forest brought his old bones back to life.

Just before sunrise he came to one of his power spots. It was under an ancient thorn by a placid lake at the edge of the forest. He sat down heavily, and gazing out meditatively over the lake started sucking his three remaining teeth, one of which, he painfully noted, was looser than yesterday.

The lake was perfectly still. The morning was fine, and the few stars still in the sky were reflected here and there in the deep, dark water.

Of all Merlin's power spots - and he had many - he liked this one best. It had a very friendly spirit.

A sudden breeze began to caress his long, wispy beard. He paid no attention. But then the breeze got more insistent and began to shake the thorn vigorously. He still paid no attention. But when a bone-dry leaf twirled down from a branch above him and balanced auspiciously on the pointed toe of his left boot he studied it intensely with a twinkle in his eye.

Merlin was a seer, a hierophant and a polyglot. He had a mythical, magical consciousness with which he could do all kinds of fantastic things. He could, for instance, with one magic word go out of his thin, stooped body and let this little leaf take him away on a journey. But *where* would it take him was the question? For lately he was having visions of a monstrous serpent that frightened the hell out of him!

Merlin had seen many strange creatures in his day, including serpents. He knew that they were very powerful creatures who should only be evoked magically with great caution, because of their supremely cunning nature. But this one needed no beckoning at all! It came entirely of its own accord, and when it did it would stay around for days, silently stalking the pale borders of his mind. Green at first, its slimy skin always turned black as it ebbed closer. And sometimes its mouth would open so wide that it threatened to devour him. But it never had...........yet!

Merlin shook the leaf from his boot. He was staying put! The breeze vanished.

Merlin then let his gaze fall meditatively upon the calm, reflective surface of the lake before him. He had only been doing this for a few moments however when suddenly the surface of the lake erupted. At first he thought it was some unusually big fish jumping. But it soon became apparent it was a swimmer.

'How the hell did he stay under for so long?' Merlin muttered as he watched the figure swim towards the shore. But once it got there it revealed itself not the strong young man Merlin was expecting, but a totally naked and very lovely girl!

Merlin fell on his side in order not to be seen. He was fascinated, not so much by the girl's nakedness or beauty as by her aura. For rarely had he seen one with such strong and striking colours. When she was fully dressed and he was about to secretly follow her - for he now desperately wanted to know more - he heard an all-too-familiar voice in his head: 'No! Arthur wants you.'

'I know,' Merlin objected, 'but what about *her*?'

'Some other time!'

Disappointed, Merlin watched the girl disappear behind a copse of ash. Sucking his teeth and grumbling he pulled on his broad-brimmed, cone-shaped hat, grabbed his big bog-oak staff and stiffly raised his stooped frame. After tightening his tattered, long grey cloak with a piece of cord he set off again.

A little later, when the great, golden orb of the sun lifted itself majestically above the low distant hills to the east, Merlin quickened his pace, for Camelot was more than three hours away, and Arthur had asked him to be there by breakfast-time!

Arthur was widely regarded as the finest and fairest of the Brittonic warlords. He regularly sought Merlin's advice, and regarded him as his 'right-hand man', for he owed much of his success as a warlord to him. Not only did Merlin pinpoint Camelot as the most auspicious place for Arthur's headquarters, but he also designed the castle there, and personally made for Arthur the beautiful Round Table at which Arthur, with his twelve best men, conducted all the important business of his militia.

'But what the hell does he want today?' Merlin irritably muttered as he trudged along over the fallow fields towards Camelot. 'Probably something to do with Jesus again.' For lately Arthur was asking a lot of questions about this god and his followers.

Mostly confined to the Roman army while it was still in Britannia, nowadays only a sprinkling of the Christian's monkish lower clergy were left. These however were often seen galloping madly about the land on horseback, proselytizing with a big black cross, desperately trying to hold onto whatever power they still possessed by gaining new converts.

Merlin simply hated them and they hated him, but Arthur wanted to know more and more.

After about a mile Merlin stopped and scanned the distant blue hills for a familiar gap. That gap was his direction, the safest way to Arthur, if indeed any way was safe nowadays. For, ever since the army left there had been a steady decline into anarchy. In the past month alone Merlin had seen three villages burnt. Some said it was the painted Picts who regularly swooped down from the north in marauding gangs, plundering everything in sight and quickly disappearing again. Others habitually blamed the Hibernians. They usually came in from the west, over the hills of Cambria, having crossed the narrow sea that divided the two islands, in their little skin-covered coracles. And of course from the south came the worst foes of all, the dreaded Saxons. Merlin himself reckoned that a lot of the ever-increasing carnage was due to in-fighting by local or neighbouring warlords, the most powerful and violent of whom was Mordred.

After traversing another two miles of marshy ground and, despite his much punctured boots, keeping his feet dry, Merlin eventually came to a familiar stile. Crossing this however he stopped suddenly and tugged ponderously on his long wispy beard. For his ranging eye had alighted, from the stile's height, upon a very straight line in the distance to his right. The grey line stretched across the pastoral landscape as cleanly and clearly as if it had been cut with a knife. It was the Roman road that connected the once prosperous towns of Isca with Aquae Sulis, towns which however were now little more than rat-infested ruins, the haunt of thieves, villains and outcasts. The road was part of the once great Fosse Way, in olden times the busiest road in all of Britannia, but nowadays the bailiwick of bandits who lived by robbing its travellers.

As he had to hurry, Merlin was tempted to take the road, for it would prove a good shortcut. After scanning the landscape again and seeing no sign of activity, he mouthed a quick petition to the Great Mother, turned back over the stile and scurried down the long ditch to the road.

Camelot was not visible from it, not with ordinary eyes at any rate. But Merlin's eyes were not ordinary. They could see more and farther. So, when after travelling without incident for about an hour he suddenly turned off the road and once more headed for the distant hills, there was no apparent reason, no obvious landmark that signalled his new direction. But with his seer's eye, Merlin had seen a distant but familiar glow, a shroud of fire-mist that afforded the hill-fort of Arthur's Camelot and its inhabitants a form of protection that was exceedingly rare. It was precisely because of this fire-mist that Merlin had told

Arthur to build his citadel there years ago.

The sun had climbed high by the time the first distinctly physical and very daunting features of Camelot came sharply into view: the darkly glinting, wet granite of the steep, defensive ridges that girded the entire fort and made it virtually impregnable. The mound itself, which was roughly triangular in shape with a broad circling dyke, was capped by Arthur's impressive castle which Merlin had also designed. Its walls embraced most of the mound's plateau, with its main gate on the escarpment to the east. Midway however, along the steep northern ridge and concealed among dense foliage was a little used postern gate. It led into the interior of the mound, which was a matrix of secret underground chambers.

This gate was built primarily as an escape route for Arthur himself, if that ever became necessary. But special people, authorized by Arthur only, were also allowed to use it, and Merlin was not the least of these.

As usual it was very quiet as he approached the narrow drawbridge which had a little watch-hut on its far side. Seeing or hearing nobody, Merlin coughed loudly. But he got no response.

Asleep again, Merlin thought. *Must tell Arthur.*

'Hello there!' he then cried.

Soon he heard shuffling from inside the hut. Then a garrulous demand, 'Password!'

'Ruhtra,' Merlin promptly replied.

A small, fat guard stumbled yawning out of the hut. When he fully opened his eyes he glared at Merlin. 'Oh, you.'

'Sorry for the disturbance,' Merlin said, tongue-in-cheek.

'Humpf.'

The man pulled the pin-lock from the wheel and lowered the narrow, rickety drawbridge. Merlin crossed.

'Not many visitors today,' Merlin mildly mocked as he watched the guard wind the drawbridge up.

Ignoring him, the guard produced from his satchel a huge iron key and opened the narrow gate in the wall. Merlin gazed into the dark interior. The daylight lit only the first few steps.

'Are the torches lit farther in?' Merlin asked.

'You'll find out soon enough,' the guard sourly replied, nodding Merlin through.

Merlin's fears were justified. Damning the unknown page whose job it was to keep the torches ablaze, he irritably picked his way through the dripping under-earth, arriving eventually at his destination more by instinct than sight, for he had done this trip many times. Lifting a trapdoor with his free hand he came up in the floor of the tower at the north end of the courtyard, relieved to find it unoccupied, which meant he didn't have to explain himself to some busybody. For he could in fact come and go as he pleased in Camelot.

Stooping to exit the low door of the tower, he entered the bustling courtyard of the castle.

Used as he was to the solitude of the forest, where he lived in hiding from the Jesus people whom he firmly believed were determined to kill him, the activity of the court always deeply engaged him - the pages running errands, the stable-boys exercising the horses, the swains polishing weapons and armour; the fighting men themselves conversing casually in twos and threes; the ass-and-carts carrying away steaming dung - all the usual comings and goings. But today one thing struck Merlin as most unusual. On a grassy bank, near the main gate, a group of children sat quietly, spellbound by the singing of a thin, ageing man, on whose shoulder was perched a pure white dove.

Who on earth can that be? Merlin wondered. *Must remember to ask Arthur.*

After climbing the stairway to the second floor of the keep he tapped with his staff on the big wooden door that led into Arthur's comfortable apartment. A page answered and took him along a corridor to the living room where, leaving Merlin outside, he entered, and formally announced the visitor's presence.

'Who is it?' Merlin heard Arthur ask.

The boy turned towards Merlin and frowned.

'It's me!' Merlin shouted.

'Aha! That's Merlin, boy. Don't you know *him*?'

The boy blushed.

'Don't worry, boy,' Arthur said from within, 'he's often invisible. Come in Merlin!'

Merlin gently squeezed the boy's shoulder as he scurried back to his post.

Arthur was standing with his back to a blazing fire. His hound, Caleb, was stretched out snoozing at his feet. Arthur had on casual, brightly coloured clothes - a green, hip-length tunic and pale yellow breeches – in the native Brittonic style but of much finer than average fabric. A jewelled belt girded his waist and a silver filigree brooch was pinned to his breast. His black, shoulder-length hair, freshly brushed, shone in the firelight. Kay, Arthur's big-boned, broad-shouldered, chief steward was standing beside him. Rarely out of armour, Kay's sword swung at his hips. They had been engaged in earnest conversation before Merlin's arrival.

'Late again,' Arthur said good-humouredly to Merlin.

'It's a long way on foot,' Merlin said, deadpan.

'Why didn't you come on Caliban, your donkey?'

'Wouldn't budge.'

'What's wrong?'

'Old age, I suppose.'

Kay was fidgeting with his sword. Annoyed at the interruption he also reluctantly realized that Merlin took precedence over him. Aware of Kay's discomfiture, Arthur caught his eye and with a nod conveyed that the conversation could continue, but later. Kay bowed and left. When his heavy footsteps had faded down the stairs Arthur put both his hands on Merlin's bony shoulders.

'Good to see you again, old friend,' he said, looking into Merlin's eyes, 'really good.'

He pulled a wicker chair to the fire. 'Here. Please sit.'

Merlin pulled the chair back. 'I'm tired, Arthur,' he said, 'but not cold.'

'Ah yes, I understand,' Arthur said, 'but we must always keep the fire going. In here, even on the warmest days, it can get unpleasantly cool, especially for Guinevere.'

'And how is the good lady?' Merlin enquired sitting down.

'Slightly indisposed,' Arthur said with a shrug. 'She has taken to her bed, I'm afraid. Just a chill, I think. If you stay around for a few days you might be able to help.'

Smelling his fingers, Merlin hesitantly asked, 'And...is there........ any news?'

The question was euphemistic. Although Arthur and Guinevere had been married for many years, there were still no children.

Arthur shook his head. 'Neither your potions nor my love is enough.....obviously,' he said resignedly. 'Sometimes I think she would sacrifice one of her beautiful limbs in order to have a child. But it's not to be, it seems. The will of the gods..........I suppose.'

'Them,' Merlin sarcastically muttered. (He was thinking

of how he had been married when he was Arthur's age to a beautiful young peasant girl whom the gods had taken from him after a few years of pure bliss, and of how he resolved when he overcame his grief to be celibate, and thereafter always jokingly rhymed to himself that 'his penis was his Venus!')

'What do you want me for?' he eventually asked.

Arthur got up and went to the window.

'Come!' he said.

Merlin joined him. They overlooked the courtyard.

'See him,' Arthur said pointing to the curious, thin man with the dove on his shoulder Merlin had seen earlier. He was still standing in the same place surrounded by the children. 'Know him?'

'No,' Merlin replied, 'but the children seem to like him.'

'Yes, and the dove follows him everywhere!'

Merlin sniffed. 'Who is he?'

'His name is Pelagius. It's a Roman name. But he's actually Hibernian. Young Percival came across him a few days ago on the road between here and Aquae Sulis and rightly decided to find out who this strange person was. Percival actually knows a little Gaelic, the Hibernian language, so he was able to deduce that Pelagius had come to Britannia especially to seek *me* out.'

'You? Why?'

'Well, firstly, Pelagius claims to be some kind of holy man, though we are fairly certain he is not a Druid. Nevertheless he has apparently received some kind of a prophecy and was instructed to come here to Camelot to deliver it personally.'

'Some kind of a prophecy,' Merlin repeated, sucking his teeth. 'Prophecy is a complicated business.'

'Precisely,' Arthur agreed, 'and that's where *you* come in.

You see, we can hardly understand the man at all! But there's no one in the land better at prophesy than your good self, hmm? And perhaps even more to the point, you can speak Gaelic, and quite fluently as I recall.'

Merlin shrugged with mock modesty.

'So,' Arthur went on, 'if you interrogate the fellow you can find out what he's on about.'

'I might,' Merlin said.

'There is however one thing,' Arthur said, 'that we do understand.'

'What's that?'

Arthur spread his hands and beamed. 'Pelagius says that I am to become King of the Britons!'

'King of Logres, eh?' Merlin said sourly.

'Yes.'

'But how many times have I told you that Logres is only a myth?'

'Ah, but there is truth in myths. *You* know that. And it was you who first told me the story of Logres, long ago, when I was a little boy. I've never forgotten it. Merlin, I want to re-establish this ancient kingdom of the Britons. That's my dream.'

'Methinks you dream too much.'

Arthur smiled and put his hand on Merlin's shoulder. 'And so long as I have you to help me, old friend, I will continue to dream.'

'Yes.........but to dream of...........of a harmonious, peaceful kingdom in this..........this godforsaken wasteland. Impossible!'

'Tut, tut,' Arthur chided. 'Impossible is a word that should *not* be in a great magician's vocabulary!'

At this, Merlin suddenly burst out laughing! His laugh was high-pitched, loud and raucous and his whole body shook. He stopped himself only by firmly stamping his staff on the floor. Caleb woke and barked disapprovingly. As Merlin wiped away tears Arthur said quietly, 'Don't *you* have a dream, my friend?'

'Magicians,' Merlin sighed, 'especially old ones, don't have dreams. They only have visions. And I stopped having good ones long ago. And I'll tell you this for nothing: you will need far more than a dream if you are to overcome the likes of Mordred.'

'No one,' Arthur said, 'knows better than I what it's like out there, Merlin. But I am doing something about it, and I intend doing lots more. Thanks to you, here in Camelot I have been able to establish a very secure base. I have a handpicked group of excellent soldiers culled from my fellow Britons who, like myself, were once employed as mercenaries in the Roman army. Unlike Mordred and most of the other warlords, I have a well-trained, experienced and obedient militia. What's more, they all share my dream and even regard me as their lord. And then there's the beautiful Round Table that you, wise old man, made for us and where, also upon your advice, I meet with my twelve best men. All this is central to my plan and I have *you,* Merlin. What *more* do I need to succeed?'

Merlin sniffed his staff. After a while he said, 'Methinks a very special weapon.'

'A dream weapon perhaps?' Arthur suggested with irony. 'I remember you also once told me a wonderful story about a famous sword....What was it called?.....The Clive something?'

'The Claiomh Solais. It's Gaelic. The Sword of Light.'

'That's it! You said whoever had it could banish a whole army in one afternoon! Was that a myth too, Merlin?'

Merlin ran a bony finger thoughtfully along his staff.

'No,' he said at length, 'that wasn't a myth. The Sword is real. But it's owned by the Hibernians.'

'Ah, the Hibernians. I could've guessed.'

'The Sword is one of their *Four Treasures*. Did I ever tell you about *them*?'

'Not that I remember.'

'Well, the story goes that they inherited them from their ancient forebears, the tribe of the Danaans. The Danaans are regarded as gods by the people at large. But the Bards secretly believe that they were magicians, and trained in the Temples of Egypt, no less. Whatever about all that, their *Treasures* are very real. They are genuine talismans capable of channelling the Spirits of the Four Elements. As well as the Sword there is the Spear of Initiation, the Stone of Destiny – known as the Lia Fáil in their language - and the Chalice of Rebirth. The Chalice was apparently stolen - they claim by a Jew! - a few hundred years ago, so they really only have three now. I am quite familiar with the Spear and the Stone, but I've never laid an eye on the Sword of Light.'

Arthur closed his eyes and imagined himself brandishing the powerful weapon.

'The Sword of Light,' he said dreamily.

Merlin looked out the window again.

'Hibernian light,' he muttered slanting his dark eyes on Pelagius.

He concentrated hard on Pelagius now, for he wanted to see his aura. Pelagius's colours however remained opaque. He was too far away. Merlin turned then from the window and once more focussed on bright young Arthur. He said suddenly, 'You shall have the Sword of Light.'

Arthur beamed. 'By the gods, Merlin, but I certainly look forward to *that*! But will you also please speak with this strange man out there for me?'

Merlin nodded.

After sharing a light meal with Arthur, Merlin went out to the courtyard and cautiously approached Pelagius. He was still standing and singing quietly to the same group of enthralled, seated children. Tall and lean, with a complexion fresh for his advanced age, Pelagius had on a long brown cloak. His straight silver hair touched his narrow shoulders. The dove was perched now on his outstretched fist. She flew up onto the castle wall when Merlin approached.

'Pelagius, I believe,' Merlin said in Gaelic, limply extending his bony hand.

'And you must be the famous Merlin!' Pelagius returned slowly in musical tones. 'For who could have a staff as black as that and a cloak with so many shades of grey?'

They shook hands cordially.

Now Merlin could clearly see Pelagius's aura. What pure colours! Pelagius must indeed be a very special person, but special in what way Merlin could not make out.

'Arthur asked me to speak with you,' he said nonchalantly.

'He doesn't understand me!' Pelagius returned, and looking down into the little white sea of adoring faces at his feet added, 'In fact, no one does here except these.'

'Can we talk?' Merlin said.

'With pleasure,' Pelagius said and after bidding 'goodbye' to the children in their own language pointed to the parapet of the castle wall. 'Let's go up there.'

They ascended the steps to the parapet and after walking along it for a while they stopped where no sentries were patrolling. Gazing out over the rolling fields and hills around Camelot, Merlin said quietly, 'You prophesy, I hear.'

Pelagius's dove alighted on the wall beside him. Cryptically he replied, 'I am a Christian.'

Merlin froze! Had he known this he would not have agreed to talk! But before he could say anything else Pelagius presciently continued, 'And fear not. I am not the kind of Christian who wants to kill you.'

'Well, I'm very glad to hear it!' Merlin sarcastically returned. 'And what, pray, kind of Christian might you be then? Aren't you people all the same?'

'No. Without going into details there are essentially two types of Christians these days: Roman Catholics and Pelagians.'

'Then you must be the leader of the Pelagians!'

'Correct. More to the point however, I'm a heretic.'

'So what's that?'

'Years ago I lived and worked in Rome as a Christian teacher. But the Roman clerics didn't like me or my teaching. It was too free-spirited for them.'

'Too Hibernian, eh?' Merlin prodded.

'You could say that. Anyway, they accused me of paganism. They also gave me my cognomen, Pelagius, which means "the strange one from overseas." Then a hugely influential writer and Catholic bishop called Augustine, got involved. He stirred up the Roman clerics against me so much that they hounded me out of their city. I went then to other cities in the Empire and gained many followers. But the Romans feared my teaching and pursued me. They wanted me dead. They still do. That's a heretic!'

Merlin grinned. 'Why have you come here?'

'Arthur can help me. And I can help him. Merlin, listen. Ever since the Emperor Constantine made Christianity legal the Christians have grown in strength. This will only increase. But right now there is a great battle brewing over the truth of the Godman Jesus. Your friend Arthur needs to be on the right side if he is to realize his great dream.'

'Your side, I suppose!'

'Yes.'

'Why?'

Pelagius held out his fist and the dove landed on it. After a ponderous silence he cryptically declared, 'Because I have the Holy Grail.'

'What the hell is that?'

'The Grail is the magic power of Jesus the Christ. That's all I can say.'

Merlin sucked his teeth.

Pelagius shook the dove from his fist. 'Rome must not win this coming battle!' he solemnly declared as he watched the bird soar. 'The future of civilization depends on it. You must tell Arthur all that I have said.'

Merlin gripped his staff.

'And speak to no one except Arthur about the Grail,' Pelagius continued. 'It has many enemies.'

Merlin grunted.

'There's one thing more,' Pelagius said.

'What?'

'In Hibernia there is a secret Temple where the Grail is kept. That is also where I live. You must at some time in the near future seek out this Temple. Finding it will be absolute proof that Arthur is destined for great things.'

'Arthur! What about me?'

'Time alone will tell that. But Arthur will be king.'

A tremor shook Merlin's frail body. He closed his eyes then and in a dark corner of his mind once more caught a glimpse of that monstrous serpent.

Patrick and the Holy Grail

Pelagius returned eventually to Hibernia, but every time Merlin came to Camelot after that the Grail figured prominently in his conversations with Arthur. Arthur was utterly intrigued by it. He sought out books by Pelagius, read them all carefully, but found nothing about the Grail in them. He dearly wanted to know more and urged Merlin to seek out the Temple. But Merlin prevaricated. 'If *you* don't, I will try myself,' Arthur once good-humouredly threatened. 'You'd be wasting your time,' Merlin returned. 'You don't know Gaelic!'

And then, as if somehow mysteriously connected with the Grail, rumours started spreading that dark Mordred, Arthur's arch-enemy, was poisoning the wells.

In a vast area around the ruined hill-fort of Sorbiodunum where Mordred was reputedly setting up new headquarters, people were dying of strange diseases. Lancelot, the most conscientious and experienced of Arthur's men, was the first to bring the rumour to his attention. Merlin was with Arthur at the time.

'What the hell does Mordred want?' Arthur angrily said to Lancelot. 'To create a bloody kingdom of dead-men?'

'He knows no other pleasure but killing, Sire,' Lancelot returned. 'An evil spirit moves him surely.'

'Many of these wells are holy places for the peasants,' Merlin pointed out.

'I know,' Arthur said. 'Don't they all worship their old gods and ancestors there?'

'Mordred wants to kill not only our people's bodies,' Lancelot said, 'but their very souls.'

'Draw up a list of wells,' Arthur instructed Lancelot, 'and we shall investigate tomorrow.'

'Consider it done, Sire.'

The next day they set out on the expedition. Arthur rode his mare Llamrai at whose feet Caleb trotted. They were on the road to Aquae Sulis. Beside Arthur, Merlin rode proudly on a big borrowed stallion, his long grey cloak billowing in the wind. With one hand he gripped the reins, with the other held erect his big black staff.

These days Arthur never left Camelot without an escort. So, behind him and Merlin, at a distance, Kay and Percival rode abreast, fully armed. Up ahead Gawain and Lancelot rode, similarly attired. While one or two of the men disappeared every so often off the road to scour the surrounding countryside, Arthur chatted amiably with Merlin.

They were a few miles out from Aquae Sulis when Gawain came trotting towards them. Upon reaching Arthur he bowed.

'Sire,' he said to Arthur, pointing, 'we believe there is a well up there in off the road, just behind those trees.'

'Is it safe?' Arthur queried.

'We saw nothing,' Gawain replied.

'Right, let's go!'

Caleb ran ahead. A track off the road led up an incline towards a clearing in the trees. As they approached it Merlin, who had become very alert and responsive to his new surroundings, said to Arthur, 'This well is dedicated to the goddess Sulis.'

'How do you know?' Arthur asked.

Merlin pointed to one of the trees they were passing.

'It's a tree, so what?' Arthur said.

By jabbing his staff Merlin directed Arthur's eye to a tiny strip of red cloth fluttering gently in the breeze on one of the tree's lowest branches. Soon he saw similar strips on other trees.

'You miss little, my friend,' Arthur said. 'But I would never have thought that a goddess could be so primitively honoured.'

'The superstitious have strange ways,' Merlin haughtily replied.

As they trotted into the clearing they were confronted by a horrible sight.

Caleb was sniffing wildly at everything. The area around the well was littered with dead birds and broken vessels. Rats scurried about in the undergrowth and vultures were ominously perched on low branches of the trees.

'Ye beasts!' Arthur cried, dismounting. 'What a stench!'

'Go over there, Sire,' Gawain said from his mount, pointing to Percival who was dismounted by the well's wall and gazing down sorrowfully at something.

When Arthur joined him he saw a handsome young peasant woman lying dead. Yellow bile was hardened on her blue-black lips. The grass around her was caked with blood. A broken water-jug lay by her outstretched, open hand, and on her breast her naked, dead baby. Arthur looked away in anger and disgust. Caleb, his front paws on the well's low wall, barked at the floating corpse of a bird.

'Shall we bury them here, Sire?' Percival enquired, still gazing at the woman.

'Yes,' Arthur replied. 'But not now. Cover them with branches and come back later with more men and spades.'

He turned to Lancelot who had dismounted and was standing beside him. 'Have this well sealed up immediately,

Lancelot,' he said, 'and post a sign saying POISONED'.

'Yes, Sire, straightaway,' Lancelot said.

'Arthur!' Merlin called from the far side of the well.

Arthur joined him.

Merlin was looking at a word that had been hastily daubed with blood on the side of the well: ARTHUR. 'Mordred wants the people to think you did it,' Merlin said.

'He's a hideous monster,' Arthur hissed. 'He'll not get away with this.'

The vultures stirred uneasily on the trees.

'Come!' Arthur said. 'Let's get out of here.'

CHAPTER TWO

THE TEMPLE OF THE VIRGINS

Loosely robed in a gown of green Persian silk, the tall, stately figure of Morganna, High Priestess of the Temple of the Virgins on the tiny island of Avalliona, moved serenely along the island's steep western cliff. Every evening she walked alone here, where her thoughts turned easily to Atlantis, which long ago had sunk below these deep, vast waters.

Often, on cloudless evenings, her ageing but handsome face would brighten when she saw the indigo strip of Hibernia on the horizon to the south. At such times Morganna would sigh, 'Ah! Hibernia! What a lovely sight.' Sometimes she fancied that she could even see the castle of Dunseverick.

Dunseverick was the capital of the ancient Hibernian kingdom of Dal Riada, of which Avalliona, the Western Isles and some of mainland Pictland was now part. Avalliona however had a unique, autonomous status within Dal Riada. There were many reasons for this, not the least being that the Druids believed it to be the only piece of Atlantis that had not sunk during the Great Flood thousands of years ago. In their eyes therefore it was a sacred sanctuary. And this was also why in more recent times it had come into possession of the talismanic white Stone of Destiny, and the Spear of Initiation.

For Avalliona was not only a neutral ground between the Gaels and the Britons, but also between the tribes of Hibernia herself. Internecine wars had often been fought in the past over possession of the Gael's *Four Treasures,* most especially over the Stone of Destiny; and the placing of them by the Gaelic Druids in Avalliona had substantially reduced the risk and incidence of war.

Although Morganna was a Briton, she was privileged with the task of crowning the kings of Dal Riada while they stood on the sacred Stone. She relished this task, for she was very fond of these people, who were so different from her own race, but with whom she was however united through a mutual and deep love for the Great Mother.

The Great Mother was of course known the world over and had many names. The Britons called her Don and the Gaels Danu. Nowadays however, due to the Romans' hatred of the Druidic religion, her only surviving Temple in these parts was in Avalliona.

Simply constructed of rough, wooden boards, with a yellow thatched roof, the Temple of the Virgins was also the only building of note on the sparsely populated island. In it

Morganna, who was Arthur's step-sister, attempted to keep the cult of the Mother alive by training up young priestesses.

Merlin sometimes sent her candidates, the most recent of whom was a very special young virgin named Vivian. He used spy on her as she swam alone in the lake near his forest hut and became so utterly enthralled by her aura that one morning he followed her home. There he struck up a relationship with her father who eventually accepted Merlin's offer to have the girl trained as a priestess. 'But be careful,' the father warned, 'she's a handful.'

Vivian had arrived at the Temple only seven months ago, but was already advanced enough to receive, this very evening, her first degree of initiation! It was most unusual! On the one hand Morganna had rarely known a pupil with such a profound gift of The Sight; but rarely also had she known one so precocious.

When Morganna returned from her walk she was not only surprised to find Vivian in the Temple, but appalled. For the girl was............... dancing!

'You should *not* be here at this time, Vivian,' Morganna scolded. 'You should be quiet in your hut, praying.'

Furtive as a hunted hind Vivian ran back to her hut. There she threw herself on her mattress and rolled her head about for a long time. She tried hard to pray, but couldn't. Eventually she got up and started dancing again.

A half-hour before midnight, when Morganna called at Vivian's hut she found her asleep on the floor.

Morganna smiled. 'Vivian,' she said, touching her face softly, 'wake up. It is time for your initiation.'

Vivian sat up and rubbed her eyes. 'I tried, Mother!' she cried. 'I tried!'

'I know you did, my child,' Morganna said. 'Praying is hard. But after tonight you will find it easier. Believe me.'

Morganna led Vivian then to a small room off the main part of the Temple where three of the other Virgins prepared her for initiation. First they bathed her in sweetly scented water, then anointed her mouth, breasts and vagina with holy oil. After this they placed a long white veil over her head that reached to her feet, while all the time murmuring chants and prayers specially designated for these purifying rituals. When finished, they led her into the Temple where the entire congregation of blue-veiled Virgins sat silently in rows facing the altar, heads uniformly bowed.

Morganna stood erect and proud in her scarlet robes behind the big, black marble altar. A serving Virgin stood each side of her, one holding a smoking incense burner and the other the white, gold-tipped Spear of Initiation. In front of the altar was the Stone of Destiny to which Vivian was led by her helpers. Leaving her standing on the Stone, they joined the main congregation.

Vivian was trembling. She wanted desperately to dance again. But she knew she must only pray.

After a short silence Morganna took the censer from the server while the other server held out the sacred Spear. Morganna then dowsed the Spear in the sweet-smelling smoke. The censing complete, she took the Spear in her own hands and began a long rhapsodic incantation. When this ended one of the Virgins came from the congregation and removed Vivian's veil. Morganna then silently touched all the anointed parts of Vivian's naked body with the Spear's golden tip. Then she commanded, 'Open thy mouth.'

Vivian obeyed, and Morganna touched her tongue with the Spear.

'Blessed be the organ of love, truth and justice,' she declaimed.

Vivian closed her eyes and swallowed. A flame instantly shot up and down her spine. She warmed to it, thrilled to it, gave herself up body, soul and spirit to it. When however she eventually opened her eyes again she did not see the Spear. Neither did she see the altar, nor even Morganna herself! She saw nothing except a huge green Serpent! It gazed at her with flaming red eyes and wide-open mouth!

Vivian was no stranger to visions. She had had them since childhood. But this one was different. She had never seen anything vaguely like it before. A Serpent! And was that a grin on its slimy, scaly face? One half of her was repelled, the other half drawn.

The Serpent's tongue flashed in and out of its mouth like a jet of flame. The head came so close that Vivian feared the tongue might slash her face. But the grin remained. Then a voice issued from the Serpent's mouth. It was a strange, high-pitched, feminine voice, and said, 'Seek me, O Virgin, above all else. I am the source of all human knowledge and power.'

Vivian gazed in awe at the beastly face. Timorously she enquired, 'H....how can I have your power?'

'Firstly, you must learn my *name*,' the Serpent coyly answered.

'Wh....what is your name?'

But then there was a flash, so bright that Vivian had to close her eyes. She did not know how long she closed them for, but when she eventually opened them again there was only Morganna standing before her. Now she was resting the Spear on Vivian's head.

'Have you had another vision, my child?' Morganna asked.

Vivian nodded.

'Then you must tell me about it.'

In the days and weeks that followed, the green Serpent came to Vivian often, but silently, and more in dreams than waking visions. Morganna knew that each of her neophytes would, as part of their initiation, have unusual experiences. But the more she heard of Vivian's visions the more perplexed she became. Merlin, she reasoned, was undoubtedly correct in his assessment that the girl had something very special in her makeup. She had indeed inherited The Sight to a remarkable degree. But as she climbed up the ladder of initiation and began to show her true colours, Morganna wondered whether in the long run she would've been better off without her.

CHAPTER THREE

THE HERETICS

The leaves of the old sycamores that lined the low wall of the cemetery near the chapel where Patrick strode impatiently up and down, glinted yellow and gold in the early autumn sunshine. Lengthening shadows darkened the path as the sandaled feet of Patrick's huge frame noisily crunched the gravel. He tugged often and ponderously on his curly red beard and stopped occasionally at the chapel to peer through a crack in its old wooden door.

Although Patrick was a bishop he neither felt nor looked like one. Only recently consecrated, his humble nature made it hard for him to become reconciled to his new status. He had on a grey, very soiled monk's cowl and had just come from hewing wood in the monastery garden. The only thing which indicated his new spiritual status was the ring on his right index finger. It was of purest red gold, inset with a beautifully cut emerald, the gold itself engraved with his name and the Christian sign of the Chi Rho. This ring had been placed on Patrick's finger at his recent consecration, and presently he had an appointment with Germanus, his superior, to receive the rest of his official insignia.

How long more? Patrick wondered as he paced the path. But it was difficult to say, for these days Germanus prayed harder and longer than ever.

Although in his younger days Germanus was an officer in the Roman army, nowadays he acted as the esteemed Archbishop of Auxerre, in which town in Gaul the monastery was situated. The chapel was part of the monastery where Germanus lived with his community of Roman Catholic monks. He prayed hard these days because he was deeply worried about the Church. In the outside world the Empire was crumbling away, and if something was to be rescued from the chaos, if something of the pure old Roman spirit were to be preserved for future generations, it could only be done through the Church.

But for the Church to be strong, its doctrines and beliefs must be uniform. Heresies of every hue must be crushed. And there was no greater heresy conceivable than that of the Pelagians! It was instigated by a Hibernian called Pelagius, in which country, Germanus was reliably informed, Pelagius now lived, after being hounded out of every other major city of the Empire where the Catholic religion was strong, most especially Rome.

In Germanus's eyes there was only one way to deal with this heresy and that was to dispatch a Roman bishop to Hibernia, a man with the authority of the Pontifex Maximus himself. But because the current one, Pope Celestine, was dragging his feet badly on the matter, Germanus had recently gone to Rome to personally seek permission from the Pope to send one of his own monks to Hibernia to do the job. This was Patrick.

'But he's not even a priest, never mind a bishop!' the Pope impatiently snorted after listening to Germanus make his case for Patrick.

The Pope was ensconced, richly robed, on the high ornate throne of his opulent audience chamber in St. Peter's Basilica. Germanus stood humbly below him.

'I know, Holy Father,' Germanus meekly agreed. 'But I have come to seek your permission to bestow on him these Orders.'

'Can he pay?' Celestine asked patting his large stomach. He was enormously fat.

'No,' Germanus replied. 'He is a poor man. I will actually have to give him money when he goes to Hibernia.'

Celestine belched. 'Can he even write?'

'Not very well, but he speaks our Latin adequately. But here is the key point, Your Holiness: he actually knows and can speak fluently the difficult language of these Hibernian barbarians!'

'How strange!' the Pope said. 'Explain.'

'He actually lived in Hibernia for some years when he was young,' Germanus informed. 'He was taken there as a boy slave. But with the guidance of an Angel - or so he says - he escaped. After that he wandered around Gaul, eventually making his way to our monastery where we made a proper monk of him. And now he is very eager to return to Hibernia, because he believes the selfsame Angel wants him to go there to preach the gospel! He's got tremendous zeal, Your Holiness. He loves the Lord dearly. He's the ideal man for the job. I believe that once he gets to Hibernia he will quickly find the ringleader of the heresy.'

'Pelagius,' Celestine said, yawning.

'The very one.'

'And what do you propose to do then with Pelagius?'

'I will have him assassinated, Your Holiness.'

'Patrick doesn't seem like the assassinating type to me,' the Pontiff sniffed.

'No, indeed. He is a simple sort, really.'

'So you'll send someone else to do the dirty work?'

'Yes. Once we locate the damn heretic I'll either bring him to your good self in chains or I'll have his head cut off straightaway in Hibernia. Whatever you wish.'

Celestine grew tired of Germanus. Making the sign of the Cross over him he eventually dispatched him with the decree, 'You have my permission to deal with Pelagius, his heresy and his heretics in whatever way you see fit.'

Then he snapped his fingers at his nearby secretary for the next audience to commence immediately, for it was nearing dinner time and he was getting very hungry.

Germanus came home from Rome very happy. He hastily conferred Holy Orders on Patrick. Soon afterwards he invested him with his bishop's ring and was now about to put the final touches to the whole procedure.

Patrick had moved a distance from the chapel and was going to climb the steps to the parapet of the monastery's wall when he heard his name called in a shrill voice. He turned to find the small, gaunt figure of Germanus framed in the chapel doorway. He was shaking his crozier reprovingly.

'Running away again,' Germanus sharply scolded as he shuffled towards Patrick. (He had a limp from birth.)

'Your Grace,' Patrick said apologetically, 'I didn't know how long you'd be. I.......I was......'

'Running away,' Germanus insisted.

Upon reaching Patrick Germanus lifted his hand and

Patrick dutifully kissed his gold ring.

'Impatience is a vice, Bishop,' Germanus said when Patrick straightened up. 'It must be tempered with its virtuous opposite.'

'Patience,' Patrick said deadpan. (He was all-too-familiar with the predictable nuances of Germanus's moral philosophy!)

'Correct. Now, tell me, how are the preparations for your journey to Hibernia going?'

'Well, Your Grace.'

'And have you informed those two poor innocent young monks I am allowing you to take along?'

'I have.'

'Good. Now come with me.'

They walked by the side of the chapel, passed under the leafy sycamores and soon came to an arched doorway at the back of the main body of the church. Inside it a dark narrow passage led to the dimly lit scriptorium where two very old monks were huddled over sheets of parchment, busily at work with their rulers, inks and quills. They looked up in unison. Their aged faces bore a remarkable similarity.

'Leave us for a while,' Germanus said dismissively. 'Get yourselves some fresh autumn air.'

With a practised suppression of resentment against their superior's notoriously abrupt manner, the monks shuffled out, glad however of their temporary release.

'Sit there!' Germanus ordered, jabbing his crozier at one of the vacated stools.

After whipping a cover from a nearby wicker chair which was reserved specially for him, Germanus fell heavily into it, closed his eyes and sighed deeply. After a few moments he opened his eyes again, slanted them on Patrick, and gripping his crozier said, 'I take it that you have secured a safe sea-passage?'

'To Londonium only, Your Grace. From there we will have to make our own way to Hibernia.'

'Hmm. And is there a *precise* date of departure?'

'Yes. The middle of next month.'

'Good. Now listen to me carefully. We have spoken of this before, but I must remind you again. The very first thing you do when you arrive on the island of Hibernia is to seek out the ringleader of this Pelagian heresy, Pelagius. Find out where his headquarters is and make it your highest priority to get full dispatches to me. I will give you enough soldi to pay, or bribe, whoever you need. Understand?'

Patrick nodded.

'Then you will baptize all Pelagius's followers into our Roman Church and instruct them in the one true faith.'

'The gospel,' Patrick said.

'Yes.'

'Does Pelagius not know the gospel, Your Grace?'

'Oh, I don't know what he knows! All I am certain of is that he is an arch-heretic. Some say he is even a sort of... .of..... What do you call those damn pagan priests?'

'Druids.......?'

'Yes. A Druid. They even say he's one of those.' Germanus threw back his head and gave a mock, high-pitched laugh. 'Christians, how are you! Sorcerers, serpent-worshippers and devils all.'

'I believe,' Patrick said, 'that you are going to give me a gospel book.'

'Of course. Of course,' Germanus said. 'But remember... ..patience! First things first. Now, stand up.'

Patrick stood and Germanus raised himself stiffly from his chair. Resting his crozier against a scribe's desk he ambled to a corner of the room where from a table he took a mitre. Made of high quality purple taffeta, he proudly placed it on Patrick's head saying, 'Bishop Patrick.'

Then he stood back admiringly and with an uncharacteristic smile added, 'Yes, that will surely make those savages in Hibernia take notice.'

Patrick felt awkward. Was he supposed to say something? He remained silent

'Wear it there all the time in Hibernia, you hear?' Germanus commanded.

'Y....yes, Your Grace.'

Germanus went to the table again and took from it a little book.

Presenting it to Patrick he said, 'Your gospel.'

'Oh, thank you most dearly, Your Grace,' Patrick said enthusiastically. 'This is what I was waiting for.'

'Remember, it's the gospel of *Peter*, the one true gospel. There are far too many so-called gospels doing the rounds these days.'

'Didn't Saint John write one?'

'I don't know and I don't care.'

Germanus snatched the book back from Patrick and after rapidly finding a particular passage continued, 'Listen to this. Jesus is speaking to his closest Apostle, Peter. I quote: "You are the Rock and upon this Rock I will build my Church. To you I give the keys to the Kingdom of Heaven." These are the most decisive words that Jesus ever spoke.'

'If I may be permitted to say so,' Patrick boldly declared, 'I find your exegesis somewhat....well, heterodox.'

'Exegesis! Heterodox! My God, but these are mighty big words! Where the hell did you learn *them*?'

Patrick grinned. 'Augustine.'

'Hmm. Well, my reasoning is perfectly orthodox. And I'll tell you why. The apostle Peter was the first Bishop of Rome. See? The universal Church of Christ has its origins *there* and nowhere else. Not in Alexandria, not in Carthage, not in Antioch, and certainly not in godforsaken Hibernia, but Rome, Rome, the eternal city, the city of God. So convert those heathens to *this* gospel of Peter and no other - *Saint* bloody Peter, the first Bishop and Pope of Rome. Understand?'

'Yes, Your Grace,' Patrick said, but a worried look came over his face.

'What's the problem now?' Germanus irritably demanded.

'As far as I remember,' Patrick replied, 'only the Druids are allowed to read or write, or even *have* books in Hibernia, and they are the most powerful people in the land.'

'Then dammit, tell them you're a Roman citizen or something!'

'But the Druids hate the Romans, Your Grace. It would a dangerous thing so say.'

'But it's a dangerous mission you're going on, Bishop,' Germanus sharply returned. 'You'll have to take risks, many risks.'

'I suppose so........'

'No, no. Suppose nothing. You will *have* to take risks. Full stop. You must have confidence and courage, man. Courage!'

Repeating 'courage' many times Germanus hobbled back to the little table. From it he now took a piece of embroidered cloth. Offering it to Patrick he said, 'Now this is the stole of your high priestly office.' Pointing to the embroidered symbol of the Chi Rho on the cloth he continued, 'This was the sign by which our great Christian Emperor Constantine defeated the pagans. Kiss it.'

Hesitantly Patrick kissed the sign and Germanus placed the stole around Patrick's shoulders. Germanus then brought a crozier from the table. Beautifully made of carved ebony, it had a crook of fine filigree silver. Handing it to Patrick Germanus said, 'This is the sign and symbol of Rome's authority. The aim of your mission is nothing less than to establish in Hibernia the authority of His Holiness, Pope Celestine, and the Canon Law of his Holy Roman Catholic Church. Got that?'

Nodding, Patrick took the crozier. Then he mumbled, 'I remember, Your Grace, that....the people of Hibernia were very.....very different to us. All this regalia might.....might....'

'I know they're different,' Germanus interrupted. 'They're all bloody illiterate! That's the difference.'

'I mean, Your Grace........I remember that they were also very free-spirited.'

'Free-spirited? What the hell does that mean?'

'Well....free-spirited in....say....art, religion, law, you know, even......dare I say...... in s....s....'

'In what?'

'Sex!'

Germanus went purple! Raising his voice he cried, 'Jesus man, but isn't that the whole bloody point!'

'But, Your Gra....'

'Don't argue with me! If they're free-spirited then I say they are far too damn free-spirited! Listen. That fellow Pelagius they're all raving about over there was probably sex mad.'

'Yes, but the Druids......'

'Shag the Druids! We're talking about Pelagius.'

'Sorry.'

'Just because that fellow got to Rome and made something of himself there after learning to read and write, he thought he could do everything. Free will was all he could ever think or write about. Free will my backside! It's an illusion.'

'Is it?'

'Yes. And I'll tell you why. Because our great Christian scholar, Augustine, whom you've obviously read, said so. Augustine put Pelagius in his place! Augustine was dead right when he said in his book about Pelagius that he was full of Hibernian porridge.'

'Porridge, Your Grace?'

'Shit, Bishop!'

'Shit, Your Grace?'

Germanus was exasperated. He sighed. Then looking condescendingly down his dagger nose at Patrick he said with a forced calm, 'It's an old Etruscan word, Bishop. For your enlightenment it means *excrement*.'

'Oh, yes. Of course.'

With his temper rising again Germanus repeated, 'Excrement, Bishop. That's all Pelagius ever preached or wrote. Now listen.' He jabbed Patrick's chest with his ringed index finger. 'Your job is, one, to find that heretic Pelagius, and two, to bring those poor illiterate yobs in Hibernia that he's leading astray into the one true fold. And keep me well informed of everything, you hear? Everything.'

But Patrick felt foolish. He looked warily at his crozier in one hand, his book in the other then up at his tall hat. What was this all about? Was all this dressing up really about his beloved Jesus? What could he say? His eyes fell to his dirty toes that poked awkwardly out of his ragged sandals. Memories of that enchanted time long ago he had spent as a boy in Hibernia came suddenly flooding back, memories of magical adventures he had had with his old Druid master, Miliuc, memories that blended seamlessly with stories Miliuc had told him of ancient gods and heroes, of magic cauldrons, of stones that could speak, of swords that could banish armies, of spears that bled, and countless other mysteries.

Was it all just a dream? Patrick asked himself now as he had many times before. But no, he concluded, he really *was* there. All those strange and wonderful things really *did* happen.

'Are you listening to me?' he heard Germanus growl.

'I am, Your Grace,' Patrick evasively replied. 'To every word.'

CHAPTER FOUR

INITIATION

It took Merlin over two weeks to make the long, difficult and dangerous journey from his hut in the Forest of Elfham to Avalliona in the far north. He made this journey every year around Lughnasadh, the time of the autumn festival, on his donkey, Caliban, in order to officiate at the ceremony in which a new group of neophytes, having completed their training under Morganna, would receive their seventh and final degree of initiation, and thereby be inducted into the priesthood of the Great Mother.

Although Avalliona was part of the Gaelic kingdom of Dal Riada, officiating at this ceremony had always been in Merlin's hands. He had performed it for longer than he cared to remember, even before Morganna had become High Priestess and no one had ever questioned his worthiness. By this late time of his life it had become routine.

On the journey he remembered many of the fine young women he initiated in his long career and his thoughts inevitably turned to the current batch of neophytes of which one in particular he simply could not get out of his mind: Vivian.

From the very first moment his seer's eyes beheld her over three years ago he knew she had that special quality of soul which, though immature, if properly nurtured would render her capable of becoming a fine priestess. Since then he had seen her once a year and it was obvious that her spiritual faculties were responding exceedingly well to the training she was receiving from Morganna in Avalliona. She truly possessed The Sight to a very remarkable degree. But there was more to her than this. Much more. There was in fact something utterly unfathomable about her, something Merlin often pored over, but something that his age-old wisdom could never quite get to the bottom of.

Avalliona was situated in the Hibernian Sea, about a day's boat trip from a little hamlet on the north-western coast of Pictland, way beyond the great wall the Roman Emperor Hadrian built long ago to keep the Picts out of the Roman's vast territories in the south.

When Merlin finally arrived at the hamlet he left Caliban, as he had done for many years past, in the care of the wife of the same, trusted ferryman, Murdoch, who always took him across to the island.

Murdoch was a tiny man who reminded Merlin of a wren. He was also mute. But he rode the huge waves and handled the oars of his light, skin-covered coracle with such superb skill that Merlin considered him a natural magician.

As if shielding it from unworthy eyes, the island of Avalliona was perennially shrouded in mist. It was said that the Druids spread it as a form of protection for the island's invaluable possessions, the Stone of Destiny and the white Spear of Initiation. It was however a mist that Murdoch's bird-eyes seemed to penetrate, for the island always suddenly appeared, and in sharp detail, out of nowhere.

The sun peeped out from behind a great towering bank of snow-white clouds as Merlin stepped nimbly, staff in one hand, knapsack in the other, from the coracle onto the island. After signalling thanks to Murdoch who would wait in a little boathouse nearby for his return, however long it would take, he took off his broad-brimmed hat, wiped the sea-spray from his face and gave inward thanks to the Great Mother for his safe arrival.

With knapsack secured on his back he set off in the direction of the Temple of the Virgins which was clearly visible in the sunshine, it being the only building of any size on the flat island, and pure white.

He had been here many times before and knew by heart which turns to take on the matrix of muddy tracks that led eventually to the Temple.

Morganna had been watching for him from mid-morning and when she eventually spotted the conspicuous, grey-clad figure, her blue eyes lit up like stars and she rushed with outstretched hands to greet him.

'Dear Merlin,' she said beaming, 'how wonderful to see you again!'

Without speaking, Merlin leant his staff carefully against his chest and took both her hands in his. He kissed each of them gently, then her cheeks.

'Morganna,' he said at last, his dark eyes uncharacteristically moistening as he gazed softly upon her handsome, ageing countenance.

'And how are *you*?' Morganna asked tenderly.

'Bruised all over,' Merlin complained.

'Good heavens! Why?'

'I keep bumping into things.'

'Can't you use your magic to avoid them?'

'I forget.'

Morganna laughed. 'Our air here will do you a power of good,' she said good-humouredly.

Taking his staff again, Merlin said, 'I'm getting too old for all this Morganna. Methinks I will need stronger medicine than the air of Avalliona if I'm to do *this* particular journey again.'

'Nonsense!' Morganna countered and arm-in-arm led him towards the Temple.

'And how are all your young Virgins faring?' Merlin asked.

'Oh, at the moment very excited.........about *you*.....especially the seven you are turning into priestesses.'

Merlin grinned. Morganna continued, 'And tell me, how is my dear stepbrother Arthur, faring? Does he still dream of the lost kingdom of the Britons?'

'Oh yes,' Merlin replied, 'but as you are well aware, he fights even better than he dreams.'

'As a boy, you know, he dreamed of little else but Logres, thanks to you and your stories. But of course his father Pendragon was also a very powerful chieftain before the Romans got their military claws into Cambria.'

'Indeed. Arthur's blood is the best. And I help and advise him, for his father's sake if for no other. Which reminds me, have you seen my old Gaelic friend, The Gobán, lately?'

(The Gobán lived in Dunseverick and Merlin knew he was the Druid guardian of the Sword of Light.)

'Yes,' Morganna replied, 'I saw him just last month. He stayed here for a few days. Why do you ask?'

After a short silence Merlin said very slowly, 'I want the Sword of Light.'

Morganna stopped and glared at him. 'What? You want The Gobán to give *you* the Sword of Light! Are you mad or something?'

'Something, preferably,' Merlin returned vaguely, 'but I want the Sword for Arthur. I promised it to him.'

'You promised! And what on earth makes you think that The Gobán will give you, or Arthur for that matter – Britons! - one of Hibernia's four great *Treasures*?'

'A spirit!' Merlin replied tapping his forehead with his staff. 'A very lively spirit makes me think it.'

'Merlin! You don't understand. You don't know these Gaels.'

'I do. Am I not speaking their language....sort of?'

But Morganna shook her head vigorously. 'You don't know them as *I* do. I've been crowning their kings ever since I became High Priestess here and I knew them well long before that. They are fiercely nationalistic. And as for The Gobán.........'

'Madam,' Merlin testily interjected, 'my spirit informs me that nationalism is a thing of the past. Now that the Roman army is gone for good, the Britons and the Hibernians should forget their ancient tribal animosities and unite to fight a new beast that is rising rapidly in our midst. It is, I fear, even worse than the Roman She-Wolf. Britannia herself is becoming a veritable wasteland. We badly need a saviour. It might be Arthur.'

'But, my dear Merlin,' Morganna sighed, 'I repeat: he is *not* a Gael. If The Gobán gives you the Sword of Light I'll.....I'll.......'

'Resign?' Merlin said with a wicked grin.

Morganna forced a smile and taking his arm back they walked again.

They entered the Temple's neatly flagged courtyard through a towering pair of ancient oaks. Full-berried rowans dotted the yard's edge where numerous out-houses were also erected. Of these Morganna's private dwelling was the most conspicuous, due to its tall, round shape and distinct aspect: it directly faced the Temple's arched doorway to which it was connected by a pure white, pebbled pathway, bordered with small evergreen shrubs, some still in flower.

'You must be tired,' Morganna said. 'I'll take you to your quarters.'

They were heading for one of the smaller out-houses which was reserved especially for Merlin and contained all the accoutrements of his profession when Merlin suddenly stopped and said, 'Oh wait! Take me to Vivian first.'

'If you wish,' Morganna said. 'But the question is: where is she?'

They were standing near a sundial. Morganna glanced at it. 'She's probably in the sacred grove praying. She goes there every day around this time, now that the apples are ripe. Come.'

'How is she?' Merlin enquired as they headed out of the yard again.

'She's changed, Merlin. Not nearly as flighty as she used to be. She also keeps to herself more and more. And now that she's about to become a priestess, a certain strangeness has come over her.'

'A *strangeness*?'

'I can't describe it in any other way. You'll just have to see for yourself.'

As Morganna anticipated, they found Vivian in the sacred grove which was situated just outside the courtyard to the north. There was an old story that a powerful avatar once came to the island to die and his staff, planted over his grave, had grown into this apple tree. The grove was surrounded by a cluster of little wooden huts, in which the Temple Virgins lived.

Vivian was on her knees beneath the tree, her head bowed.

'Vivian,' Morganna said quietly from a distance.

Vivian lifted her head slowly to the tree as if *it* had spoken.

'Vivian,' Morganna said louder, and the Virgin turned.

'Mother,' she said, surprised, though her bright eyes quickly turned to Merlin. She stood up.

Small of stature and smooth of brow, Vivian had long jet-black hair, sallow skin, huge violet eyes and a small, impish mouth.

'Master Merlin,' she said, curtsying.

Merlin nodded, but a beam from her incredible eyes made him grip his staff. He glanced at the tree. Its branches were laden with golden fruit of which he would later personally pick one for her and all the new priestesses. These would then be solemnly consumed as part of the initiation ritual.

He returned his gaze to Vivian.

'Are you prepared,' he earnestly enquired, 'for your final initiation when you will be received into the communion of the Great Mother?'

'I am, Master,' Vivian replied, and instantly an apple fell from the tree with a lively plop onto the grass between them.

'It is the first to fall,' Morganna observed.

'It's Vivian's,' Merlin said as he stooped stiffly to pick it up.

'Come, Merlin,' Morganna said impatiently, 'I'll bring you to your room straightaway. You must be weary.' Addressing Vivian she went on, 'Vivian, go join you colleagues. Now that Merlin is here there is much preparation to be done for the ceremony.'

'I had not finished my prayer, Mother,' Vivian said, adding coyly, 'when I was......interrupted.'

'Finish it quickly then,' Morganna said. 'You've been here long enough.'

'Yes, Mother,' Vivian replied, but she was looking at Merlin.

'Come,' Morganna repeated and drew Merlin briskly out of the grove.

Morganna was right! The air of Avalliona revived Merlin! As the days passed, and the preparations for the initiation ceremony drew nearer, he felt a vigour reminiscent of his youth. He relished seeing the Temple decorated by the Virgins with branches and all sorts of freshly picked flowers, while on the altar itself, alongside the white Spear of Initiation lay seven perfect golden apples.

However, the day of the ceremony dawned gloomy and wet. A howling wind swept menacingly across the flat little island. The proceedings were to begin at noon, but despite the foul weather, all morning the blue-cloaked Virgins worked ceaselessly to put the finishing touches to the Temple's interior. They moved swiftly and earnestly about, singly or in groups, in and out of the Temple, back and forth from their huts, sometimes briefly visiting the sacred grove, heads always determinedly bent to the wind, carrying things, talking or giggling, and sometimes chanting or singing.

Then all went very quiet. The wind dropped and the sun came out.

Suddenly the silence was broken by the sound of a horn, bright, clear and high. It was noon sharp! Morganna had blown the horn from the Temple doorway. It signalled the commencement of the ceremony.

Like butterflies rising to the first rays of a summer sun, the Virgins immediately swarmed out of their huts and gathered in the sacred grove. From there they walked in solemn procession along the winding pathway to their Temple. Inside it they found their seven colleagues to be initiated standing solemnly in front of the altar. These were clad in transparent white veils from head to foot. The rest of the Virgins, in blue veils, sat on plain wooden benches neatly arranged in a crescent around the altar.

As well as the sacred Spear and the apples, on the altar was a huge, lit, beeswax candle and Merlin's grimoire, his invaluable book of spells and incantations. The Stone of Destiny was placed, as it always was on the floor in front of the altar and, like the kings of Dal Riada when they were being crowned by Morganna, each Virgin to be initiated stood upon it. The Virgins were however not going to receive a crown, but the sacred wound of initiation.

Behind the altar Merlin, in the full regalia of a Hierophant, stood, utterly transformed. His flowing white robe reached to his feet, its copious folds pleated at his waist by a thick purple belt with a huge gem-encrusted buckle. A large, embossed breastplate hung from his neck, while over his shoulders and crossed in front just below his diaphragm was a bright red stole, richly embroidered with multi-coloured astrological symbols. Finally, his brow was capped by a crescent of pure gold, the embossed ornamentation of which displayed the Heavenly Eagle, that ancient, holy symbol brazenly usurped by the Romans for their own materialistic purposes, but here, precisely in this ceremony, brought into its proper use and legitimate power.

Morganna, also attired in her finest priestly robes sat solemnly behind Merlin on a throne-like, carved wooden chair holding her horn, while two serving Virgins, faces veiled, stood in the wings, one holding the smoking censer, the other the lustral water and the holy oil. As the ceremony progressed, Merlin several times blessed and dowsed the Spear with incense, sprinkled it with lustral water and finally anointed its golden tip with the holy oil.

Vivian was the last to be initiated. Barefooted and trembling, with eyes closed and hands piously joined, she took her stand on the Stone of Destiny. Morganna rose from her throne, came in front of the altar and from the hem lifted Vivian's veil, fully exposing her left side. Merlin took the Spear then and after a long incantation gently pierced Vivian just below her diaphragm.

Up to this point Merlin's words and actions had been clear and strong, his thoughts pure and concentrated fervently on the Great Mother. Suddenly however, as a little bead of blood swelled on Vivian's wound, the old Serpent reappeared! It crept stealthily out of the backwaters of Merlin's mind, took hold of Vivian's aura, and once again filled his entire vision, challenging and threatening him. Green at first, then as usual turning dull and slimy all over, it rose up behind Vivian's veiled body and from above her head flashed its flaming red eyes at him.

Exasperated, Merlin cried, 'Who are you?'

There was a short silence. Then in a strange, high-pitched voice the Serpent replied, 'Naas is my name.'

A thousand questions flashed through Merlin's mind but they could be neither asked nor answered now. That would be an utter violation of the sacred rite. Desperately trying to banish the all-intrusive vision, he barely managed to complete the ceremony, but immediately afterwards fled to his room and collapsed.

Such apparitions often drove Merlin mad, a condition that could sometimes last for days or even weeks. But he was always capable of returning to himself in the end. The impression that the Serpent left on him this time however was so sharp and lucid he feared it might consume his sanity entirely and spawn a species of madness that would endure even beyond the grave!

There was, he felt, only one sure way of staving off such an abominable threat. He must at all costs find out who or what the Serpent Naas was.

CHAPTER FIVE

THE SWORD OF LIGHT

Dunseverick was the seat of the Hibernian kings of Dal Riada. The kingdom was founded around the time of the birth of Jesus by the great Conor MacRiada of the northern Cruithni. For centuries prior to Conor many great battles and even full-scale wars were fought between the Cruithni of the north and the Gaels of the South over possession of the *Four Treasures* of the Danaans, the ancient, semi-divine rulers of the land who by all accounts emanated from the Temples of Egypt. The Gaels eventually won the day, and in full possession of the magical *Treasures* established their rule and culture over the whole of the south of the island, pushing the Cruithni back as far as they could into the north.

The Cruithni however claimed direct descent from the Danaans and, egged on by their Druids, never ceased their warring efforts to regain possession of their *Treasures*. When Conor became King he amassed a powerful army, built a great fortress at Emain Macha and waged war on the Gaels like never before. Cormac MacArthur, a powerful king of the Gaels whose headquarters was in ancient Tara, was Conor's greatest enemy.

Conor eventually defeated Cormac, repossessed the *Four Treasures* and soon afterwards was crowned the first High King of Hibernia. His primary focus then was to keep the Romans out of the island. For they, having firmly established their power, law and culture in the southern part of Britannia were, precisely at this time busily trying to conquer Pictland, or Caledonia as they called it. Once they achieved that they would, Conor reckoned, inevitably set their imperial eyes on Hibernia and conquer her from Pictland. He therefore enlarged his army, moved his headquarters from Emain Macha to Dunseverick - a highly strategic spot on the northern Hibernian coastline - erected a formidable castle there and built a fleet of sturdy ships.

The Romans however found it impossible to conquer Pictland, eventually gave up trying, and so Hibernia too remained free of them.

Over the subsequent centuries the Gaels of the south and the northern Cruithni intermarried and the whole of the island became Gaelic. Conor's specific legacy however was the great Gaelic kingdom of Dal Riada which nowadays was ruled by King Fergus and comprised much of north-eastern Hibernia, most of the western islands of Pictland, including Avalliona, and vast swathes of western mainland Pictland itself.

Weather permitting, Dunseverick was about two days' boat trip from Avalliona. On the day that Merlin wanted to get to Dunseverick however, the weather was not permitting. For the same irascible wind that blew on the day of the initiation ceremony had returned with a vengeance. Merlin however had great faith in his hardy little ferryman, Murdoch. This shaman of the seas could, he reckoned, cross any water he wished in his tiny craft. All he needed was a little 'encouragement' which Merlin duly, if tactfully, provided. And so once more they rode the monstrous waves with Merlin irritably threatening them with his staff as often as they threatened him with their great gnawing surges.

They sighted Dunseverick just as the wind was dropping and dusk was descending on the third day. The castle shone like a lighthouse, its many torches having just been lit around its staunch and forbidding battlements.

The harbour was patrolled by King Fergus's soldiers, one of whom dimly discerned the approaching coracle while it was still a distance out. He stood carefully monitoring the little craft as it approached the jetty.

'What business have you here, strangers?' he shouted as Murdoch deftly lassoed a rope around a virtually invisible bollard high above him. The soldier spoke in the rough dialect of the region which Merlin knew and spoke himself. Holding his hands to his mouth Merlin shouted, 'My name is Merlin. I am an old friend of The Gobán's. Do you know him?'

'Of course,' the soldier returned, 'everyone here knows The Gobán. Where have you come from?'

'Avalliona!' Merlin shouted.

'Are you a friend of Morganna's?'

'I am.'

'Then you are welcome.'

The soldier kicked a rope ladder down and Merlin and Murdoch climbed up.

'This is Murdoch,' Merlin said after regaining his breath, 'but he doesn't speak.'

'My name is Niall,' the soldier said extending his hand to Merlin. As Merlin grasped it the soldier eyed his staff. 'Are you a Druid then, sire?'

'You could say that,' Merlin replied, deadpan.

'The Gobán has many Druid friends,' the soldier informed.

'Sure wasn't he one himself in the days of yore,' Merlin said, and added under his breath, 'before he got too fond of the grub.' Then full voiced again he asked, 'Is The Gobán here at present?'

'I believe so,' the soldier answered.

'Will you take me to him then?'

'Not now. He will be asleep. He retires very early, sire, and it's impossible to wake him once he falls asleep. You will see him in the morning surely. He awakes early. But right now I see that you and your companion are in dire need of some refreshment and nourishment. You look as if you have just crossed the Styx.'

Mmm......, Merlin thought, *so the young fellow knows a bit of the old Greek. Interesting.* 'We have in a way,' he dryly replied.

Chatting as they went, the soldier took Merlin and Murdoch to a draughty lodging house in the outer ward of the castle. There he left them in the hands of its lean but attentive steward, promising to send a page first thing in the morning to take them to The Gobán's quarters.

After drying out in front of a huge log fire they were given a hearty meal of cold mutton, buttered bread and sweet mead by the steward. Then he took them up a winding, stone stairway to a small room at the top of the house overlooking the sea.

Dog-tired from the sea-crossing and unused to the luxury of a feather mattress, without even removing his boots Merlin collapsed onto the mattress and fell instantly into a deep sleep. Despite the sharp snoring whistles of Murdoch who was but two feet from him, he slept like a corpse.

He awoke the following morning to the sound of loud banging on the door. Grunting and groaning he arose, opened the door and was greeted by a shining pageboy in apple-green tights and a bright red jerkin.

'I want Mister Merlin,' the boy said. 'I have to take him to The Gobán straightaway.'

'Straightaway,' Merlin repeated sarcastically, trying to open his eyes. 'What's the hurry, boy?'

'Oh, please Mister,' the boy said shifting on his feet, 'I have so many other duties this morning, I don't know if I will be able to do them all. Is Mister Merlin here, *please*?'

'He's coming,' Merlin said hobbling back to fetch his staff. 'Hold your horses.'

Silently bidding Murdoch, who was now awake, to wait for his return, Merlin went back to the boy and said, 'He's here at last.'

'You?' the boy quizzed.

'Me. Go!'

The boy smiled happily and they set off down the stairway. He led Merlin into the main courtyard of the castle and through its north gate. Outside the castle walls they soon came to a drawbridge over a deep inlet which separated the promontory on which the castle was built from the mainland. A fine mist was blowing which made the sea's horizon invisible. After crossing the bridge they climbed up steep steps until they came to a plateau. On this was the carefully laid out, extensive walled gardens of the castle.

'The Gobán lives over there, Mister,' the boy said when they passed through the garden gate. He was pointing to the south-facing corner where a long, yellow-thatched, mud dwelling stood out against the whitewashed wall.

'Is he awake?' Merlin asked.

'I don't know, Mister,' the boy replied. 'I'm not allowed to go near his house at all.'

'Well, thank you, boy,' Merlin said patting the boy's head, 'you've done well.'

The boy bowed, ran away, and Merlin picked his way through beds of cabbages, leeks and beans until he came near the house. Its door was open, but four big hairy men were sitting silently on the wet grass in front of it. They seemed to be playing a game with pieces of sticks.

'The gods be with you,' Merlin said at a distance, but the men totally ignored him.

'That's a mighty fine morning,' Merlin then tried. This time he spoke in the roughest accent he could muster in the hope of a better response. One of the men then cast a huge lazy eye over him, but said nothing.

'Is The Gobán within?' Merlin enquired, forcefully now.

All the men looked up. They appeared hung over.

'He's at his breakfast,' one of them growled. 'What do you want?'

'I want to speak with him. I am a friend of his,' Merlin replied. 'An old one.'

A deep, well-fed voice suddenly sounded through the open door of the cottage, 'Merlin! It's you! I can hear you. Come in! Come in!'

The hairy men looked puzzled. Shrugging, the biggest of them nodded Merlin through with a flick of his head.

The dark interior of the oblong, single-roomed cottage was

lit by a fire at one end. The other end was curtained off. Near the fire, on the floor, huge, bald-headed, jovial-faced Gobán was stretched out on a mattress. Guardianship of the Sword of Light had, over the years, made him proud and indolent, so that nowadays he didn't practise his Druidic profession at all. He was surrounded by chunks of roasted meat and piles of vegetables on plates of various sizes. Wiping his mouth with the back of his puffy white hand he said, 'I saw you in my dreams last night, Merlin. I was expecting you. Good to see you.'

He extended his hand to Merlin who observing its greasiness refrained from taking it and tapped it lightly instead with his staff, saying, 'Good to see *you*, old friend.'

'Sit down,' The Gobán invited pointing to cushions on the floor opposite him. 'Have something to eat.'

'No, thanks,' Merlin replied as he lowered himself stiffly.

'You're too thin,' The Gobán said with a laugh. (Merlin was aware of how The Gobán always joked at the beginning of their occasional meetings. But he knew The Gobán was secretly afraid of him.)

'It's all relative, is it not?' Merlin said.

'Ah, wise Merlin. It is surely.'

The Gobán had on a cloth-of-gold bedroom robe, the type worn by Roman aristocrats, which though of the largest possible size was still too small, so that much of his flabby white flesh was visible, for he had nothing at all on underneath. His feet too were bare. Licking his fingers he asked, 'And how is old Britannia faring, now that the Roman dogs are gone, eh?'

'Not good,' Merlin replied. 'The army took the Law with them. There is chaos. Utter chaos.'

'Ah, sure a little bit of chaos is not such a bad thing, is it? It breaks out here in Dal Riada regularly. And it gets our men, our soldiers I mean, properly exercised. But our Fergus never lets it last too long.'

'Despite our longstanding distaste for the Romans,' Merlin said, 'they at least left us with a deep desire for law and order.'

'Then get yourselves a good strong king like our Fergus. Or an emperor even!'

'I believe we may have such a one.........in the making.'

'Who, pray?'

'A young man called Arthur. He was a commander in the Roman army. He is a lover of peace and has a fine sense of justice, and has gathered about him an equally fine body of ex-army men. He has turned them into a strong militia and fired them with his ideals. They all show excellent promise, especially Arthur. But he's young. He still dreams a lot.'

'Dreaming is not such a bad thing either, is it, wise Merlin?'

'It depends,' Merlin said distractedly, 'on what you see in your dreams, I daresay.'

'Well, I certainly saw *you* last night in *my* dreams,' The Gobán said as he picked up a dripping rib. 'Now, Merlin, to business,' he continued, biting into the meat. 'What brings you to these parts, eh? Not my dream, but my *gut* tells me you did not cross that stormy ocean simply to pay The Gobán a friendly visit. You have some other purpose. What is it, pray?'

'Young Arthur needs help.'

'What kind of help?'

'Hibernian help,' Merlin said.

Although Merlin had never seen the Sword of Light he knew that The Gobán kept it in his house in a sort of shrine. It must, he reckoned, be behind the curtain. Jabbing his staff in its direction he said gravely, 'Arthur needs the help of the gods, the Tuatha de Danaan, to be precise.'

The Gobán's countenance darkened. He stopped chewing, swallowed slowly and laying down his meat said emphatically, 'There is a problem here Merlin, an old one, and you know it very well.'

'Indeed I do,' Merlin returned with a sigh. 'The Hibernians and the Britons have different Mothers.'

'Precisely! Danu is the Mother of the Hibernians and Don is the Mother of *your* nation.'

Merlin had heard the argument many times before. It was one of the Hibernian bards' favourite means of separating their nation from the Britons, and it wearied him to the bone. He had no time for these semantics, these theological nuances, this insularity of the Hibernians. To him the worshipful Mother was the same great *Mother of All.* That, in fact, was the only name by which he ever invoked her in ritual.

'But,' Merlin countered, 'don't we all have the same *tongue*? Don't we all speak the same language......more or less? Language, man! That's the thing.'

'No,' The Gobán impetuously returned. 'The *Mother's* the thing.'

'Listen to me, Gobán,' Merlin said tapping his forehead with his staff, 'the *Spirit of the Time* tells me that the nations must co-operate. The Roman She-Wolf may be gone, but there is another, even worse beast rising in our midst. I can sometimes even see it with my own eyes. It will devour us all if we don't learn to act *together*.'

Merlin pointed his staff directly at the curtain. 'I want it for our young Arthur. Nay, I *demand* it.'

'Never!' The Gobán cried. His jowls were red and trembling with anger. 'Never! Impossible.'

Merlin stood up and shook his staff at The Gobán.

'Nothing,' he shouted, 'is impossible for Merlin of the Britons! Nothing!'

The Goban sprung up. 'You can't have the Sword, I tell you!' he roared. 'And I'll show you why.'

He dashed to the far end of the room where he pulled open the curtain. Although Merlin had never seen the Sword of Light he had heard much of it. He imagined it to be lying here now on an elegantly carved table, cushioned on oriental brocade or some such exquisite fabric. But what he saw shocked him severely. It was a crude, even ridiculous sight: a huge, square block of granite into which was stuck something that could only be the fabulous Sword, for what *was* visible of it - its golden hilt and part of its great silver blade - shone with all the brilliance of the sun.

'The Sword of Light,' The Gobán announced.

'How.....how in the name of all the gods of Hades did it get like that?' Merlin cried.

'It's a long story,' The Gobán replied. 'It was being abused. Worse, it was in danger of being stolen. I couldn't take the risk. I got Balor to put a spell on it.'

'Balor! You mean you invoked the Evil One to protect the Sword of Light?'

'Yes. It's for the good. No upstart can ever misuse it again. He must have *real power* if he is to pull the Sword from the stone.'

'And who, may I ask, decides who tries?'

'Me, who else?'

'I have to try!

'No.'

'Yes, by the gods. Yes!' Merlin cried and attempted to push past The Gobán.

The Gobán stayed him. 'No.'

Once again Merlin raised his staff threateningly at The

Gobán. He also let out a long, loud incantation.

The Gobán slunk back.

Merlin approached the Sword unimpeded. Still chanting and waving his staff about, he felt a tremendous power rising in him. He closed his eyes, prayed hard and after touching the Sword's hilt lightly with his staff, grasped it. And to his supreme delight and the utter astonishment of The Gobán, the Sword slid out of its spell-bound, granite encasement as easily as it would out of a custom-made scabbard!

The Sword of Light was his. This Sword was for Arthur.

CHAPTER SIX

GUINEVERE

Though now long dead, Arthur's father, Pendragon, had been a tribal chieftain in the hill country of Cambria. While he was alive he commanded wide respect, even as the Roman army occupied and controlled vast swathes of the Cambrian lowlands. Pendragon brought up all his children according to the ancient customs and had Arthur judiciously betrothed to Guinevere, the daughter of a neighbouring chieftain, when both she and Arthur were still very young.

Guinevere was a little older than Arthur, and although they hardly knew one another when the match was formally made, they nevertheless formed a close and sweet friendship, and after puberty fell deeply and passionately in love.

Guinevere grew into an extraordinarily beautiful woman of whom Arthur was immensely proud. Her beauty was notorious throughout the land. She inspired Arthur into great ambition, so much so that while he was still young, and in defiance of his father's vehement objections, he enlisted in the Roman army as a mercenary soldier. Although he missed Guinevere enormously because of this, their lovemaking grew all the sweeter, for he was allowed to return regularly to his tribe on leave. However, in the army he eventually forsook his tribal roots and like many of the Roman soldiers took up the religion of Mithras. This meant that when the time for his marriage to Guinevere eventually arrived, he insisted upon it being enacted according to the Mithraic rite.

In the religion of Mithras marriage was considered a sacrament. Divorce was prohibited except in very special circumstances. For this, if no other reason, Guinevere from the beginning cultivated a deep loyalty to Arthur, a loyalty reinforced by fidelity. But, in truth, the passion had long gone out of their relationship. It had in fact ended soon after the marriage. It sometimes seemed to Guinevere that Arthur had even lost interest in having a child by her! Nowadays, with the Romans long gone from the land, his dream of Logres ruled every aspect of his life.

One afternoon in winter, while Arthur was away from Camelot, Guinevere lay forlornly on her feather bed wondering how she would fill the rest of the dreary afternoon. She was fully dressed with a large, red fox-fur thrown loosely across her long, shapely legs. There was an upturned, open book by her side, and a bored look on her lovely face. Periodically she ran her splayed fingers through her hair. This hair, her finest feature, was long and thick, its colour the deep, rich, red-brown of freshly turned soil, its texture soft as sea-foam.

Every so often her wide, sensuous mouth opened slightly in a half-yawn at which moments she also reached for her book again. She had read it many times; in fact it was the only book she ever really read. It was written by a wise and knowledgeable old man she once met on a journey with Arthur to Pictland and was all about the sunken island of Lyonesse, from where, the old man authoritatively informed, her own ancestors originally came.

Lyonesse was originally part of Atlantis, a continent which once existed in the Western Ocean but sank in the Great Flood of thousands of years ago. Guinevere's forebears had been kings and queens of Lyonesse, the old man said.

Ah! To be Queen of Camelot! Now there was a thought that warmed Guinevere's blood on days like this; cold days and nights of winter as she waited for Arthur's return. For he was gone yet again, responding to some call or other. Such expeditions he constantly undertook in pursuit of his great dream, the dream of bringing the ever-multiplying warring factions of his ancient nation into some kind of understanding of the need for a common goal of peace. It was, alas, a dream that for Guinevere turned the battle, not the bed, into Arthur's first love.

Guinevere took up her book again. But her attention was soon deflected by a gentle tapping on the door of her bedchamber.

'Come in!' Guinevere said, and Erecura, her old, trustworthy, but down-in-the-mouth waiting-woman entered.

'What is it, Erecura?' Guinevere asked.

'It is Lancelot, ma'am,' Erecura replied, her eyes cast disapprovingly sideways. 'He wishes to see you.'

'There's nothing *very* unusual about that, is there,

Erecura?' Guinevere testily questioned.

'No, ma'am,' Erecura noncommittally agreed.

'Where is he?'

'In the library.'

'Tell him I'll be there presently,' Guinevere said.

When Erecura left, Guinevere sprung gingerly from her bed and stood in front of her full-length mirror. Tidying her hair, she thought *But he was only here yesterday.* She smoothed creases on her blue satin gown. *Perhaps Erecura thinks he is calling a little too often.* She stepped forward, and buttoning up the white lace neck of her gown said with a wry smile to her reflection, 'Perhaps Erecura is right.'

She threw a shawl over her shoulders, pulled on a pair of thick woollen socks and made her way to the library which was a few doors from her bedchamber. When she silently entered its open door she found Lancelot in full armour standing with his back to her running his fingers over some leather-bound books on the shelves. He turned slowly when she purposely gave a little cough.

Though by no means an old man, Lancelot was the most experienced and respected of Arthur's militia. He was however much older than Guinevere, but by how many years precisely she had never found out. *Yet surely old enough to be my father*, she sometimes thought after a conversation with him. She had had a troubled relationship with her own, long-dead father, but Lancelot was nothing like *him.* In fact, if she was truly honest, she found Lancelot's tall, strong, though much scarred body, coupled with his mature, handsome looks, very attractive.

Because of his fastidious nature, Arthur always left him in charge when he was away. At such times Lancelot considered it his primary duty to keep a regular check on Guinevere's well-being.

As Guinevere gazed upon him now the thought flashed through her mind about how much gossip there was in Camelot as to why he never took another to wife after his divorce some years previously from his Roman wife, Imelda. *Divorce, of course, is easy under Roman law,* she inwardly sighed.

'Lancelot!' she declared, her sensuous lips stretching to a one-sided smile. 'How good of you to call......again.'

Placing his hand upon his sword, Lancelot bowed. 'It is my pleasure always, ma'am, to call on you. You are well, I take it?'

'Yes. Quite,' Guinevere said. 'Will you have a seat?'

'No, ma'am. There is too much to attend to.'

'Camelot is a complicated place,' Guinevere proffered.

'Yes. And it has so many valuable possessions!'

For an embarrassing moment Guinevere thought he was referring to herself! She was relieved when, pointing to the shelves behind him, he continued, 'Like these books.'

'Ah yes,' she instantly agreed. 'They are surely valuable, Lancelot.'

'It took Merlin many years to build up this library.'

'We are terribly grateful to him.'

'Are you aware that some of them badly need cleaning?'

Guinevere changed colour! 'No,' she confessed. 'I wasn't. I'll tell Erecura straightaway.'

A white dove suddenly landed on a nearby windowsill. They both looked at it silently. After a few moments Guinevere asked, 'Any news from Arthur?'

'Well, ma'am,' Lancelot replied, 'as you probably know, he has gone on a covert operation with Gawain and Kay to Sorbiodunum.'

'Yes,' Guinevere said, 'but I'm not sure precisely why.'

'He is investigating a report that Mordred is setting up

his headquarters in that ruined Roman hill-fort. If this is true it poses the greatest threat yet to Arthur's own plans.'

'Mordred,' Guinevere reflected. 'I have heard Arthur speak of him. He seems..........well.....difficult.'

'You may say that again. It is said that he wants to be king of the Britons, but I say he is a veritable child of the Devil.'

The dove flew away.

'When will Arthur be back?' Guinevere asked.

'A scout is due in Camelot this very day, ma'am. We shall have definite news for you, and everybody else, then.'

'The men miss him dearly, don't they?' Guinevere said walking casually past Lancelot to the bookshelves.

'We certainly do,' Lancelot agreed.

Guinevere ran her long index finger down the fat spine of a volume by Cicero. Wincing at the mark she left on the book she turned to Lancelot and eyeing the green tip of her finger said, 'Thank you, Lancelot.'

'My pleasure, ma'am,' Lancelot said, bowed and left.

For a long time Guinevere stood gazing idly at the open door, sucking her finger.

CHAPTER SEVEN

THE HOLY GRAIL

According to the genealogies of the Hibernian Bards Pelagius was descended from a southerly branch of the Novantae, an ancient tribe of Western Pictland, a sept of whom had migrated to Hibernia hundreds of years ago and established a line there.

Pelagius was proud of his heritage because he knew that during the Roman occupation of Britannia it was the Novantae who initiated a defensive alliance with their northerly neighbours, the Caledonii. This alliance eventually grew into a powerful, nation-wide tribal federation that actually kept the Romans from ever conquering Pictland and from which the Roman name for the country, Caledonia, subsequently derived.

Pelagius was born to peasant parents in Hibernia. But it was known from many signs accompanying his birth that he was a special child. So the Druids, who were all-powerful, and occupied every important profession in the land, took him from his parents and educated him. They did this with every child who showed promise of becoming a member of their cult.

Their system of education was based exclusively on the word. Becoming a Druid was intense, long and arduous. The Druids owned many fine but secret libraries and Pelagius learnt many strange and wonderful things denied to the masses, especially the arts of reading and writing, and not just in his native tongue, but in various other languages also. He enjoyed learning and looked forward to being fully initiated into the Druidic Order. However one day in a library he came across a story about Jesus and was enthralled. He desperately wanted to know more. But because he found no other reference to Jesus in any of the Druids' libraries he questioned his teachers. They however emphatically denied possessing any more knowledge of Jesus than what was written in the one enchanting little story Pelagius had found. Pelagius was not satisfied. He sensed that the Druids knew more but were afraid to tell him, why he could not say. Then one day he learnt from a total stranger that an important new religion called Catholicism had grown up around the figure of Jesus in Rome. This, Pelagius decided, was the reason for the Druids' reticence! For if Catholicism ever came to Hibernia it would surely undermine their authority!

Keeping these thoughts to himself Pelagius conceived a long-term but secret ambition to go to Rome. Considering it wise to first finish his education, he did, and when the time eventually came for his induction into the Druid Order he astounded everyone by refusing. Ostracized then by both his teachers and his tribe, he borrowed gold from a few admiring friends and set out on the long journey to the great city.

In Rome his accent and odd appearance were the subject of much ridicule and gossip, but because he was such a remarkably well-educated young man he did well. In the vast libraries of the city he found scores of books on Jesus, all of which he studied carefully. He came to the firm belief that Jesus was the new God of mankind, and became utterly devoted to him. Eventually he became more knowledgeable about Jesus than even the most erudite of the Catholic priests in Rome. They then tried to ordain him as a priest, but he refused. He wanted, he argued, to relate to Jesus in his own Hibernian and freedom-loving way. He wrote many letters and books about this which made him famous among the Roman *literati*, and as a result gained many followers. However, the Catholic priests came to detest him. They accused him of being a latter-day Gnostic. His following nevertheless grew, and grew so large that he posed a threat to the ever expanding power of the priests in Rome. And so they expelled him from their city, condemning him as a heretic.

Pelagius then went to Alexandria which boasted the finest library in the entire world. There, recognizing and appreciating his vast knowledge, the authorities allowed him to lecture on Jesus. But when the hugely influential Catholic writer and Egyptian bishop, Augustine, heard about this he started a virulent campaign against Pelagius. He denounced him in public meetings, in numerous books and regularly in church sermons. This resulted one day in a blood-thirsty Catholic mob chasing Pelagius out of the library and through the streets of Alexandria. He was forced to flee for his life into the Egyptian desert.

In the desert Pelagius found a cave and lived in it. He

ate very little and talked to few. But he made friends with the wild animals and birds, and one bird in particular - a small white dove - was a source of great comfort to him. It lived with him in the cave and followed him wherever he wandered.

Life was very hard in the desert. Pelagius missed teaching and talking to people about his beloved Jesus, but his austere way of life deepened his love for his divine Master. More and more he prayed to him, often all day and all night without interruption. Then one night as he knelt in prayer, a strange, handsome, but very earnest-looking young man stood suddenly before him. He was dressed in a long shimmering robe of pure black silk. In his hands he held an indescribably beautiful crystal Chalice. It contained an ethereal rose-coloured liquid. From the Chalice all the colours of the rainbow rayed.

Pelagius was astonished. 'Who are you?' he asked.

'I am a Messenger,' the young man replied. 'My precise name I cannot yet reveal to you, but you will know it in time. Now however I must ask *you* a question. Have you heard of the *Four Treasures of Hibernia*?'

'Yes,' Pelagius obediently replied. 'I was educated by the Druids in Hibernia.'

The young man smiled knowingly. 'Yes. And therefore you must also know that the Chalice of Rebirth is the missing *Treasure* of Hibernia.'

'I do.'

'Well, this is it.'

With awe and wonder, Pelagius gazed upon the lovely Vessel.

The Messenger continued, 'This Chalice is not available to the profane, but only to those whose soul has been purified through suffering. It contains nourishment for both men and gods. This nourishment is the meaning of life. I now offer it to you. Will you take it?'

'Yes, of course,' Pelagius answered.

The young man then held out the Chalice and Pelagius took a sip. The effect was indescribable. It was as if he had drunk the very sun!

'What is it?' he asked.

'It is the Blood of the Risen One,' the Messenger solemnly informed.

Pelagius's hands flew to his mouth! Suddenly he felt as if he had committed some terrible sin!

But the young man smiled serenely and said, 'Fear not, for all men are sinners. But this Chalice contains the cure for their sickness.'

There was a high flat stone on the cave's floor which Pelagius used as a table. The young man carefully placed the Chalice on the stone and in silence they contemplated its great beauty. Eventually the young man went on, 'Listen now to the story of this Chalice. Long ago when Jesus of Nazareth was a young man, he knew that this Chalice existed in a strange and distant land to the west called Hibernia. When he grew up and began his ministry he dearly hoped that he might one day use the Chalice in ritual meals he often had with his twelve closest followers, the Apostles. Now, among his close followers was a man called Josephus of Aramathea. Josephus was a tin merchant who in the time before the Crucifixion of Jesus travelled all over the Empire, including to Hibernia. A few years before Jesus died Josephus planned a trip abroad which included Hibernia. So when Jesus learnt of this he asked Josephus would he try to procure the Chalice for him. Josephus would do anything for his Master and instantly agreed. So, when Josephus arrived in Hibernia, Jesus inwardly guided him to a Druid called Altus who was the guardian of the Chalice in Hibernia. Jesus had already appeared to Altus a short time before in a dream, and convinced him that it was right and proper to give the Chalice to Josephus. So, in this magical way Josephus succeeded in his task. He got the Chalice, brought it back to Jerusalem and the Master used it many times in sacred rituals with the twelve, but most especially at the Last Supper on the evening before he died. Josephus was not an Apostle, so he was not at this last meal. Nevertheless, he remained responsible for the Chalice, and after Jesus died on the Cross collected some of Jesus's blood in it from a wound in his side. Now, after the Resurrection, Josephus, the twelve and others used the Chalice at special agape or love-feasts they had commemorating the divine Master. And when Josephus himself died, the Chalice was carefully guarded by Jesus's ever-growing number of followers and has, for more than four hundred years, been used in various parts of the Empire where the Pistis Sophia, that is, the sacred, secret, and initiation wisdom of the Master Jesus was taught. Increasingly however it has become the focus of evil powers whose objective is to destroy it. The place it can be best protected from these evil powers is its original home, Hibernia. And you, Pelagius, have been chosen to accomplish this very special task. Do you accept?'

'Wholeheartedly,' Pelagius replied.

The young man continued, 'Then I hereby appoint you the earthly guardian of this heavenly Vessel. You must leave for Hibernia with it immediately. The dove will go with you and guide you to a secret, sacred place where you must build a temple for this holiest of all things on Earth.'

'A temple?' Pelagius queried.

'Yes, the Temple of the Risen One. An Angel of the Lord will instruct you.'

'I will gladly do all this,' Pelagius obediently promised.

'Guard this Chalice with your life,' the Messenger said.

Soon afterwards he departed with the words, 'Feed the sheep.'

Pelagius immediately left the desert and returned to Hibernia with the Chalice. Although he was a native of this land he had been away for so long that he now felt a total stranger. Nevertheless he was determined to fulfil his promise to the Messenger. And as the Messenger himself had said, the dove led him to a lonely but very hallowed place where he knew he must build the Temple. It was at the foot of a high mountain. In the mountain Pelagius found a secret, dry cave where he lived with the Chalice for many months. He drank often from it but its contents never diminished. An angelic voice told him to be patient.

He moved about the land very cautiously. But the dove directed chosen people to him. These Pelagius instructed in the mystic gospel of Jesus. And although he said nothing of the Chalice, all these people were deeply inspired by Pelagius, his knowledge, wisdom, and especially his sanctity.

When they were about twelve in number Pelagius, with them, started collecting stones. The dove pointed out each and every one. When eventually there was a great pile of them at the foot of the mountain the voice told Pelagius to start building. So, one by one he and his companions started placing the stones on top of one another. The voice directed every move.

And so, in this miraculous way the Temple was eventually built! It was only then that Pelagius told his pupils about the Chalice of Rebirth. It was brought down from the mountain cave in a beautiful ceremony and placed in the Tabernacle of the Temple. The whole Temple now took on a wonderful and mysterious glow. During this ceremony Pelagius also renamed the Chalice. He called it the Grail, taking the name from the Latin word *gradalis*, which means gradual. For he knew that only after much hard, patient, and inner work would anyone be able to see it from now on.

Pelagius's pupils became known as Grail Initiates. Over the years their numbers grew, but they remained far fewer than was needed to combat the growing wickedness of the world. Then one night at prayer in the Temple the angelic voice told Pelagius to seek out one called Arthur of the Britons. Arthur was destined, the voice said, to become a great king and would be supremely helpful to the future of the Grail Quest.

That was the reason Pelagius went to Camelot years ago. And although he did not get to know Arthur then, he made the Quest known through Merlin, Arthur's great friend and adviser.

Merlin never forgot his conversation with Pelagius, and Arthur continued to urge him to seek the Grail. Many times over the years Merlin started out on the Quest but gave up due to unexpected and sometimes even impossible obstacles. However, after acquiring The Sword of Light from The Gobán in Dunseverick he reckoned that the omens would never be better. And anyway he was actually *in* Hibernia! He would simply *have* to try again!

With the Sword secure in its scabbard, which The Gobán had reluctantly given him, Merlin wrapped it up in a blanket and with this bundle tied to his back set out in search of the Temple. He remembered that Pelagius instructed him to speak to no one about the Temple or the Grail, so he didn't. The only thing he knew for certain was that the Temple was somewhere in the south of Hibernia. Pelagius had however given him one clue. 'You are nearly there,' he had said, 'when you see a tall, stony, conical-shaped mountain.'

Merlin walked in a southerly direction for many days through thick mist, taking shelter under sprawling oaks and sleeping rough in animal huts or wherever he could lay his head. However, the mist only got thicker and eventually so thick that he wasn't even sure if he was headed south! (And in such mists his magic was useless!) But suddenly one morning he woke up to find the mist totally gone! Now everything in the landscape stood out magically in crystal clear detail. Scanning his surroundings Merlin soon became aware he was on high ground.......and near the foot of a conically shaped mountain! He got very excited!

He skirted the mountain in a westward direction. Then after rounding a rocky outcrop which tediously blocked his vision for an unnaturally long time, suddenly..........there it was: the Grail Temple!

Tucked away in a forest clearing, in a valley directly below him, beyond a narrow, racing river, a low, pap-shaped, green forested hill rising softly behind it, the Temple was profoundly striking. It comprised two circular structures, one about twice as large as the other, the two merging slightly, and ingeniously capped by intersecting domes. Built on a hillock above a small settlement of daub and wattle huts, and pure white apart from the roof which was green, it shone like the sun.

'By the gods,' Merlin grunted, 'this man is a Pythagorean or I'm a Jew!'

He had not seen anything vaguely like it before! Was it even real? He dashed down the hillside, several times nearly falling into pools of brown bog-water. Wet and muddy he eventually reached the darkly racing river. A rickety, wooden swing-bridge spanned it. He stopped at it and took some deep breaths.

'I think it's real!' he said grasping the rail.

Calmly then he crossed the bridge and made his way slowly along a track through the little huts. Hooded figures, some possibly female, in loosely-fitting, long white cowls flitted silently but busily about; others were toiling in a patchwork of fields that covered the rising ground behind the Temple. Yet others were working in yards or gardens by the huts. Many stopped and stared at the stooped, grey-clad figure with the long wispy beard and broad-brimmed hat, an awkward bundle on his back and a big black staff in his hand.

'I'm looking for Pelagius,' Merlin enquired of one of the workers, a wide-eyed young man who was weeding a patch of vegetables. He studied Merlin with squinting eyes before silently replying by pointing his finger at the Temple. 'Don't blink or it might disappear,' the young man mysteriously advised.

'Thank you, I won't,' Merlin said and continued on his way.

The young man kept staring.

Acutely aware of the many pairs of eyes following him, Merlin climbed up the winding pebble path to the Temple to survey it at close quarters.

The material seemed to be white marble, but Merlin wasn't sure. He studied the amazing, double-domed roof. *Slate? Silver*? It shimmered green. *What the hell kind of stuff could it possibly be?* He walked all around the Temple. It had no widows and only one door. This too was white and had three steps up to it. It was in the larger of the two circular constructs and faced east overlooking the huts below. On the door was painted a bright red, four-petal rose.

Merlin mounted the steps and was admiring the simple beauty of the rose when he suddenly felt a tap on his shoulder. He turned and was startled to find Pelagius standing beside him. Pelagius smiled wistfully from inside the hood of his long, snow-white cowl. On his outstretched left fist his white dove was perched.

'You found it at last,' he said quietly, slowly pulling down his hood. 'I had almost given up on you.'

Tall, gaunt and erect, he looked older but even more other-worldly than when Merlin first met him in Camelot.

Merlin tugged at his beard. 'I was doing something up north,' he confessed, 'so I said to myself it's now or never.'

Casting his eye very deliberately over the awkward bundle on Merlin's back, in characteristically slow and carefully measured tones Pelagius said, 'This Temple is not easy to find. You did very well.

'There are many places that are hard to find,' Merlin said, thinking of Avalliona.

'Yes, but *so* many people set out on the path to this Temple and fail to find it.'

'I'm different,' Merlin haughtily returned.

Pelagius smiled. 'I feel certain you will be well rewarded.' he continued, 'I was expecting you.'

'What?' Merlin exclaimed. 'Today?'

'Yes. I had a vision. I'll tell you more later. But first,

I'm sure you'd like to look inside.'

'Oh yes!' Merlin said enthusiastically.

After gently shaking the dove from his fist and contemplatively watching her in flight, Pelagius turned to Merlin and said softly, 'She speaks sometimes, you know.'

'I'd watch her then, if I were you,' Merlin replied.

Pelagius smiled, took from his belt a huge iron key and opened the door.

Inside the Temple was dim. The only light was from a flame on a pure white altar. The flame was tiny but gave a remarkable light in that it lit up only the altar itself and what was directly above and below it. The altar was on a raised platform, reached by three steps and was placed directly beneath the larger of the two intersecting domes. A small book was the only other object on it. The air was clean, fresh and faintly perfumed. After locking the door Pelagius took a taper from a nearby shelf, lit it from the altar flame, and began lighting torches that jutted from the Temple walls. Around the altar were now revealed a number of carved columns, supporting the cupola above. The space beneath the smaller dome also became visible. In it was a pure white cube, about the size of a small house. It too was surrounded by carved columns reaching to the cupola. The cube's only feature was a low door which curiously had no handle. It shone however like gold and directly faced the altar.

'The altar flame,' Pelagius informed as he lit a torch, 'is also the Grail Flame. It comes from the sun. The Greeks call it holy fire. We call it Holy *Spirit* fire. It will only go out if and when the Temple outlives its usefulness, or you could say, dies. It represents the life of the Temple. It was the gift of an Angel at the Temple's dedication.'

'An Angel?' Merlin queried as he strode enthusiastically about, stopping here and there to examine various carvings or inscriptions on the wooden pillars.

'A god if you want,' Pelagius said.

'The god of the Grail, I suppose,' Merlin said as he counted the pillars: twelve under the large cupola, seven under the small.

'Of course,' Pelagius said.

'Jesus then,' Merlin challenged.

'Oh no! Jesus was much more than an Angel.'

Merlin's head quivered on his long thin neck. 'But you actually *know* this ....this Angel..... I mean you've.....?'

'Met him?'

'Yes. Have you *seen* him, or........or her?'

Pelagius smiled condescendingly. 'But Merlin, are you perhaps pulling my leg?'

'Never!'

'But surely *you*, of all people, know that angels or gods are not subjected to the interminable tortures that we, poor creatures, must suffer regarding *sex*?'

'Well,' Merlin conceded, sucking his teeth, 'I suppose.......'

'And yes, I have seen this Angel. But I *hear* him more than see him.'

'Him?'

'Merely a figure of speech. I prefer "him" to the impersonal "it".'

'Hmmm. I suppose,' Merlin said, now jabbing his staff at the large white cube beneath the small dome 'your.....your Grail thing is in there?'

'Yes. That's the Grail Tabernacle. '

'Can I......perhaps.......?'

'Oh no,' Pelagius instantly returned, 'you have first to be initiated.'

'But I *am* initiated!' Merlin irritably retorted.

'Yes, but certainly not into the secrets of Jesus.'

Merlin went red! 'Then at least tell me what this Grail is?'

'You can only know that by serving it.'

Merlin grunted and went up very close to one of the pillars. Squinting at a figure carved on it, he said, 'Looks like Helios, the Greek's Sun-God.'

'You *are* a clever man, Merlin!'

'Why Helios?'

'Jesus, or should I say his holy Christos *spirit*, comes from the sun. That this Sun-Spirit would some day incarnate on the Earth has been known to the followers of Zarathustra in the East from the most ancient times. The Grail contains all the wisdom of the East.'

'Contains? Is the Grail a vessel of some kind then?'

Realizing his injudicious choice of words Pelagius replied simply, 'Represents.'

Merlin snorted, went to another pillar and tapped it with his staff.

'I see,' he haughtily declared, 'a sign of the Babylonian Zodiac is carved on each of these pillars.'

'These pillars represent many things,' Pelagius replied. 'Twelve is the number of the starry cosmos.'

'I know.'

'Mmm. But these pillars here most fundamentally represent the twelve Apostles. Have you heard of them?'

'No.'

'They were the inner circle of Jesus. To them he gave his most secret and powerful teachings. Through them the new faith and the new Law will eventually be established over the whole world. At the moment however, only a few of the Apostles are really known.'

'Like who?'

'Well, let's say Peter and John. The Romans follow Peter. But we follow John.'

'Why? What's the difference?'

'In a nutshell, I am a reincarnation of John.'

'How the hell do you know that!?'

'Simple! My Angel told me.' Pelagius pointed to the book on the altar. 'And there,' he continued, 'is the only book I wrote here in Hibernia. However, wrote is not quite the word. It was channelled.............by my Angel. It's my gospel, the Book of the Grail. I use it for the instructions of my Grail pupils.'

A serpent carved on one of the pillars under the smaller cupola suddenly caught Merlin's ranging eye. He immediately ran to it.

'These seven pillars also represent many things,' Pelagius informed as he watched Merlin carefully examine the serpent, 'but most especially the seven planets. That one is Mercury.'

Merlin faced Pelagius. This was a chance not to be missed! 'Have you ever heard of a serpent called Naas?' he queried.

'My, my, but you really are a *very* knowledgeable man,' Pelagius replied. 'How in the Lord's name do you know about Naas?'

'It doesn't matter. Just tell me what *you* know.'

'Naas is actually Hebrew for serpent. There is a remnant of an old Christian Gnostic sect who hang out somewhere in the Syrian Desert who worship the serpent and are known as The Naasenes. They are actually one of the few original Gnostic sects still in existence. The Gnostics generally were wiped out by the Romans well over a hundred years ago.

However, the Naasenes persist, and like many Christian schools - my own included I might humbly add - try to gain followers. The Naasenes also send their initiates all over the world. I believe there are even some of them here in the south of Hibernia. But heaven forbid that they will expand! For they have no idea of the true Christ. As far as I'm concerned, they represent nothing less than a demonization of Christianity! They worship the old serpent Lucifer, or one of his hosts. Lucifer is nothing but a fallen angel, and they think by worshipping him they are worshipping the Christ! It's monstrous!'

Merlin looked worried. 'Thank you,' he said abruptly, 'I think I've seen and heard enough for one day.'

'As you wish,' Pelagius said.

He took one of the torches from the wall and doused it in a large bucket of water near the door. As he passed Merlin with another torch to douse he stopped and once again very deliberately eyed the odd bundle on Merlin's back.

'You know,' he said, 'my Angel told me that you have come here directly from Dal Riada.'

Merlin froze!

Pelagius continued, 'And that somehow you have acquired the Hibernian's Sword of Light.'

Merlin turned away.

'Jesus said, "I am the Light of the World," ' Pelagius quietly said, 'and my Angel also said the light of this Sword can become the light of Jesus if it is passed through the Grail Flame on this altar here.'

Merlin spun round. 'And what then?' he barked.

'With the Sword, Arthur could turn his twelve closest men into *Christian Knights*.'

Merlin sucked his teeth furiously. What in the gods' name was he supposed to do now? He began to tremble. A word involuntarily escaped his lips: 'Jesus.'

Pelagius smiled. 'Yes,' he said. 'And can you do something to help him?'

A terrible sense of helplessness suddenly overcame Merlin. Resignedly he rested his staff against the altar steps. Then stiffly loosening the bundle from his back he laid it on the floor, opened it and took the Sword from its scabbard. Its incongruous beauty drew a loud gasp from Pelagius.

Reluctantly Merlin handed the Sword to Pelagius. With it Pelagius ascended the steps to the altar. There he raised the shining blade solemnly above his head, looked up to heaven, closed his eyes and prayed. Opening his eyes again he brought the Sword down and slowly passed it through the Grail Flame. The great blade shone brighter than ever. The whole Temple was ablaze with it.

Once again Pelagius raised the Sword above his head. This time he loudly declaimed, 'Let this great *Treasure* of the Hibernians now become yours, O Lord. And let Arthur of the Britons wield it for the good of all man- and womankind, for ever and ever.'

Immediately a voice resounded deep and strong from inside the Grail Tabernacle: 'Amen.'

Pelagius bowed his head in thanksgiving.

Merlin however didn't hear the voice. But in the deep and holy silence that followed it he saw that familiar but formidable Serpent again.

CHAPTER EIGHT

THE MISSION

Patrick was a big, bearded, fresh-faced, muscular man in his early forties when he set out from his monastery in Auxerre for Hibernia, charged by his superior, Germanus to stamp out the Pelagian heresy and convert the Hibernians to the 'one true faith.'

With a purse-full of Roman soldi, dressed in a warm, woollen cowl, crozier in hand, with the gospel book, purple mitre, embroidered priestly stole and a fine silk soutane in his knapsack - all brand new and given him by Germanus - Patrick stood on the day of his departure at the gate of the monastery in Auxerre and received Germanus's farewell blessing with a sprinkling of holy water that, Germanus said, was consecrated by no less a person than Pope Celestine himself. Beside Patrick stood Ignatius and Benedictus, two young novice monks of Auxerre whom

Germanus allowed Patrick to take with him as companions and assistants, but only after Germanus had thoroughly indoctrinated them into the evils of the Pelagian heresy.

Neither Ignatius nor Benedictus knew much about the world beyond their monastery walls. But that did not bother Patrick, for he always saw worldliness as a danger to faith. Benedictus and Ignatius possessed the finer virtues of piety and loyalty, and in their zealous, youthful love for the great new Godman, Jesus, Patrick saw a fresh and beautiful reflection of his own deep and abiding love. Their faith could only grow through a mission like this.

Germanus's parting words were, 'Baptize all those poor Hibernian yobs now, you hear?'

'We'll do our best, Your Grace,' Patrick replied and they set off.

One morning, a few days into their journey, they were sitting by a river preparing breakfast, when an old beggar-man suddenly appeared and held out his bowl. Ignatius immediately broke his bread and put some into the bowl. The old man quickly gobbled it but continued to beg. Patrick then opened his purse and to the astonishment of his two young companions put one of the gold coins into the bowl! The old man immediately whipped it out, gazed at it ecstatically, dropped his bowl and ran away.

Ignatius, a thin-faced, serious young man, ponderously watched the beggar until he disappeared into the wood from which he had emerged. Then he asked, 'Father, will we not need all the coin for our journey, and especially when we get to Hibernia?'

Patrick looked gravely into the young man's eyes and raised his eyebrows as if to say, 'Anything else to add?' When Ignatius remained respectfully silent Patrick ruefully continued, 'Perhaps you should have become a merchant instead of a monk, hmm?'

Ignatius was embarrassed. Patrick then opened his knapsack and took out the gospel book, and pressing his big thumb down on a page said, 'Listen to this. It's about the twelve Apostles and their mission. Chapter ten, verse five: "These twelve Jesus sent out with the following instructions: provide no gold, silver or copper to fill your purse, no pack for the road, no second coat, no shoes, no stick." '

He looked up. 'The moral,' he continued, 'is this, my young friends: on our mission we are going to follow the gospel to the letter. Understand?'

The young men nodded.

Patrick put the book down by his side on the grass then and bit hungrily into his bread.

But Benedictus was frowning at the fine leather boots Germanus had given him for the journey. Eventually he asked, 'Father........it also says...........no....no......'

'No what?'

'No shoes.'

Patrick scratched his curly red beard and studied the inquisitive young face.

'Mmm,' he muttered, 'does it, now?'

Benedictus nodded hesitantly.

'It means no *second* pair of shoes,' Patrick informed.

Benedictus frowned but remained silent. After a few thoughtful moments Ignatius pointed to the beautiful ebony, silver-tipped crozier by Patrick's side and said, 'But is that not *really* a stick, Father?'

Patrick stopped chewing and raised his eyes to heaven. After swallowing he took the crozier in his hand and looked it up and down.

'It's a *Roman* stick,' he said to Ignatius with raised eyebrows.

'Still a stick, Father,' Benedictus challenged with a big smile.

'By Jove,' Patrick declared, energetically slapping his thigh, 'but I believe I've chosen two fine young philosophers to accompany me on my mission!'

He looked at the crozier again and suddenly saw the ascetic old face of cantankerous Germanus. An irresistible impulse suddenly took hold of him. He stood up, raised the crozier above his head and to the utter astonishment of his young companions shouted, 'Yes, by God, it *is* a stick!' and flung it into the racing river. Then he held his hands in the air, inquisitively eyed the young men and asked, 'Anything else?'

Benedictus laughed heartily. Ignatius however worriedly watched the crozier float down the river. When it disappeared he slowly turned to Patrick and asked, 'But Father, how will you make the Hibernians know you are a Catholic bishop now?'

Patrick took his purse in his hand then and jangled it tauntingly at Ignatius. 'I'll bribe them.'

'Are you serious, Father?' Ignatius said.

Patrick sat down. 'I don't know,' he said, 'but the Hibernians won't need to know I'm a bishop, Catholic or otherwise. That was Germanus's idea.'

'But the Pelagians, Father,' Ignatius challenged. 'Archbishop Germanus said that we, that *you*, must have the authority of Rome to....to....'

'Stamp out the Pelagian heresy, right?'

'Yes.'

'That too was the Archbishop's idea, not mine. But I played along with it because I needed both his permission and his gold to get to Hibernia. My real mission was always simply to return to Hibernia to preach the Word of the Lord because I was asked by an Angel to do so in a dream. I know nothing about Pelagius or the Pelagians apart from what Germanus said. And all I remember from him is that they are accused of making far too much of human free will. It doesn't seem to me to be much of a heresy. In fact I rather like the idea of free will. Anyway, when we get to Hibernia we will find out for ourselves what this Pelagian business is all about. Until then, forget it.'

'But the Catholic Bishop, Augustine,' Ignatius persisted, 'believes that it is a mortal sin to......'

'Forget about Augustine too!' Patrick interjected in a raised voice. 'I read some of his books. He was nothing but a guilt-ridden misogynist. He also had baptism on the brain! Germanus was simply trying to brainwash both of you with his Catholic dogma. But we are not going to imprison ourselves, our *minds* in all that stuff. If necessary we'll start our own bloody religion!'

'Sorry, Father,' Ignatius said, 'I was only....'

'Listen to me! We are not going to Hibernia with hatred and venom in our blood for something we don't understand. We are going only to spread the peace and love of the Lord that is in our hearts. Do you both get that?'

Benedictus nodded enthusiastically, Ignatius more thoughtfully. Softly then Patrick continued, 'Let us not, my young friends, think of ourselves as heresy-hunters or even preachers, but as *farmers,* and the Word of the Lord as our seed.' He took up the gospel book again and tapped it with his finger. 'This is all that matters. This is the Word of God, and we are its servants. Understand?'

Ignatius and Benedictus nodded obediently and they all continued their meal in a contemplative mood, quietly listening to the flowing water, the chirping birds and the full rich sounds of nature surrounding them.

This early morning meal by the river, and the encounter with the beggar, set the tone for Patrick's missionary pilgrimage to Hibernia. Even before he embarked on the ship that took him and his companions across the Gallic Sea he had sold his mitre, his embroidered stole and silk soutane and had given the money away to beggars. Even some of his gold soldi he exchanged for bronze and copper and distributed them in a similar fashion.

They crossed the sea without incident and after disembarking at a tiny port on the southern shore of Britannia set out in a north-westerly direction, following a map supplied by Germanus on which the disused Roman roads were marked.

However, after seeing too many signs of the devastation being wreaked by the feuding warlords they abandoned the roads for a less clear-cut route and arrived much later than they originally hoped at the port of Segontium in Cambria. By then they looked like beggars, their cowls torn and soiled, their boots punctured and their feet blistered.

In Segontium Patrick searched for a ship bound for Hibernia, a difficult task, for although the people spoke a language similar to what Patrick knew from his boyhood in Hibernia, here it was a rough dialect of which he understood little. Nevertheless he eventually managed to secure a passage on a merchant ship where, because it was short of slaves, and despite paying a hefty fare, they were expected to work alongside the slaves feeding the cramped cargo of cattle and pigs.

It was a stormy crossing. The ship rolled and heaved, and

the animals and their dung splashed constantly about. The task of feeding them however brought Patrick powerfully back to his boyhood when he worked as a slave in Hibernia. Immersed once more in these earthy smells, he richly remembered his years in captivity. He prayed often now, as he did then. And if he wasn't praying he was planning how to preach the Word of the Lord to the Hibernians.

Though he had been their captive, he remembered the people of this land with deep affection. And although through his Christian eyes they now appeared as uncultured and illiterate pagans, he nevertheless felt deep down that if the Word of the Lord was fed to them in the right way, they would take to it like babes to mothers' milk.

As the ship rolled and reeled, as the animals bellowed and shat, as Ignatius and Benedictus vomited and wished themselves dead a hundred times over, the holy fire of Jesus flared like a sun in Patrick's heart, so that by the time they reached Hibernia, in his mind he saw the entire island ablaze with the light of his Lord Jesus Christ.

CHAPTER NINE

THE ROUND TABLE

When Merlin eventually returned from Hibernia to Britannia he did not go straightaway to his hut in the Forest of Elfham which he would've dearly loved to, for he was weary to the bone after his long journey. But he had with him the precious cargo of the Sword of Light, and the only place for that was Camelot. So there he went, and precisely to the beautiful room of the Round Table which comprised the entire top floor of the castle's keep.

Like many other aspects of Camelot, this room and everything in it, was designed by Merlin. Its twelve evenly spaced windows, each with a different coloured glass, imparted to the room an ethereal quality. Between each window a long elegant tapestry hung depicting heroic scenes from Greek and Roman literature. In the centre of the room was the Round Table which Merlin made from a very special ancient oak he found in the Forest of Elfham. On Merlin's advice, meetings of the Round Table were reserved for twelve of Arthur's best and most trusted men and he made the Table round, he said, so that they would all feel equal.

He took the Sword from the scabbard, placed it in the centre of the Table and sent immediately for Arthur.

'I promised you a dream weapon, remember?' Merlin proudly said, pointing to the Sword when Arthur entered the room.

Arthur was stunned! 'It's absolutely magnificent!' he gasped.

'You can see it has real power, can't you?' Merlin said.

Arthur grasped the Sword's hilt. 'I can *feel* it, my friend.'

Enthusiastically he sliced the air with the flashing blade. Then dropping it he said, 'But I find it hard to believe that the Hibernians gave *you* one of their famous *Four Treasures*!'

Merlin shrugged. 'Oh, I wouldn't exactly put it like that. It's a long story. It's yours now anyway.'

'But won't they want it back?'

'Mmm. That's a good point.'

'Merlin, did you *steal* this?'

'No, no. Merlin's no thief!'

Once more Arthur brandished the Sword. Then smiling he brought it down lightly onto Merlin's bony left shoulder.

'Will this help me build my kingdom?' he asked.

Merlin brushed the Sword from his shoulder, took it from Arthur and laid it carefully back on the Table.

'Sit down,' he said.

They both sat down then, and for a long time Merlin spoke about Pelagius and the Grail Temple, and of how Pelagius believed that the Sword should be brought into the service of Jesus and the Grail. When he finished Arthur asked, 'Did you actually get to see this mysterious Grail?'

Merlin jumped up and walked about, pulling agitatedly on his long wispy beard. When he eventually stopped he looked Arthur in the eye and said firmly, 'No. But whatever the Grail is, it is my reluctant but considered opinion that in the long-term interests of Britannia the instructions of this holy man of Jesus and Hibernia should be followed.'

Arthur picked up the Sword again. 'How can I disagree?' he said brandishing it.

The next day Arthur gathered his twelve around the Table and showed them the beautiful Sword. When all the gasps of astonishment died away, Merlin, who was also present, gave the men a brief history of the weapon. Then Arthur spoke. 'I firmly believe the Sword of Light's destiny is with us,' he said and went on to tell of its connection with Pelagius and Jesus, while, acting on Merlin's instructions, saying nothing about the Grail. As he feared however, his speech was not greeted with unanimous favour. For, like Merlin, many of the men hated the Christians. Kay was particularly vociferous.

'How the hell can we even *think* of allying ourselves with those damn Catholics!' he cried. 'They're all possessed, half bloody mad! You've seen them yourself, Arthur, galloping around our land with their big black crosses. They're an evil death-worshipping cult!'

Arthur responded to Kay's outburst by turning to Merlin. Merlin then spoke at length about what he had learned from Pelagius about the two types of Christians. 'So, whatever about the Roman Catholics,' he concluded, 'the Round Table has nothing to fear from the Hibernian Pelagians.'

Lancelot then spoke, and although he was privately critical of Arthur's close association with Merlin and was nihilistic regarding the gods generally, he praised the Sword of Light eloquently. Because of this the men eventually arrived at a consensus, and it was decided that the famous blade should become part of the Round Table.

Arthur was delighted! He got up, took the magnificent Sword in his hand and asked each of the men to come forward and stand before him. 'Bow your head,' he commanded, and keeping in the forefront of his mind all of what Merlin said about Jesus, the Sword, and especially the mysterious Grail, he touched each man on the shoulder with the Sword's point. Then he said, 'Raise your head.' When the man did this Arthur solemnly pronounced, 'You are now no longer a mere soldier of the Round Table, but a *knight*, and you will be called *Sir*. By the power of this Sword you will serve the ideal of the Good always.'

Meetings of the Round Table were not fixed. They could be called at any time, but only by Arthur. He usually called them at times when the warlords were stepping up their activity. Keeping them, their movements and their pillaging in check was Arthur's day-to-day concern. Thus, when a few weeks after receiving the Sword, he returned from a covert expedition in which he gathered more information on Mordred, he immediately called a meeting. It would be a very special one, the first at which the Sword was present.

It was springtime. Outside the castle walls little clumps of primroses bloomed in marshy fields while all along the dyke surrounding the fortress yellow daffodils bobbed their heads merrily in a gentle breeze.

In the castle, in the room of the Round Table, the magnificent blade lay solitary and resplendent in the centre of the Table, ethereally reflecting the gently shifting light of the tall coloured windows through which the rays of the morning sun poured abundantly.

One by one the Knights entered the room and took their seats. Lancelot however sent his apologies. He had a bad cold and was confined to bed.

The chief item on the agenda was Mordred, the longest and sharpest thorn in Arthur's side.

'He is growing in strength at an alarming rate,' Arthur informed after opening the meeting. 'He has gathered around him many of the most brutalized men in the whole of Britannia and has moved his headquarters to the old abandoned Roman hill-fort of Sorbiodunum. He has furthermore started poisoning wells in a vast area surrounding Sorbiodunum while at the same time spreading rumours that I am doing it, and that I am also poisoning the rivers! This causes many of the country-folk to flee to the fort where they know that the river Twiss springs. This is precisely what Mordred wants! He imprisons the people there. He builds up his brutal militia by allowing the men to freely rape the womenfolk. Any who refuse are killed. He is also currently forging alliances with other warlords of his own ilk.'

'What does he feed the poor bastards in Sorbiodunum on?' Sir Kay asked.

'Rats, I believe,' Arthur replied, 'and if the rats run out he sometimes even kills and eats the smaller children! The place is a living hell.'

Drumming his fingers rapidly, Kay said, 'The man has the mind of a dog and the soul of a rat.'

'Indeed,' Arthur agreed. 'He claims to be a member of our

noble Brittonic race, but I don't believe it. Merlin says he is a child of the Beast. Yet he has ambitions to be king of our people!'

'He must be mad!' Sir Gawain said.

'Why don't we just kill him and be done with it,' Kay said clenching his fists.

Sir Percival, who was sitting opposite Kay and had been gazing pensively upon the great Sword, looked up.

'Why must you always think kill, kill, kill?' he challenged Kay. 'There are other ways of defeating an enemy you know.'

'I am aware, boy,' Kay sharply returned, 'of your feeble philosophies, and I have oft listened to your faulty strategies. You know what I think of them.'

Arthur held up his hand. 'Please, gentlemen,' he interjected, 'not so soon! We must fashion our talk to be worthy of this Round Table. Let us speak to one another as friends, eh?'

Turning directly to Sir Kay, Arthur continued, 'I know it might be difficult for you, but please don't address our newest knight, Sir Percival as *boy*. I'm certain he doesn't like it.'

Percival smiled. Arthur continued, 'Anyway, it's not that simple, Sir Kay. Killing Mordred I mean. His militia is enormous. Much bigger than us. And he never leaves Sorbiodunum now, on foot or on horseback, without being surrounded by a veritable wall of bodyguards.'

Percival asked, 'Sire, to whom does this Sword really belong?'

Arthur stretched out his hand and gently touched the Sword's hilt. 'What do you think, men?'

'It's Merlin's,' Sir Pellinore suggested.

'No, no. It's Arthur's,' Sir Bors countered.

'Hear! Hear!' a few of the Knights cheered.

Arthur then stood up and took the great blade in his hand. 'Let us say,' he said, 'that the Sword belongs to the gods. Does that answer your question, Sir Percival?'

'Aye, Sire,' Percival said.

At that moment Guinevere entered the room! All the Knights immediately arose and bowed respectfully.

'My dear Guinevere,' Arthur said, frowning. 'We did not expect *you*.'

'I've just finished it,' Guinevere said, proudly holding up an exquisitely embroidered sheath for the Sword's scabbard. 'I couldn't wait to show it to you all.'

She came to Arthur.

'It's beautiful,' he said touching the sheath. 'The colours, threads and patterns are all perfectly chosen. Put it down beside the Sword, my dear.'

Guinevere went to the Sword but deftly slipped the great blade into it, then smiled wryly at Arthur.

'Thank you, my love,' Arthur said firmly, suggestively glancing at the open door.

But Guinevere did not move.

Slowly, one by one, the Knights sat down. Then Guinevere went to the door, closed it, and to the astonishment of all returned to the Round Table and sat on Arthur's lap! Embarrassedly, Arthur whispered in her ear, 'What has you so giddy today, my dear?'

After giving him a quick kiss on his forehead Guinevere whispered, 'I'm bored, Sir.'

Some of the Knights blushed, others smiled. Kay however, remained predictably stern. Guinevere turned from Arthur and addressed them all, 'Gentlemen, do you think you can stand the presence of a lady for a little while?'

Everyone looked at Arthur who responded by whispering

in Guinevere's ear, 'You can't sit here.'

'I can sit on that empty chair,' Guinevere whispered, pointing

'That's Lancelot's.'

'I know, but he's in bed, isn't he?'

Guinevere went then to the empty chair and after pulling it from the Table looked questioningly at Arthur. He nodded hesitantly. Guinevere sat down and the meeting resumed, much changed in tone and content. Guinevere, however, remaining as exquisitely quiet as only a woman can be.

CHAPTER TEN

AN UNEXPECTED VISITOR

It was midwinter and snowing hard. Shivering uncontrollably, Merlin was sitting by a wood fire in his smoky little hut in the Forest of Elfham. He was considering going back to bed out of which he had just got, after being confined to it for many days, coughing. His big, white, hairy cat, Ariel, was lying at his feet. Her long tail wagged irritably because the fire was nearly out. Suddenly she sprang onto the table and immediately there was a tapping on the door.

Merlin scratched his head. *What, or who could it be? Possibly a badger, a fox, or, by the gods, even a wolf!* He was amazed at how brazen these latter creatures could be, especially this time of the year when they roamed the forest floor in packs for food. They often tried to push the door open!

Tap. Tap. A little louder.

Merlin lifted himself reluctantly from his rickety old armchair, took the rush-lamp from the table and went to the door where, peeping through a crack in it saw that it wasn't an animal but a human being.

Merlin's abode in the Forest of Elfham was supposed to be a secret. He built it over a decade ago after becoming convinced that the Christians were out to kill him. He felt safe here. He only told Arthur and a few of the older Knights where it was, as well as Morganna.

He studied the figure outside carefully. It was small and snow-covered, huddled up in a huge bearskin and carrying a knapsack. Merlin felt no danger and opened the door slightly. The aperture at the top of the bearskin, from which issued a curling stream of breath, was too small to reveal the face, but from it Merlin heard a weak voice, 'May I come in?'

Ariel, who had been intensely observing these developments from the vantage point of Merlin's table hissed at the sound of the voice and the hairs on her spine stiffened into a perfectly pointed arch. Merlin observed this and became suspicious. Nevertheless he replied to the stranger's request by opening the door wide and stepping hospitably aside. The figure brushed passed him quickly and stood by the dying fire.

Ariel hissed again.

'It's all right, my dear,' Merlin said softly to the cat as he closed the door. Then addressing the figure he continued, 'Now stranger, how can I help you?'

The figure slowly pulled the fur from around its face and Merlin nearly jumped out of his skin!

It was Vivian!

The traditional practice of Morganna was to dispatch all her new priestesses, as soon as possible after their final initiation, to various parts of Pictland and beyond, where they were expected to administer and foster the ancient Mother cult to the best of their ability. This Morganna did as usual and without difficulty with six of the seven Virgins after the most recent ceremony. But with Vivian it was different. She argued. She did not, she said, want to go to the east of Pictland, where Morganna wanted her to go. And when Morganna asked why, Vivian said there were Romans there. And only when Morganna made a perfectly plausible case for there being Romans *nowhere* in Pictland did the truth come out.

'I want to speak to Merlin,' Vivian revealed, 'before I go *anywhere.*'

'*Master* Merlin,' Morganna irritably corrected, aware that lately she had to correct the young priestess on this and many other matters nearly every time they conversed.

'Master Merlin,' Vivian said reluctantly.

'He may not come to Avalliona ever again,' Morganna cautioned. 'He's gone too old.'

'Then I will go to him,' Vivian asserted.

'But no one knows where he lives!' Morganna declared.

'*You* do,' Vivian instantly returned, and with such certainty that Morganna felt she could not deny the statement.

The two priestesses glared at one another. When the intensity of Morganna's stare drove Vivian's huge eyeballs into the corners of their sockets, Morganna sternly asked, 'Why do you want to see him?'

'I have questions that only he can answer,' Vivian said, now nervously twisting strands of her hair around her fingertips. 'I *must* see him.'

Perhaps it's not a bad idea, Morganna suddenly thought. *This strange one is, after all, Merlin's protégé. He surely will know what to do with her. For I don't.*

After more sharp exchanges Morganna concluded she was wasting her time extending the conversation.

'Very well then,' she conceded with a sigh, 'see him, if you must.'

Reluctantly then she disclosed Merlin's whereabouts, charging Vivian not to reveal it to anyone.

That was over three weeks ago. And here she was!

She flashed a coy smile at Merlin who immediately ran for his staff. When he got it however, he started trembling.

'H...how...did you find out wh....where I.......I.....lived?' he spluttered.

'Morganna told me,' Vivian casually replied dropping her knapsack on the floor.

'Sh.....she shouldn't have,' Merlin said. 'Never!'

Vivian grinned impishly. 'But she did.'

Ariel hissed again.

'Can you do something about the animal?' Vivian asked, brushing snow from her bearskin and shaking out her long black hair.

Reluctantly, Merlin shooed the cat into his bedroom and closed the door.

'I'm flipping freezing,' Vivian said rubbing her hands.

Merlin plucked a log from a basket and threw it on the dying fire. Then standing back he took a long deep breath, blew at the embers, and a huge orange flame jumped immediately up!

'Sit down,' he then said pointing to the only other chair in the room.

Vivian pulled the wobbly chair near the fire and warmed herself at the leaping flame. After a few minutes she loosed the bearskin around her shoulders, self-consciously revealing the curves of her firm young breasts.

Merlin, who had remained standing, demanded, 'What do you want?'

Gazing into the flame Vivian said dryly, 'The wound you gave me hasn't healed.'

Merlin dropped his staff! He never heard such a thing before! What in the gods' name was she talking about?

'My initiation wound,' Vivian firmly repeated, looking at him, 'has not healed. It has on all the other girls. Why not me?'

'I...d....don't know,' Merlin confessed, picking up his staff.

Vivian jumped up. 'Here, I'll show you.'

She was about to throw off her bearskin when Merlin shouted, 'No! Wait!'

'All right, don't panic,' Vivian said. 'It doesn't bleed much.'

She sat down again. Merlin sucked his teeth frantically.

'Why do you always suck your teeth?' Vivian testily queried.

Merlin ignored her.

Suddenly there was a loud *hee-haw, hee-haw*, so loud it rocked the hut.

'Your cat makes a god-awful racket,' Vivian said when the noise died down.

'It's Caliban,' Merlin muttered, pointing to the byre which was attached to the outside gable wall. 'My donkey. She's in there. It's feeding time. But she can wait.'

Hee-haw, hee-haw.

Vivian pinned Merlin with her gaze. 'Tell me,' she asked, 'why do you think my wound bleeds on Fridays only, and at three o'clock in the afternoon *precisely*?'

'I don't know,' Merlin replied.

'You should,' Vivian brazenly returned.

Merlin's staff was vibrating. What audacity! What shameful insolence!

'You know the name of the green Serpent, don't you?' Vivian stated ominously.

'What if I do?' Merlin returned.

'Well, you could tell me its *name*!'

'Why should I?'

'My vision would improve.'

'Your vision, I believe, is pretty good already.'

'The green Serpent is very powerful, isn't it?'

'Serpents usually are.'

Vivian looked at Merlin curiously. Then suddenly she bared her teeth! He had never seen them before and was shocked. They were uniformly sharp, like little fangs!

'I want its power,' she hissed, 'and *you* can get it for me.'

'H.....how?' Merlin said stifling a cough.

Vivian jumped up again. 'What's its FUCKING name?'

Merlin went green! He had never heard this word before. It went through him like a spear.

He turned disdainfully from her and silently prayed to the Great Mother. Had he made a terrible mistake in making this wild young one a priestess of the cult? he asked. Did he not do enough spiritual research before he made the decision?

'Come on,' he heard Vivian say, 'the name, the name.'

Tell her, an all-too-familiar voice in Merlin's head said.

'Naas,' he eventually conceded.

'Good. Anything else?'

'She is worshipped by Christians who call themselves after her: The Naasenes.'

'Christians! For fuck's sake!'

'Where the hell did you get this expletive from?' Merlin angrily demanded.

'From the Serpent,' Vivian smirked. 'Who else? But you say *her*?'

'Yes, her, her, her. The green Serpent is f......f...... female.'

'What makes you think that?'

'Oh, for the gods' sake!' Merlin cried. He tapped his mouth with his staff. 'Its voice.'

'Huh. And where are these Naasenes located?'

'In the East, in Egypt, Syria, places like that. Very far away.'

'Shit!' Vivian cried, stamping her feet.

'But there are some in Hibernia,' Merlin added.

'Oh.'

Suddenly Vivian gripped Merlin's shoulder. 'Oh, Merlin, Merlin, I must go to Hibernia straightaway. I *must*.'

Merlin brushed her hand disdainfully away and threw back his head.

'No priestess of the cult,' he haughtily declared, 'can leave our island of the Britons without *my* blessing. You will die as soon as your feet touch Hibernia's soil if you do not have it.'

'Then give it to me.'

They stared silently at one another for a long time. Merlin knew in his heart that she would go, even without his blessing. Better let her have it then, he decided.

Normally he gave his blessing by laying his hands on a person's head and reciting an appropriate incantation. With Vivian however he could not bring himself to do this. Instead he took his staff in both hands and slowly raised it until it was horizontal and directly in front of Vivian's face.

'Kiss it,' he commanded, 'if you want my blessing.'

Vivian ran her fingers tauntingly along the staff. 'Your *blessing*, Merlin?'

'Yes, kiss it.'

Perfunctorily Vivian kissed the staff.

'You may go to Hibernia,' Merlin said gravely. 'Find out all you can about these Naasenes. But I solemnly charge you to come to me immediately upon your return to these parts. I must be the first to know all you have learnt about the green Serpent. Understand?'

'It will be as you wish,' Vivian said and bared her teeth again.

CHAPTER ELEVEN

LANCELOT

Lancelot's Roman wife, Imelda, died childless. Since then he lived alone in a little house in Camelot with hypocaust heating. Arthur always left him in charge while he was away on one of his frequent expeditions. Keeping some kind of order in the land, or even the hope of it alive, was Arthur's main task, but keeping order in Camelot itself was also a big and on-going challenge. And although Arthur would have liked to take Lancelot along on expeditions, it was more expedient to leave him in charge of Camelot. In Arthur's experience it was only Lancelot who had the depth of character, maturity, and skill to deal with the various kinds of problems which occurred while he was away, not the least of which was interpersonal rivalry between the Knights. The latter must always be quickly resolved if the ideals of the Round Table were to be kept alive.

Lancelot's house was situated across the courtyard, directly opposite the castle's keep. There it was his deep pleasure after a hard day's work to polish his sword while meditatively sifting the day's events.

Late one evening when Arthur was away, and Lancelot was engaged in this very occupation he was surprised to hear a gentle tapping on his door. He had no idea who it could be, for no one ever called on him at such an hour unless it was an emergency. It was almost midnight and had been raining hard for hours!

Lancelot cocked an ear. The tapping was repeated. Whoever this was or whatever the reason for the call it was definitely *not* an emergency! If it was, the knock would be louder and accompanied by a voice, an anxious voice calling his name. That was what amounted to a protocol for emergencies, which inevitably occurred from time to time. But if this was an emergency it was an odd one!

Lancelot opened the door. The strange cocktail of emotion he experienced at the sight that greeted him then was something he would never forget for the rest of his life.

It was Guinevere!

She had on a black cloak with the hood up. It was dripping wet and muddied at the hem.

'May I come in?' she asked with a wan smile.

'Of.....of course, my lady,' Lancelot distractedly replied.

'I'm sorry for calling so late,' Guinevere said, timorously entering the room. 'I was afraid you might be....be.....well.....'

'Is anything the matter, ma'am?' Lancelot asked, closing the door.

A little pool of water formed on the stone flags around Guinevere's feet. Lancelot suddenly realized there had not been a woman in his house for years!

'It's so wet out,' Guinevere said staring at the pool of water. 'I've been walking about for ages.'

'Why, my lady?' Lancelot pressed.

'I don't know,' Guinevere replied. 'My thoughts......my......'

'Your thoughts, ma'am?'

'My........difficulty..........' she went on, sighing and untying the cords of her cloak. But she did not finish her sentence.

'Here, allow me,' Lancelot said.

As he removed the cloak, Guinevere turned and caught his gaze. She said something with her eyes that both attracted and confused him.

He hung the cloak on a wall hook. Guinevere gazed at his polished sword on the table. From the wall Lancelot studied her. *What an incredibly beautiful face*, he thought, *but so lonesome*. He came forward saying, 'Will you have a seat, ma'am?' and pulled a chair from the table. Guinevere looked up.

'Call me Guinevere,' she said into his eyes.

'Why, yes, ma'am, of course,' Lancelot returned and added with an uncertain smile, 'Guinevere.'

She sat down and glanced around the little room. It was neat, clean and tidy as she expected.

'How many servants have you?' she asked running her fingers through her thick hair.

'Two, and a page,' Lancelot replied.

'Where do you eat?'

'All the Knights eat together in the dining room off the kitchen on the ground floor of the keep. Arthur often eats there too.'

'Oh, yes, of course.'

After a pause Lancelot asked, 'Did anyone see you knocking on my door, ma'am......I mean, Guinevere?'

'No,' Guinevere replied, 'I don't think so. Why do you ask?'

'Well....it's most....un.....unorthodox.'

'Oh, yes. I see. I'm sorry. I suppose it is. No. Don't worry.'

There was a stool by the wall behind Guinevere. As Lancelot passed her to get it in order to sit beside her she reached out suddenly, took his hand and held it tenderly on her shoulder. Lancelot froze. He was about to pull his hand away when she rubbed her cheek against it. She did not look at him. Then she touched the hand with her lips.

Lancelot's heart pounded! His Knight's honour was at stake! This lady was Arthur's. No one in Camelot, especially the Knights, ever dared think of her otherwise. *She can never be your lover*, a loud voice said in his head, *never*.

But then she kissed the hand, and when it still did not move he felt the touch of her warm, wet tongue. His blood caught fire! And in that instant all the chivalry that lived in his noble soul yielded to something infinitely stronger: the hunger for love.

His head bent slowly and he kissed her hair.

CHAPTER TWELVE

HIBERNIA

It was early autumn when Patrick and his companions crossed the sea from Cambria to Hibernia. The reeking boat arrived at its destination on a cloudy morning after a short voyage. The place, a large settlement situated on the estuary of a gently flowing river, was slapdash, topsy-turvy, and thronged. There were several ships docked along the rickety wooden quay, all being either loaded or emptied of assorted cargos of livestock, fish, furniture, wine, grain and much else including gangs of yellow- and black-skinned slaves.

Even before he disembarked Patrick's attention was arrested by a pungent smell that immediately transported him back to his boyhood time in this strange land, the smell of burning peat. It was all-pervasive.

On the crossing Patrick worried that he might not

remember the language well enough to convincingly preach the Word of the Lord. Upon disembarking therefore, he mingled with the merchants and initiated conversations by deploying common phrases he remembered well. At first all his interlocutors seemed to be talking gibberish. Nevertheless Patrick persisted and after learning to distinguish native from foreign merchants found to his delight that the language came rushing back to him.

The place, he learnt, was called Dubh Linn, which meant the Black Pool. But why a river estuary should be given the name of a pool was the first mystery he encountered in a land whose people he was soon to discover revelled in mystery, and made an art of misinformation.

He eventually left the dockside and wandered with his companions up and down the broad street and few filthy lanes that comprised the 'town centre.' He soon picked up all the information he needed including the whereabouts of the only bathhouse and the cheapest boarding-house. Towards evening, after a much needed bath they made their way to the boarding-house which was a tall, narrow, three-storey building just off the busy 'main street' of the town. It was built of blackened wood and jammed between a single-storey tanner's workshop and a fish merchant.

'I need a room for two nights for myself and my young companions here,' Patrick said slowly in the native tongue to the cross-looking woman who opened the boarding-house door. She was small, barrel-shaped, and smothered in a huge greasy apron. Wiping her puffy hands on the apron she examined Patrick, Ignatius and Benedictus with slanted eyes. Then she shrugged. Unable to read her body language, Patrick produced a bronze sestertius from his purse and studied the woman's face.

It lit up! And Patrick immediately knew that if this was

anything to judge by, his purse of coin would go far in Hibernia!

After whipping the coin from him the woman waddled up a creaking stair and led them to a dark, musty room on the top storey. It was empty apart from a bunk bed on one side and a straw mattress on the floor. A hole in a wall was more for air than light.

'It's a bit small,' Patrick modestly commented.

'It's the only one available,' the woman harshly responded. 'Full up today. Lots of ships in, ye know.'

'Have you any...........?' Patrick struggled to remember the word for blanket but couldn't. Then he drew a large square in the air.

'No,' the woman said and abruptly left, banging the door.

Ignatius was carefully examining the lower mattress of the bunk.

'It's just as well,' he said.

'What is?' Patrick enquired.

'That she doesn't have blankets. The fleas would be worse.' He swiped at one. 'They breed in blankets.'

'Well, we can expect worse than fleas in this country,' Patrick stoically observed. 'Remember lads, we're at the very edge of the world.'

'Does that mean we might fall off if we go too far?' Benedictus asked.

'Possibly,' Patrick returned. 'But I believe myself that the world is round, although Germanus says that's heretical.'

'We won't worry about him anymore, Father,' Benedictus proffered.

'Good lad,' Patrick said. 'Now choose your bed.'

'Ah, no, Father,' Benedictus said, 'you choose first.'

'All right,' Patrick said, 'I'll take the mattress on the floor.'

'And we'll toss for the bunks,' Ignatius said. 'Can I have a coin please, Father?'

Patrick gave Ignatius a coin. Benedictus won the toss and choose the lower bunk. Soon all were lying stretched out, glad of the respite.

There was a long silence. Benedictus eventually broke it.

'Some of those people down there at the docks,' he said 'were half-naked. Did you notice?'

'Of course we noticed,' Ignatius testily responded.

'And some of them paint their bodies too,' Benedictus added.

'Yes,' Patrick put in, 'but *they* were not Hibernians. Those painted ones are called Picts. They are traders from the north of Britannia, or Caledonia as the Romans call it.'

'They look a bit frightening,' Benedictus said.

'Do you think the native people here perform human sacrifices, Father?' Ignatius asked.

'I never saw any human sacrifices when I was here as a boy,' Patrick drowsily replied, 'but they do sacrifice certainly. They are quite religious really.' He yawned. 'But get some sleep, boys. You'll need it. We have a big day tomorrow.'

Early next morning Ignatius awoke to loud hissing. He got up, quietly went to the hole in the wall and peered out. Nobody was about, but the lane below had turned into a patchwork of muddy puddles. Two huge grey hounds, their long shaggy hair stuck to their bodies from the rain, were fighting with a pack of screeching gulls for morsels of rotten meat and mouldy crusts, while a fat, black pig watched from a distance, contentedly munching.

'It's raining,' Benedictus said with a yawn.

'God bless your eyes,' Ignatius sarcastically returned.

Patrick, who had been lying awake for some time thinking about his mission, said, 'Can you see the sky, Ignatius?'

'No, Father,' Ignatius replied. 'Just the clouds.'

'What colour are they?'

'Very dark.'

'Grey or black?'

'Nearer black than grey, I'd say.'

'Mmm. Not to worry. The sun might be shining before you know it. The weather here is worse than women.'

Benedictus laughed. 'What do you mean, Father?'

'Patrick sat up and stretched. 'Unpredictable,' he said.

'Did you ever have a woman, Father?' Benedictus boldly enquired.

'Now, now,' Patrick returned, 'we have to concentrate on our business here.'

'Business, Father?' Ignatius said returning from the wall.

'Mission is the word, Ignatius. You're perfectly correct.'

'Does the greasy woman do breakfasts?' Benedictus wondered, yawning again.

'When the rain stops,' Patrick said, 'we'll look for a tavern. The Hibernians love to drink, so there's bound to be lots of taverns around. We'll search for a good one to eat in.'

'When the rain stops,' Benedictus repeated resignedly. 'I'm hungry.'

'And so am I!' Patrick snapped. 'Sit up, boy.'

Benedictus sprang up.

'Blow your nose,' Patrick ordered.

As Benedictus obediently blew his nose Ignatius sat down beside him and Patrick took from his knapsack the gospel book. After removing its protective woollen cloth he read, as he had done every morning and evening from the beginning of their journey, a long passage to which the young men listened with rapt attention.

'You'll both know the whole book off by heart in no time,' Patrick said good-humouredly when he finished.

'I know a lot of it off by heart already,' Ignatius boasted.

'Yes,' Patrick said, 'and I think maybe we should all learn it all off by heart.'

'Why, Father?' Benedictus enquired.

'I know from my time spent in slavery here,' Patrick replied, 'that books are illegal for ordinary people. Only the Druids are allowed to read or write. And the Druids are all-powerful here; they are not only the priests, but also the lawyers, the police, the judges, the whole shebang, and they practise magic to boot.'

'Magic!' Benedictus exclaimed. 'You mean the Druids are magicians?'

'I do indeed. And many of them pretty good ones. And by good I don't mean that they always *do good* with their magic. Not by a long-shot. What I mean is that they really can work what we, as Christians, would rather call miracles. With their hocus-pocus they keep a kind of magic grip on the mind and imagination of the whole nation. It's a mighty strange place this, boys. We'll have to tread very carefully.' Patrick slowly tapped the gospel with his index finger. 'But I firmly believe,' he solemnly continued, 'that there is no better magic in the whole wide world than what's in here.'

Ignatius was thinking hard.

'What are you thinking?' Patrick asked.

'Oh, it's just that I remember Archbishop Germanus saying there were many other versions of the Jesus story, that's all,' Ignatius replied.

'And I'm sure our dear old heretic-hunting archbishop is

right,' Patrick agreed. 'But it's all the same story nonetheless. The *facts* of the gospel are all the same and that's what really matters. And what are the facts, boys?'

'Jesus died on the Cross and rose from the dead,' Benedictus enthusiastically answered.

'Correct. But you're missing something, aren't you?'

'I suppose so,' Benedictus said shrugging.

'Ignatius,' Patrick said, 'what's he missing?'

'That Jesus was God, Father.'

'Yes. But *is* God. And not *a* god, but, as you say, God, full stop. But what else?'

'He was........sorry, *is*, also a man,' Ignatius replied.

'Absolutely right. Jesus *is* the prototype of a new race of human beings, the first man-God, and we are the first of his offspring. From now on there can be no other God but him.'

Patrick closed the book and placed it beside him on the mattress. Winking, he said, 'Lesson over.'

After a ponderous pause Ignatius asked, 'What's the plan, Father?'

'Good question,' Patrick replied. 'It's as follows. I found out yesterday that there are very few towns or hamlets here in Hibernia. This place we are in now might in fact be the *only* town of any size on the whole island. Imagine! Most of the land is either marsh, bog, or densely forested. It's quite unlike the landscape we were used to in Gaul or Britannia. I also found out that there are only four roads here in Hibernia, believe it or not. Only four! The rest are nothing but tracks. The four roads go north, south, east and west, as you might expect. The eastbound one ends here, but they all begin in a place called Tara which must make it the most important place on the island. Someone told me the High King lives there. So we go there first. I'd like to talk to this fellow.'

'Sounds exciting,' Ignatius said. 'How far is Tara?'

'A few days on foot, I reckon,' Patrick replied.

'I've never met a king,' Benedictus chuckled.

'Neither did I,' Patrick said. 'But whatever happens in Tara, boys, before we start preaching this gospel of ours we have first to find out a bit about the politics of this place. For instance, we were told by Germanus that there are Christians already here, and he says, or thinks, they are Pelagian heretics. So we have to find out precisely what that means. The old Archbishop is not so worked up about them for nothing. So we have to know what we're up against.'

'Shall we leave today?' Ignatius asked.

'No,' Patrick replied. 'Today we will take it very easy. We will mingle with the throng. You two can pick up some words of your new language, and we will all try to get the feel of this mighty strange land we are going to be in for a long time to come. Then after a good night's sleep we will set out first thing in the morning for Tara; hail, rain, or snow.'

A ray of light suddenly shot through the hole in the wall and magically lit up the gospel book by Patrick's side.

'Look, my young friends!' Patrick eagerly declared. 'The blessèd sun speaks. Let us go seek the Bread of Life. It's breakfast time!'

CHAPTER THIRTEEN

MORDRED

Arthur's fame continued to grow throughout the land of Britannia. It became a widespread practice that if the inhabitants of a village, town or townland needed help in either warding off a marauding gang, or release from the brutal tyranny of some local farmer-turned-warlord, a trusted person would be discreetly dispatched to Camelot to seek Arthur's assistance, requests to which he not only quickly responded, but relished.

Armed with the Sword of Light, Arthur these days often felt invincible on the battlefield, for truly the weapon seemed to have a mind, a power, and a life all of its own, so that the very threat of its use was enough to chase away a warlord and his militia.

The people began to talk of him as their king. But Arthur himself knew that a king without an army is no better than a king without a crown. And although the Sword of Light and the Round Table gave him advantage over his enemies, his militia remained just that, a militia. It was not an army. Before ever therefore he could make legitimate claim to be King of the Britons, and thereby truly begin to realize his dream of Logres, he knew he must first have a recognized and legitimately constituted army. And so, with Merlin's advice he set about forming it.

In the villages, towns, or townlands where he was called to help, he would not return to Camelot before appointing competent men to take charge of the area's defence. They in turn trained up younger men in military skill, distilled discipline and made weapons. As time passed and this industry bore fruit, Arthur began to organize training sessions at convenient locations throughout the land, and soon enough under his guidance and direction the semblance of a national army of the Britons took shape.

It would however be some time before it could be fully deployed. And such deployment would be absolutely necessary if Arthur's arch-enemy was to be overcome: Mordred. For, as Merlin, Arthur and the more mature knights fully realized, Mordred was not only very powerful, but was nothing less than the very embodiment of Evil.

Tall, sinewy, with long greasy black hair, Mordred's skin had the colour of wet straw and the texture of uncured cowhide. What drove him was an intense hatred of Arthur. And the stronger Arthur became the more intense did Mordred's hatred grow.

He often sat in his scruffy tent in Sorbiodunum, fingering his multiple scars, or scratching the ever-itchy ugly hole where his left eye used to be, trying to hatch out the perfect plan for Arthur's elimination. It was, alas, no easy task!

Nevertheless, a familiar voice in his head simply got louder and louder: 'Kill the bastard. Kill him.' But how, how?

One day as Mordred sat thus brooding in his tent a black shadow fell across the floor in front of him.

Mordred jumped. 'What the hell!' he cried. For there was no one else in the tent!

'Don't worry,' an eerie voice came from the shadow. 'You know me.'

'I....I....never...,' Mordred stammered, making for the door.

'Wait!' the shadow shouted.

Mordred froze.

'There is no point in running,' the shadow said. 'Up to this you have only heard me as a voice. Now you can actually *see* me, that's all, ha, ha!'

'Wh....who are you?'

'My name is Sorath. I am a Prince of Hell.'

Mordred relaxed. 'What do you want?' he asked.

'What do *I* want!? No, no, the question is, what do *you* want? And you want to kill Arthur, right?'

'Yes.'

'But you don't know how!'

'I have ideas.'

'Well, here's one you'll never better. Forget about all your petty farmer-warlords. Form an alliance with somebody really powerful.'

'Like who?'

'Hengist the Saxon!'

Mordred's thoughts raced. He was being forced to think the unthinkable. Form an alliance with Hengist!! Was he going mad?

A great problem for Britannia even during the Roman occupation, the Saxons lately had spawned this Hengist, their most vicious and powerful warlord yet. With the Romans gone, he had even managed to establish a settlement on the southern shore of Britannia, so that the area had become known as the Saxon Shore.

'What's your problem?' Sorath asked.

'The Saxons are the greatest enemy of....of.....'

'Of who?'

'My....my race.'

'Oh, shag your race! *Power* is what matters. Listen. Hengist can bring shiploads of experienced, war-hungry warriors from Saxony here to Britannia at the drop of a battleaxe. Together with him you will easily eliminate Arthur, and become King of the Britons!'

Mordred grinned wickedly. Trying to avoid the Shadow he nervously paced the tent. Then suddenly he stopped.

'What is it?' the Shadow asked.

'Would not Hengist want to be King of the Britons after the defeat of Arthur?'

'No, not at all. The Britons would *never* tolerate a hated Saxon as their king.'

Mordred gripped his sword. It felt alive.

'The crown is for you only, my boy,' Sorath said. 'Go get it!'

The Shadow disappeared. There was no time to lose. Mordred knew that Hengist spoke his own language. So he shot out of his tent and quickly found his most sycophantic henchman - a courageous, block-faced young fellow called Mullo – and sent him off on his big chestnut stallion immediately to find Hengist and deliver him a simple message: Let's talk.

Mullo rode south non-stop for three days. Eventually, after many escapades, he arrived at Hengist's settlement, a vast, dreary sprawl of tents scattered about a muddy estuary. Quickly becoming an object of suspicion, a crowd gathered round Mullo. He spoke the only word he knew of their language, 'Hengist'. After repeating it several times someone shouted 'Briton' and the crowd grew wild and angry. This stranger was an enemy! They were about to pull him from his horse when a tall, thin, sharp-featured man of uncertain age, stepped calmly from the crowd. He had slanted black eyes, wiry grey side-locks, and, in striking contrast to the ragged attire of the crowd was dressed impressively in a long black frock-coat, a black fur-trimmed hat and a black smock with an odd, white, circular collar. With a single hand-gesture he restrained the entire crowd. Then looking up at Mullo and pointing to himself he said in a clear, authoritative voice, 'Sighard.'

Mullo pointed to himself, said, 'Mullo,' and putting his hand to his mouth and flapping his fingers added, 'Hengist.'

He breathed a sigh of relief then as Sighard took the reins of his horse and with another hand-gesture caused the mob to melt miraculously away. He led Mullo up a muddy embankment towards a tent, conspicuous by being the tallest and largest by far in the settlement.

'Hengist,' Sighard said pointing to the tent.

Mullo dismounted. Signalling, 'wait,' Sighard entered the tent and from inside Mullo heard his name mentioned in a short conversation. When Sighard reappeared he took the horse's reins and told Mullo to go inside.

Big, bushy-bearded Hengist was lying on cushions on the tent's floor surrounded by a group of his men in similar positions. They were all eating, and drinking ale freely from huge earthenware jugs. Dressed in rough linen jerkins and short leather battle-skirts, they had knives and axes fixed to their belts and black-crossed wooden shields by their sides. Some of them had horned helmets. None moved or made any attempt to acknowledge Mullo except Hengist. He looked up and gruffly enquired in Brittonic, 'From whom do you carry a message?'

'From Mordred of the Britons,' Mullo replied.

In his own tongue Hengist repeated this sarcastically to his men who burst into uproarious laughter. When it subsided Hengist asked, 'And what, pray, *is* this message?'

'He wants to talk to you.'

Hengist repeated this and once more the men exploded into laughter. When it stopped Hengist lifted himself drunkenly from his cushions and prodded Mullo in the chest.

'Tell Mordred,' he said, 'I don't *talk* to Britons, I only *kill* them. Now get the hell out of here while you are still alive, Briton.'

Mullo dashed out. However, as he whipped his horse's reins from Sighard, who had been listening attentively, Sighard restrained him.

'Wait,' Sighard repeatedly pleaded.

Reluctantly Mullo waited. Sighard then re-entered the tent where he began another conversation with Hengist which was again punctuated by raucous laughter. Sighard himself, however, never laughed and gradually his voice became sharper and eventually dominated the conversation. Mullo heard the words Rome, Catholic and Jesus repeated many times.

When Sighard eventually re-emerged he took the horse's reins again and signalled Mullo to go back inside, assuring him it was safe.

Mullo went in. The men were still stretched out, but they

now had their backs turned and were muttering quietly among themselves. Hengist was standing with his thick legs apart holding a jug of ale. After disdainfully looking Mullo up and down he lifted the jug and drank deeply from it. Then wiping his mouth with the back of his hand he said, 'Tell your leader I will meet him, Briton.'

'Thank you, sire,' Mullo brightly returned. 'When and where will.......?'

'And tell him,' Hengist interrupted in a raised voice, 'to come alone.'

'Y....yes, of course. B....but where and...?'

'The Butchers' Tavern in Londonium.'

'Wh.....where exactly is....?'

'He knows.'

'Yes.....sire. And when?'

'Midday, a week from today.'

'Thank you,' Mullo repeated and turned quickly to go.

'Wait!' Hengist shouted.

Mullo stopped. Hengist put his jug down, came towards Mullo and prodded his chest so hard he pushed him through the door-flap. Outside Hengist hissed, 'And tell Mordred, if he brings anyone with him I'll kill them all, including himself. You get that, Briton?'

'Yes, sire,' Mullo said, and whipping the reins from Sighard mounted and galloped away as fast as he could.

CHAPTER FOURTEEN

THE WAGES OF LOVE

The organization of Arthur's army took him increasingly away from Camelot, to remote parts of the island, to ramshackle hamlets in the foothills of Cambria, or to distant, crumbling Roman towns where even though the original Romanized population might be sparse, the Brittonic tribes of the hinterlands would often gather to engage in some basic bartering. He went anywhere he might find young men willing not only to share his dream, but fight for it. And wherever he found such men he organized them into military cohorts.

He always left Lancelot in charge of Camelot when he went on these expeditions, a thing that nowadays invariably stirred up a great conflict in Lancelot's soul, a conflict that had its genesis in Lancelot's house that fateful moment when the deliciously soft moist warmth of Guinevere's lips first touched his pock-marked, love-starved skin. Soon after that they made love, and always then when Arthur was away.

The affair, however, sunk Lancelot into a deep inner turmoil. Many times he tried to break it off but couldn't. Her seductive power bordered on the divine. The result was that Lancelot's soul became a kind of quagmire where a veritable beast crawled about, a hungry hound that often barked at him in clearly audible words.

Which do you value most? it would immediately demand when Arthur told him he had to leave him in charge for a while, and Lancelot knew that yet again he could have her. *Which? Arthur's brotherhood or Guinevere's love? For surely you realize you cannot have both!*

I don't know, Lancelot would weakly reply.

Thus while outwardly mouthing words to his lord, Lancelot would be engaged in an intense inner dialogue. Half of him would be listening to Arthur's instructions, the other half guiltily dwelling on her, on her luscious lips, her soft, milky breasts, her delicious scent, and most of all her taste.

You don't love her at all, you fake! the hound would bark. *Your so-called love is merely lust!*

No, no, Lancelot would argue, *that's not true. Lust is of the body only. But Guinevere has something more. I love something in her soul.*

Soul my backside! Your love is pure, unadulterated, lust!

It's all her fault! Lancelot would then snap back. *She should never have tempted me in the first place! You either yield to a beautiful woman's freely offered love, or you go mad.*

But Arthur's lady! Come on! Wake up, you fool!

And so on.

Oh, if Lancelot could suffocate that beast he would! But it was not possible! He must live with it. It was, it seemed, the price of his love.

For Guinevere it was different. She was a woman whose extraordinary beauty was matched by an equally extraordinary sexual desire, one indeed that bordered on nymphomania. For her, Lancelot was an excellent lover. He was compatible, confident, and rough. More than anything else it was the overall *hardness* of his battle-scared body that she found most attractive.

He did not kiss much, but the merest press of his fingers on her flesh, or the merest touch of his teeth on her neck or face, was always the first rung on a soaring ladder of ecstasies. Though his thick arm and leg muscles were sometimes as cold as his iron sword, they invariably set her skin on fire; and his gritty nails digging into her body, drove her dangerously on and up into places of ever-sweeter delights. So that when his penis was full and huge inside her and he was about to release his white-hot seed, she always had to stuff her mouth with her thick brown hair, each of his thrusts making her bite all the harder to prevent herself screaming with pleasure. For she must not scream! Not in Camelot! It would betray her great secret: a love passionate beyond all telling; a master lover exquisite in his sensitivity to her body's deepest desires and longings.

'Arthur must *never* find out!' Lancelot emphatically declared after making love one night in bed with her when Arthur was away. 'Never ever.'

The affair had gone on for far too long. Lancelot harboured a growing, even desperate feeling that he must end it before it was too late.

'You worry too much, dear Lancelot,' Guinevere coyly

replied, twisting the wiry black hairs of his chest around her elegant, white fingers.

'I worry with just cause,' Lancelot said. 'I will fall on my sword if Arthur ever finds out.'

'That's a bit extravagant, dear, isn't it?' she said.

'I mean it.'

She gazed at him. 'Good heavens, but I think you do! But he'll never find out, believe me.'

'How can you be so sure?'

'Well, for one thing I always give the keep sentry the night off when I come to you.'

Lancelot ran his index finger along her thick luscious lips.

'Is that all?' he asked.

'No. I also make absolutely certain that there is no one moving about in the courtyard before I knock on your door.'

'What about the sentries patrolling the parapet?' Lancelot asked, his member steadily stiffening again. 'Do you remember them?'

'Yes, I do,' Guinevere said, resisting him slightly, 'mostly.'

'Mostly?' Lancelot questioned. He kissed her hard brown nipples.

'But there are so few of them on duty after midnight,' Guinevere protested, 'and, as you know, I never come to you before midnight.'

'They have eyes like golden eagles,' Lancelot said. 'That's why we pick them for sentry duty. We always check their eyes first.'

'They are always looking *outside* the castle,' Guinevere insisted. 'That's their job, isn't it? They have no interest in what is going on *inside*.'

When Lancelot was mounting her yet again, she suddenly pushed him off. Surprised at her strength, he sensed danger.

'What's the matter?' he asked.

Guinevere got up.

'Where do you get it all from?' she asked with vague contempt.

She put on the silk, scarlet robe he had bought for her recently when he was in Londonium and which he kept in his house especially for her use on these illicit nocturnal visits. Apart from emphasising the stunning contours of her nakedness, it also leant her a distinct air of authority when she wore it.

'Well?' she repeated.

'From the capital of heaven,' Lancelot replied with an uncharacteristic, nervous laugh. He held out his hand. 'Old men have more of it. Come!'

'Wait,' she said. 'I have something to tell you, something very important.'

A frisson ran through Lancelot as she got in beside him. She lay silently on her back for a while staring at the ceiling.

'Tell me, my darling, quickly,' Lancelot said touching her beautiful face with the back of his hand.

After kissing the hand perfunctorily Guinevere said to the ceiling, 'I'm pregnant. I'm going to have your child.'

Lancelot's fingers froze. Slowly she turned her head towards him. Her big black eyes fell on him like stones.

He took his hand away, got up and slowly put on his long, linen nightshirt. Staring at the floor, he walked about agitatedly for a long time. *You knew all along this would happen, you fool,* the hound hissed at him. Eventually he looked up and asked, 'Are you absolutely sure?'

'Absolutely.'

'And how do you know it's not....?'

'Arthur's? Oh, I know, believe me. We do it so rarely...........'

Gazing at her, he wrestled helplessly with his emotions.

'It's easy to tell,' she continued shrugging off his penetrating gaze. 'The child is yours.'

'How long?' he asked.

'About three months. I'm surprised you haven't noticed.'

'You'd better go,' he said suddenly.

'I had to tell you, of course,' Guinevere said getting up.

'Thank you,' Lancelot abruptly replied. 'We will speak again soon. But go now. Please.'

He opened the door slightly. There was a full moon. He closed the door again.

As Guinevere silently dressed he came up behind her and kissed her shoulder. She turned, smiled hesitantly and said, 'You'll like it. It'll be a boy. He'll be a great warrior, like you.'

'Or Arthur,' Lancelot feebly returned.

'Merlin will know for certain,' she said.

'Oh, keep him out of it!' he testily retorted.

Pulling up the hood of her cloak Guinevere kissed him on the lips. 'For you, yes.'

Lancelot opened the door.

'It's clear,' he said after checking the courtyard, 'but there's a full moon. Be quick and careful.'

As she slipped by him she said, 'Don't worry, my love. Everything will be all right.'

After closing the door Lancelot leant his head heavily on it. He felt numb. He wanted to shout; he wanted to pound the door with his fists; but he could do nothing. After a while he turned away, began pacing the floor and heard the hound inside barking louder than ever before.

Outside in the courtyard, concealed by the half-open door of the stable where his horse was, young Sir Percival had for some time been leaning quietly against the doorpost contemplating the moon. As was often the case on nights of the full moon, he could not sleep. So he got up, dressed, and went outside to be with his horse awhile. From where he stood the beams of the moon sometimes made Lancelot's house visible; so that when at one point its door opened and a tall hooded figure come out, he was very perplexed. It was so unlike Lancelot to have visitors at all, and such a late-night one! One would've thought the old Knight would be fast asleep at this hour!

Stealthily Percival followed the hooded figure as it flitted along the cloisters. And when it entered the keep, flew quickly up the stairs, and soon afterwards a light appeared in Arthur's quarters on the second floor, Percival, to his astonishment and deep consternation, concluded that that figure could have been none other than Arthur's most noble, beautiful, and virtuous lady, Guinevere.

CHAPTER FIFTEEN

TARA

It was raining heavily on the morning when Patrick and his companions set out on their journey from Dubh Linn to Tara. The road was deeply rutted and riddled with big muddy potholes. Progress was slow, for often they had to shelter for hours under roadside trees.

They travelled mostly on foot, but when bumpy rides on ox-drawn carts were offered from farmers or peasants they availed of the opportunity to relieve their sore feet, though their sore backsides afterwards hardly compensated.

The road was more a track than a road. Having continually to avoid sprawling marshes, racing rivers, raised bogs and dark, brooding forests, it looped and doubled back on itself like a labyrinth. It bore not the remotest resemblance to the straight, wide and expertly constructed paved Roman roads of Gaul or Britannia, although along the way Patrick observed sporadic attempts at cobbling, usually in places where the road passed a settlement or hamlet.

However, unlike many of the Roman roads nowadays, it was safe. That, at least, was the report. 'There's no robbers on this road,' Patrick was emphatically informed by a ragged, pipe-smoking peasant on whose cart he and his companions travelled for a few bumpy miles. 'We is all honest people around here, stranger.' The man went on to inform Patrick that he was a travelling merchant. But when Patrick examined his merchandise - an unseemly pile of tin cans, rags, rusty axes, and god-knows-what, all half-covered with damp sackcloth - he concluded the real reason there were no robbers was there was little worth robbing!

Patrick delighted in refreshing his memory of these people's simple life and ways, and he let not an hour pass but added to his growing storehouse of such knowledge. For, before he started preaching to them he wanted to know as much as possible about their occupations and preoccupations, their laws and customs, their stories and legends, but most of all their gods. Like their land, the people were extremely poor. But also like the poor everywhere, they were both generous and loquacious.

'What gods are worshipped in Tara?' Patrick asked a tiny, haggard old woman in whose tumbledown cabin he and his companions were sheltering at one point while the old woman prepared a meal for them. She had offered it freely after Patrick had engaged her in a conversation by a well near which she lived.

'Oh, the Tuatha De Danaan do be worshipped up there, mister,' the old woman replied as she stirred a great pot on a turf fire in the middle of the dirt floor of her cabin. There was no chimney hole, so the door was left wide open to let the smoke out.

'The Tuatha De what?' Patrick questioned. (He spoke through his fingers because of the smoke.) 'Danaan,' she replied. 'The People of Dana. Them's the gods they worship up there, mister. That's the way it used be anyway.'

'Dana is the Mother of the gods then?' Patrick said.

With the back of her hand the woman wiped a large drop from her nose which was about to fall into the pot. She sniffed and stirred a few times before melancholically replying, 'Aye. The Mother. The Mother of the gods and the Mother of Hibernia. Thems the old gods, mister, and they're the best, if y'ask me.'

Curious as to which of them she favoured or even worshipped herself, but thinking it impolite to ask, Patrick tactfully changed the direction of the conversation.

'I hear the High King lives in Tara,' he said.

'Oh, yed be wrong there now, mister. Who told ye that? He doesn't live there at all. But he was *crowned* there. Shure aren't all the High Kings crowned there? And they're all buried there too.'

Disappointed by this news, Patrick asked, 'Do you know where the High King lives then?'

The old woman shook her head. 'No, but he comes there every Beltane, that's all I know.'

'Beltane?' Patrick queried.

'In the summer, the beginning of the summertime, mister. And he comes then with a great crowd of people - musicians, harpers, jugglers, poets, dancers, and people selling all kinds of things, mister, lovely things altogether. Oh, it's then I wish I had a bit of gold or silver! But I go anyway. Shure everybody goes in the springtime, for there does be great teeaas entirely, great.'

'And the rest of the time?' Patrick asked. 'Does nothing happen in Tara between the King's visits?'

The woman scooped out some gruel from her pot into a small stone bowl. As she placed it before Patrick she bent close to him, looked him in the eye and in conspiratorial tones revealed, 'Oh, there does be quare things going on up there in Tara these days. It's not like the old days at all, at all, so it isn't, mister.'

Straightening up she went on, 'There's no respect anymore. No respect. That's what I think.'

'What's the problem?' Patrick queried.

The woman shook her head and clacked her tongue.

'Oh,' she said, 'shure won't yez see for yerselves if yer going there? Yez don't need me to tell yez, so yez don't.'

She placed bowls of gruel before Ignatius and Benedictus. When she turned and went to fetch a big jug from a shelf Benedictus pointed to his bowl and grimacing at Patrick silently mouthed, 'What is it?'

'I don't know,' Patrick whispered in Latin, 'but eat up. You'll have to get used to it, whatever it is.'

The woman came back and poured out thick buttermilk into battered tin mugs.

'So, good woman,' Patrick asked, 'tell me the name of your great High King?'

'Leery, mister. That's his name.'

'And what's he like?'

'I never met him.'

'Yes. But what does he *look* like?'

The woman raised her knobbly hands above her head and looked up stiffly.

'I see,' Patrick said.

'And there's always seven big Druid fellows around him, mister,' she informed. '*Seven*, all bigger even than himself.

Ye can't get anywhere near that King. Ye have to keep well back from *him*. Shure don't ye have to do everything them Druids say, whether they're big or small!'

'Everything?' Patrick queried, tongue-in-cheek.

'Aye,' the woman said resignedly. 'Everything.'

'Are there any Druids living in Tara?' Patrick asked.

'Oh, yed never know who yed meet there, mister. Be careful now.'

When the rain eventually stopped they set off again. It was around midday on the fourth day of their journey when suddenly the pools and potholes disappeared, the road widened and for the first time appeared to be properly maintained. Now it was covered with sandstone pebbles professionally pressed into a hard, even surface. Patrick sensed they were at last nearing the famous place.

The road passed then between a long, narrow lake and a dark wood. As they came to the end of the wood they saw ahead two identical, cube-shaped stones, about two feet high, placed precisely opposite one another on each side of the road.

'Marking stones!' Patrick exclaimed. 'We're nearly there, boys.'

They quickened their pace and soon reached the stones. Suddenly the entire landscape changed! They were utterly astonished! A vast green plain rolled out before their eyes like a magic carpet. Its circumference was clearly delineated by hundreds of low, evenly spaced but irregularly shaped stones. Exactly from the marking stones the road turned dazzling white and cut straight across the rich verdure which was dotted with sheep. There was a gently rising hill at the plain's centre, its plateau capped by a white circular mound from the centre of which, silhouetted against the cloudy sky, a huge, tall object, rose conspicuously up.

'Is all this real,' Ignatius asked, slack-jawed, 'or am I dreaming?'

'It's Tara!' Patrick said, gleefully absorbing the pastoral scene which reminded him of long ago when he was a shepherd-boy.

'What's that thing at the top of the hill?' Benedictus asked.

'Probably a standing stone,' Patrick replied. 'The pagans worship sticks and stones.'

'It's a pretty big stone,' Ignatius observed, 'a little Tower of Babylon. I suppose that's where the kings are crowned.'

'Or buried maybe,' Patrick suggested. 'Come, let's go see!'

However, as they were about to pass between the marking stones they all suddenly felt dizzy. At the same moment a crisp, sharp voice shouted: 'Stop!'

'Wh.....what's happening, F....Father?' Benedictus cried, staggering about.

Out of nowhere an unbelievably small man with a long, white, pointed beard, reaching to his feet, appeared. He was tightly clad in a bright-green, two-piece costume, a green conical cap, his trews neatly tapering into bright red, sharply pointed ankle-boots. He stood staunchly with his little legs apart, between the two marking stones, his fists on his hips.

'What are you doing here?' he testily enquired.

'Well..........we are.......you know........visitors,' Patrick weakly replied. 'We heard a lot about Tara ......and....and....'

'You cannot enter the sacred sanctuary of Tara,' the man sharply interrupted, 'without uttering the password.'

'I'm afraid I don't know it,' Patrick meekly confessed.

'Then you can't go, can you?' the man sneered.

He jumped deftly up onto one of the marking stones and gazed contemptuously at them from his perch.

'Can you perhaps make an exception for us?' Patrick foolishly pleaded. 'We've come an awful long way............'

The little man shrugged and made odd shapes in the air with his hand. His dizziness gone, Patrick was inspired to take out his purse. The little man watched curiously as Patrick produced a silver coin. He held it up to him questioningly. But after squinting at it the little man arrogantly shook his head.

'Gold,' he declared, 'only gold!'

Reluctantly Patrick produced one of his precious soldi. The little man studied the coin carefully.

'Two,' he eventually said.

More eager than ever to explore Tara, Patrick took another gold coin from his purse and dropped them into the green man's tiny cupped hands. Then the little green man hopped down.

'Kiss the stones!' he commanded.

When Patrick and the boys had courteously complied, the little man said, 'Liarg is the password.' Then after sticking his finger in his mouth he pointed to the sun which had suddenly appeared. Slowly he moved his finger to a westerly point.

'Before the sun is there,' he continued, 'be back here,' and tapped one of the stones.

'Thank you,' Patrick said. 'We will.'

Sniffing the coins, with unexpected ease he pushed one of the marking stones on its side and disappeared uncannily beneath it.

Bewildered but anxious to move on, Patrick and the boys immediately set off on the white road towards the hill.

'Was that little man really real, Father?' Benedictus asked.

'I told you before we came here,' Patrick replied, 'that it's a mighty strange place, didn't I?'

'You did, Father,' Benedictus agreed, 'but.....'

'But you better get used to it. That's all. Now, we mustn't waste time. Come!'

At the base of the hill the road narrowed into a footpath spiralling upwards. Upon reaching the top a vast panorama of the surrounding countryside greeted them. The plateau itself was green, flat as a lawn but featureless apart from the totally dominating white mound at its centre, a construct of white marble stones, all perfectly arranged in the shape of an upturned basin. From its centre rose the object they had hitherto only seen in silhouette.

It was indeed a standing stone. Of polished grey granite, it was expertly sculpted into a giant, erect phallus, its split, bulging head painted bright, blood red.

Benedictus fainted! Laughing, Patrick caught him before he hit the ground! Ignatius took his arm. After a few moments he came to.

'These pagans are a funny lot,' Patrick comforted, 'and their gods are even funnier at times. Are you all right, lad?'

Benedictus nodded.

The plateau was still and silent. The sky suddenly darkened. A black raven appeared and landed on the phallus.

Ignatius sniffed the air. 'Incense,' he said.

Patrick sniffed, then frowned. 'You're right! But where's it coming from?'

They followed the scent to the back of the mound where they discovered a small opening. Its lintel and side-stones were decorated with numerous roughly carved symbols. Stone steps dropped steeply from the opening into the hill's interior. Flickering, distant light indicated torches along the narrow descent.

Patrick studied the symbols.

'These are very ancient, boys,' he informed. 'They were carved thousands of years ago.'

'Thousands? Benedictus gasped.

'Yes, by the pagans.'

'What do they mean, Father?' Ignatius asked.

'All kinds of things,' Patrick replied fingering one of the spirals. 'This must be a symbol of the sun. The Druids worship the sun, you know.'

'Isn't Jesus a symbol of the sun too?' Benedictus asked.

'Jesus isn't a symbol of anything,' Patrick corrected. 'He's a man like me or you.'

'He's a god,' Ignatius added.

'God, no a,' Patrick qualified.

'He's really real, Father,' Ignatius said with a grin.

'We're going round in spirals,' Benedictus quipped.

'That's enough theology for today, boys,' Patrick said, cocking his ear to the opening. 'Listen!'

Chanting echoed faintly from the depths.

Patrick said, 'Are you ready, boys?'

'A...are you sure it's safe, Father?' Benedictus stammered

'What's the password?' Patrick questioned.

Benedictus screwed his face in frustration.

'Remind him,' Patrick said to Ignatius.

'Liarg,' Ignatius said.

'Good,' Patrick said. 'You're safe, Benedictus, as long as you remember the password. All right?'

Benedictus nodded.

'Ignatius, you're the timekeeper,' Patrick said winking. 'Keep your eye on the sun.'

'What, down here?'

'Yes. Imagination, boy. That's what you need in Hibernia!'

They began their long descent. The deeper they got the stronger the incense became and the louder the chanting. Nearing the bottom they saw a closed wooden door ahead. To one side of it a tall man stood still as a statue. He had on a long, green cloak and was holding a staff in his right hand. Beardless, his black hair, oddly shaven from ear to ear at the front, hung to his shoulders.

'Your first Druid, boys,' Patrick whispered while they were still out of the man's earshot. 'Be careful now. Let me do the talking.'

The Druid's lean countenance stiffened as they approached. He gazed questioningly at them.

'Liarg,' Patrick said quietly.

The Druid's eyes slanted. After a few moments he said firmly, 'You're late.'

'I know,' Patrick said apologetically. 'Forgive us.'

The man looked Ignatius and Benedictus up and down several times before it dawned on them to say

'Liarg.' When they said it in perfect unison a faint smile crossed the man's lips.

'We had a....a... mishap on the way,' Patrick lied.

The Druid relaxed, opened the door and nodded them through. Once more they were amazed! Although the light was dim and they were slightly overcome by the incense fumes, they now found themselves standing on the highest of numerous, descending, concentric rings of steps, thronged with seated people all gazing silently and intently upon a colourfully robed man with a bedizened, conical hat in the brightly lit central arena at the bottom of the steps. In a feat of pure architectural magic, the entire interior of the hill was transformed into a packed amphitheatre!

'It's real,' Patrick whispered to Benedictus whose eyes were glazing over.

'It's amazing,' Ignatius said quietly.

Because they were on the top steps they were able to make their way unobtrusively to a seat with a good view. The arena below was delineated by a circle of low, uniformly rounded stones, but totally dominated by a huge black stone cross in the centre. On one side of this was a raised wooden platform with a lectern and a book. On the other side of the cross was a big, flat stone with an indented surface containing burning charcoal. Beside this a robed attendant stood, intermittently sprinkling the charcoal with incense.

Patrick soon spotted that the colourfully robed man in the arena was holding a little white wand in his right hand.

'That's an oriental wizard or I'm not a Christian,' he whispered to the boys.

Suddenly, upon a sign from the wizard a rousing chant went out from the crowd.

'We're just in time,' Patrick said and after listening closely to the chanting added, 'By Jove, that's Hebrew!'

'What are they saying?' Ignatius asked.

'I'm not sure,' Patrick replied, 'but I know the cadence. It's definitely Hebrew.'

The wizard then walked slowly around the edging stones chanting and waving his wand over them. One by one they all turned bright green! And as the chanting grew louder, more rhythmic and pulsating, slowly but astoundingly the stones melded and transformed into a huge green snake!

Benedictus grabbed Patrick's arm.

'Easy, boy,' Patrick said, 'easy now.'

The serpent began to move! At the same time attendants

dowsed all the torches and the entire amphitheatre was eerily filled with the serpent's green light. Its eyes shone like red-hot coals, and its thin, darting tongue flicked in and out of its wide, grinning mouth. In perfect obedience to the commanding words of the wizard it moved slowly in from the periphery of the arena.

With the audience responding with increasing enthusiasm to the wizard's words, through a slow spiralling movement of his wand the wizard drew the serpent towards the black cross up which it slid and rested its head on top. Its long green tail formed a glistening spiral around the cross's base.

All went totally silent then as the wizard seemed to hold the serpent in place with his little wand.

Suddenly a petite figure emerged from a door under the steps! Though covered from head to foot in a blue veil, it was nevertheless obvious that the figure was female, for the veil was transparent and her body was totally naked underneath. Slowly she approached the raised wooden platform, mounted it and opened the book on the lectern. Then parting the veil from her face she began to speak.

'I read,' she said, 'from the holy gospel of Jesus, chapter three, verse thirteen: "No one has ascended into heaven except the one who descended from heaven, Jesus. And just as Moses lifted up the serpent in the wilderness, so must Jesus be lifted up, so that whoever believes in him may have eternal life. For the gods so loved the world that they gave to it Jesus who gives to those who follow him eternal life." ' After a short pause she addressed the audience directly. 'This is the word of the gods.'

She turned then towards the cross and pointed. 'Behold the Lord Jesus.'

The audience roared ecstatically.

The woman then came down from the lectern and completely cast off her veil. Kneeling reverently before the cross she kissed the serpent's tail. Then she stood up, faced the audience and above the roaring cried, 'Jesus, we love you!'

A wound in her side was visibly bleeding.

It was Vivian!

CHAPTER SIXTEEN

THE DEVIL'S PACT

Londonium was the largest town in Britannia. Many would say it was the *only* town, for most of the others were little more than rat-infested ruins. Londonium however was different. Reputedly founded in ancient times by the god Lud, the town was heir to a heritage that pre-dated the Romans by hundreds if not thousands of years. And this heritage undoubtedly helped it survive the chaos which followed the Romans' withdrawal. Londonium actually managed to keep alive a semblance of that ancient spirit which the Greeks called *demos* and the Romans *civitas.*

Semblance, however, is the operative word. For, while there was indeed law of sorts, it was minimal, and its enforcement cruel and arbitrary. The 'peace of Londonium' was patchy and fragile, but the town nevertheless functioned because of it. There was for instance a town wall which, though crumbling in many places, had guarded gates; it also had real streets and alleyways, houses with roofs, shops with goods, bartering markets, amusements, and of course ale-houses.

The most popular of these latter, and much-frequented establishments was *The Butchers' Tavern*, a tall, flat-roofed, three-storey building with a very narrow door above which a signboard bearing the establishment's name in faded painted letters swung and squeaked constantly in the breeze. The popularity of the place was due as much to the undeniable quality and strength of its ale as to its general reputation.

As the tavern's name implied, its origins could be traced back to the butchers of the town. During Roman times they had formed a guild, established the tavern as their meeting place, and as a result became a powerful group in the body politic. However, after the withdrawal of the army, with an eye to both survival and profit, they successfully adopted and promoted a policy of neutrality regarding the various warlords and their on-going feuds; and out of this neutrality there was established in the course of time a custom that whenever a Brittonic warlord came to Londonium (be he well-known or simply on-the-rise) he was to receive as much hospitality as he required in *The Butchers' Tavern*. And although the butchers had long since sold the tavern and found a new meeting place, the custom was still observed. Nowadays the tavern was privately owned by a man called Calder.

Arthur, who was well aware of the place and even had spies there, never set foot in it, considering it little more than a conspirators' den. Mordred on the other hand went there often and was indeed given royal treatment.

Whenever he arrived with his henchmen, all of the tavern's sleeping space was immediately and unceremoniously cleared, and Mordred's men installed for as long as they wished.

Hengist frequented it too. Hengist, of course, was not a Briton. But he was so powerful that Calder felt compelled to make an exception. Unlike Mordred however, Hengist never arrived unannounced. Aware of his alien status he usually took the precaution of sending word ahead with a scout that he was on his way. But when one day Calder received word that Hengist was not only coming, but that he was coming to meet Mordred, it was as if Calder had been hit by lightning! He frantically interrogated Hengist's scout for several minutes hoping it was a bad joke. But it wasn't! Hengist was definitely coming, was definitely meeting Mordred, and it was all about to happen in a couple of hours' time, at midday!

Tall, skinny and nervous, Calder hardly knew what to do. Hengist and Mordred in the tavern at the same time! Even the dogs in the street knew that these were not only two of the most powerful warlords in the land, but also fierce enemies! Moreover, the scout informed that Hengist wanted the meeting to be *private*! Calder had had such a demand before, and it meant only one thing.........

He immediately emptied the tavern. Luckily, because it was morning and he didn't have many customers - just the usual few drunks - he had little difficulty. Once the place was cleared he bolted the door, ran upstairs, and wringing his hands continually, anxiously watched the street outside through a crack in the wooden wall.

Mordred often brooded on the difficult conditions Hengist had set for this meeting. But his procrastinations were just as often dispelled by Sorath who, after his first ominous appearance, came regularly to Mordred filling him with dark resolve. So, at the appointed time he rode to Londonium, alone and unarmed, and arrived exactly on time at the tavern.

A number of horses were tethered to a railing outside, while two huge, heavily armed men leant idly against the tavern's doorpost. They watched Mordred cautiously as he approached and became very alert when he dismounted and tethered his horse beside the others. By their matted yellow hair and bright blue eyes, Mordred knew they were Saxons, Hengist's men.

He stood before them, pointed to himself and said, 'Mordred.'

The men looked at one another and after a quick exchange in their own language one of them knocked loudly on the door. Calder opened. Recognizing Mordred, he nervously beckoned him in and bolted the door again. Then he ran to the counter and watched.

Hengist was sitting behind the only table in the drab tavern, all the others having being cleared for the meeting. The table was long and in the centre of the dirt floor. Hengist was flanked on either side by a few of his men, all awkwardly seated and armed with axes and knives, fixed stares on their hairy faces. Three others stood behind Hengist, holding spears and black-crossed, wooden shields. Directly in front of Hengist an ebony-handled, silver dagger was stuck upright into the table. Hengist pointed to a vacant chair opposite him. Mordred sat down. Hengist snapped his fingers then and Calder quickly came with a jug of ale and two mugs and placed them on the table.

When Calder returned to the counter Hengist slowly filled the mugs. He pushed one of them towards Mordred who responded by lazily scratching his empty eye socket. Hengist shrugged and drank. After wiping his lips he said, 'I hear, Briton, you want to talk to me.'

Mordred took a sip of his ale and replaced the mug carefully. 'Yes,' he said slowly.

'Then start talking!' Hengist growled.

'Are you aware that Arthur is.......?'

Hengist banged his fist on the table. 'Damn Arthur!' he roared.

Mordred ignored the outburst and sipped his ale. Licking his lips he calmly continued, 'His army will soon be ready to fight.'

'What of it?' Hengist contemptuously spat. 'I can deal with *him*.'

Mordred shook his head.

'State quickly, what's on your mind, Briton?' Hengist said.

'More than simply *dealing* with Arthur. *Eliminating* him.'

'How?'

'How many men have you?'

'Two thousand.'

'I have more. Arthur could muster fifteen hundred at the most.'

'So?'

'Together we would have no bother ridding this land of him for good.'

Hengist studied Mordred with slanted eyes. 'And.....?'

'And you could establish your own independent state, a fully legitimate Saxon principality here in Britannia.'

Hengist grinned. He turned to his men and repeated what Mordred said in their own language. They laughed heartily.

Hengist set the dagger in front of him in motion. Eyeballing Mordred, he slowly lifted the earthenware jug and drank deeply. Then after smashing the jug onto the table he tore open the front of his tunic. On his hairy chest, dangling from wire was a large, crudely fashioned, iron crucifix. He grabbed it and thrust it at Mordred.

'See this?' he barked.

'What is it?' Mordred asked, perplexed.

'It's Jesus.'

Mordred had heard of Jesus, but had never seen a crucifix. He examined the scrawny body nailed to the cross, spots of red paint indicating blood from the wounds.

'I like it,' he said coldly.

'Kiss him!' Hengist demanded.

'Why?' Mordred asked.

'Because this is where the power is now, Briton. Kiss him. Kiss him quick, and we can talk.'

Shrugging, Mordred kissed the crucifix. 'Anything else?'

Hengist drank again. 'You and your men will have to be baptized.'

'Baptized?'

'The key to Valhalla,' Hengist said blessing himself awkwardly.

'Valhalla is where your gods live, isn't it?' Mordred said.

'Yes and now Jesus lives there. I am making him head of my tribe's gods. I'll organize your baptism.'

'As you wish,' Mordred said.

Pleased at having concluded such an easy deal, Mordred

took his mug and touched Hengist's. 'Here's to Jesus,' he said, 'and the elimination of Arthur.'

'There is one thing more, Briton,' Hengist said.

'What's that?'

'I have a Jesus priest and he tells me that if I'm to be a really good follower I must change my old ways.'

'Oh. In what sense?'

'He tells me I should get married.'

Hengist repeated this to his men and they laughed uproariously, making obscene gestures. Hengist went on, 'Yes. And you know, Briton, there is only one women in this whole wide world that I think could satisfy Hengist the Saxon in marriage.'

'Who is that?' Mordred asked.

'Arthur's Guinevere. She must not be killed. We will abduct her and I will have her. All right?'

CHAPTER SEVENTEEN

PALLADIUS

Of course, what Patrick and his companions had accidentally witnessed on that portentous afternoon in Tara was a demonstration of a Naasene ritual, in fact their most potent and powerful one. And the wizard's name was Palladius.

Like his contemporary Augustine, Palladius had been a Manichean before he became a Naasene. The Manichean religion was a Persian, as distinct from a Roman, brand of Christianity and was named after its founder, the third century prophet Mani, who believed himself to be an incarnation of the One whom the very first Christians called the Paraclete, or the Holy Spirit.

From the beginning, Mani based his religion firmly on the dualistic doctrine that God was a kind of divine Twin, encompassing in his universal nature both good and evil, and Mani wrote extensive treatises on the subject. All Manichean neophytes, or *hearers* as they were technically called, were obliged to study and digest these writings, but neither Augustine nor Palladius could ever fully fathom them, could never get to grips with Mani's essential insight; and their disputations with the *electi*, or the priests of the religion, eventually forced them to abandon it altogether.

Soon after Augustine left he converted to Roman Christianity where he continued to brood long and hard on the problem of evil and in time hammered out his own distinctive theory of it. This he duly published to wide acclaim and soon became the established Catholic authority on the subject, his teaching actually being adopted as the orthodox position.

However, whereas Augustine was an intense intellectual, Palladius was nothing of the kind. After he left the Manicheans he did not have a mind to pursue the subject of evil any further and actually tried to forget about it altogether. He set off on an entirely new spiritual adventure. He reckoned he could surely find some other Jesus-based cult capable of utilizing his many talents, but without having to bother his head about the thorny problem of evil.

After much searching he came upon the Naasenes in the Syrian Desert. They based their knowledge of Jesus on a gospel book by Thomas the Twin whom they believed was one of Jesus's intimate circle of twelve. Thomas's gospel regarded Jesus as the Serpent of Wisdom. And as the Hebrew word for serpent is *naas*, they adopted it for the name for their sect.

The Naasenes combined their apocryphal gospel with a vast cabbalistic knowledge, elaborate oriental rites and richly robed rituals, and also possessed a huge lexicon of highly sophisticated meditation techniques. Their emphasis on practical magic rather than on theological nuances appealed to Palladius enormously. Like the Manicheans, their leaders or initiates were all male and celibate, and this gave Palladius a head start. He was certain he had found what he was looking for! He learnt Hebrew, studied and meditated with tremendous enthusiasm, and soon became a highly accomplished wizard.

Though small in number, the Naasenes were big in ambition, and enthusiastic evangelizers of their sect. Their initiates went all over the known world, and when the initiate Palladius one day heard of a mysterious island beyond the borders of the Roman Empire, in the farthest reaches of the far-flung West, a land whose very name conjured up for him images of spiritual mysteries older than time itself, he decided that it was the place for him.

Palladius was a handsome, middle-aged, man when he first came to Hibernia. He took with him as helpers a small group of male neophytes. He quickly learnt the local language, made it his business to befriend some influential Druids, and used his undoubted talents to impress upon them the great new power of the Serpent and the Cross. Seeing in him one who could potentially further their own power, the Druids did not collectively oppose him and even turned a blind eye to him openly using his gospel book in public gatherings. However, in this land, the very air of which bred mystery and magic, Palladius did not make much progress until one day a small but very attractive young woman stepped precociously out from an attentive group to whom he was preaching, and in carefully measured tones announced, 'The Serpent god has sent me to help you.'

Now, from the first moment of his arrival in Hibernia Palladius was struck by the frequency of odd and unexpected happenings. But this was the oddest yet! This young woman's aura had at least fifty shades of green! Positively amazing! And though her claim was outlandish in the extreme, he decided he simply *had* to investigate. He immediately abandoned the meeting and took the young woman to his tent where they sat down and talked.

She told him her name, something of her background and especially how she often had visions as a child. Further questioning revealed that she had recently become an initiated Virgin Priestess of the Mother Goddess of these lands and since then had had many visions of the great Serpent Naas.

Palladius could hardly believe his ears!

'I want to know more about this Serpent,' she firmly asserted. 'I want more than just to have visions of it. I want to smell it, touch it, lick its flesh.'

Palladius's mouth watered.

'Who initiated you?' he enquired.

'Merlin,' she replied. (For, of course, she was Vivian!)

'Merlin!' Palladius cried. 'You mean the famous Cambrian magician?'

'Yes,' Vivian said. 'Who else?' Then she added coyly, 'Say, do you want to see my wound?'

Palladius swallowed hard. 'Your wound?'

'Yes. My wound of initiation.'

'Oh, I see.'

Vivian got up and was in the act of lifting her tunic when Palladius said, 'No. Wait! First tell me how this wound was inflicted?'

'Why, by old Merlin, with his white Spear.'

'His white Spear?'

'Yes, the white Spear of Initiation. It's one of the *Four Treasures of Hibernia*.'

'And what, pray, are they?'

'The most powerful talismans in the whole world,' Vivian proudly informed. 'The Sword of Light, the Spear of Initiation, the white Stone of Destiny and the Crystal Chalice of Rebirth.'

Palladius was breathing heavily. Hibernia just kept getting better!

'Show me your wound!' he commanded.

Eagerly Vivian lifted her tunic and Palladius's eyes popped! The little red-raw wound on her side plunged him into deepest ecstasy.

'Kiss it!' Vivian excitedly demanded.

Palladius obeyed.

Vivian laughed. And when he kissed it again she laughed all the more.

Now Palladius knew for certain that what Vivian said was true! She had indeed been sent by a god, the god of purest ecstasy. He had received a heavenly helper! Now at last he was going to make progress in Hibernia. To hell with celibacy!

As Palladius fully expected, as Vivian's lover his life-force swelled enormously and his magical powers grew in great leaps and bounds. With his little white wand in one hand, his gospel of Jesus in the other, and the cosmic-channelling Vivian always by his side, now all of the planetary and zodiacal powers he could ever wish for were at his disposal and flowed with ecstatic abundance into his demonstrations. He felt he was even outdoing the great Simon Magus! All over the south of Hibernia he travelled in a luxurious caravan drawn by two splendid horses, one black, one white, capturing the minds and hearts of the simple people with his hugely impressive wizardry, a potent and highly seductive blend of the exotic, the erotic and the theosophic. He held many mass meetings, and his number of followers rapidly expanded. Everywhere he went he trained up new initiates and established groups of serpent-worshippers. Every type and class, from peasants to kings was attracted to him. And when he told them that all his power was due to Jesus, they wanted only to hear, see and know more. The Druids even allowed him the occasional use of their secret underground amphitheatre in Tara for his most powerful demonstration.

It was to one of these that Patrick inadvertently made his way soon after arriving in Hibernia. At first Patrick thought he might be witnessing a gathering of the Pelagians, for Germanus in his tirades against Pelagius often referred to him as a serpent; but Patrick soon learnt that this was not the case. Pelagianism however did, he discovered, exist in Hibernia. For he met people who professed to practise what the enigmatic Pelagius preached. 'And what precisely *did* he preach?' Patrick always asked, but the answers he received were invariably vague, apart from an assertion of a belief in the inner Christ.

After the Tara experience Patrick moved very cautiously about the island but kept mostly to its central plain. He spoke very little of Jesus, and the more he saw of the Naasenes the more reserved he became. To see the name and power of his beloved Jesus used, or in Patrick's view, *abused* in their circus-like fashion, utterly appalled him. Then one day he learnt that the more cool-headed Druids of the north did not like the Naasenes at all. Moreover there was, he also learnt, a very enlightened king up there. This was Fergus who ruled a kingdom called Dal Riada and had his castle in a place called Dunseverick. Patrick immediately set out for it with his companions.

Dunseverick was situated on the coast in the far north-eastern tip of the island. It was an easier journey than many of the others Patrick had so far made on his mission, for one of the only four roads of Hibernia led directly to Dunseverick.

When Patrick eventually got to Dal Riada he found accommodation in a tavern near Dunseverick castle where merchants and others who had business with the castle usually stayed. From these he learned much about the castle's working and through them was able to discern how best to make his approach to the King. Patrick's presence however aroused intense curiosity, and when his intentions became known the curiosity quickly yielded to suspicion, especially in the mind of the King's chief Druid. This was Eoin MacSaggart who lived within the castle compound.

Long-legged, lean and spiky-faced, MacSaggart was shrewd as a fay. Like all chief Druids, he considered it his sacred duty, according to the ancient laws and traditions of his profession, not only to advise and protect the King, but to know as much about him as possible. There were absolutely no restrictions in this regard, a situation which Fergus, an exceptionally single-minded man, accepted reluctantly.

From the first moment MacSaggart became aware of Patrick's intentions he actively opposed him. No way was he going to allow some strange Roman preacher, who was by all accounts trying to popularise some new god, access to the King's ear. Fergus on the other hand was usually interested to hear of new gods, albeit in the hope that his ever-tottering belief in them might be strengthened! Thus when MacSaggart heard that Patrick had bypassed him and had actually procured an interview with the King by bribing a close aide with Roman gold, he was livid. He ran immediately to Fergus and bitterly complained.

Serious-faced, of squat build and melancholy of mood, Fergus exuded an unmistakable aura of power. Widely respected by his army, his vassals and his people, he was fair-minded and listened patiently to all grievances brought before him. But he had less patience with long-winded MacSaggart and the Druids generally who were professionally obliged to tell him stories of the gods and heroes of old whenever they needed to make some moral, legal or political point. For Fergus was deeply interested in truth and innately suspicious of mere stories.

Taking a deep breath he said bravely to MacSaggart, 'I want to hear what this man Patrick has to say of his god.'

'But, my King, ' MacSaggart argued, 'the fellow is attempting to bring to Dal Riada a new religion!'

'I have been told,' Fergus said, 'he is not a serpent-worshipper, if that's what you mean.'

'I have my doubts,' MacSaggart returned. 'And he's definitely a Roman.'

'Roman or not,' the King determinedly returned, 'I will hear this man out.'

MacSaggart bowed his head, withdrew sullenly but resolved to fight on.

Fergus listened attentively to everything Patrick told him

about Jesus. Fergus however spoke very little during the interview and even less when it finished. But the few words he did speak were portentous. After thanking Patrick for his time and efforts, he declared, 'Come back next week and I will hear more!'

Patrick was delighted! He reckoned he had at last found what he had so fervently hoped and prayed for ever since he arrived in Hibernia: the sympathetic ear of a powerful man.

Patrick studied very carefully how best to convince the King of the truth and beauty of the great new Godman. Patrick never forgot the dream he had had long ago in Hibernia as a slave-boy, the dream in which he saw a great stone fall on him out of a midnight, rainbow-filled sky, a stone that his old Druid master, Miliuc, told him came from the sun itself. It was the dream that had awoken in Patrick a great love of God and the sun-like majesty of his divine Son, and so he used the dream, albeit with many imaginative variations of it, to impress upon King Fergus the unique goodness and power of Jesus the Christ.

It worked! Fergus invited Patrick back many times to his castle. And the more words that flowed from Patrick's mouth the more the King felt that in Palestine over four hundred years ago the Sun-god really had taken on the form of a flesh-and-blood man!

Eventually Patrick asked Fergus the crucial question, 'May I have your permission, good King, to preach this holy gospel of Jesus openly in your lovely kingdom?' At this, however, the King's down-of-mouth countenance looked more burdened than ever. 'I must consult with my chief Druid about that,' he gloomily replied.

And so the next time Patrick spoke to the King, MacSaggart was present.

'Tell my chief Druid about Jesus,' Fergus ordered

Patrick, and Patrick nervously but confidently repeated to MacSaggart much of what he had already told Fergus.

'So you see,' Fergus declared when Patrick finished, 'this man is not a serpent-worshipper. Far from it! Actually he hates them....don't you Patrick?'

Patrick nodded.

'Although this man is a Roman,' Fergus continued to MacSaggart, 'I would myself like to hear more from him of Jesus. However, I would also like him to tell *my people* about this new god. You, Eoin MacSaggart, as a representative of the guardians of all religious practice in my kingdom, have the power to prevent his happening. If you do this, however, it would......well, shall I say, *displease* me....greatly. So I ask you plainly in this holy man's presence: will you oppose him if I, as sovereign of the land, who wishes always to act not only in the interests of the people of my kingdom of Dal Riada, but in the interests of the *whole* of the island of Hibernia; will you oppose him if I grant him permission to preach his new god?'

MacSaggart stared at the floor. Eventually he shook his head. Then suddenly looking up he demanded, 'But he must not use his book!'

'Do you use books in your mission?' the King asked Patrick with surprise.

'Only one, good King,' Patrick replied. 'It's called the gospel.'

'Oh, and what does "the gospel" mean?'

'The good news.'

A rare smile brightened the King's countenance. 'Well then, don't let the people *see* your "good news." Just let them *hear* it!'

Patrick nodded delightedly and MacSaggart withdrew.

That night MacSaggart had a strange dream. In it he

saw a great pile of books burning. He watched in dismay as the flames turned the things he held so precious to ash. Then suddenly from the dying embers he saw a little white dove rising. It flew away in to a clear blue sky. When MacSaggart awoke he pondered the dream deeply, as was his duty. He was obliged to come up with a plausible interpretation of *every* dream. But no matter how long and hard he pondered this one he could not decide what it meant.

A few weeks later King Fergus donated to Patrick, for use in his mission, a derelict cowshed and some rusty tools which had outlived their usefulness to the castle. Patrick was hugely excited by this gift and thanked the King (and God!) profusely. The shed had a small stony field attached and was situated a little further along the shore from Dunseverick castle. Together with his trusty helpers, Ignatius and Benedictus, Patrick got immediately down to work. They cleaned out the cowshed, patched up the rotting thatch of the roof, repaired and re-hung the broken door; with sackcloth draped over interwoven branches they partitioned the interior into three smaller rooms, and finally they made some rough furniture out of driftwood gathered along the seashore.

In this way Patrick established his first house-community of Christians in Hibernia. And when they settled in he was at long last able to do what he had most earnestly wanted to do from the beginning: fulfil the command of his Angel and preach the word of the gospel of Jesus Christ to the Hibernians.

He travelled about Dal Riada seeking places wherever crowds gathered, at fairs, festivals or funerals. There, at some suitable spot, he spoke out from his heart the truth of

God as he knew it. He was not alone in such endeavours however and often had to compete with a variety of augurs, ascetics and part-time prophets who invariably came to such places seeking the ears, the hearts, but especially the coin of the populace. Often no one listened to Patrick and he came back despondent at night to the cowshed. At other times, however, a few would stop, and attracted as much by Patrick's imposing, bearded figure and the way he spoke as by what he actually said, listened for a while.

Patrick was particularly interested in young men. These, he reckoned, were more likely than any other types to properly receive the Word, and be able to break with the old tribal ways. If he gained the attention of such a one he would sometimes engage him in conversation when all other listeners had drifted away. Patrick would sometimes divulge the location of the cowshed to such young men, with an invitation to visit. Many did, and some were invited to stay. These, together with Benedictus, he usually sent out begging, always leaving Ignatius in charge, while he himself continued to preach.

The cowshed community was thus a poor, but eventful, and at times chaotic place in the early days. Often angry parents came to snatch their boys away and threatened to report Patrick to the Druids for child abduction! Other parents, however, were less aggressive and after a conciliatory conversation with Patrick allowed their offspring to stay, at least temporarily; and sometimes after hearing a little of the gospel story stayed themselves for a while in order to hear and learn more. Soon Sunday mornings were set aside in the cowshed for all who wanted to listen and learn. In this way also a core living group of young men was gradually established.

Thus it was that at the beginning of his mission, as well

as his main task of preaching, Patrick had daily to deal with the problem of imposing an ordered routine, such as he was used to in his monastery in Auxerre, upon the unpredictable moods, habits, instincts and rivalries of a disparate group of about twelve young men all eagerly engaged on a great new spiritual mission. Benedictus and Ignatius were a great help in this regard in that they had already been used to the monastery routine for over two years before they left for Hibernia. In Auxerre, however, they had had little contact with the outside world. It was entirely different in the cowshed community.

Early one morning of their first springtime together a few of them were digging in a flat corner of their very stony field. Patrick had instructed them to make some raised beds, for he had had a powerful vision of a vegetable garden! A scattered flock of noisy rooks flitted about the scraggy thorns that skewered the field's low hedges. In the middle distance the King's castle could be seen, stark, formidable and totally dominating the surrounding landscape.

Angus, the newest member of the community, was a petulant young man. As the newest member, he had been allocated the rustiest spade for the morning's digging! But he had never used such a tool before and was growing increasingly frustrated, finding little but stubborn rocks every time he sunk his spade more than a few inches into the soil. He eventually stopped trying and looked up. The sea-breeze stirred his wavy mop of thick red hair. He ran his freckled hand through it and gazed ponderously on the great white clouds that sailed high above the distant castle. Then he looked suddenly around at the other diggers.

'Hey,' he shouted to Ignatius, 'where's Benedictus?'

'I don't know,' Ignatius dryly replied.

'Didn't Father Patrick say he was supposed to help with the digging this morning?'

'I don't know,' Ignatius repeated.

Angus looked towards the castle again. 'I bet he's up there,' he said with a mixture of accusation and envy.

'What makes you say that?' Ignatius asked.

A grin appeared on Angus's fresh, freckled face. 'He likes our Hibernian girls, your Benedictus does,' he said slyly.

Ignatius stopped digging. He looked wearily at this latest addition to the household and wondered how long it would take to get used to the fellow.

'What are Roman girls like?' Angus asked.

Ignatius took a kerchief from his pocket and mopped his brow. 'I don't know,' he said again, 'but why don't you ask Father Patrick? Look! He's coming.'

Angus turned. Patrick was picking his way towards them through jutting rocks and tufts of wet rushes, holding up his cowl to keep the hem dry. Upon reaching the diggers they all greeted him in unison, 'Good morning, Father.'

'Good morning, my lads,' Patrick brightly returned.

He jumped deftly up onto a flat boulder that protruded like a discarded table from the nearby ditch and surveyed the work. After forcing a nod he asked, 'How's it going?'

There was an awkward but respectful silence. Ignatius broke it. 'Not bad, Father.'

Angus held up his rusty spade. 'We need something better than this, Father.'

'Bad workmen always quarrel with their tools, Angus,' Patrick said with a raised brow.

Angus shrugged. Patrick counted the young men. One missing! After another quick survey he asked Ignatius, 'Where's Benedictus?'

'Angus thinks he's up in the castle,' Ignatius replied.

'The castle!' Patrick exclaimed and looked at Angus. 'Well, explain, boy.'

Angus blushed. 'You... you see, F...Father,' he said with a giggle, 'there is this s...servant girl who works in the c...castle......'

'What about her?' Patrick demanded after stifling giggles from the others with a stern look.

'Well, Father, she comes to our meetings on Sundays and he walks back with her to the castle every time afterwards.'

'Does he indeed!?'

'Yes, Father. She's very pretty. Isolde is her name.'

'And how long has this been going on?'

'About three weeks.'

'Right,' Patrick said, wagging his finger, 'from here on no more walking girls back to the castle...or anywhere! You all got that?'

'Yes, Father,' the boys said, except Angus. He was looking grumpily at his spade again.

Patrick jumped down from the boulder.

'Remember this, lads,' he said, 'keep your mind on your work, and God will bless it all the more.'

'We will, Father.'

'Good. Now, I'll be off. See you all for our midday meal.'

'See you, Father.'

With his cowl lifted Patrick was picking his way carefully back to the cowshed when Angus called, 'Father!'

Patrick turned.

'Should we not have a house for girls too?' Angus said.

Patrick glared sternly at the pleading young face, then his countenance softened. But he said nothing and went on his way, a mood, however, of despondency gradually overtaking him as he approached the shed.

Inside, it was empty. He stood contemplatively before the

simple shrine that was set up in a corner of the common-room: a piece of clean sackcloth spread beneath a cracked beaker containing a bunch of freshly picked wild flowers, alongside which lay the gospel book. Although Patrick tried to obey MacSaggart's interdict not to use the book, he could not preach without it. It was thus his routine to set off with it each morning on foot to some suitable location to preach until noon. It was time now to go, but before picking up the book he suddenly fell to his knees, clasped his hands, bowed his head, closed his eyes and prayed.

He prayed harder and more fervently than ever. Often he felt he needed superhuman strength if he was to fulfil the call of his Angel and succeed in converting the poor people of this land to the Christ of his dreams. Prayer sometimes supplied that strength. And this morning as he prayed, not only did his despondency lift, but he was filled with an unfathomable sense of sweetness.

He opened his eyes and looked around. The warped wooden door of the shed was ajar, allowing a thin shaft of light into the room's gloomy interior. But there was another source of light! Never before was he so certain of not being alone. He turned to his left. And there, near the ceiling, on a protruding twig of the room's improvised partition he was amazed to see a small white Dove silently watching him! It was no ordinary Dove however, for it shone like a star! Patrick gazed transfixed. The bird's tiny eyes sparkled blue, yellow and green. The light from its little body poured down on him like honey. Then its breast feathers swelled and he heard a beautifully clear voice: 'I am the Comforter of all humankind. Come, follow me!'

Dumbfounded, Patrick watched the bird. The words were still echoing in his head when suddenly the door of the shed was pushed open. It was Benedictus.

The bird immediately flew out past Benedictus into the open air, but he hardly noticed, for he was not expecting to see anyone, especially not Patrick!

'Oh, Father,.....' he cried, 'I'm sorry......'

Patrick got up. 'Where were you, boy?' he demanded.

'I....I.... was searching for...fire.....firewood.'

'Don't lie to me!' Patrick snapped. 'I *know* where you were!'

Tears filled Benedictus's eyes. With a red face and head bent he confessed, 'In the castle, Father.'

'Good,' Patrick said softening his tone. 'Now, listen to me. Any time you want to go up there again you must ask my permission first. Understand?'

'Yes, Father.'

Patrick went to the door and looked out over the stony field.

'You're supposed to be helping your Brothers this morning, aren't you?' he said, gently now.

'Yes, Father.'

'Well, go to them.'

As Benedictus made off, Patrick's eyes were drawn to the ancient oak that stood proudly in the centre of the stony field. On its summit he spotted the little Dove primly perched. She seemed to be waiting for him.

'Benedictus!' Patrick shouted.

Benedictus stopped.

Patrick said, 'Tell your Brother, Ignatius, to take charge. I am going away for a while.'

'For how long, Father?' Benedictus anxiously enquired.

'I don't know.'

'I'll tell him, Father,' Benedictus said and ran to his Brothers.

CHAPTER EIGHTEEN

THE BABY

If what Guinevere found most attractive about Lancelot was his hardness, what he found most attractive about her was her softness. And though in the weeks and months after she revealed her pregnancy to him his troubled conscience tried hard and often to put a stop to the affair, her softness so delighted and soothed his body that desire always got the upper hand. Thus, he continued to enjoy her as often as he possibly could.

Especially now as she was nearing the fullness of her pregnancy, after they made love he liked nothing better than to rest his head on the big soft pillow of her belly.

'Can you hear his heartbeat?' she asked him one night in bed during Arthur's absence from Camelot.

Lancelot kissed her belly and straightened up to her. Wiping away a film of sweat from her brow, he said, 'No, but *he*?'

She took his hand and kissed it. 'Merlin told me.'

Lancelot fell back and sighed. 'But, my dear, I asked you not to involve *him*.'

'Sorry, love. But I had to. Arthur is absolutely ecstatic about the baby. We simply had to tell Merlin.'

'Damn!'

'Don't worry.'

'But are you not afraid Merlin will get......suspicious....about us? After all, he can see much more than anyone else.'

'No, I'm not afraid. Even if he did suspect he wouldn't say anything to Arthur.'

'What makes you so sure?'

'Oh, Lancelot! Merlin, more than anyone, knows the ways of our wicked old world. He would speak with *me* first, and he hasn't. And anyway, he loves Arthur too much to upset him with.......with mere suspicion.'

She raised herself up and gently tugged the curly black hairs of his chest. 'We do however have a real problem in this regard.'

Lancelot's countenance darkened. 'What do you mean?'

'Percival.'

'What about him?'

'He knows.

Lancelot sprung up. 'How, by the gods? How can *he* know?'

'He knows!'

'Are you sure?'

Guinevere nodded. 'At least, he has been deeply suspicious for some time.'

'And has *he* told anybody?'

'I don't think so. I'm working on him.'

'What on earth do you mean: working on him?'

'Lancelot, my love, you *know* what I mean. He's only a boy. I don't think he's even had it yet! I keep..... in touch with him.....you know..... I make suggestions, offers. And any time I come here to your bed now I always make sure he *can't* know.'

'What? You send him out of Camelot?'

'On some errand,' Guinevere smiled wistfully. 'I think he'll make an excellent knight.......when he grows up.'

'He's already a fine Knight.'

'Don't worry about him. Let me handle it.'

Lancelot stroked the nape of her neck with the back of his hand.

'You shouldn't,' he said vaguely, 'be making Percival.....offers.'

'No one tells the Queen of Camelot what to do,' she teasingly returned.

Lancelot flashed a rare smile. 'Don't count your chickens before they're hatched, my dearest. Arthur has a long way to go before he'll be king.'

'How long?'

'I don't know.'

Lancelot got up and paced the bedroom. 'The forces against him are mounting,' he said. 'Mordred, whom I'm sure Arthur has mentioned to you, has recently aligned himself with Hengist the Saxon. Soon Arthur's army will be ready to fight. There's one hell of a big battle on the cards, one I believe that will determine the future of our land for many generations to come. There is, however, despite the Sword of Light, no certainty at all that we can win it. The army, after all, has never been tested.'

Guinevere sighed. 'Oh, do you men ever think about anything else except wars and battles?'

Lancelot stopped pacing. He studied her. Surely she was the most beautiful woman in the world, her soft skin shining now with sweat in the candlelight, her breasts the colour of honey in the golden afterglow of their lovemaking.

'We do occasionally,' he said.

'Well, I genuinely think Arthur has forgotten about lovemaking altogether! You know sometimes now we sleep with The Sword of Light between us in the bed!'

'You're joking!'

'No. I'm deadly serious. Sleeping with it gives him power, he says. He has taken to calling it the "Sword of Jesus the Victorious." '

'Yes. I've heard that.'

'And he's also studying the gospel!'

'That's the life story of Jesus, isn't it?

'Yes. Merlin told him about it.'

'Where did he get it?'

'Kay found him a copy in a bookshop in Londonium. Now he spends nearly all his free time in the library reading it. He's searching for information on the Grail.'

'What the hell is that?'

'It's something belonging to Jesus apparently. It's the secret of Jesus, Merlin says. Pelagius has it. I'm not supposed to tell anyone.'

'But you are!'

'Yes, but darling, you're different.'

Lancelot lay down beside her again. After kissing her belly he put his ear to it.

'I can hear the heartbeat now,' he said.

Guinevere laughed. 'Tell your son about the Grail, my sweet,' she said clutching his hair. 'He'll find it surely.'

CHAPTER NINETEEN

A DINNER IN CAMELOT

A magician's is a lonely occupation. No one knew this better than Merlin. Merlin however was well suited to his profession. He was a 'lone wolf.' He liked nothing better than performing his own private rituals. Throughout his life he only conformed when absolutely necessary to the conventions of social life, assiduously avoiding most of its customary niceties. So that nowadays the only social engagements he honoured were those directly connected with his work either as a hierophant or Arthur's adviser.

He favoured the latter. Visits to Camelot were mostly pleasurable, for they were a perfect antidote to his never-ending, solitary routine of rituals, incantations and meditations. Thus one morning while out communicating with the trees near his hut in the Forest of Elfham he was pleased to see Clegis, Arthur's personal courier, approach on horseback.

'Greetings!' Merlin said.

'The gods be with you, Merlin,' Clegis returned.

'What news?' Merlin brightly enquired.

'Arthur wants you,' Clegis replied, dismounting.

'That I can tell. But for what?'

'He invites you to a dinner.'

Merlin suddenly looked irritated.

'Arthur knows damn well I don't go to dinners!' he retorted. 'I avoid them like drunken soldiers.'

'I know Arthur knows that,' the courier said. 'But he also told me to tell you that a Hibernian king will be present at the meal.'

Merlin nearly dropped his staff!

'Are you sure?' he questioned. 'A Hibernian king?'

'Yes,' Clegis returned. 'He is from a kingdom in the north of Hibernia, Dal Riada.'

'By the gods,' Merlin gasped, 'Fergus!'

'Yes. That's the name.'

Merlin had never met Fergus, but through his connection with Avalliona and Morganna knew much about him and his Gaelic kingdom.

'Have you been told the reason for this visit?' he asked.

'No,' Clegis replied.

'Is Fergus in Camelot at present?'

'No, but he is due in two days' time. Arthur says you can't miss this dinner.'

'Did he now?' Merlin grunted as he tugged ponderously on his wispy beard.

Arthur had no power of summons over him; that was taken for granted. Nevertheless, the more Merlin considered this 'invitation', the more it took on the character of a summons. And Arthur was right! How could he possibly miss being involved in such an important occasion?

'Tell him I'll be there,' Merlin said and after a little more cordial conversation the courier departed.

Merlin dashed back excitedly into his hut and after a few quick rituals which he would normally do in the evening before bedtime, he immediately set out on his donkey for Camelot. It was mid-afternoon. There was no time to lose. Before the King arrived, Merlin wanted to get as much background information as possible on the unprecedented visit. Something was in the air. Something big. Even Caliban seemed to sense it, for rarely was she so sprightly. She took him to Camelot in miraculous time, only two hours! It was unheard of!

'I received the request for the visit via Morganna,' Arthur informed soon after he arrived.

They sat together in the comfortable living room of Arthur's apartment in the castle keep. A huge log fire was blazing in the hearth, Arthur's hound basking with one eye watchfully open in front of it. Arthur had a piece of parchment in his hand.

'It's a written request,' he said, 'very proper, though in his own language.'

'What!' Merlin cried. 'Does Fergus not know Brittonic?'

'Morganna says he can speak it, whatever about writing it. And when you think about it, he would hardly come here if he *couldn't* speak it. But Fergus knew that Morganna would translate the letter for me.'

'Oh, that's the Hibernians for you all over,' Merlin scoffed. 'Nationalistic to the bone.'

'Mmm. Anyway, the letter is actually very....very....Oh, what's the word...?'

'Ambiguous?' Merlin suggested.

'No, no, that's not what I mean. Here, you know Gaelic. Read it yourself.'

He handed the parchment to Merlin. Merlin read the short letter carefully.

'He doesn't seem to be hostile, does he?' Arthur said when Merlin looked up.

'No,' Merlin agreed, 'but I wouldn't bank on it. You know these Hibernians.'

'Actually I don't. Not like you and Morganna at any rate.'

'Well, you never know with them. And this letter gives no clue as to what's on the fellow's mind.'

Arthur smiled. 'I was hoping you might be able to....to read *between the lines*!'

Merlin grunted. He shook the parchment vigorously, smelt it, held it to his ear then raised it to the light. Suddenly he began chuckling. This gradually mounted until it became a fully-fledged, riotous laughter. When it peaked Caleb got up, came to Arthur and resting his head on his master's knee watched wide-eyed as Merlin strove heroically to exorcise his laughing spirit.

When he eventually regained control of himself Arthur calmly asked, 'What is it?'

Wiping tears from his face Merlin spluttered, 'Per.....perhaps The Gob.....The Gobán told Fergus he could bribe you to give The Sword of Light back!'

'The Gobán?' Arthur queried.

'The one I got the Sword from. Didn't I tell you?'

'Oh, yes! But is it possible, that Fergus would attempt such a thing?'

'Anything's possible with the Hibernians! But remember, I, Merlin, broke The Gobán's spell. And here's another thing. It is perfectly possible that king or no king,

Fergus is a typical Hibernian idiot, and would *believe* The Gobán. They have idiots as kings over there, you know.'

'It's a strange and funny place by all accounts,' Arthur mused. 'Tell me, would The Gobán be a nickname for the King's chief Druid by any chance?'

'No. The Gobán is, ahem, actually a Druid, but he's retired. It's a wonder they didn't kill him after losing the Sword. Anyway, why do you ask?'

'Because although it says nothing about it in the letter, Morganna believes that Fergus will have to bring his chief Druid with him.'

'Oh, *I* could've told you that,' Merlin stated haughtily. 'We still control everything in Hibernia you know, including, nay *especially* the kings.'

'We?' Arthur asked with raised eyebrows.

'The Druids.'

'But you're not a Druid, Merlin!'

Merlin sucked his teeth. 'I am.......of sorts.'

'But you don't have the proper tonsure, you don't meet with them in secret conclaves, you don't wear a green cloak, you don't.....'

'I'm a Druid *at heart,*' Merlin cut in. '*That's* what matters. Now, let's concentrate. Did you get this Druid fellow's actual name?'

'MacSaggart, and he will also have to attend our formal dinner.'

'Of course! And he will watch, evaluate, and advise the King on his every word and every move. He will even regulate his breathing for him.'

'Are you serious?'

Merlin grinned wickedly. 'The Hibernians take their Druids very seriously, Arthur. And the Druids take their

Four Treasures more seriously still. This fellow probably blames *me* for stealing his feckin Sword!'

'Ouch! I see! We better tread very softly then.'

'Very sensitive stuff! But whatever way you look at it, something *big* is on the cards.'

'Indeed. And whether Fergus is a fool or not he is well aware of the risk he's taking coming here at all. He knows that Hibernians are hated here almost as much as the Saxons! So he said he will come with little or no luggage, and in disguise. We suggested Frankish scholars, and he agreed. The whole thing was arranged through Morganna and is a secret. Only my twelve Knights know the truth. For nothing, as you know, is kept secret from the Round Table. And I also informed the Knights that I will have no *private* meetings with the King. Hence the importance of the dinner.'

'You're a clever young man, Arthur,' Merlin mused.

Twisting the large gem-encrusted ring that adorned his right index finger, Arthur confessed, 'If that's true Merlin, I owe a lot of it to you.'

Merlin shrugged with mock modesty. 'I do my best.' He held the parchment up to the light again. 'Hey,' he cried, 'this is not in the King's hand!'

'How do you know?' Arthur asked.

'The signature is different from the text. The text was probably dictated by Fergus to your man, the Druid. This proves a thesis I've long held that we are still the only ones who can write or even read over there. That's another reason why Fergus needs to bring MacSaggart.'

'This is very useful knowledge, Merlin,' Arthur said taking the parchment back. 'And I'm really glad *you* are coming to the meal. I'm going to need you badly.'

Merlin shrugged and changed the subject abruptly. 'How is the good lady?'

'Oh, fine. You'll have a look at her while you're here, I hope.'

'Of course.'

'That last potion of yours was certainly good stuff!'

'Potion? What potion?'

'The green, slimy stuff you gave her last year. Remember?'

'She said it didn't work!'

'No. Not then. But she kept half a bottle of it and took it all one night a few months ago in desperation. She didn't tell me, of course. I wouldn't have allowed it.'

Merlin looked suspicious. 'The whole half-bottle in one go, eh?' he muttered, sucking his teeth. 'Should've killed her.'

'But it didn't. And it worked, Merlin. That's the main thing.'

Merlin sniffed. 'What will you call the child?'

'We want you to name it.'

Merlin bowed but said nothing.

A scout brought news to Arthur of the pending arrival of the guests. They were spotted on horseback a few miles south of Aquae Sulis and two Knights were immediately dispatched to escort them to Camelot. To avoid dangerous speculation about Hibernian spies and the like, it was put about in Camelot that two Frankish scholars had requested shelter on a journey they were making up north.

Rumours nevertheless were inevitable, and so the visit was scheduled to be short. The evening after the guests' arrival was set aside for the formal dinner, and they were to depart the following morning.

Arthur involved Merlin in every detail of the dinner's planning.

'There should be *seven* people at the table,' Merlin said after studying some astrological charts he had brought with him, 'and don't ask me why.'

'But you do know why, of course?' Arthur said.

'Yes. But it would take all morning to explain, and we don't have all morning, do we?'

'How about a hint?'

'Seven is the number of the roving stars.'

'Aha! I see. Now, seven also means that we need to think of two more, for I had only *five* in mind: you and me, Guinevere and our esteemed guests.'

'You're a born Pythagorean,' Merlin jibed.

Ignoring the jest, Arthur asked, 'Who do you.....or your, ahem, charts suggest we invite to make up the magic number?'

Merlin buried his head in his charts again. After a while he looked up. 'The youngest and the oldest of your Knights should do the trick,' he said. And....'

'......Don't ask why?'

'Yes.'

'I won't.'

'Good.'

'The youngest and the oldest,' Arthur mused. 'Hey, that means Lancelot and Percival! I like it.'

Merlin grinned. 'Now, about the actual seating arrangement.'

'Very important!'

'It must be thus: you and Guinevere will face each other at each end of the table, and the King and MacSaggart on one side will face me on the other, flanked by your youngest and your oldest Knights.'

Arthur closed his eyes in order to visualize the constellation. When he opened them he said, 'You need to eyeball MacSaggart, right?'

'You keep getting better,' Merlin chuckled. 'I want to see *exactly* what's in that particular Hibernian's tight little mind.'

Merlin ordered virgin boar for the main course. So a fat young pig was quickly slaughtered, duly roasted, and many other delicacies were brought out for the occasion. The meal was to be held in the small, elegant, but rarely used dining room of Arthur's apartment; rarely used, for Guinevere nowadays - heavy with child - often had her meals alone, and sometimes even in bed, while Arthur ate with his Knights.

At the appointed time for the big event Guinevere, Arthur and Merlin seated themselves expectantly on the carved, high-backed chairs at the long, rosewood table in the dining room. Soon afterwards the other guests arrived at the keep's door and were escorted by a page up the stairs and directed to their seats according to Merlin's astrologically informed arrangement. Freshly cut flowers in large Grecian vases adorned the room. A log fire blazed in the hearth.

Arthur opened the proceedings by remarking how unusual it was to have as guest in Camelot someone who was not only a king, but a Hibernian one! Britannia, he said, had neither seen nor even *had* a legitimate king of its own since before the Romans occupation hundreds of years ago! It was therefore both an honour and a pleasure now to be dining with one. And after a few more perfunctory words about the general, post-Roman situation in Britannia, he invited a response from Fergus.

Fergus stood up. Placing his thick fists very deliberately on the table, and leaning slightly towards Arthur, in good Brittonic he said, 'I am most honoured to be here and to have made your acquaintance, Arthur of the Britons.'

He spoke in a low, grave voice, with a strong Hibernian accent, and his assured poise and distinctive tone immediately revealed him as no fool but a serious and intelligent man.

Arthur nodded politely. Then Fergus turned to Guinevere. She was radiant in a red, low-cut gown, and basking in the light of so many admiring male eyes.

'And to you, my lady,' the King continued, 'I bring greetings from all the fair maidens and noble ladies of Dal Riada.'

Guinevere smiled, but as she did so, gently with her foot touched Lancelot's which was next to hers, trying at the same time to catch his eyes. But he refused to look in her direction.

Addressing the whole table now, the King continued, 'I bring greetings to you all, not only from my own kingdom, but from the fair land of Hibernia herself. For although we have many kings in Hibernia, our own kingdom of Dal Riada is the most peaceful and prosperous, and this, perforce, allows me to speak for the entire island.'

MacSaggart nodded vigorously. Fergus turned again to Arthur. 'You are becoming very famous among my people, Arthur,' he said. 'You are greatly.....what shall I say....*exciting* the imagination of our Bards. We are hearing many stories of your Knights and your Round Table.'

Arthur acknowledged the compliment with a modest

spreading of his hands. 'I hope and trust,' he proffered, 'that these are.....*good* stories?'

'The Bards,' Fergus ambiguously returned, 'will make a good story out of *anything*.'

'Anything?' Arthur questioned.

'Yes,' Fergus said, 'but of course the *Four Treasures* are one of their favourite themes.'

Arthur looked anxiously at Merlin whose body language said, 'Say nothing'. Fergus continued, 'The Bards lament, understandably, that the Sword of Light has gone from Hibernia; but even more so do their Druid colleagues.' - Fergus glanced at MacSaggart who bowed in agreement. - 'In fact,' Fergus went on, 'I think it's fair to say our Druids more than lament it; they resent it!'

Arthur, Lancelot and Merlin exchanged uneasy glances.

'However,' Fergus continued, 'whatever about the legitimacy of the Sword's removal here to Britannia, I must immediately put your minds at rest that that precise question is not the purpose of my visit.'

Arthur gave an audible sigh of relief.

Guinevere found the conversation boring! She kicked off her shoes and caressed Lancelot's leg with her petite toes. Now he was thoroughly nettled. Percival spotted his unease and, purposely dropping his napkin, ducked under the table to retrieve it. What he saw confirmed a long held suspicion. When he sat up again he glared accusingly at Guinevere. She blushed, then went pale. Lancelot, however, was unaware of what had happened.

Merlin became impatient. 'Pray tell us, King,' he testily enquired, 'what *precisely* is the purpose of your visit to Camelot?'

Fergus turned to MacSaggart. 'Perhaps,' he said, *'you* would like to inform him?'

MacSaggart looked surprised. After a moment's hesitation he drew the King's ear to his mouth and a secret concourse began.

Taking this as an opportunity to serve drinks, Arthur snapped his fingers at an attendant page who whipped a jug from a nearby trolley and quickly filled all the silver beakers on the table with red wine.

When the secret concourse concluded, Fergus took a sip of his wine and said, 'My lady and gentlemen, before I tell you about the precise reason for my visit to Camelot I must first give you some background information. Now, the first thing is that a very strange and dreadful mania is spreading throughout our dear island. Our people are abandoning the old traditional Gaelic gods of our forefathers and are taking up a new and woefully seductive form of religious worship. This new cult has come, we believe, either from Egypt or the Orient. But it takes the hideous form of the worship of a great Serpent.'

'Jesus!' Merlin involuntarily cried.

Fergus looked stunned!

Arthur said modestly, 'Merlin, my chief.......ah...adviser, is very well informed, King Fergus.'

'Obviously,' Fergus said, 'for Jesus is precisely what they call the Serpent!'

Sucking his teeth, Merlin asked, 'How widespread is this new cult?'

'Oh, it is spreading rapidly in the south of the island,' Fergus informed. 'Even the old High King, Leery, has taken to it recently, I believe. But we in the North are opposed, always have been, but even more so since the appearance of the white Dove.'

'The white Dove?' Merlin enquired.

'Well recently,' Fergus explained, 'a white Dove came to my Druid here,' - he turned to MacSaggart - 'in a vision. It *was* a vision, wasn't it?' - MacSaggart made no response. - 'Whatever it was,' Fergus continued, 'this Dove was, *is* a very remarkable creature. Eoin has never been quite sure whether it was a vision or not, but that doesn't really matter, for the point is that this Dove could *speak*. And she spoke very clearly and prophetically about the Serpent. She said the Serpent will poison the soul of our Hibernian nation unless we do something about it, and do it fast. This Serpent, the Dove announced, must be banished from Hibernia at all costs! She further revealed that this can only be done if a man by the name of Patrick is empowered to do so.'

'You are full of mysteries, King Fergus,' Merlin said with a hint of sarcasm. 'Who, pray, is this Patrick?'

'Patrick,' Fergus replied, 'is a Roman who in my kingdom preaches a thing called the gospel.'

'Oh, well *that's* no mystery,' Arthur said. 'We are quite aware of it here.'

'My husband,' Guinevere interjected to Arthur's embarrassment, 'studies it all the time.'

'The serpent-worshippers also preach the gospel,' Merlin added.

'That may be,' Fergus said, 'but Patrick is definitely *not* a serpent-worshipper. And this makes all the difference. He actually opposes them vehemently.'

'Have you heard of Jesus followers called the Pelagians?' Merlin asked.

Fergus frowned. 'The name rings a bell.' Turning to MacSaggart he asked, 'Do we have Pelagians in Hibernia, Eoin?'

MacSaggart nodded. 'Some.'

Fergus said to him, 'Isn't Pelagius the one you, I mean the Druids, taught when he was young and then humped off to Rome and created a big stink over there about Jesus and got up a lot of people's noses?'

'Yes. That is correct,' MacSaggart dryly confirmed. When he added nothing more Fergus said to Merlin, 'I think that's about all we know. Why do you ask?'

Merlin was about to reveal that Pelagius was now back living in Hibernia when his tongue became stuck to the roof of his mouth! He took it as an act of the gods! The Grail was a secret, and the less said about it the better! When after an embarrassing silence his tongue loosened again he blandly said to Fergus, 'Oh, I'm simply curious about these Christians, that's all,' and turning to Arthur said with his eyes to let the matter of Pelagius drop.

'The Christians are indeed a growing force everywhere,' Fergus continued, 'but to get back to our mysterious white Dove; Patrick, she says, has been sent by Providence to Hibernia to preach the *truth* of the gospel, not a poisonous, cock-and-bull version of it. The Serpent-worshippers will engulf the entire island, the Dove says, unless Patrick becomes like a Druid. Those are her very words, *like a Druid*, isn't that right, Eoin?'

MacSaggart nodded vigorously. Fergus continued, 'So the question then is, how can we follow the Dove's instructions and make Patrick *like a Druid?* Well, he has no staff! So Eoin here says we must give him one! And quick! Eoin further says, or the Dove - I don't know which, but that doesn't matter for the moment - that this staff *must* be no ordinary staff, but one that is suffused with the light of the... ..well, let us say the *missing* Sword. *That* is the point! That will surely make Patrick *like a Druid*, and that precisely is the purpose of my visit here.' He turned to MacSaggart again. 'Perhaps Eoin you would now wish to speak?'

MacSaggart sprung up. Long-faced, sharp featured, with a complexion the colour of mouldy cheese, his huge pointed ears poked mysteriously through the red matted hair of his half-moon tonsure.

'Over the past few months,' he said in clear Brittonic, in a high-pitched voice, 'I have spent much time speaking to many of the oldest members of my profession in Dal Riada.' His eyes were half-closed and he seemed to draw his words from the air through the long curling nails of his nervous, trembling fingers. 'I have informed them,' he continued, 'of my.....my....the vis....the visitation of the white Dove, and all are agreed that it was an authentic prophetic experience. So I can confirm that we, the Druids of Dal Riada, will support Patrick. Even though he is a Roman, he acts independently and assures us that he will have no truck with the imperial power in Rome. We are therefore allowing him, on certain conditions, to preach his Jesus.'

He sat down abruptly. Fergus rose again. 'So you see, Arthur,' he said, 'we have come to you not with hostility in our hearts, but with a petition. My Druid believes that if this man Patrick is endowed with the power of the Sword of Light it will be for the good of us all. For we have a common enemy now. These snake-worshippers are spreading like an insidious vermin through the soil and soul of Hibernia, and if this disease has not already reached Britannia, it will soon. The snake-worshippers will apparently stop at nothing in order to spread their poisonous faith. They are led by a masterful oriental wizard who often puts our Druids to shame - magically speaking, I mean. He is called Palladius and he is ably assisted by a voluptuous young priestess who has deserted her very own, native Mother cult and joined this new religion.'

On hearing this Merlin started sucking his teeth frantically.

'Do you know this priestess's name?' he demanded.

'No,' Fergus replied.

'Have you ever seen her?'

'Once only, and it was enough.'

'Describe her.'

And as Merlin fully expected, the King described his problematic protégé, Vivian, in every, and perfect, detail.

Merlin closed his eyes. Once again he saw the Serpent! But here he sensed an opportunity to banish it once and for all.

He made a snap decision! Opening his eyes and looking directly at MacSaggart he haughtily announced, 'I, Merlin of the Britons, will make a staff for this Roman preacher, and I will make it from the wood of the same oak from which I made Arthur's Round Table. I will furthermore devise a ritual, and invest the staff with the power of the Sword of Light. I will then go to Hibernia and personally present it to this Roman, Patrick.'

This fervid announcement was met with a long, ponderous silence during which MacSaggart's mouth dropped open so wide he became lock-jawed!

And because no one else spoke Merlin got up and abruptly left.

CHAPTER TWENTY

A TOUCH OF MADNESS

Germanus, the irascible Archbishop of Auxerre was livid. It was over two years since he dispatched Patrick to Hibernia to root out the Pelagian heresy; yet in all that time he had received from him not a single, godforsaken word!

Germanus felt utterly betrayed. He had personally groomed the monk, ordained him, financed him, invested him with the consecrated power of Catholic Rome, and what did he get in return? Sweet shag all!

What could possibly have happened? Germanus suspected the worst: Patrick himself must have fallen victim to the doctrinal poison. For there were reports that the Pelagian heresy was simply overrunning Hibernia, and that it had even spread to nearby Britannia! From there stories were reaching Germanus about one called Arthur, a charismatic and powerful young warlord who was supposed to possess a magic sword (what utter nonsense!) and who was, apparently, destined to become King of the Britons. He too had taken up the Pelagian cause!

Where was it all going to end? Gaul itself would be next! Each new development felt like a nail being driven by some foul devil into Germanus's old flesh.

All the news was brought to him by his sycophantic, middle-aged secretary, Lupis, a tall, dark-shaven, poker-thin deacon with a big hooked nose. Lupis however was always circumspect about bringing the latest regarding the heresy to his superior because of the powerful effect it could have on him. But the news kept getting worse! So that when Lupis one day told the venerable old man that he just received a report that the Pelagians in Hibernia were now worshipping Jesus there in the form of a serpent, Germanus literally went mad!

They were in the scriptorium of the monastery at the time. Germanus ran around the little room banging his fists against the wall, roaring like a biblical bull and frightened the two permanent scribes there into running for their lives. Lupis ran with them, but while the others hid behind bushes in the monastery garden Lupis remained outside the scriptorium and watched through its half-open door. Eventually the old man ran out of his mad steam and fell in an ignoble heap onto the floor. Lupis then dragged him to his bed where, when he eventually regained consciousness, the monastery doctor ordered him to indefinitely remain.

Germanus reluctantly agreed, but on condition that Lupis would continue to brief him on Church matters, and especially report every little scrap of news about the spreading Pelagian heresy.

'Then you better sleep with this,' the monk doctor

stoically advised handing the Archbishop his crozier, diagnosing that *it* now was the only medicine that would help Germanus tame his demons.

When, long ago, Germanus was an officer in the Roman army he could give unrestricted vent to these dark beings. When he became a monk however, he was obliged by Canon Law to sublimate them through prayer, fasting, and sundry austerities. But the heretical Pelagians were stirring them up again like mad!

And the more Lupis told him about Arthur of the Britons the more convinced he became that it was on Britannia he must now focus if he was to succeed in his increasingly frenzied personal crusade. Lupis made it his business therefore to compile increasingly detailed intelligence reports for Germanus regarding what was happening in Britannia.

'There is even a Saxon settlement on the southern shore of Britannia now,' he informed Germanus one morning while he was still confined to his bed.

'Arthur must be their greatest enemy then,' Germanus opined.

'Indeed, Your Grace. And they too have a very powerful leader. Hengist is his name. But you'll be glad to hear he and his men have all been baptized recently.'

'What!' Germanus cried. 'The barbarians...........baptized?'

'Yes. It's a new idea, from Rome. They say it is better to have the barbarians on our side than against us.'

With one eye closed Germanus studied his secretary.

'Mmm,' he eventually conceded, 'I suppose they're right.'

'The barbarians are the way forward, Your Grace.'

'This Hengist fellow is very powerful, you say?'

'Very, Your Grace. And just think of this: what if he gets

some other powerful Brittonic warlords to oppose Arthur, and we......?'

'.....And we baptize *them* too?' Germanus finished with a grim smile. He gripped his crozier. 'Yes, yes, by God! Get them *all* on *our* side.'

'It may be our only hope of defeating Arthur, Your Grace. For, as I understand it, in order to defeat the Pelagians we must defeat Arthur. On the other hand if we do not defeat him, we might end up with a totally heretical Church on our very doorstep.'

Germanus grimaced. 'But there's a problem here, isn't there, deacon? I mean are not these Saxons little more than an ill-disciplined, ale-drinking rabble?'

'Granted. But the Church can give them order, direction. As you know, we Roman Catholics possess expertise in all areas of life, not just in religion.'

'Are you thinking perhaps of *military* expertise, deacon?'

'I am indeed, Your Grace. Did not over half our bishops serve as officers in the army, your good self included?'

Germanus's thin lips stretched into a self-satisfied smile.

Lupis shuffled his feet. 'Your Grace' he hesitantly suggested, 'do you think.........I mean could you not.........well........consider....?'

'Going to Britannia *myself*?'

Lupis beamed! 'Oh, Your Grace, we could raise an army.........from the monasteries here in Gaul. We could bring some proper Roman Catholic order into this ragbag Saxon force!'

Germanus gripped his crozier. He felt a vision coming on. 'I'd have to get back up on a horse!'

'Faith can move mountains,' Lupis proffered.

'And I'd have the Pope behind me. Celestine wouldn't object, would he?'

'Never!'

'And you'll come with me?'

'Of course, Your Grace.'

Germanus kicked his feet in the air.

'By God,' he cried, 'this is just the medicine I needed! Go tell that damn doctor that I'm recovered.'

And shouting 'Praise the Lord!' he jumped out of bed.

CHAPTER TWENTY-ONE

THE GRAIL MESSENGER

Patrick felt compelled to follow the little white Dove that had mysteriously appeared and spoken to him on that fateful spring morning in the cowshed of his budding Christian community in Dal Riada. She led him then on a strange and mystical journey.

Losing track of time he travelled on foot through a misty landscape of dark forests, high mountains, sodden marshes, tumbling streams and racing rivers. Never for an instant losing sight of the bird as she perched conspicuously on rocks, trees or bushes, and patiently waiting while he scrambled over obstacles to get to her, she led him up bracken-covered hills and down rocky slopes. Then suddenly, as he was descending a tall, conically shaped mountain, his vision began to change. The bird hovered before him and spread her wings farther than ever before.

They grew huge. Drawn into this feathery whiteness, Patrick felt as if waking from a dream. And soon he saw not the bird anymore but a pure white *building*.

With difficulty he focussed. The building seemed to hover in the middle distance. Built on a hillock beyond a darkly racing river that divided a sparsely inhabited valley, it had a sparkling double-dome roof. In its simple elegance Patrick thought it the most beautiful thing he had ever seen.

He had been led to the Grail Temple!

Cautiously he made his way down the mountainside, half expecting the Temple to disappear at any moment. *Perhaps*, he thought, *this is all just a dream.*

The little settlement was shrouded in sleepy silence. He saw no one as he crossed a rickety wooden bridge spanning the river and climbed the hillock. Upon reaching the Temple door he was surprised to find it slightly ajar. Carefully pushing it he peered inside.

The interior was aglow with soft light emanating from the altar beneath the large cupola. The air was beautifully perfumed.

Patrick did not see Pelagius at first. He was standing perfectly still behind the altar in his snow-white cowl, hood down, silently reading his book in the light of the Grail Flame. When he heard Patrick he looked up.

'Ah, Patrick,' he said slowly, 'you have arrived at last. I was expecting you.'

Patrick was startled. 'H...how do you know my name?' he stammered. 'Wh...who are you?'

'Come in, please,' Pelagius said gently, closing the book.

Patrick tentatively approached the altar and Pelagius descended from it extending his right hand. 'You know me. Or at least I am sure you have *heard* of me. I am Pelagius.'

Patrick was overwhelmed. 'Pelagius the her.....her.....?' He couldn't finish.

'Heretic?' Pelagius said. 'Yes. That's me. It's what the Romans call me, unfortunately.'

As they shook hands Patrick felt a strong current of energy entering him. In the monastery in Auxerre he had heard and read much about the Christian saints. They were extremely powerful Christ-Initiates who were believed to have existed mostly in the early Church, but Patrick prayed earnestly that some day he might meet one, and now he felt his prayers were being answered.

'Where am I?' he asked. 'And what is this amazing place?'

'I suppose you are still wondering, is it real?' Pelagius said.

Patrick smiled.

'I know how you feel,' Pelagius went on, 'but you should be aware that this building is just a sign, a shell if you like. It's what happens *in it* that's important. It has a history.'

'Please tell me.'

'I will, but it's a long story.'

The Saint took a huge key from his belt and locked the Temple door. He then drew two plain wooden chairs from the wall and they sat down.

'The first thing you must know,' Pelagius said, 'is that this building is neither a church nor a chapel. It is a Christian *Temple*. Properly speaking it is the *only* one of its type in the world. However, it exists as a kind of spiritual embryo in the minds and souls of all true followers of Jesus. Even if it were destroyed today it would still exist, and this is because the Temple is the reliquary of that object which partakes of *both* worlds. Here we possess the most spiritual and sacred object in the whole wide universe.'

'And what is that?' Patrick eagerly enquired.

Pelagius then told him about the *Four Treasures of Hibernia,* of how the Druid Altus had given to Josephus the Jew the Chalice of Rebirth, of how Josephus had collected the precious blood of Jesus in it after he died, of how he, Pelagius himself, had lived in a cave in the Egyptian desert as a fugitive hermit, hiding from the Romans, and was there given the Chalice by a Messenger of God with the instruction to bring it back to Hibernia where it belonged; and finally of how the Temple came to be built and how the Chalice was now known as the Grail, the supreme object of spiritual initiation.

Patrick listened with ever-mounting excitement.

'It's a fabulous story,' he said. 'You know, I lived and worked as a slave-boy in Hibernia when I was young and my Druid master told me many stories, and I had many wonderful dreams. But none of them beats this. May I see the Grail?'

But Pelagius smiled sadly. 'I'm afraid,' he said, 'a very definite kind of preparation has to be undergone before *anyone* can actually see it. Don't get me wrong! I am sure you are personally worthy, but you are not *ready* yet. Seeing the Grail demands a lot of *inner* work.'

'I pray a lot,' Patrick said meekly.

'And that's very commendable! But I will teach you to *meditate.* That's how one learns to see the Grail. Don't worry. You will see it. You will surely drink from this cup of the gods. But the Grail has many enemies and must remain a secret. You must go on preaching. For it is vital that the warm and simple-hearted people of this ancient land be rescued from their pagan darkness. Recently they have taken in great numbers to worshipping the Serpent.'

'I've seen them! The Naasenes!'

'Yes. Christians, how are you! They are even worse than the Catholics, if you ask me. Christianity cannot, *must not* be made into a circus, a moneymaking racket!'

'You must tell me what to do.'

'What gospel book do you use for your preaching?'

'Peter's.'

'Oh yes, you would, for that's the ones the Romans always use, isn't it? Look. I'll make you a copy of my Book of the Grail. It's the only book I wrote here in Hibernia. You can use *that* from now on. All right?'

'Wonderful!'

'You must of course never refer to it as the Book of the Grail, just, "John's book" or simply "the gospel".'

'John's book?' Patrick queried.

'I am a reincarnation of Saint John!'

'You mean the one that Jesus loved?' Patrick asked with astonishment.

'Yes. But I cannot go into details now. You must progress a little on the Grail path first.'

'I am mad to spread the word of Jesus,' Patrick affirmed.

'I can see that,' the Saint said gazing into Patrick's eyes. 'You know, Christianity actually began long ago in Palestine through people living together in life-communities; love-communities they actually called them.'

'I have started a little community in the kingdom of Dal Riada,' Patrick excitedly revealed.

'Ah, very good.' Pelagius stroked his chin. 'Now, I also think you should distinguish yourselves in some outward way. We, the Grail people, don't of course, make ourselves outwardly known, for reasons I've outlined. But you can.'

'How?'

Pelagius thought for a moment, then wagging his finger said, 'Make the sign of the cross with ash on the forehead of all your followers from now on.'

'I'll start straightaway,' Patrick declared

'And call yourselves Culdees.'

'What does that mean?'

'The Servants of the Living God. And also wear only white cowls, like me. I have a few spare ones I'll give you when you're leaving.'

'Excellent!'

The distant sound of a bell caught their attention and they listened in silence. After it chimed exactly seven times Pelagius went slowly to the door, unlocked it and left it ajar. Returning to Patrick he said, 'I will also give you some Grail mediations before you leave. If you practise them daily your inner vision - what the Orientals call the Third Eye - will open eventually. You will see the Grail surely.'

Patrick rubbed his hands enthusiastically. He was about to ask for more advice when the white Dove suddenly flew in through the open door. She landed on the altar beside the Grail Flame.

'The Grail Messenger,' Pelagius said with a winning smile.

He made a tiny sound in his mouth, held out his fist and the bird landed on it. Then suddenly a shadow fell across the door and it slowly opened wider.

'Look,' the Saint said, 'I am also expecting someone else this fateful morning.'

A stooped male figure with a big black staff stumbled in the door. A long thin bundle was tied awkwardly across the figure's shoulders giving it the appearance of a huge, scary bird. A bony head swivelled on its long, thin neck and when the piercing eyes of its gaunt yellow face spotted Pelagius and Patrick near the altar, it snorted.

It was Merlin!

CHAPTER TWENTY-TWO

ZEALOUS MONKS ON THE WARPATH

Because Germanus of Auxerre was such an enthusiastic army man in his younger years, he remained a soldier at heart even long after he joined the monastic Church. Indeed, to that institution he brought all the zeal, courage and determination of an ancient warrior. He practised his Rule's severe austerities unstintingly and to such a degree that in time he became prone to visions, for such are the notorious side-effect of asceticism. Thus, ever since his clever secretary, the deacon Lupis, planted in his old brain the potent idea that he should go to Britannia *himself* to deal with the dreaded Pelagians, he had a *recurring* vision of the Archangel Michael leading a great army into battle against the heretics.

When the vision first came he was in bed, confined there on doctor's orders. But the vision resulted in his frail, thin body, stiff with age and weak from endless ascetic practices, revivifying. Long-forgotten memories of his prime suddenly flooded back and the spirit of youthful action once more gripped his decaying innards.

Lupis actually felt he was witnessing a kind of Lazarus event when he saw his master rise miraculously from his sickbed, and donning his colourful episcopal regalia, with eyes blaring, mount the monastery's big white workhorse - it was over a decade since Germanus had ridden! - and gallop madly about the monastery grounds, scaring the animals, scattering the birds and seriously discommoding the few old monks who dutifully and quietly tended the extensive gardens.

Galloping about like this Germanus hatched out his plan for a great Catholic army. He abandoned his regular, daily schedule and set up a new one. Monkish meetings, monastic duties, hourly prayer, nightly scourging, prostrations in the chapel, and even the enactment of the recently invented ritual of the Mass itself, all now took second place to the business of forming the Jesus army of his visions.

It was a task Germanus relished more than any he had ever undertaken. He would not even bother to wait for approval from the Pope! Not that even *he* could now put Germanus off! For the Divinity itself would have had to intervene for *that* to happen!

In these days Lupis conferred with his master daily. To all the abbots of all the monasteries in Gaul and beyond, and to some even as far away as Egypt, Lupis soon dispatched a circular letter. The letter was of course dictated by Germanus, in which firstly the heresy of the Pelagians was outlined in simple, clear language: it denied the grace of God and that was tantamount to denying God himself! As was well known, the heresy originated in Hibernia but was now a disease rapidly spreading. This malevolent movement threatened the very existence of the Roman Catholic Church if it was not soon eradicated. In case the abbot didn't already know, he was further informed by Germanus that the hub of this heretical movement was now in Britannia and centred upon the charismatic young warlord, Arthur of the Britons, who had a national army at his disposal, all Pelagians to their rotten core! Thus, if the Church was to be rid of this Pelagian poison the very first step was to eliminate Arthur. Germanus therefore proposed to raise an army in Gaul, a holy army of Catholic monks led by ex-officers of the near-defunct imperial army. This new army would then join its Saxon allies in Britannia, and by provoking Arthur into an all-out confrontation would be sure to eliminate him. A Catholic king of the Britons, obedient to the Pope of Rome, would then be installed in Britannia. He would soon subdue Hibernia which Rome had so far failed to do, and thus the problem of the cankerous heresy be fully and finally solved.

Germanus rounded off each long letter requesting the abbot send to him as soon as possible a list of those monks in his monastery whom he considered fit, willing and able to join this great venture. Germanus himself would, of course, act as commander-in-chief of the holy army.

Another similar but more individualized letter was sent to all Germanus's associates and colleagues from his time in the army, old friends and acquaintances who were still alive, requesting from them as much support - material, moral or financial - for the project as they could muster.

The response to these letters from the abbots was swift,

generous and encouraging. The lists of pledged and potential monk recruits to the proposed army grew daily. The response however, from the disintegrating official Roman army was less encouraging. Much was promised in coin and kind, but personal commitment was lacking. A few retired ex-officers, mostly ageing farmers now, signed up, but only one of these had, in Germanus's eyes, any real potential. This was Romulus, an elderly, diminutive but very alert man, who in splendid contrast to his brightly shining bald head sported a huge snow-white moustache. Like Germanus himself when he was in the army, Romulus had had command of a cohort. Unlike Germanus however, Romulus had spent a lot of time in Britannia and would therefore be extremely useful.

And so Romulus became Germanus's chief adviser. With him and a few others he set up an 'army council' and they got down to business. The dedicated old monks of the scriptorium were once more unceremoniously tufted out of their work-place and the scriptorium itself turned into a war-office. Soon enough, outside the monastery walls, on a great expanse of scrubland, the huts, tents and assorted buildings of an army camp sprung up as day by day more and more of the promised monk recruits poured in from all over Gaul and beyond. The excitement was positively paranormal!

The 'army council' tapped old imperial contacts for the procurement of weapons and armour, rusty or otherwise; also for animals, old or young, and whatever else was going. Stuff poured in in cartloads from all over. Even old ships were promised, for nowadays many of them lay idle in ports throughout the Empire, some needing only basic repairs to be brought into a condition capable of crossing the short channel from Gaul to Britannia.

A vital part of the overall plan was the Saxons on the Saxon Shore. A trustworthy alliance with them was essential to success. That they were baptized was, of course, a big plus, and a cultivation of the Catholic connection was inevitably the way to go. Contact with Rome soon revealed that their main priest was a man called Sighard.

And so an extra special letter, very different in content to all the others Germanus wrote at this time, but similar in its bellicose tone, was duly delivered to Sighard on the Saxon Shore. Aware that Sighard and the Saxons at large might not be interested in, or impressed by the technicalities of the Pelagian heresy, Germanus adopted a more general approach, arguing that for the overall good of the Catholic Church, if there was soon to be a king of the Britons he must be a *Catholic* one, and one moreover who had the full and unambiguous approval of the Pope in Rome! In no way did Arthur qualify for that approval! He was a Pelagian and therefore a heretic pure and simple! He must be eliminated! In the letter a strong hint was also dropped that Sighard could soon become the first Archbishop of the Britons! He was sternly summoned to Auxerre to discuss these matters.

The chief part of a Catholic priest's training, if the candidate was not of Roman origin, was the learning of Latin. Many so-called barbarian men found this a taxing task, but Sighard, possessing neither a specifically religious temperament nor a particularly bright intellect, found it doubly difficult. But he learnt in the end. However, when he received Germanus's letter he had to read it very slowly, and many times over, before the full sense and import of it struck home. But when it did he got very excited.

He immediately dashed to Hengist and explained to him the letter's content. Hengist, who saw in Roman Catholicism his best opportunity yet for the advancement of his tribe, readily agreed to all that Sighard proposed and Sighard set out straightaway for Auxerre.

He arrived at the monastery less than a week later, mud-spattered and tired from his long ride from the coast. After resting overnight in a vacant monk's cell, the next day Germanus received him in the spacious reception room of his private apartment in the monastery. Germanus was sitting legs apart on his big throne-like chair, decked out in full episcopalian attire including the diadem, his white-gloved hand gripping his bejewelled crozier. Lupis was sitting attentively on a three-legged stool by his side, quill in hand, ready to take notes.

'We did not expect to see you so soon,' Germanus said, holding out the back of his gloved hand for Sighard to kiss his ring. (An interpreter was not necessary, for both Germanus and Lupis could speak the Saxon's dialect.)

'These.....are pressing times.....Bishop,' Sighard said tentatively after kissing the ring.

'*Arch*-bishop,' Germanus crossly corrected, thinking that these Saxons still had a lot to learn about their religion.

'Oh,' Sighard said, and uncertain of what to do next offered Germanus the crude iron crucifix that dangled from his neck to kiss.

Irritably dismissing the gesture, Germanus pointed to a nearby velvet-covered chaise-longue upon which Sighard sat down awkwardly, fearful that his mud-spattered cassock might soil the lovely thing!

'Your Grace,' Germanus said.

'Pardon?' Sighard returned.

'Your Grace, is how one addresses an archbishop.'

'Oh, I see.'

'Now, tell me, how many men have already received Holy Orders in your tribe?'

'Three, Arch....Your Bish.....sorry, Grace,' Sighard replied, 'including me, and two in the making.'

'Then you'll need a proper bishop. I'll write to the Holy Father immediately and nominate yourself.'

The black slits of Sighard's smouldering eyes studied Germanus.

'Thank you.....Your Grease,' he said, but...but.....'

'GRACE!'

'Sorry! Grace.'

'And no buts or arguments,' Germanus growled.

'Of course!'

'Now, to business. You've studied my letter, I take it?'

'Yes, I have, and Hengist our leader.........'

'The Pope in Rome is our leader!'

'Well then, Hengist, our *Saxon* leader, has also considered your letter and......and....how should I put it...?'

'Put it whatever way you bloody well like!'

'Well, let me say this, Your Arse.......sorry, Grace, if what I observe here in Auxerre is anything to go by, and your plans for the new army continue apace, I can assure you Hengist will welcome it with open arms when it arrives in Britannia .'

'I'm very glad to hear it.'

'As you may know, he has already formed an alliance with Mordred, and if....'

'No, I haven't heard of this alliance,' Germanus cut in. He shot a quizzical glance at Lupis who shook his head in surprise. To Sighard Germanus continued, 'An alliance with who did you say?'

'Mordred.'

'And who the hell is Mordred?'

'Well, Your er....Ar........Grace, he is, apart from Arthur, the strongest of the Brittonic warlords.'

'We are told that Arthur is the strongest.'

'But that has yet to be decided!'

'Indeed! And how many men has this Mordred got?'

'About two thousand, we believe.'

'And what about all the other little farmer-warlords of Britannia?'

'I think that when word spreads of *your* army's imminent arrival in Britannia in order to oppose Arthur, then many of these petty warlords will join *our* alliance.'

'They'll have to be baptized first!'

'Yes, but we must also keep in mind that Arthur receives very cunning council from one called Merlin.'

'Isn't he one of those damned old shaman types you still have over there in Britannia?'

'Yes. But not so much in Britannia as in Hibernia. There are lots of his type still at work there.'

'The Druids, blast them!'

'Yes, and they have a.....a certain kind of power, Your...Your...Graw...Grey. I mean there is even talk of Merlin having procured for Arthur from them a, well........a *magic sword.*'

'I've heard that too! Pagan bloody superstitious nonsense!'

Sighard agitatedly pulled the wiry grey hairs on his leathery face. 'I'm not so sure about that,' he said. 'Merlin cannot be so easily dismissed.'

'Jesus Christ will dismiss him!'

Sighard nodded but continued to pull the hairs of his face.

Germanus went on, 'And remember this too. Our army here is already drilling and will soon be ready for full-scale manoeuvres. Ten fully fitted-out and thoroughly seaworthy ships are standing by in Bononia ready to take the army across the Gallic Sea. We will soon be able to notify you of the *precise* date of our arrival. So have this....this.... What's the fellow's name again.....?'

'Mordred?'

'Yes. Have him, all his men and whoever else you can muster up for our side, have them all assembled on the Saxon Shore once you receive our notice. We'll tell you where precisely. We'll bring enough buckets so that we can baptize them immediately we arrive. After that I will lead the army on the march.'

Germanus screwed up his face and leant forward on his 'throne', so far he nearly fell off! After steadying himself he snarled, 'The Catholic Church, believe me, will soon be rid of this Arthur and the Pelagian pestilence once and for all!'

CHAPTER TWENTY-THREE

THE STAFF OF JESUS

Merlin was a man of his word. At the special dinner in Camelot he said he would make a staff for the Roman preacher, and he did. Moreover, he made it from the wood of the same ancient oak that he had, many years previously, made the Round Table. And, as he also promised, when the instrument was fully carved, in a specially devised cabbalistic ritual he nicked it three times with the Sword of Light, thereby investing it with the magic power of the famous blade. Then, after asking Arthur to tell Clegis to feed his donkey while he was gone he set off for Hibernia from Camelot on foot with it bundled on his back.

He crossed the sea from Cambria to Dubh Linn in a buoyant mood. For he earnestly hoped that the fulfilment of his double promise to the preacher and the King of Dal

Riada would rid him of the Serpent once and for all. Alas, it was not to be. For, from the first moment his feet touched Hibernian soil he felt that beast closer than ever.

He quit the gritty settlement of Dubh Linn quickly and soon found an animal track leading in a north-westerly direction. He kept moving all the time, day and night, afraid even to sleep, for he often felt pursued by a veritable brood of vipers! Then one evening at dusk in a wood, when he was about to collapse with tiredness, a little white Dove suddenly appeared out of the gloom on a low branch near him. The bird glowed with a wonderful translucence and remained still as a statue. But when Merlin inspected her at close quarters she came suddenly alive, flew up and landed on another tree a short distance away. A little cloud surrounded her and Merlin was inexorably drawn into it. Then in a magical time-warp he was swiftly transported by the bird to the Grail Temple where finding the door invitingly open he entered and saw Pelagius and Patrick standing beside the altar!

'Ah, Merlin, my friend, come in,' the Saint said, 'I was expecting you.'

Turning to Patrick Pelagius continued, 'Patrick, this is Merlin, a very famous man indeed from Britannia. You must surely have heard of him up in Dal Riada?'

Patrick nodded. The peasants indeed had told him many stories about Merlin, and Patrick often wondered what he was like in real life. Now, as this strange, dishevelled, bird-like creature with the big black staff stood before him, Patrick winced.

'Hello,' Patrick said politely.

Pelagius said, 'This, Merlin, is Patrick, the Roman preacher of whom, I believe, *you* have heard much.'

Eyeing Patrick suspiciously Merlin muttered a greeting.

'Merlin, I think,' Pelagius said to Patrick, 'has something of great importance and power for you.'

Merlin sniffed, limped forward and laid his staff carefully against one of the carved pillars. After loosening the bundle from his back he opened it and proudly displayed the new staff. Patrick was confused.

'I have no need of a pagan staff!' he complained.

'But you need *Merlin's*,' the Saint said emphatically. Snapping his fingers at Merlin, he continued, 'Here. Give it to me.'

Merlin grudgingly handed Pelagius the staff. He studied it carefully. It was slightly taller than himself, highly polished, with the face of a lion expertly carved on its crook.

Nodding approvingly Pelagius said to Merlin, 'Nice piece of work. But a lion?'

Retrieving his own staff, Merlin responded deadpan, 'Inspiration.'

'First-class inspiration then,' Pelagius brightly commended. 'For Jesus sometimes refers to himself as the Lion of Judah!'

Merlin grinned. 'Judah?'

'That was his tribe.'

'Give the staff to *him*,' Merlin muttered, jabbing his own staff at Patrick.

'I will,' Pelagius said, 'but first I must do something with it.' He pointed to his Dove which was perched on the altar beside the Grail Flame. 'There,' he said to Merlin, 'is the Grail Messenger. She did her work well, eh?'

'Agreed.'

'She guided Patrick here at the very same time as yourself! For he too has only just arrived.'

'She must fly pretty fast!'

'No. She simply has bi-location. And she can also speak.

Did she speak to you?'

'No, and you shouldn't leave her there on your altar. She might soil it.'

'Oh, *she* doesn't soil *anything*. She's an angel-bird. And speaking of angels, last night mine appeared to me and foretold your coming today.'

'Your Angel knows a thing or two,' Merlin said smelling his fingers.

'Yes, and he also said, "Merlin's gift must be infused with the Grail power so that its wood becomes the very Word with which the forked tongue of the Serpent and its evil hosts will be banished forever from the fair land of Hibernia."

'I hope so,' Merlin gloomily responded.

'Brother Patrick,' the Saint said, 'our friend Merlin here has made this staff specifically for you, and what is more he made it from the wood of a very special tree, an ancient, holy oak, one that his Druid ancestors in Britannia used to worship. Isn't that right, Merlin?'

'Aye,' Merlin said. 'No serpents ever got up *that* feckin tree!'

To Patrick Pelagius continued, 'Merlin here is chief adviser to a young warrior in Britannia by the name of Arthur. I'm sure you've heard of him too up in Dal Riada.'

'Indeed I have,' Patrick said. 'The people speak of Arthur as if he was a great hero of old. But they also say he possesses of one their *Four Treasures.*'

'And they are perfectly correct! The Sword of Light. Merlin here took it.......or should I perhaps say, *procured* it for Arthur a few years ago. And this staff has been invested with the light and power of this famous Sword, isn't that right, Merlin?'

Merlin grunted in the affirmative.

'So,' Pelagius said to Patrick, 'I'm sure you now realize

the uniqueness of this gift of Merlin's. Will you accept it?'

'I will,' Patrick reluctantly agreed.

'Good. Now, please observe very closely.'

The Saint then mounted the steps to the altar where he passed the staff slowly through the Grail Flame while reciting a long and solemn invocation. When this ended he said to Patrick, 'Come forward now, Brother, and touch this staff with your ringed finger.'

Patrick mounted the steps and touched the staff. Miraculously, he felt Jesus closer than ever! However, as Pelagius now presented Patrick with the staff a sharp sound, like a baby's shriek was heard! From where had it come? Soon a big split was discovered in Merlin's staff! He was furious.

'Perhaps you would like me to pass it through the Grail Flame?' Pelagius consolingly offered.

'I've kept my promise,' Merlin irritably retorted. 'That's enough for you....for your.....'

'Jesus? Pelagius said, and slanting his eyes added sternly, 'We'll convert you yet.'

But Merlin recoiled from the Saint's gaze and ran out of the Temple! He ran all day and all night and eventually got lost. Somewhere in open country he gravitated to a halt and raising his cracked staff to the stars, angrily summoned a god to his assistance. But none came. He struggled on, and feeling wearier than ever before in his long life he eventually arrived back in his little hut in the Forest of Elfham. There he soon went to sleep, and slept for many days. But he had terrible nightmares. In many of these Vivian figured as a monstrous, ravenous pythoness determined to devour him. And even when he awoke he found no relief from his ever-mounting fears.

Patrick however was never happier. Although in the south of Hibernia the Naasenes continued to thrive, now, armed as it were with Merlin's magic, Patrick's preaching took on a great new dimension. His voice became deeper, richer and projected much farther. He felt strangely but wonderfully empowered by Merlin's gift, more confident than ever about his mission and hugely enhanced in his determination to spread the truth of his Divine Master's message.

The people of Dal Riada took more and more notice of him. They began to ask one another, 'Is this big man a Druid or not?' For he certainly looked like one! But what he was saying was entirely new to their ears. He spoke of a god whose sacrifice would end all the suffering of mankind and who promised his followers a return to *Tir-na-nOg*, the long-lost Paradise of Happy Youth the Bards spoke much of. This was theirs if they but obey one commandment: 'Love one another.' It was indeed a wonderful promise but a very strange commandment. Yet the people listened.

Then one day a blind man came up to Patrick out of a crowd and asked to be healed. For Patrick this was a turning point. He had never been asked such a thing before. He was shocked, embarrassed, and hardly knew what to do. He was however certain of one thing: he could not possibly turn the man away! So he gripped his staff, closed his eyes, and concentrating the whole of his mental and spiritual power into a short prayer, he asked the supreme God, in the name of his Son, Jesus the Christ, that this man be healed. Then he gently touched each of the man's eyes with his staff.

The man fell to the ground! Patrick thought he had killed him! But a few moments later the man sprung up and ran about touching everything, embracing everybody and ecstatically crying, 'I can see! I can see!' And all the people believed him, and believed also that if Patrick was a Druid then he was the most powerful one they had ever seen.

Everyone in Dal Riada, and many beyond, began talking about Patrick after that. He made converts simply by touching people on the crown of their head with his staff saying, 'Receive the Holy Spirit of Jesus the Christ'. Many went into ecstasies at the touch and Patrick studied these ecstatics carefully. With specially chosen males he would also lay on his hands and place a cross of ash on their forehead. These became the Culdees who expanded his first community. They grew rapidly in number so that the cowshed soon became too small to house them all. Around it tents and improvised dwellings of various sorts and sizes mushroomed. Encouraged and directed by Patrick, the enthusiastic Culdees dug trenches, drained the rushy field, and cleared away most of its ubiquitous rocks and stones. The vegetable garden, long ago began but till now showed little promise, suddenly blossomed and proved very productive.

King Fergus was so impressed by all this that after a few seasons he granted the community two more fields, plus some cows, pigs, goats and sheep. With the sheep's wool a weaving workshop was begun where white cowls were made for the Culdees and other products for sale at markets. With the accumulated pile of rocks and stones the cowshed was transformed into a substantial and very solid meetinghouse where interested people gathered to learn about and celebrate the new God and his universal law of love. A low wall was also built around the community.

Patrick was so emboldened by all these developments that he defied MacSaggart by openly reading from his book at these meetings. MacSaggart grew envious. He came to severely regret having allowed himself to be pressured into helping Patrick at all and bitterly complained to Fergus of Patrick's breach of the conditions under which he could preach in Dal Riada. But Fergus in the meantime had grown ever fonder of listening to Patrick and admonished MacSaggart forthrightly, 'This man is not to be impeded in his work in any way in my kingdom,' he angrily declared, 'and you can tell *all* your colleagues that!'

Although Patrick never knew where the Grail Temple was geographically located, he could always get to it whenever he wished. All he needed to do was pray to Jesus then set off in a south-westerly direction from Dal Riada, keeping the Grail thought firmly in his mind. Sooner or later the spirit Dove would appear and lead him directly, swiftly, and magically to the Temple's door.

Patrick went there often to consult with the Saint who imparted to him more and more secrets of the Grail. A deep hunger grew in Patrick to really see and touch the sacred Vessel but Pelagius cautioned that that could only happen at a propitious moment. 'Patience,' Pelagius said, 'was the highest of all the Grail virtues.' From his own perspective however, Pelagius was very pleased with the success Patrick was having in spreading the Word of Jesus in Dal Riada, and of how Patrick took on board all the advice, instructions and suggestions he received in the Temple.

One day however, when Patrick entered the Temple he found Pelagius in an uncharacteristically despondent mood. He was standing in his snow-white cowl, hood up, at the altar, lethargically turning pages of his Grail book. The Dove was perched on his shoulder, but seeing Patrick she flew to the nearby roof of the Grail Tabernacle.

After exchanging greetings Patrick tactfully enquired as to the reason for Pelagius's despondency.

'Oh, Brother,' Pelagius sighed, 'I have just received a report from one of my Initiates in the south that MacBran, the most powerful king in Munster, is the latest king to succumb to the spiritually seductive charms of the Naasenes. I don't know where all this is going to end.'

Patrick felt an uncharacteristic anger rising. 'I will go down there myself!' he declared, shaking his staff.

Pelagius lowered his hood and came down from the altar. He gripped Patrick's arm.

'But there is even more, Brother. I have also received a report from another Initiate in Gaul that your old superior in Auxerre has amassed a huge heretic-hunting army!'

'What?' Patrick cried. 'Germanus? An army? Impossible! Sure that old man can hardly even ride a horse!'

'Oh, but the report is true! My Grail Initiates *never* give false information! Your disowning Germanus probably drove him mad! Some raging devil has probably taken possession of him. Believe me, there is a Catholic army all set to invade Britannia. Its intention is to overthrow our great friend and ally, Arthur. Germanus now regards him the ringleader of "the Pelagians", as he calls us. And if he succeeds it will only be a matter of time before the Catholics will come here to Hibernia!'

'Oh, my Jesus,' Patrick cried, 'and they'll bring their horrible black cross of death with them!'

'They will surely. Death! That's all they know about. Oh, Brother, I fear neither Merlin, Arthur's army, nor the Sword of Light will be of any use against such dark opposition.'

Patrick stamped his staff on the floor. 'I will go to Britannia myself!' he declared. '*I* will help Arthur!'

But the Saint shook his head. 'No, Brother. That is not the answer. You are an instrument of peace. But here we are dealing with war!'

'What can we do then?'

Pelagius walked about agitatedly with his head bent. Then looking up suddenly he said, 'I believe we have but one hope of overcoming the terrible evil that is rising in our midst. The highest of all the Grail powers must be invoked!'

Patrick frowned deeply as Pelagius took two wooden chairs from the Temple wall. He placed them directly in front of the Tabernacle's golden door above which the white Dove was still perched, silently watching.

'Sit down,' he said. 'It's time I initiated you into the deepest of all the secrets of the Grail.'

Patrick rubbed his hands enthusiastically as they sat.

'You have heard,' the Saint said, 'of the Spear of Initiation, haven't you?'

'Yes, it's one of the *Four Treasures of Hibernia.* You told me before.'

'But I did not tell you *its story*, only the story of the Chalice of Rebirth. You will remember that Altus was the Druid guardian of the Chalice, but after receiving a vision of Jesus on the Cross he gave it to Josephus of Aramathea.'

'Yes, I remember. How could I forget!'

'Well, I did not tell you that Altus was also guardian of the Spear of Initiation. Now, listen very carefully. Long after Josephus returned to Jerusalem with the precious Vessel, Altus had another vision. It occurred when the day of the Crucifixion was drawing ever closer. In this vision Altus saw a Roman centurion piercing the side of Jesus on the Cross with a white spear. Now when Altus looked closer he was shocked to find that the centurion was himself! When the vision dissolved he troubled greatly over its meaning but in the end decided that the gods were instructing him to go to Jerusalem with the Spear of Initiation and pierce the side of Jesus with it! Altus could not understand why he should do such a strange thing, but neither could he bring himself to disobey the gods. So he went to Jerusalem, and on the day of the Crucifixion disguised himself as a centurion, and when Jesus died he ran up to the Cross, quickly pierced Jesus's side with the Spear and ran away again. Now, later on that same fateful Friday, when Jesus was taken down dead from the Cross, Josephus came along with the Chalice in order to gather some of the Saviour's precious blood in it. Jesus's blood had dried on all his wounds except the Spear wound. But from that there flowed in abundance, a sweet smelling substance that seemed to be part water. Josephus had no difficulty filling the Chalice. Afterwards Altus returned to Hibernia with the Spear, but he became very silent and withdrawn. He would speak to no one, and when his Druid colleagues eventually discovered that he had given the Chalice of Rebirth away, they killed him. This killing however stirred up great unrest among the tribes. The Chalice was missing and the Spear was now without a proper guardian! Fearing a renewal of the kind of intertribal warfare that had occurred in the past over the Lia Fail, which had long been placed in Avalliona for protection, the Druids decided to do the same with the Spear. So it was given to the High Priestess of Avalliona who soon began to use it in initiation ceremonies. Jesus appeared to Josephus in Jerusalem in his old age and told him of these events. Josephus afterwards travelled to Avalliona where he died. His staff was planted over his grave and became the tree that the Virgins of Avalliona now worship. The true story of these happenings however has, over the centuries, been lost to legend, but the Spear has remained in Avalliona ever since.'

The Dove flew from her perch above the Tabernacle door towards the altar. Patrick and the Saint watched in silence as with outspread wings she hovered uncannily above the Grail Flame, a very beautiful but mysterious sight.

Pelagius said quietly, 'Do you know what all this means, Brother?'

After a moment's reflection Patrick slowly replied, 'Only the Spear has the power to overcome the great Evil rising in our midst?'

'Precisely.......but how?'

'It must be passed through the Grail Flame!'

'Exactly. And then?'

'Arthur must have it?'

'Yes! It *must* be on his side.'

Patrick kissed his staff.

'I will,' he suddenly declared, 'go to Avalliona! I will somehow get the Spear from Morganna and bring it here. After you consecrate it I will take it personally to Arthur.'

The Saint spread his hands gratefully and smiled. 'Oh, thank you, Brother, you are surely sent to me from heaven!' He embraced Patrick. 'I will pray fervently at this altar that the peace and power of the Christ will be with you on this most important quest.'

CHAPTER TWENTY-FOUR

MERLIN'S TOOTH

When Guinevere's pathological boredom sank to crushing depths she usually assuaged it by strolling with a few of her lady companions through the muddy, smelly streets of Camelot, or more satisfyingly up along its high paved ramparts where she knew many of the patrolling sentries by name and all of whom greeted her as if she were a queen. It was a powerful panacea for her boredom!

But the baby in her womb was almost better. Every time it kicked now she imagined it as a little Lancelot, for was not that battle-hardened body of his soon to become the very outgrowth of her own?

When the day of Guinevere's labour finally arrived it was long and hard. Camelot's fussy but fiercely efficient old midwife came quickly, and reeled off instructions to

Guinevere like an army officer readying his men for battle. Guinevere moaned, groaned and cried, but she was determined not to scream, and didn't. The midwife however, almost did once, and was quite as relieved as Guinevere when the little head finally came between the vulval lips. Then after cutting the cord with a knife as old as herself the midwife held the baby upside down and with one eye examined it carefully all over. 'Perfect!' she adjudged, wiping sweat from her brow. She presented it to Guinevere saying that it was 'as good a job as I have ever done, my lady.'

Guinevere's smile betrayed an indescribable sense of relief! At the same time however she had to suppress a flash, a *guilty* flash of repulsion as she focussed for the first time on the pink little thing. Overall she was pleased that it was male, and the warmth that began to suffuse her deflated body as the tiny new-born instinctively sought for her breast, quickly drowned out all other thoughts and feelings. For this was something entirely new. This was pure joy, and soon it reigned over all.

Lancelot's feelings however were mixed. Although there was a corner of his soul which took pleasure in seeing the little thing occasionally, his conscience would not allow him ever to express that pleasure, and he viewed the baby primarily as an embodiment of his guilt.

Arthur on the other hand was ecstatic and wanted immediately to inform Merlin and hear the baby's name. But he would have to wait! For Merlin had resolutely stipulated that he should not be informed of the birth until twenty-one full days had elapsed. This irked Arthur tremendously. For he had not seen or heard from the old magician for months, and apart from the fact that Merlin was to name the baby, Arthur badly needed advice on many and increasingly important military matters.

Therefore it was precisely at sunrise on the morning of the twenty-second day after the birth that Arthur dispatched his personal courier, Clegis, to Merlin in the Forest of Elfham with news of the baby's arrival.

Clegis got to Merlin's hut around midday but found its surroundings oddly littered and untidy. After getting no response to repeated knocking on the door Clegis forced it open and found Merlin asleep in his bed.

'Are you not well, sire?' Clegis asked after waking Merlin.

Opening one eye with difficulty, Merlin sourly replied, 'I have been known to be better.'

News, however, of the baby's arrival enlivened him and he sat up.

'Arthur says you must come immediately,' Clegis said.

'Did he now?' Merlin dryly returned.

'And you're to bring your charts.'

'Charts? What charts?'

'He didn't say, sire.'

'Huh. Oh, very well. Tell him I'll be there as soon as I can.'

Merlin had difficulty waking Caliban who, like himself these days slept far too much. When he got her fully awake he went back into the hut, dipped into his boxful of charts under his bed, took out the first one that came to hand, plunged it into his cloak pocket and set off for Camelot.

Arriving at the fortress three hours later he gained access in the usual way by the postern gate where a new and friendly young guard agreed to look after Caliban until his return.

He found Arthur seated at the table in the library of his apartment, studying a book. Dressed casually, with his favourite filigree brooch pinned to his brightly coloured tunic, Caleb, crouched on all fours, was alert as a sphinx at his feet.

Arthur got up and embraced Merlin warmly.

'Congratulations!' Merlin said.

Arthur beamed. 'Thank you, old friend.'

'Fatherhood's the thing,' Merlin said.

'I'll send for Guinevere soon,' Arthur said, 'but let's talk first.' Suddenly his countenance altered. 'Hey! Where's your staff?'

'Holy smoke!' Merlin returned. 'I forgot it.'

'But isn't it dangerous for you to go about without it?'

Merlin sighed. 'Oh, I suppose you're right. But I'll survive.'

Arthur touched Merlin's sleeve. 'And, I've never seen your cloak so dull. It's absolutely colourless. What's the problem?'

Merlin pulled distractedly on his wispy beard. 'It must be the light,' he said.

'No. It's *you* my friend. Now please tell me, what's the matter?'

'There is something in the air that doesn't agree with me,' Merlin muttered and deflected Arthur's attention by pointing to the book he was reading. 'What is it?'

Arthur held up the small, skin-bound volume. Merlin eyed the barely legible letters on its heavily soiled covers.

'Mmm. Latin,' he said, fiddling now with one of his teeth, the one that was about to come out. 'The, Gosh...Gosp.....'

'*The Gospel according to Thomas the Twin*,' Arthur informed. 'Kay found it for me in Londonium.'

'Ah, yes. That. Any good?' 'It's amazing,' Arthur said. 'I've never read anything like it. It's positively unique. You simply have to read it.'

Merlin shook his head. 'I'm too old for new stories; and

as for new gods.......'

'Oh, but this one is different.'

'I know. That's the problem.'

Merlin took the book from Arthur and read a few lines. Handing it back he said, 'Anyway the Latin is lousy.'

'Merlin,' Arthur emphatically asked, 'are you *afraid* of Jesus?'

'I don't know.'

Caleb barked.

'Magicians,' Arthur said looking at his hound, 'shouldn't be afraid... of....of....They just shouldn't be afraid, full stop.'

Merlin sat down heavily. 'How's the baby?' he asked.

'Oh, mother and baby are fine,' Arthur said and picking up a small bell on the table rang it. A page immediately entered. 'Tell Guinevere,' Arthur said to him, 'to come here with the baby as soon as is convenient for her. And tell her Merlin is here.'

'Yes, Sire,' the boy said and was about to run off when Arthur shouted, 'Wait! Take Caleb with you.' To the dog he said, 'Dinnertime, eh?'

Caleb barked enthusiastically and followed the page down the stairs.

Arthur started pacing. 'Jesus tells us to love one another,' he said, 'that's all. It's not the god Jesus you should be afraid of but those damn Catholics.'

'Now you're feckin talking!'

Arthur sat down and looked Merlin anxiously in the eye. Then grasping his arm he said, 'Oh, Merlin, the times are changing so rapidly. I need you more than ever. There's a Catholic army gathering in Gaul, and increasing rumours that it's coming here to join the Mordred-Hengist alliance. Now the Catholics want to kill me as well as you!'

Merlin smelt his fingers. 'And are *you* afraid?'

Arthur sat back and sighed. 'I suppose I am.......a little.'

'Fear keeps you on your toes.'

'Aye,' Arthur replied brightening, 'and the smell of a battle!'

'And you have the Sword of Light.'

'Indeed! Which reminds me; did you bring your charts?'

Merlin groped inside his cloak and produced a tatty roll. He threw it on the table. As he did so however there was a knock on the door.

'Guinevere,' Arthur excitedly whispered; then loudly, 'Come in, my dear!'

The door opened. But it was Lancelot!

'Oh,' Lancelot said eyeing Merlin.

'It's all right,' Arthur said. 'Come in!'

Lancelot bowed to Arthur who pulled a chair out from the table saying, 'Please, sit down.'

After seating himself - stiffly, for he had his iron leggings and breastplate on - Lancelot placed his right hand characteristically on the hilt of his sword.

'Any more news?' Arthur asked.

'I have indeed, m'lord,' Lancelot replied, 'and it's not good.'

'We have to hear it anyway. Come!'

'I have just received a report from the south that ten ships were spotted heading for the Saxon Shore!'

Arthur boxed his palms. 'That's it!' he cried getting up. 'The rumours are true! The Catholics are coming. How old is this report?'

'Very recent.'

'Then they are probably already here. Gentlemen, I believe the real test of our strength is about to begin.'

Merlin was sucking his teeth furiously. The loose one finally came out! He held it up.

'It's an omen,' he wistfully announced.

Arthur glared at the old yellow tooth. 'Good or bad, my friend?'

'Good for some,' Merlin evasively replied and put the tooth on the table beside the chart.

'My Lord,' Lancelot said, 'I think the real question now is: where are we to engage the enemy?'

'Indeed,' Arthur said sitting down.

Lancelot leant towards him. 'And *we* can dictate that, Sire. But we must be very quick. Now, I've just been studying some old Roman maps I have in my house and I think......'

'Merlin has brought his charts,' Arthur interjected, touching the roll on the table.

Lancelot grimaced, offended by being overruled in favour of Merlin whose magic often repelled him.

'But, Sire....' he complained.

Arthur held up his hand. 'Merlin,' he boasted 'will surely tell us where is the best theatre to stage this last great battle of ours - for that, I think, is what it will be – won't you Merlin?'

Merlin grunted as Arthur pushed the chart towards him. 'Open it, friend.'

Merlin pulled the string of the chart and it sprang open. He expected it to be an astrological chart but was surprised to find it was a map he had made over forty years ago, one he had put a great deal of time, knowledge and effort into. It identified and pinpointed exactly all the most theurgically potent places in the large area of Britannia between Camelot and the Saxon Shore. These were places where the Druids had conducted their rites of initiation in very ancient times. Many of the places were outwardly insignificant nowadays - no more than a pile of ivy-covered stones - but they were still very potent, a potency which Merlin could not only sense but accurately evaluate. This map had in the course of his career often proved very useful. And as he perused it now he was pleased to recall it was the same one he had used many years ago to identify Camelot for Arthur as the place to build his fortress.

'It's a good omen, ' he muttered.

'What is?' Arthur asked.

'The tooth,' Merlin said and took it up. Putting it to his dagger nose, he sniffed it. Then he pulled a long hair from his white beard and tied it around the tooth. With the tooth suspended over the map he closed his eyes and for several moments murmured an incantation. Suddenly the tooth began to vibrate. He stopped chanting then and lowered the tooth onto the map. Opening his eyes he touched a spot on the map with his little finger.

'Here,' he announced, 'is where you should engage the damn Catholics.'

Arthur examined the spot carefully.

'Badon Hill!' he declared.

He got up and paced the room, thoughtfully twirling his big gold wedding ring. Eventually he started nodding. 'It's perfect!' he declared looking at Lancelot. 'Do you know the place?'

'Well enough, Sire,' Lancelot replied.

'Frankly, Sir Lancelot,' Arthur said, 'I cannot think of any spot in the whole of Britannia with such excellent and all-round strategic advantages for us. Sure, we can have the entire army assembled there within the week. The Catholics won't even have found their bearings by then!'

'Mmm,' Lancelot said looking at the map. 'It's about halfway between the Cambrian borderlands and Londonium.'

'Yes,' Arthur said, 'and only about a morning's march in off the old Roman road. It's perfect. It would have taken me more than a week's intensive study of all the excellent maps here in this library to come up with such a place to engage the enemy.' - He pointed to Merlin who was sucking his two remaining teeth. - 'But he's done it in two minutes. *Two minutes*! The man's a genius, Sir'.

He's a sorcerer, Lancelot thought, then said, 'I fear we will be greatly outnumbered.'

'That may be,' Arthur said, 'but from what I hear, this Roman army was very quickly assembled from the Catholic monasteries in Gaul. Sure they're probably all bloody monks for Jove's sake! They're not soldiers!'

Lancelot forced a deferential nod.

'*My* army,' Arthur continued, 'may be smaller, but it's well trained.'

Lancelot said, 'Then it's a question of how to lure them to Badon Hill, I suppose. That, I suggest, Sire, with respect, would not be at all easy.'

'Oh, I don't know about that either, Sir Lancelot,' Arthur contested. 'You're remarkably pessimistic today! What's the matter? Have we not lured many an upshot warlord's militia into convenient places before, and rid ourselves of them quickly enough? And many's the time it was Merlin here who advised us how to do it. I think we can rely on him again.'

Addressing Merlin, Arthur humorously enquired, 'Can you throw a spell or two for us over this ragbag of monks and gobs that are assembling on the Saxon Shore and calling themselves an army, my friend?'

Merlin grinned but said nothing.

The door opened suddenly and Guinevere entered. Radiant in a flowing, full-length, cloth-of-gold morning-gown, she held her sleeping baby, swaddled in a snow-white woollen shawl, to her fulsome breast. Lancelot rose with difficulty and bowed. 'My lady,' he said.

Guinevere blushed, her eyes turning quickly from Lancelot to Merlin who remained seated. She smiled at him and he nodded.

'Please, my dear,' Arthur said, pulling a chair from the table, 'sit.'

But Guinevere ignored him and went to Merlin. She held the sleeping baby to him.

'Have you ever seen anything so beautiful?' she asked.

'No,' Merlin dryly replied, studying the baby's aura. *Mmm*, he thought, *it's a love-child.* But then he was quickly shocked! There was something in this aura which distinctly stated that this was *not* Arthur's child! Who's then? Long years of studying auras had taught Merlin that only the eye's aura could give him the answer he sought. But the baby was fast asleep.

Lancelot was nervous.

'Shall we begin mobilization, Sire?' he asked.

'Immediately,' Arthur confirmed.

Lancelot rose and made for the door.

'But, Sir Lancelot,' Guinevere coyly called, 'don't you want to know what name Merlin gives to..... our...to this little darling?'

'I will find that out soon enough, m'lady,' Lancelot stiffly replied. Addressing Arthur again he continued, 'By this time tomorrow, Sire, every division of our army within one hundred miles of Camelot will be on the move and the rest the following day.'

'I firmly believe you, Sir,' Arthur said. 'Set to.'

Lancelot bowed and went out.

'Merlin,' Guinevere said, 'I believe that the most valuable

thing this child will possess for the whole of his life will be the name *you* give him.'

'Your words,' Merlin testily returned, 'may be wiser than you think.'

He got up and went to the window. Looking out over the courtyard he mumbled, 'If I am to properly name this child I will need to see its eyes.' Then turning abruptly he commanded, 'Wake him, madam!'

Guinevere gently shook the baby but it merely dribbled. Then she tickled its tiny pink palms for several seconds, but still to no avail.

'I'm afraid I can't,' she said at length. 'Sometimes he sleeps so deeply he frightens me.'

Merlin came to her then and gently touched a spot on the baby's temple with the small finger of his left hand. Instantly the baby's eyes popped open. Merlin absorbed himself in them and immediately the startling thought, clear as a blackbird's call in spring, came to him: *This child is Lancelot's.*

Merlin had a cultivated, if censorious, habit of never allowing his eyes to dwell for long on Guinevere. For he invariably found her alarming beauty stirred up his precious fluids far too easily! And after all, a magician's trump card was self-control! Nevertheless he now faced Guinevere squarely and for several long seconds drank her in. Then he kissed the baby quickly but tenderly on the forehead.

And in that auspicious moment the name was delivered.

'Galahad,' Merlin said.

Guinevere smiled.

'Galahad,' she repeated slowly to the baby. Its eyes shone like big blue suns.

Arthur was watching from behind.

'What does this name mean?' he asked.

Merlin turned and gazed with sadness upon this young scion of the Britons. *When will he know the truth*? he asked himself.

'It's cabbalistic,' Merlin said, 'from the Hebrew. It means something old, pure, hard and strong.'

Merlin looked into the big baby-blue eyes again and saw there now only his own reflection.

'And this child,' he prophesied, 'will need all of these qualities if he is to overcome the beasts that will pursue him. He will I fear need to be super-human.'

'He will be,' Guinevere said and kissed the baby.

CHAPTER TWENTY-FIVE

THE MONK'S RULE

The architectural plan of Dunseverick castle was as roughly conceived as it was solidly executed. It was built of great blocks of grey granite hewn with the most primitive tools out of the sheer, wind-lashed cliff-face of Dunseverick many centuries ago. Its draughty dining hall was wide and long, with a bumpy, stone-flagged floor, a very high ceiling and a number of irregularly placed windows, some of which, remarkably, had panes of thick, opaque glass; remarkably, for glass was a rare and expensive commodity in Dal Riada, one that had to be imported from Britannia, Gaul, or even farther afield. This latter fact also explained why some of the windows were merely large apertures which were boarded up in winter. In summer, of course, the boards were removed, but eating then could be a hazardous affair, for birds often entered and flew unnervingly about, or perching themselves on the high sills hungrily observed the diners.

The large oblong table in the hall was usually generously laid for dinner with copious amounts of bread, butter, roast meats, milk, beer and whatever seasonal fruits and vegetables were available.

The attendees at dinner included, apart from the King himself, his grey-haired but diligent wife Aoife, a few of his many children, and his chief Bard, musician and Druid. Sometimes there were special guests, and Spanish wine was then produced.

King Fergus often invited Patrick to dine with him, and on such occasions, when all the other diners had drifted away he liked to sit alone with Patrick and question him about his faith and hear him speak of his beloved God.

'Did Jesus teach reincarnation, like our Druids?' the King pensively enquired of Patrick during one such after-dinner conversation. It was winter, so birds were not a distracting problem. They were sitting on generously cushioned wicker chairs by a roaring log fire in the empty dining hall. Patrick was savouring this rare comfort, for conditions in his community, while improving, were still primitive. King Fergus had a fur-lined, crimson cape around his drooping shoulders.

Patrick also greatly valued these conversations, for they offered him rare opportunities to make requests and ask concessions of the King for the expanding Christian mission. And after Patrick's recent visit to the Grail Temple the most urgent of these requests was for the King's permission to visit Avalliona.

'I am convinced Jesus did teach reincarnation,' Patrick answered. 'After all, Origen taught it, and he was privy to books and knowledge about Jesus that have long disappeared.'

'Origen?' Fergus queried.

It was Pelagius who told Patrick about this writer who castrated himself for the love of Jesus and whose beliefs and teaching about the divine Master impressed Patrick greatly. Moreover, Pelagius believed he himself was a reincarnation of the Apostle John.

The King wanted to pursue this matter further, but Patrick, anxious to press his own urgent request, changed the subject.

'Your Highness,' he said, 'you will remember that I have on a couple of occasions previously asked for your permission to take my mission to the island of Avalliona.'

Fergus was perturbed by this sudden change of subject, but because he greatly valued and respected Patrick, he was forgiving. Looking at him ponderously with his big watery eyes he said, 'I remember very well, good Patrick. But Avalliona is, as I also told you, a very special place.'

'Can it be more special than Jesus?' Patrick braved.

Fergus carefully pressed a burning lump of peat into the fire with his boot. Yellow flames and red sparks shot about.

'Morganna might not agree!' he said.

'Jesus loved women!'

'That's hardly the point! Morganna, remember, is the foremost defender of the old faith in these parts. She is formidable. I fear you are not fully aware of the possible consequences of your request.'

'Your Highness, let *me* decide that. All I know is that I must speak to her about Jesus.....for her own good.....for the good of the old faith.'

'Well, whatever about Morganna, what I *am* certain of is that MacSaggart would vehemently disapprove!'

'All I need is *your* approval, King Fergus. I can deal with your chief Druid in my own way.'

'Aye! And *he* will deal with me in *his* own way.......if I overrule him! I've seen him kill people with words alone!'

'But his words will not kill *you*, good King, if you take the word of Jesus into your bravely seeking heart. The power of the word is now with *him*.'

Shuddering, Fergus pulled his slipping cape up his shoulders.

'MacSaggart tells me,' he said, 'that you are defying him by openly reading from your book....your ...gosh......gossip....What's it called again?'

'Gos....pel,' Patrick informed. 'Yes. I'm afraid so. And I hope your High......'

'Oh,' the King interrupted, 'I'm not too worried about that really. But I *am* worried about your interest in Avalliona. I was crowned by Morganna there you know. All our kings are, standing on the old Stone of the Danaans, the Lia Fail. Odd, isn't it? Hibernian kings being crowned by a Briton. But we take an oath of allegiance to the Great Mother. And then of course they also keep the Spear of Initiation over there in Avalliona. You know about that thing too, I'm sure.'

Patrick nodded nervously but remained silent.

The King continued, 'Personally I never know what to make of the Druids' magic. All I know is that it works.'

Looking at his staff which was lying against a wall nearby Patrick mused, 'Jesus is the best magician of all.'

Fergus meditated on the leaping flames. After a while he said, 'Some of the stories the Druids tell of that Spear of theirs makes my hairs stand on end.'

'I've heard some of these stories,' Patrick said coyly.

'Aye, but wouldn't you want to be half-mad to believe them!'

'Oh, I don't know. Jesus himself told lots of stories. Stories often have truth in them.'

'Pfff. Truth! What is truth?'

'Jesus said, "I am the Truth." '

'Words. Words. Words.'

'But his word guides, fulfils and nourishes. He also said, "I am the Bread of Life." '

'Your Jesus never fails to surprise me with the brevity and boldness of his words, good Patrick.'

'No one ever spoke like him before, Your Highness. That's why they killed him!'

The King laughed. Then he nodded to the empty table behind them. 'Did you notice anything?' he cryptically enquired.

'Do you mean that Eoin MacSaggart wasn't present at the meal?' Patrick asked.

'I do indeed. He's disappeared. No one, apparently, knows where he is. A law unto himself! Oh, it's not *very* unusual. He's disappeared many times before. It's one of his many skills! But he always reappears sooner or later, and for that I am thankful. The older I get the more I realize how much I need him. He's the only one I can ever fully rely on to throw light on the intractable problems that tribal religion constantly raises for me and my kingdom.'

'There can be no true religion from now on without Jesus,' Patrick said emphatically.

The King went silent for a long time. Patrick eventually broke it, 'May I go to Avalliona, Your Highness?'

'Yes,' the King suddenly replied, surprising Patrick.

'Oh, thank you most heartily!' Patrick cried.

'But don't tell MacSaggart.'

'That you approve?'

'Yes. Anyway I can't get his approval, can I, for he isn't

here? For all I know he might even be in Avalliona!'

Patrick smiled. 'Your decision is good, wise and just. And if MacSaggart challenges it you have a perfect defence!'

The King laughed again. Then throwing a log on the fire he said, 'I bid you good evening, Patrick.'

Patrick got up, bowed, took his staff and went to the door. When he reached it the King called over his shoulder, 'Be sure to let me know how you get on in Avalliona.'

'I will surely, gracious King,' Patrick replied and went out.

Patrick had told his community that he would stay overnight in the guest room of the castle - something he often did when visiting Fergus - and would not return until the following afternoon, which was a Sunday. However, because he could not sleep, he got up during the night and made his return journey in darkness on foot along the coastal path. He arrived at sunrise.

On Sunday mornings people came to the community from far and wide to join in its prayers, chanting and other Jesus-inspired activities. These mostly took place in the old cowshed which had recently been transformed into a substantial meetinghouse.

When Patrick arrived he made straight for it. It was overflowing with people. Many stood outside. Upon being recognized, a passage was respectfully cleared for him, and when he entered he immediately sought out Benedictus, for he wanted to speak with him. However, it was Ignatius he first saw, for he was standing conspicuously at the lectern on a raised platform in a corner of the room addressing the crowd who were listening attentively.

Since Ignatius's arrival in Hibernia he had developed into not only a convincing lector, but also a very persuasive orator. His explanatory talks on the Lord's revelation which he always gave after his gospel reading on Sunday morning, and which he was obviously doing at this moment, were always eagerly anticipated and energetically discussed afterwards. Already possessing the art of calligraphy which he acquired in the monastery in Auxerre, Ignatius was also now an excellent copyist and was teaching others the art of writing. Patrick had recently even set up a little scriptorium in the community where under Ignatius's precise instructions and Patrick's overall guidance copies of the gospel were being lovingly made by a carefully selected few of the more capable Culdees. Copies however were only made of Pelagius's gospel book, for the more Patrick studied this the more he realized its unique nature. Compared to it, all the other gospel books Patrick ever read paled into insignificance.

Happily, MacSaggart was not yet aware of this development. He was bound of course to find out eventually, and Patrick shuddered every time he thought of it. For this germinal scriptorium, Patrick firmly believed, had the potential not only to revolutionize religion in Hibernia, but the whole of Christianity, nay, it might alter the entire course of human history!

Inside the meetinghouse the Culdees, distinguished from the rest of Ignatius's listeners by their white cowls, were sitting on the floor around the raised platform from which Ignatius spoke. The other listeners were on improvised chairs, standing or leaning against the wall. Patrick first searched the Culdees but could not see Benedictus. Then he scanned the general crowd and eventually spotted Benedictus in a dark corner at the back of the room. He was without his cowl, and the young servant girl, Isolde, from the castle was standing beside him. She came to the Sunday gatherings regularly and Patrick often saw them together. Once or twice Patrick had spoken to her. She was pretty, charming and intelligent, a pick of the freshest flowers of feminine beauty that this green land produced in abundance, and obviously a virgin, albeit a wise one.

Patrick wanted to talk to Benedictus about her but he could never bring himself to it. Now however he would have to.......for they were holding hands!

Patrick slipped out. A low stone wall with a wooden gate leading onto the coastal path enclosed the various huts, dwellings, workshops and garden of the community. Outside the gate the visiting crowd tethered their donkeys and carts, horses and hounds. From a discreet distance behind one of the huts, Patrick watched the gate until the meeting ended.

Benedictus and the girl were nearly the last to emerge from the meetinghouse. And even when most of the throng had dispersed they lingered for a long time at the gate, talking quietly or silently looking into one another's eyes. Eventually Isolde went on her way, twice turning back to wave before she finally disappeared.

Like Ignatius, Benedictus too had changed since his arrival in Hibernia. In Auxerre he was, in his own way, just as enthusiastic about Jesus as Ignatius. But whereas the Hibernian experience seemed to sharpen Ignatius's enthusiasm into a fiery zeal, it softened further Benedictus's melancholic temperament. Hibernia, Patrick feared, was proving more attractive to Benedictus than Jesus, especially as the prism through which the young man was now viewing her was this very lovely, red-headed virgin, Isolde.

Patrick did not talk to Benedictus then, but a few days later, when he was setting out on his vital trip to Avalliona he decided to take Benedictus with him. He had so many things to say to this young man, but hardly knew where to start. Journeying together, he reckoned, would provide both opportunity and inspiration.

The purpose and destination of the journey was kept secret. For it, Patrick hired a local fisherman called Manaan who had been to Avalliona before and who also sometimes attended the Culdee's Sunday gatherings. Patrick trusted him to keep his promise of silence. Manaan undertook the journey singlehandedly, rowing his little skin-covered coracle with amazing speed and energy over a blessedly calm sea. But it was very cold.

In the narrow craft, wrapped tightly in wolf-skins, Patrick sat in front of Benedictus, similarly wrapped, with Manaan ahead of them rowing furiously. The second night of the journey was frosty with a full moon magnificently mirrored in the dun dusk of the water. Patrick spoke sporadically in Latin over his shoulder to Benedictus, but there were long silences broken only by a sudden shouted observation on the seascape from Manaan in his rough local language. Sometimes he would slow his rowing and quietly chant an old sea-song, its rhythm attuned to his gracefully moving limbs. Occasionally a bank of cloud passed in front the moon and all went suddenly pitch dark.

'Where are we going anyway, Father?' Benedictus asked during one such darkness.

'Whatever about you, my child,' Patrick ponderously replied, 'I think I am on the most important journey of my life.'

Benedictus laughed. 'You're joking, Father?'

Unseen, Patrick shook his head. 'You've heard of

Avalliona, I'm sure.'

'Oh yes,' Benedictus brightly replied, 'the people who come on Sundays are always talking about that flipping place. It sounds weird!'

'That's where we're headed!'

'Holy Moses! Really?'

'What did you hear about it?'

'That the people there practise black magic!'

'I see.'

'Is that true, Father?'

The moon reappeared. Patrick looked up. Quietly he said, 'We will find out shortly, won't we, boy? Are you afraid?'

'I......I'm all right,' Benedictus replied huddling himself.

'Don't be afraid,' Patrick said.

Suddenly gripping his staff he inwardly prayed: *Jesus, inspire me to speak your wisdom.* Then spinning round he faced Benedictus. 'I saw you without your cowl last Sunday.'

Benedictus bit his lip. 'I......I was.....'

'Don't you know, ' Patrick said firmly, 'that you are *never* to be seen without your cowl, inside or outside the community? Wearing it must become an *absolute habit.*'

'I....I'm sorry....'

'I have made three golden rules for my Culdees. Do you remember them?'

'Yes.'

'What's the first one?'

'Obedience. I'm sorry, Father.'

'Sorrow is not enough. Disobedience is a sin. It requires repentance.'

'Then I repent.'

'Indeed you may! But I'm not sure I can forgive you! Anyway, what is the second rule?'

'We can own nothing ourselves. We must share everything, like the first Christians.'

'Right. And the third?'

'Chastity.'

'Correct. Now, on Sunday last I also saw you with the girl, Isolde, again.'

Benedictus went scarlet! 'Oh, Father.....I.....'

'Have you kissed her?'

Benedictus closed his eyes. He appeared about to cry.

'Have you?' Patrick insisted.

'Yes,' Benedictus confessed.

'How many times?'

'Twice.'

'And now will you please tell me this: how on earth do you think you can practise the virtue of chastity if your head is filled constantly with love thoughts of Isolde and her kisses, eh?'

'I don't know, Father.'

'Well, *I* know. My Culdees are *Servants of God.* That's what the name means, in case you've forgotten. I require *total commitment* to this service from *all* my Culdees.'

Benedictus opened his eyes. They were filled with tears. He said, 'I love Isolde, Father.'

Patrick sighed and turned back to his normal position. He suddenly saw cranky old Germanus in Auxerre and shuddered at the thought of becoming like *him*! He gazed at the silver moonlight on the glassy-smooth water and watched the rhythmic, hypnotic motion of Manaan expertly plying his age-old craft.

'I love you too, Father,' he heard Benedictus softly say after a long silence.

A dark patch appeared on the horizon indicating that they were approaching Avalliona.

'I know you do,' Patrick mildly responded, 'but you must also know this: a Culdee can have neither two loves nor two masters. So you'll have to choose which one you love most and want to serve, and you must choose soon, my son.'

CHAPTER TWENTY-SIX

INVASION!

Twice or three times every day, Archbishop Germanus of Auxerre galloped Caesar, his big white carthorse, up and down the fields outside his monastery walls where his army was training for combat. He was pleased with the great number of monks who enlisted for his crusade, but regretted that so many of them were little more than fresh-faced, pimply youths. On the other hand, the divine enthusiasm they displayed for their sacred mission warmed the cockles of his old heart.

Germanus thought long and hard about how to tap that enthusiasm, how to channel it to a purely *military* advantage. Eventually he got the idea of a battle-cry.

The imperial army never had a battle-cry, but during his time in the army Germanus was always impressed with how the pagans used it. Once their cry was raised they would be seized by a super-human courage, and totally ill-equipped for battle with their primitive axes, pikes and clubs, would hurl themselves headlong against the Roman army, sometimes to outrageous and unlikely victories.

If it worked for the barbarians, Germanus thought, *it should also work for me.* The question then was what sort of a battle-cry would be appropriate for Christian monks?

One night as Germanus lay awake in bed thinking about this, his innards were suddenly gripped. He jumped out of bed and started pacing his bedroom. 'Battle-cry, battle-cry' he kept chanting like a shaman. And eventually an ancient Hebrew word came to him: *Hallelujah.*

He spoke it slowly at first: Hall-el-u-jah. Yes! This had rhythm, spunk, power. It came clean and sharp off the tongue. He said it again, louder, quicker. 'Hallelujah!' This time it felt like a veritable slash of Michael's sword! So he repeated it faster and louder still: 'Hallelujah! Hallelujah! Hallelujah!' He then closed his eyes and had a splendid vision of his entire army of monks chanting it. Oh yes, yes! This was surely a divinely inspired battle-cry! Louder and louder he shouted it. Oh, how heroically he then saw his monks hurling themselves against those horrible heretics!

Hallelujah! Hallelujah! Hallelujah! Praise be to the Lord forever and ever, amen!

It was nearly sunrise. Germanus dressed quickly and dashed out to the training fields where he had the habit of addressing his men *en masse* before breakfast. He did this through a megaphone from a high wooden tower erected specially for the purpose in the centre of the largest of the training fields. 'The Pelagians are the very scum of the earth,' he would roar at the top of his shaky but amplified voice. 'They know as much about Jesus as the backside of the bloody moon! They believe in nothing but a devil's cocktail of heretical doctrines, and indulge in evil practices. They defy the Holy Father, are a disease on the pure white body of Jesus, an ugly scar on his lovely face, and, worst of all, a cancerous growth on the One, True, Holy, Roman Catholic Church. They must be cut off and consigned to the flames of Hell,' and so on. And when he had finished a similar rant on this particular morning he raised his fisted right hand in the air and shouted, 'Hallelujah!'

The response he got was such that he had to plug his ears for joy!

Even sober-tempered Lupis was enthusiastic! He decided after hearing it that the army must also have its own distinctive banner. But what should be on it? He prayed hard for inspiration, and the answer came in a rare visionary flash: a black cross in a white circle against a scarlet background. He quickly sketched it out and ran with it to Germanus.

'The meaning of the black cross,' Germanus observed as he studied it, 'is obvious. But the white circle?'

'The Holy Spirit, Archbishop.'

'Aha! And the red?'

'The sacrificial blood!'

Germanus shook his crozier with delight. 'Oho!' he declared. 'We'll make a visionary of you yet, deacon Lupis. Have the banners made up right away.'

Spirits were high! However, so many monks enlisted that there was not enough armour to go round! Nevertheless everyone had a weapon of some kind, however primitive. What they lacked, Germanus thought, *Hallelujah* would make up for. And when parading with their attractive new banners flying, while at the same time practising their battle-cry, *Hallelujah!* sometimes resounded so powerfully in Germanus's old ears that he felt it could collapse the very walls of Jericho! It certainly regularly sent him flying into the chapel to prostrate himself before the Holy Bread in thanksgiving!

Eventually Germanus decided that his army was ready to fight. So, he picked a date for sailing to Britannia and dispatched a sea-scout to Sighard, the Catholic priest of Hengist's camp on the Saxon Shore, with the vital information. Soon afterwards, on a windy day in March he set sail from Boulogne-sur-Mer in western Gaul on the largest of his ten ships. The fleet was a motley mix of refurbished cargo and merchant vessels plus a few dilapidated warships, each carrying about three hundred monk soldiers.

Because there was a good wind behind it, the fleet crossed the choppy channel in a few hours and soon entered the Bay of Burnam which encompassed the abandoned Roman harbour of Portus Adurni. Though Germanus had been reliably informed that the stone piers there were crumbling, and most of the wooden bollards rotten, and that because of all this disembarkation would be difficult, Germanus nevertheless took the risk. He was acting on the advice of Romulus.

Romulus had been a commanding office in Britannia before the army's withdrawal. He therefore not only had a good knowledge of Britannia's terrain, but still possessed the maps he used there as a serving officer. After studying these, and aware of the overall situation in Britannia, he strongly recommended Portus Adurni as the best of a bad lot of possible places for landing the fleet, and the Archbishop agreed.

The wind was rising steadily when the fleet entered the bay. Protocol however required that anchor first be dropped in order to allow a party of the army's principals to go ashore to greet and meet the leaders of the foreign alliance. A small entourage therefore which included Romulus, Lupis and a few of the young monks (who were all instructed to bring buckets and ropes!) set out in a launch from Germanus's ship for the pier. Germanus himself, gold-tipped crozier in hand and impressively decked out in full episcopal regalia, sat like a painted prow at the head of the little craft. Irritably, he had to hold his tall, richly embroidered mitre in his free hand for fear of it being blown away.

There was no difficulty mooring the craft, but after placing his mitre unsteadily on his head Germanus had to be helped up the steep, crumbling steps to the pier. Once on it he found himself facing a small group of men at a distance. They comprised Hengist, with Sighard and Mordred on either side of him; a few paces back from Mordred stood three more stern looking Catholic priests with black woollen skullcaps, their long cassocks fluttering in the wind; behind Sighard three of Hengist's biggest and hairiest men stood fiddling uneasily with their axes and swords.

Germanus quickly ordered his entourage into a pre-arranged formation and then stepped forward a few paces.

Sighard spoke first. 'Welcome to Britannia, Your....em... ..Graw....'

'Grace, Grace,' Germanus impatiently finished.

'Oh yes. Sorry. Grace,' Sighard said. (He spoke in the Britons' tongue which all parties understood.)

Germanus held out his white-gloved hand, demanding his gleaming emerald ring of office be kissed. Sighard came forward and after bowing, obediently did his clerical duty.

'This is Hengist,' he then said, pointing to Hengist, 'the leader of the Saxons here in Britannia.'

Germanus squinted. His eyes were never good, and with the salt wind blowing into them now all he saw was a large, hairy egg-shape.

Sighard whispered, 'It's best to do what he asks, Your Grace.'

Looking offended Germanus growled, 'Tell him to come forward!'

Sighard beckoned Hengist. He swaggered up to Germanus, his crude iron crucifix dangling on his hairy chest. Germanus winced at the bear-like vision. They glared at one another. Germanus raised his ring to be kissed, but Hengist farted. Grinning, he kept fingering his crucifix.

'Brother-in-arms,' he said at the end of an awkward silence, spreading his hands. 'Welcome to Britannia.'

A sudden gust of wind snatched Germanus's mitre from his head! All watched anxiously as one of the young monks noisily dropped his bucket, and running frantically after the mitre, retrieved it just before it blew over the edge of the pier. Hengist's men tittered as the monk obediently tried to place the mitre in Germanus's ringed hand which had remained suspended in the mid-air, still waiting to be kissed. Eventually he took the mitre and the monk returned to his place.

Hengist pointed to the fleet out in the bay. Ink-black clouds were banking up behind it.

'There's a storm brewing,' he said. 'Better get them in quickly if you don't want to be blown back to Gaul before you've even arrived, ha, ha!'

Germanus turned disdainfully from Hengist and addressed Sighard in low tones. 'Is that one-eyed fellow there the pagan warlord… Mur….Mer…..Oh, what the hell's his name?'

'Mordred,' Sighard informed. 'Yes. That's him. He …he, Your Grace might kiss…..'

'Oh, that doesn't matter. Just tell him to come.'

Sighard beckoned Mordred who now sauntered forward.

'You wish to be baptized, I believe?' Germanus said.

Nonchalantly, Mordred nodded.

'Kneel down!' Germanus ordered.

After throwing a questioning glance at Hengist who implied 'just do it' with a flick of his head, Mordred went down on one knee. Germanus then shoved his mitre into Sighard's hands and snapped his fingers at the group of young monks behind him. 'Water!'

One of the monks dropped his bucket over the pier, filled it quickly and brought it to Germanus. Giving his crozier to the monk and taking the bucket, Germanus threw its contents over Mordred. He then made the sign of the cross, closed his eyes and mumbled a prayer.

'Get up,' he said when finished.

But Mordred didn't move! Hengist's men started laughing. And when Germanus looked down he saw to his horror that Mordred was drying his face in his episcopal robes!

'Get up!' Germanus angrily repeated.

Mordred got up slowly and wiped his eyeless socket with the back of his hand. His leathery face displayed no emotion.

'Anything else?' he coldly enquired, scratching his crotch.

'Say amen.'

Reluctantly Mordred muttered, 'Amen.'

'You're a Christian now,' Germanus said.

Hengist clapped.

'Where is your army?' Germanus asked Mordred. 'I mean your militia? They're next.'

A white sandy beach ran eastward for miles along the coastline. Mordred pointed lazily towards it. In the distance an amorphous black blob was visible. Smoke curled up from it. For a moment Germanus thought it some kind of indigenous, dragon-like beast!

'Fifteen hundred fighting men, all hungry to kill,' Mordred said.

'And where are *your* men?' Germanus asked Hengist.

Hengist pointed to the hill behind him. It was a little inland from the pier. On it was a large abandoned Roman fort. Men were visible sitting on crumbling walls, others casually walking up or down the pot-holed road leading to the fort's battered gate; yet others were riding around the foot of the hill on horseback.

'We've been here a few days,' Hengist said. With exaggerated politeness he added, 'We were waiting for you… ..Your Grace. As you can see, it's a big place…… lots of room for you.'

'How many men have you?' Germanus snapped.

'About the same as him,' Hengist said pointing to Mordred who had slunk away to his horse which was tethered nearby. 'And on the march more will join us.'

'We have three thousand,' Germanus boasted.

Hengist rubbed his hands. 'Did you hear that?' he shouted to Mordred who turned and forced a grin.

Hengist said, 'That means we'll outnumber Arthur by at least four to one! He hasn't a hope in Hades.'

'Hell,' Germanus corrected. 'And where is Arthur's army?'

'There are small units of it all over the place. But he

knows what's happening. As far as we can tell, he is currently headed in the general direction of Aquae Sulis.'

Germanus snapped his fingers at Romulus who now joined him.

'What's the name of that place again?' Germanus asked Hengist.

'Aquae Sulis,' Hengist replied.

'Do you know where this is?' Germanus asked Romulus.

Romulus nodded. 'North, north-west. About a hundred miles.'

'More,' Hengist corrected.

'Venta Belgarum is nearer, isn't it?' Romulus said to Hengist.

Hengist nodded.

'Has Arthur got men there?'

'No, the town's a rat-infested ruin.'

'What about Sorbiodunum? That's a little further west. Has he men there?'

'No,' Hengist pointed to Mordred adding, 'but *he* has.'

'Good. We'll go there first.'

'Exactly what I was thinking myself,' he said and shouted to Mordred, 'To Sorbiodunum first!'

Mordred shrugged.

'He agrees,' Hengist said. 'And by the way, when we get there I will be able to tell you *exactly* how and where to lure Arthur. You see, there is this.......'

'Wait!' Germanus put in. 'First things first.' To Mordred he shouted, 'Hey, move that thing, that militia of yours up here onto the pier as quickly as possible! I want to get this bloody baptism over with before the storm breaks. Then we'll moor the fleet.'

Mordred mounted his big black stallion and rode off towards his camp on the beach. He returned soon afterwards at the head of his militia, a loosely marching formation of huge hairy men of all ages, many half-naked and daubed with paint. Germanus arranged for about a hundred of them at a time to be brought onto the pier. He performed the sacral act of baptism quickly by walking through each group making rapid signs of the cross in all directions, while mumbling prayers and drenching them with seawater, a copious supply of which was kept up by a busy chain of obediently bucketing monks.

Soon after this, with much difficulty and great excitement, but without major mishap, the fleet was moored and the monkish army successfully disembarked. Guided and instructed by its few old, ex-imperial army officers, the youthful army chaotically but quickly moved with all its equipment, animals and supplies up the hill into the abandoned Roman fort where together with speedily erected tents, the ruins provided shelter from the storm which eventually broke.

A leadership group was formed the next day, and after hammering out a command structure, and agreeing a few basic points of strategy, two days later the army of the triple alliance set out marching on the old Roman road towards Venta Belgarum. Germanus's division took the lead.

The sky had been washed bright blue by the storm, but the wind still blew. Progress was slow, for the road was full of pot-holes and strewn with debris. Rocks, boulders and fallen trees regularly blocked the way and the paving was sunk steeply in many places. But spirits were high.

Germanus, as commander-in-chief, rode out front on Caesar. Though Lupis tried to discourage him from doing so, Germanus insisted on bringing the monastery's carthorse, arguing that it was the only horse he trusted not to throw him. Determined also to keep up Catholic appearances at all costs, despite the weather and hazardous riding conditions he remained clad in his episcopal robes. He even had a holster made for his crozier so that he could carry it while riding; he also had a string sewn into his mitre. This, securely tied under his chin, allowed him to wear that important appurtenance too, even in the wind!

As the army meandered its way slowly along the abandoned road, every so often Germanus would raise his fisted hand and punch the air. It was the recognized sign for the raising of the monks' battle-cry. And every time Germanus heard it he thanked God dearly.

Halfway between Portus Adurni and Venta Belgarum it went suddenly dark! Big black clouds rolled in mysteriously from nowhere and blocked the sun. Germanus watched enthralled as slowly the clouds stretched and expanded into the form of a black cross.

Germanus prayed and the cross got bigger. Soon he saw Jesus nailed to it! Germanus prayed harder, then, as he hoped and expected, the blood began to flow from the precious wounds. Oh, how he loved those wounds! The blood poured down like heavenly rain, on him and his whole army. And the moment it touched his tongue he raised his fist ecstatically and the monks' *Hallelujah!* went through him like a host of heavenly spears.

The blood flowed more and more freely. Germanus's member went stiff as a spear, its hot head pulsating rhythmically in unison with the chanting. His heart pounded, his eyes watered, and this mouth frothed.

Germanus laughed and cried. Never before did he feel as hot and happy as this, not even in his virile youth! And never in all his time in the Roman army did a battle smell as sweet as the one that was about to begin, the one that would rid his Church of the worst scum that God's earth ever produced: the Pelagians.

CHAPTER TWENTY-SEVEN

THE SPEAR OF INITIATION

Seldom was it so cold.

Morganna, High Priestess of Avalliona, awoke just before sunrise, got up and dressed. After throwing a fur-lined cloak over her shoulders she went to the front door of her house, opened it and looked about. The brightening sky was still pierced here and there by a few straggling stars. The thatched roof of the Temple of the Virgins, which directly faced her house, and everything else in sight was coated with a thin garment of glistening white frost.

Morganna fastened her cloak, walked away from her house, out of the Temple precinct and picked her way carefully down the narrow cobbled path to the cliff's edge. There she stopped and gazed calmly out over the dark green ocean. Soon, like a god awakening, she saw the huge shining eye of the winter sun rise above the eastern horizon. Reverently she watched his first beam strike her beloved, white-frozen island like a holy lance, and for a few magic moments turn it into a shining rose-coloured jewel. Spontaneously she gave thanks to the Great Mother.

When the sun was fully up Morganna returned to the Temple and went into the sacred grove. There she stood by the tall, cone-shaped apple tree, absorbing herself in the cold, glistening beauty of its naked, frosted form. Her thoughts strayed then, as they often did, to the holy man who planted this tree here so long, long ago. Was he perhaps a god? she wondered.

When she returned to her house she found that her servant Virgin, Elaine, already had a bright log fire burning in the hearth of the living room. Morganna sat by the fire where her questioning thoughts continued. She was troubled by many things lately. Why for instance did the apple tree last season produce so few fruits? And why was it becoming so difficult to find suitable recruits for the priesthood? The tradition held that fifty was the precise number of Virgins who must always serve the goddess of the Temple. But this year for the first time ever that auspicious number was not met!

And then there was Vivian! Last summer she turned up unexpectedly at the Temple, after no one had seen or heard from her for years. Morganna hardly recognized her. Vivian kept aloof, participated in none of the Temple activities and rarely spoke. Neither Morganna herself nor the Virgins knew what to make of her. Nevertheless Vivian was treated courteously and accommodated comfortably, as was befitting a past initiate of the Temple, but all were glad that she only stayed a short while. However, when Morganna discovered a few days after Vivian left that Merlin's grimoire was missing, she came to the only possible conclusion: Vivian had stolen it!

Acutely aware of the importance of this theft, Morganna had personally made the long journey south to inform Merlin. She wanted to do this, however, in Arthur's presence, and so went directly to Camelot. Merlin was not there at the time and was sent for, and while waiting Morganna had some rare and precious time alone with her beloved stepbrother. From him she first learnt how Vivian had become a priestess of the Naasenes.

'And who or what are the Naasenes?' she enquired.

'An old Christian gnostic sect,' Arthur informed, 'which is having a revival in the south of Hibernia. Merlin told me. But they are being opposed there by a Roman Christian preacher called Patrick. And, dearest sister, I have to tell you that I fully support this man.'

Morganna was shocked! 'So you've become a Christian since I last saw you!'

Arthur nodded. 'Of sorts. I'm studying the book of Jesus, the gospel.'

Morganna had long known of the Christians, but, like Merlin, avoided them like the plague. She had in fact taken up the position of High Priestess in Avalliona precisely because she felt she could foster the endangered cult of the Great Mother in safety from them in that sanctuary.

'What inspired you to make this strange conversion, brother?' she enquired.

'Undoubtedly,' Arthur replied, 'the Sword of Light has something to do with it. But do not be troubled. Your knowledge of the Christians is mainly based on the Catholics. But although Patrick is a Roman he is not a Catholic. He is a Pelagian.'

Arthur went on to explain the difference, and concluded by saying, 'You know, good sister, the more I learn of Jesus, the more flesh he puts on my dream of Logres.'

From this conversation Morganna sensed that great changes were afoot not only in her beloved step-brother, but in the very soul of her nation, and she promised Arthur to think differently about Jesus.

When Merlin eventually arrived and was informed of the theft of his precious magic book he fell to the floor in a heap! Morganna and Arthur actually thought he had dropped dead! He had however, merely fainted. When he eventually came to he sat for hours silently staring into space and sucking his gums. (All his teeth had fallen out recently!) Then he started crying! 'That w...was my ma...magic grammar,' he sobbed. 'S...she has stolen my v....very heart. All the b....best spells I ever cast are in that b....book. Oh, ye gods and beasts, that w....woman is surely a demon! I will c....curse her! I will!'

'Oh, no,' Morganna protested, 'please don't curse her! If you do you may bring a curse on all my Virgins.'

'How c.....could I have made such a mistake initiating her?' Merlin sobbed. 'How, t...tell me, how?'

'I don't know, dear Merlin,' Morganna comforted. 'All I know is that cursing her won't help. Shush now.'

Because Merlin seemed unable to walk, Arthur offered to put him up in Camelot. But Merlin insisted that he must go back to his hut. He said he had something very important to do there. He was eventually carried the whole way. Morganna feared he was dying.

She was roused from her ponderings suddenly when Elaine entered the room and curtsied.

'Good morning, Elaine,' Morganna said. 'What is it?'

'Gracious mistress,' Elaine said, 'there is someone to see you.'

'What?' Morganna declared. 'A visitor? So early in the day?'

'Yes, mistress, a man.'

'A man? And what, pray, is his name?'

'He would not tell.'

'What then does he look like?'

'A Druid, I'd say.'

'Oh dear! And where is he now?'

'In the waiting room of the Temple. He asked to be left there until your return.'

'Well, bring him to me here, straightaway.'

When Elaine went out Morganna dashed to her bedroom and changed quickly into a long, occasional gown of green silk. Her handsome face looked puzzled as she brushed her close-cropped auburn hair. 'Not Eoin MacSaggart again, I hope,' she said disdainfully to her reflection in the mirror. She disliked the King's Druid intensely.

Elaine returned a short time later with the visitor, and a cold, chaste thrill went through Morganna. This big bearded man did indeed look like a Druid, but never before had she seen one in a white cowl with a cross of ash daubed on his forehead!

It was Patrick!

He had reached the island just before sunrise, and left Benedictus and Manaan with the boat at the jetty. He then made his way along one of the many winding paths leading to the little Temple which was clearly visible from the shore because of the flatness of the island. He had arrived when Morganna was out on her walk.

She and Patrick bowed graciously to one another.

'My name is Patrick,' Patrick said in Morganna's language.

'Ah, Patrick,' Morganna returned, nodding her head slowly. 'I see. My brother Arthur told me about you. You are the Jesus preacher, aren't you?'

'That is correct, High Priestess,' Patrick confirmed. 'I have come from Dunseverick.'

'Not to preach to me, I trust!'

'I am sent by God.'

'Good heavens! By Jesus, I suppose?'

'No. His Father.'

'Oh, but doesn't he also have a mother? Why didn't *she* send you?'

'The mother of Jesus is a human being, like you, High Priestess. Her name is Maria.'

'Mmm. And what does this name mean?'

'Star of the sea.'

'Well, it's a good name for the mother of a god!' - She scrutinized Patrick's staff. - 'Now what, pray, does this lion symbolize?'

'Life,' Patrick modestly replied, 'the Life of the heart. Jesus said, "I am the Way, the Truth and the *Life*." It is written in the book of Jesus.' - Patrick pointed to a small leather satchel attached to his belt. – 'Here.'

'Would that be the *gospel* by any chance?' Morganna queried.

'Yes. Did your brother also tell you about this?'

'A little. And many other strange things besides.'

'Well then, did he tell you that Merlin, whom I believe you know perhaps even better than your step-brother, made this staff?

Morganna was startled! 'Good gracious, no! He did not!'

'He was perhaps afraid, High Priestess. But it's true!

This staff is made from the same ancient holy oak from which Merlin made Arthur's Round Table.'

Morganna stepped back. 'Why have you come here?' she crossly demanded.

'Not to *preach* to you,' Patrick said calmly, 'but to *demonstrate* the power of the great new God.'

'And how, pray, do you propose to do that?'

'With the Spear of Initiation, which you possess.'

'Good heavens! And what may I ask has the Spear of Initiation got to do with Jesus?'

'Far more than you realize. There is something vitally important you should know about this Spear.'

'What do you mean? Something *vitally important?* I know *everything* about it! The Druids imparted all there is to know to the High Priestess when they left the Spear here for safe keeping long ago. This knowledge has been passed down to me.' – She tapped her head. – 'It's all in here.'

Patrick shook his head.

'What then do I not know?' Morganna demanded.

'May I sit down?'

Morganna snatched a chair from the fire and set it firmly down beside Patrick. When he was seated she stood by the fire and fixed her gaze on him. She listened intensely then as he told her the whole story of Altus and the Spear, but he said nothing of Josephus and the Holy Grail. Towards the end of the story Morganna became anxious. She wrung her hands continually and walked agitatedly about. Almost overcome, she pulled a chair from the nearby table and sat down. Patrick went to her then and put his hand gently on her shoulder.

'There is nothing to fear from Jesus, High Priestess, believe me,' he said. 'His incredible and mysterious truth must be made known to all men and all women the whole world over. He dispels all darkness. He also said "I am the Light of the World." Now please, take me to the Spear and I will demonstrate to you his cosmic power.'

Morganna looked painfully into Patrick's eyes. What a strange fire was burning there! Again she felt that cold, chaste thrill. She sighed, got up heavily and said simply, 'Come!'

A few of the Virgins were already busily at work in the Temple, tidying, cleaning, polishing its various objects, and arranging its accoutrements and furniture according to the ritual needs of the day ahead. When Morganna entered with Patrick she dismissed them and led Patrick directly to the Lia Fail which, as always, was on the floor in front of the steps leading to the altar. She bowed before the Stone.

'Don't step on it!' she cautioned as she ascended the steps, beckoning Patrick to follow.

The altar was made from a single, huge block of black Caledonian marble. The only object on it was the holy Spear of Initiation. It shone like a pure white vein running through the marble. Patrick's soul was deeply pierced as his eyes beheld this beautiful thing that had been thrust into the very body of his Lord on the Cross of Golgotha.

'It has never left this altar,' Morganna affirmed, 'not while I have been High Priestess.'

Patrick said, 'Take up the Spear.'

Slowly Morganna lifted it.

'Hold it out over the altar,' Patrick instructed, and as she did so Patrick uttered a short prayer. Then he touched the Spear with his staff. And with supreme wonder they watched as a little drop of bright red blood appeared on the gold tip of the Spear. When it was fully formed the drop separated slowly from the Spear and slid through the air like a glistening ruby. When it touched the altar it spread out and quickly disappeared.

Morganna replaced the Spear on the altar. She turned then and gazed with a mixture of awe and sadness into Patrick's eyes.

'Take it,' she said suddenly.

He kissed her forehead. 'The Peace of the Christ be with you.'

'There is one condition,' Morganna added.

'Yes?'

'Whatever you have to do with it, when you are finished the Spear must be returned to Avalliona and this altar. This is its true home. Nothing will ever change that.'

'I fully agree, High Priestess,' Patrick said and took up the Spear.

CHAPTER TWENTY-EIGHT

A VISION

Despite the poor condition of the old Roman road, Germanus's army made good progress on its northerly march. When it reached the outskirts of the ruined town of Venta Belgarum there was some discussion as to whether it should enter the town. But when scouts returned with information that it was infested by black rats as big as cats the camp was made outside the town.

Despite the good progress however, the march was beginning to get on Germanus's nerves! A side-effect of this for him was more frequent visions. And on the night that camp was established outside Venta he had an exceptionally powerful one. At least he *thought* it was a vision, because not only seeing a little white Dove that shone like a star, but hearing it *speak*, which is what actually happened, could *only* be a vision, couldn't it?

At the time Germanus was lying wide-awake on a straw mattress in his private tent. His eyes were bloodshot, his cheeks sunken and his short, lame leg in pain. The wind was blowing hard. The tent had been insecurely pegged and Germanus continually cursed the monk who had erected it, for he feared it would lift off at any moment. The rain beat down on it mercilessly. The noise was deafening.

Suddenly the Dove appeared! It squeezed in brazenly through a tiny aperture in the tent's door-flap, which was made by the wind's constant biting at the flap's lacing. Germanus shot bolt upright. The tent had been dark, but now it was as if a very bright lantern had suddenly been lit! The bird perched herself boldly on the top of Germanus's mitre, which was standing staunchly on a chair beside his mattress.

Germanus blessed himself and prayed. Then he reached for his crozier, held it upright and fixed his beady black eyes firmly on the bird.

This was no hallucination! This Dove had all the luminosity of a divine *vision*! Then suddenly, in a clear but strange, high-pitched voice Germanus heard the words, 'You want to defeat these damn heretics, don't you?'

Now, this was *absolute proof* of the miraculous nature of what was happening!

'Oh, yes!' Germanus cried. 'Can you help me?'

'Indeed I can,' the voice returned. 'Badon.'

'P...pardon?' Germanus stammered.

'The Hill of Badon. That's where you should lure Arthur to.'

Suddenly Germanus was perturbed! 'Where is that, for God's sake?'

'Only a few more days' march.'

'But why the Hill of Badon?'

The bird hopped onto Germanus's crozier and looked down powerfully upon him. 'Everyone, everything, and every place on earth,' he heard, 'has its own spirit, Archbishop. And not all of them are friendly. But the spirit of Badon is a friend of yours. It will be able to take your side there, no bother. The Holy Spirit cannot guarantee such a thing in any other place in Britannia. So, only on the Hill of Badon will you be absolutely assured of victory over that foul fellow, Arthur. Now that's gospel.'

Germanus gripped his crozier tighter than ever. The bird flew back to his mitre.

'Then that's where we'll head for,' Germanus enthusiastically promised.

'Excellent!'

The bird then flew to the door, hovered a moment, said 'Goodbye' and disappeared.

It all happened in a flash! But it was surely the flash of God! After a few quick prayers of thanksgiving, Germanus got up, threw his long waterproof cape over his shoulders, lit a lantern and went out. He scurried, head bent to the raging wind, along the narrow path between rows of flapping tents even more poorly erected than his own, until he came to Romulus's. A forlorn, rain-soaked monk acting as sentry let him in without questions.

Romulus was asleep on his mattress on the ground. Germanus held the lantern close to his face and shook him vigorously. Waking, Romulus yawned, sniffed and began chewing his big white moustache. Blinking, he growled into the glare, 'Who's there?'

'Me,' Germanus said, 'your commander-in-chief.'

'Oh.'

Romulus sat up.

'Archbishop,' he said rubbing his eyes. 'But....but what time is it?

'Time to get up,' Germanus said. 'I want to see your maps.'

Romulus scratched his bald head.

'Archbishop,' he said, 'I've never seen you without your crozier before.'

Germanus was shocked! In truth, he had forgotten it! Lifting up the lantern he weakly explained, 'I had to carry this. Now get up!'

Unperturbed because well used by now to Germanus's ratty temperament, Romulus yawned again and took his time getting up. After putting on his greatly oversized, grey dressing gown he stoked the dying embers of his little stove.

'Sit down please, Archbishop,' he yawned.

'I'll stand, if you don't mind,' Germanus returned.

Romulus threw a log into the stove.

As Germanus placed his lantern on the tent's table he asked, 'Have you your maps here?'

Tugging the hairs of his huge snow-white moustache, Romulus said with the shadow of a grin, 'You have an idea, Archbishop?'

'Are they here or not?' Germanus superciliously returned.

'Oh, I go nowhere without them,' Romulus replied, pointing to a big wooden box under the table. 'And I also rarely let them out of my sight. As Caesar said, "The map's the thing". I have over a hundred of them. Now, pray tell me Archbishop, which one do you want?'

'Do you know the Hill of Badon?'

'Yes,' Romulus said stooping stiffly for the wooden box. Lifting it onto the table he continued, 'Badon is far north of here. It is a low hill with a broad plateau. The foothill is densely wooded to the north and west. It's about a day's march through very rough terrain off the road between Calleva and Corinium.'

He rooted in the box, found a roll, untied it and spread it out.

'There it is, Archbishop,' he said pointing.

Germanus studied the map.

'I don't see Camelot,' he complained.

'Not on it, I'm afraid. It's much further south.'– Romulus pointed to a spot off the map. - 'About here I'd say.'

Germanus straightened up. 'We go to Badon!' he emphatically declared. 'We'll engage Arthur there.'

Romulus raised his brow. 'But that's a complete change of direction!' - He pointed to the map again. - 'Badon is north from here. We will have to take this road to Calleva. Sorbiodunum is due directly west.'

'I'm not blind,' Germanus said. 'Nevertheless, Badon it is.'

'But Archbishop.... Mordred has dozens of local warlords and their militias waiting to join him in Sorbiodunum. He'll not agree.'

'You forget, Romulus,' Germanus sternly countered, 'that the man has been baptized. He is on the side of Jesus now, and *I* speak for Jesus, no one else. Mordred has no choice. He will obey me. We start for Badon, tomorrow.'

'And if he doesn't obey?'

'Then to hell with him. And to hell with his painted friends too. We'll go without them. And as for that other brute, Hengist – he'll come, don't fear. He'll obey. He knows his oats, that one. He's got nothing to lose and everything to gain by being part of this enterprise.'

'But Arch.....'

'Arch my bollocks! Convene the leadership group first

thing in the morning! That's an order! I'll be there.'

Romulus shook his head slowly and rolled up the map. Tying its string he asked with raised eyebrows, 'Why?'

'Why what?' Germanus snapped.

'Why Badon?'

'God told me.'

Romulus forced a grin. Germanus picked up his lantern, and as he was going out turned and repeated emphatically, 'God!'

'Don't forget your crozier in the morning,' Romulus said dryly.

'Sun-up,' Germans said and disappeared into the gale.

CHAPTER TWENTY-NINE

A HARD JOURNEY

'I can't describe it, Father. Really. It's like I become a flipping flame or something. I don't know. All I know is I feel so happy I want to die.'

Benedictus was talking about Isolde's kisses! He was, amidst hottest blushes, responding to Patrick's very probing questions. Patrick listened with a mixture of amusement, curiosity and empathy.

They were sitting together in Patrick's new and very solidly built stone cell. Lately the Culdees were busily building similar cells for themselves and all the new members whose numbers were increasing daily. King Fergus supplied the stones from his private quarry.

Patrick's was the first cell to be completed. Apart from the two wooden stools that Patrick and Benedictus were sitting on, plus a straw mattress and a few basic essentials, the only other object of note in the cell was the Spear of

Initiation. It lay on the floor by the wall concealed beneath a piece of clean linen. It had been there for over a week. No one knew of it except Benedictus who had promised faithfully not to speak of it to anyone.

Recently the building programme consumed most of Patrick's time, but he was determined to take the Spear to the Saint at the first available opportunity. Meanwhile it often filled his cell with strange and powerful vibrations. Like now. Does Benedictus feel them? Patrick wondered.

Discreetly Patrick pointed to his groin. 'What about this?'

Benedictus swallowed. 'I try not to let her feel it,' he innocently confessed. After a pregnant pause he pleaded, 'Is there something wrong with me, Father?'

Patrick smiled and shook his head. His suspicions were confirmed: the boy was largely unacquainted with the facts of life! He explained the basics and concluded by saying, tongue-in-cheek, 'Sex is the darkest of all the divine mysteries.'

'I had a funny feeling it was,' Benedictus blurted.

'Do you have a sense of shame when you masturbate, my child?' Patrick enquired.

Benedictus blushed again. 'Yes, Father.'

'Good. A sense of shame is crucial to spiritual progress. Now, to business! You'll have to get married.'

Benedictus frowned then nodded.

Patrick continued, 'And I think you know what *that* means.'

'I can't be a Culdee?'

'Correct. As I told you before, my Culdees *must,* like me, be single-minded and totally unattached - so that they can devote their love-lives whole-heartedly to the person and the cause of Jesus. Married people cannot do that. Their first duty is to love one another. For what, my child, is marriage?'

'The sacrament of love, Father.'

'Well put! And what is a sacrament?'

'An act of God.'

'Precisely. And in our context an act of God that unites two people spiritually and physically in dutiful love. However, don't lose heart! There is no reason why there cannot be an associated movement of lay or married Culdees. They could not of course be actually *called* Culdees, nor wear our distinctive white cowls, nor could they be marked with the cross of ash on their foreheads. However, after you and Isolde marry, you can be the first members of this new movement. Now, how about that?'

'Oh, that's fantastic, Father! Thank you.'

Patrick tugged thoughtfully at his curly red beard. Then he said brightly, 'We'll call this new movement – after your good self – the Lay Benedictines of Good Tidings; the LBGTs for short.'

'Sounds very futuristic, Father! I think we and the Culdees might even change the flipping world!'

'Aye. But we must change ourselves first, my son, mustn't we?'

Benedictus laughed. 'Isolde will be over the moon! She *wants* to get married, you know. She said so.'

'I can imagine.'

'And she's an orphan. So all we need is the King's permission.'

'Right! It's all settled then,' Patrick said getting up. 'We'll have the wedding soon. And you may continue to wear the Culdee habit until then.'

'Thanks again, Father.'

A few nights later Patrick had a prophetic dream. In it he was walking through a gloomy wilderness. It was dusk.

Suddenly a flash of lightning split the sky spectacularly apart and through the crack a bejewelled blue chariot came rushing. It was drawn by a pair of prancing, gold-gleaming horses with silver manes. The wilderness lit up as the chariot descended. It drew alongside Patrick and stopped. The charioteer was a squat, dark-skinned young man, but beside him stood a tall and stately figure robed in a long garment of purest, snow-white wool. He stepped deftly out of the chariot. He looked very like Pelagius! His eyes blazed and he spoke in fiery words, 'Bring me the Spear of Initiation forthwith! Momentous things are happening in the world! Unless the Spear *immediately* passes through the Grail Flame, all will be lost.'

Patrick tried to say, 'Yes, I will,' but couldn't. The words stuck in his mouth like lumps of wet clay. He awoke still trying to speak. Once fully awake however he carefully reviewed the dream. Then the words in it came back clear as a bell. Momentous things! Whatever could they be? He got up. He would set off for the Temple with the Spear without delay.

It was early morning and nobody was about yet in the community. Patrick dressed quickly, wrapped the Spear in sackcloth for the journey and tied it securely to his back. Then he packed his satchel, fixed it to his belt, and, staff in hand, crept stealthily to Ignatius (who slept nearby in his own half-finished cell) to inform him of his departure.

'I'm not sure how long I'll be,' Patrick said after waking him.

'All right, Father,' Ignatius said yawning, 'but where are you off to this time?'

'I can't say. Sorry. And I suspect I will be away longer than usual.'

'Oh dear! It sounds like one of your mystery trips again!'

'You could say that.'

'Can it possibly have something to do with.........the Temple?' Ignatius cryptically enquired.

Patrick was shocked! He never spoke of the Temple or the Grail to his Culdees, or to anyone!

'What about the Temple?' he queried with slanted eyes.

'You disappear so often, Father, and no one knows where you are! Rumours are only to be expected. There's talk of some strange Temple in the south. That's all.'

After a brief reflection Patrick said, 'I can't say anything at the moment. I'm in a great hurry.'

'All right,' Ignatius said. 'But what's that odd looking thing on your back?'

Patrick put his hand on Ignatius's shoulder and looked him in the eye.

'I'll tell you *everything* when I get back,' he said solemnly, 'and that's a promise.'

'I'll hold you to it. I hate rumours.'

'And so do I. But my promise will have to suffice for the moment.'

'Thanks.'

'Look after my Culdees while I'm gone.'

'I will surely, Father.'

'Goodbye, my son.'

As usual when setting off for the Temple Patrick prayed fervently to Jesus. *Perhaps this time*, he prayed *I may be permitted to see the Grail.*

Soon the Dove appeared to guide him as it had done many times before. The journey this time however was different. Acutely conscious of the Spear on his back, Patrick had not travelled far when he noticed its weight increasing. At the same time his vision blurred and he had difficulty keeping the bird in sight. The weight continued to increase and several times he nearly fell under its burden. Once he even felt he could not continue. But the thought of the Grail kept him going.

Eventually the Temple came into view, and never was he happier to see it. With greatest difficulty he climbed the hillock to the door and was utterly relieved to find it ajar. He stumbled through, fell in a heap on the floor and immediately blacked out.

When some time later he came to he found himself sitting by the Temple wall on an armchair. His staff was leaning against the chair and Pelagius was standing in front of him holding the Spear of Initiation upright in his right hand.

'Congratulations, Brother,' the Saint said softly.

Patrick looked around and gave a deep sigh of relief. Then light-heartedly he said, 'You've got yourself a staff at last, Brother.'

Pelagius smiled and gazed proudly at the Spear. 'You could say that.'

'Is it heavy?' Patrick asked with irony.

'Not any more. Here, feel it.'

Patrick got up and took the Spear.

'As light as a feather!' he exclaimed.

'Indeed,' Pelagius said taking the Spear back. 'And watch this.'

He threw it up in the air where it floated magically for a moment before returning to his beckoning, outstretched hand.

'How on earth do you *do* that?' Patrick queried wide-eyed.

'I have already passed it though the Grail Flame! And there was not a moment to lose. Black priest-magicians in

Rome were trying to rob it of its power and nearly succeeded. But they didn't, did they?'

'Was that you or your Angel I saw in my dream?' Patrick enquired.

'In dreams what's the difference? However, I can tell you I prayed hard to my Angel recently that you'd bring me the Spear most urgently. If you had put it off a moment longer, believe me the Spear would have become far too heavy for you. Only the gods know what would've happened then.'

'Can you see your Angel?' Patrick asked.

'Sometimes.' The Saint threw the Spear up again and it hovered. 'But at the moment I can *feel* him more than see him.' - Pelagius tapped his forehead. – 'In here.' When the Spear returned to his hand he continued, 'Strength of thought. That's the hardest but most powerful part of the whole initiation process.'

'It was the thought of the Grail that got me here,' Patrick confessed.

'I believe you!'

'In the dream you, or maybe I should say your Angel, spoke of momentous events.'

'Yes. For my Angel has also revealed to me recently what is happening in the outside world. The Beast is rising rapidly.'

'The Beast? What Beast?'

'The Antichrist! The Evil One.'

'You mean the devil?'

'There are many devils, my Brother. Some of them temped Jesus, but he overcame them all. But now that he lives in his etheric, or *risen* form, only *one* of them is allowed to oppose him. That is the Sun Demon. His name is Sorath, and he has taken possession of a human called Mordred in Britannia.'

'Who is Mordred?'

'He is, and has always been, the arch-enemy of Arthur of the Britons. And, as you know from various conversations we have had here in the Temple, the future of our Grail movement depends a lot upon Arthur. Listen, Brother. The Catholic army has arrived in Britannia and has sided with this monster. And only this Spear can deal with *him*. So, will you now take this holy instrument to Arthur as you promised?'

Patrick took a deep breath. 'I will,' he bravely replied.

'Good. The spirit Dove as always will guide you. You must save Arthur of the Britons, for Jesus, for Hibernia and the Holy Grail.'

They embraced warmly.

'I think this may be your final test,' Pelagius said when they parted. 'Pass this and you will surely be allowed to drink from the sacred Vessel.'

CHAPTER THIRTY

THE BATTLE OF BADON.

As Lancelot promised, within a week of the landing of the Roman Catholic army on the Saxon Shore the various little units of Arthur's army scattered throughout Britannia had mobilized. Soon afterwards news was received that the invading army had joined forces with Hengist and Mordred and were marching north. It was the cue for Arthur and his men also to commence marching. Camelot then became a hive of industry as every available pair of hands was put to the service of the Knights as they prepared for battle.

'He'll be able to say dada by the time you return,' Guinevere said to Arthur when he came to say goodbye to her. Galahad was sucking her breast. Arthur was in full battledress, replete with blue-plumed, silver helmet, and the Sword of Light sheathed in Guinevere's exquisitely embroidered scabbard, at his side. He kissed her tenderly.

'Take care, Roman soldier,' she said humorously.

Arthur smiled. 'I merely use what they taught me,' he said, '....for the love of Logres.'

'You look magnificent, love. Come back safely!'

Arthur gripped the Sword. 'With every thrust I will be thinking of you.'

Guinevere nodded. 'And Galahad too. He's the future.'

Arthur kissed the baby's head.

'But listen carefully now to me, my dearest Guinevere,' he said. 'Whatever you do, don't venture outside the castle walls for one moment while I'm gone. Mordred, I'm certain, will have men watching the gate. We have heard that you are in grave danger of being abducted. If I don't return soon after the battle, leave with the baby by the secret postern gate. I have appointed a reliable man who will assist you and take you to a safe place. His name is Lamorak.'

'Oh, don't be so pessimistic, Arthur,' Guinevere chided. 'You'll win this battle.'

Arthur sighed. 'But without Merlin I.....I.... Oh, my dear, I'll miss him so much. I was so depending on him.'

'Good heavens! What's the problem?'

'I sent for him but he wouldn't come! It's the first time ever he refused. Clegis, my courier, said he was in bed and wouldn't get up. He wishes me all the best in Badon. Fat lot of good that'll do me!'

Guinevere gently touched the Sword. 'This will make up for him.'

'I'm not so sure any more. I've always depended on him.......on his magic, to some degree at least. Now I'll just have to *hope* for it I suppose. In any event the battle must go on. Farewell, my dear.'

Each of Arthur's twelve Knights had fifty men under him. Each Knight also had command of a number of the army's national units with which they liaised through local officers-in-charge. Lancelot coordinated all communications through an efficiently organized network of scouts who also supplied intelligence regarding the location, manoeuvres and movements of the advancing Catholic army.

There was cloud about, but the day was dry and fine when the 'Camelot division' marched out of Camelot. Each unit was headed by its own commanding Knight on horseback, with the supply wagons and carts taking up the rear.

They were about two days into their march towards Aquae Sulis when a scout appeared suddenly over a hill to the right of the company. He rode down and drew up alongside Arthur and Lancelot who headed the march. Handsome and mud-spattered, the youth was totally out of breath.

'This young man looks like he has news for us,' Arthur said good-humouredly to Lancelot.

Lancelot nodded and Arthur held his hand up, the signal to stop marching.

The scout rose in his saddle and bowed.

'Well,' Arthur said, 'out with it, lad.'

'Sire,' the scout said, 'the Catholics are not marching in the direction you anticipated.'

'What?' Arthur exclaimed. 'You mean they are not coming towards Sorbiodunum and Camelot?'

'No, Sire. At Venta they headed directly north towards Calleva.'

Arthur looked at Lancelot with astonishment. Lancelot was seriously studying the youth's muddy face. 'The whole army?' he questioned.

'Yes, Sire. I made sure of that. Before I left they were already a few miles on. It's not a decoy.'

'Good work, scout,' Arthur said. 'Freshen yourself up, get some fresh supplies, and return there as quickly as you can.'

'What do you make of it?' Arthur asked Lancelot when the march resumed.

'Very odd,' Lancelot replied.

'But at least they're going in the right direction..... *for us!*'

'Agreed.'

'But we won't know what's really happening until they get to Calleva. If they go for Corinium then, methinks our work will be much reduced.'

'Halved, Sire.'

'No! Quartered, Sir Lancelot! Quartered!'

At various pre-arranged junctures along the road to Aquae Sulis all of the national auxiliary units that had been so instructed, joined the Round Table division, so that Arthur's army grew gradually to almost twice its original size. Arthur's hope was that the enemy would believe this was his full strength. But it wasn't.

From the outset he knew he was going to be greatly outnumbered. Intelligence reports from Gaul had long indicated this. Therefore the element of surprise was vital. From his time in the Roman army he had learnt that a key element in all military strategy was to conceal one's true numbers from the enemy. For this reason, and confident that Merlin would be able to lure the enemy to Badon Hill, Arthur had instructed all his crack units to strategically locate and conceal themselves in the woods around Badon Hill. Many of these units were small, comprising no more than a few score men; but their discipline, intelligence and skill, as well as their expert marksmanship made them crucial in Arthur's overall strategy.

He was not far from Aquae Sulis when news arrived from Calleva that the Catholics had, as hoped, turned north-west towards Corinium.

'They are with us,' Arthur said teasingly to Lancelot, pointing to the sky.

'Who?' Lancelot dryly enquired.

'The gods.'

'Oh, them.'

Arthur shook his head in dismay. 'Dear Lancelot! You have such exemplary valour and courage! The men *so* look up to you, and yet you equivocate *eternally* about the gods! Don't you believe in *anything*?'

Lancelot flashed a grim smile. 'Sometimes,' he muttered. (He was of course thinking of Guinevere!)

From Aquae Sulis Arthur's army continued along the road towards Corinium. Near that ruined town further news arrived that the Catholic army had set up what looked like a fixed camp about a mile east of Badon Hill. Arthur immediately established camp himself in order to await the enemy's next move. But it soon became clear that the Catholics were not moving. It was then Arthur thought that a bit of Merlin's hoped-for, absentee magic was being delivered! For more and more it seemed that the enemy was trying to lure *him* to Badon, and not the other way round!

A few nights later in the camp, alone in his tall, spacious tent, Arthur drew the Sword of Light from its scabbard and stared at it pensively for a long time. Once again he contemplated this extraordinarily beautiful gift of Merlin, this *Treasure* of the Hibernians which was helping him so wonderfully in his efforts to realize his dream.

'It has the power of the Grail,' he mused aloud.

But what on earth was this Grail? Not even Merlin

knew! One thing was certain though: this Sword had been consecrated to the great cause of the Godman from Galilee, Jesus.

Though not a religious person, the more Arthur learnt of Jesus the more attracted to him he became. Nowadays he always brought his gospel book with him wherever he went. He took it now from his satchel, opened it at random and his eyes instantly fell on the verse: 'Jesus said, "I have come not to bring peace, but a sword." ' Arthur was startled! It was as if the book was speaking directly to him! He put it slowly down, grasped the Sword and thrust it firmly into the ground. Kneeling before it then as if it were the Cross of Christ he kissed the shining blade and was instantly filled with a fiery enthusiasm for battle.

This enthusiasm continued to grow, so much he couldn't sleep. Straightaway after sunrise he called Sir Kay and Sir Lancelot to his tent. After revealing his inspired state of mind to them he emphatically declared, 'So you see, gentlemen, I will never be more ready and eager to engage the enemy!'

Lancelot and Kay did not disagree and the rest of the twelve were immediately summoned to the tent. Arthur spread a map of Badon Hill on his table; the Knights gathered round, and for hours they discussed every aspect of the pending battle.

'Everything depends on what position they take up on the Hill,' Arthur said. He had to speak loudly for it had started to rain heavily and became noisy.

'*If* they take up positions,' Sir Kay shouted. 'Might not the bastards let us go up first?'

'I doubt it, Sir Kay,' Arthur returned, somewhat wearily. 'It wouldn't make sense.'

'Mordred *never* makes sense!' Gawain said with a laugh.

'That may be true,' Arthur said, 'but Hengist does! Look men. They're almost bound to move first, being nearest to the Hill. They will want to find and take up the best possible positions. *That* makes sense! We'll wait.'

A breathless young scout, saturated with rain, dashed into the tent and bowed.

'I suspect we might not have long to wait,' Lancelot said.

'Well, scout?' Arthur said.

'Sire,' the scout informed, 'the enemy have struck camp!'

'Wonderful!' Arthur exclaimed. 'Anything else?'

'A leading group exited the road just south of the Hill and went up it.'

'Any indication what position they are taking?'

'Yes, Sire. I waited for the first few men to arrive on the hilltop before I left, and I noted they were clearing ground to the west.'

'Excellent! You're a fine scout, boy. You'll make a good knight someday. Now get back to your post as quickly as you can.'

'My dear Sirs,' Arthur continued when the scout left, 'this is the best possible news!' – He pointed to a spot on the map. – 'They are taking up position here. It's the most likely one, because they will have the woods at their rear and left flank for cover, and also for possible retreat. However, it also means that my worst worry is assuaged, for it clearly indicates that they don't know about our woodsmen!'

He clapped his hands triumphantly.

'Woodsmen?' Kay queried.

'It's our code-word from now on for our units hidden in the woods.'

'I see,' Kay said, 'but do *they* know what's happening? For they'll not see very much from the bottom of the Hill, in the woods, will they?'

'Well, if they don't,' Arthur returned, 'they will pretty soon. Lancelot! Get word of these crucial developments to your officers-in-charge in the woods as quickly as you can. And also inform them that we'll be on the Hill by midday tomorrow, at the latest.'

Lancelot dashed out. Then after a quick, light meal with the rest of the Knights Arthur gave orders to strike camp.

Although the rain continued to pour relentlessly down, spirits were high. The division arrived on the plateau of Badon Hill ahead of schedule early the following morning. The sight that greeted them however was daunting. The Catholics were well placed and spread out panoramically at a distance.

The great brown mass of Germanus's sparsely armed monks, their rain-soaked cowls stuck to their young bodies, formed their front line, with Hengist's and Mordred's better armed men slightly behind them in two big but separated groups. Germanus, in full episcopalian regalia, galloped up and down on his big white carthorse, waving his crozier about and shouting at his monks to keep in line.

Arthur shuddered. He realized he was outnumber by at least seven to one!

A slight dip in the ground near the middle of the plateau made a natural battle-line. Arthur's division, under the expert direction of the Knights, quickly began angling themselves into coordinated phalanxes. The auxiliary units took up frontal positions to make or meet initial charges. From beyond the line the Catholics watched anxiously and became restless as the highly disciplined formation of Arthur's army silently and swiftly took shape.

Battle etiquette however, dictated that no aggressive moves be made until Arthur's army finalized its formation.

When it eventually did a tense, silent hiatus developed. But this soon came to an end when Germanus galloped out a short distance from his men, turned, stopped, closed his eyes and punched the air with his fist.

'Hallelujah!' now rose up, weakly at first, but with each new jab of Germanus's fist and each repetition of the cry it grew louder, filling Germanus's ears with this sweetest of all sounds and stirring his old loins into a divine, wrath-filled longing for victory. When the cry reached fever pitch he turned Caesar to face Arthur's army. Now he aimed his crozier directly at *it* and bellowed at the top of his croaky voice, 'Forward, my soldiers, for Jesus, for God and for Rome!'

The great roar of 'Hallelujah!' now seemed to rock the very ground as swarms of yelling, club-wielding monks surged forward. But it was all too much for Caesar! As the monks flashed passed, the old carthorse took fright, bolted, and up went the Archbishop! He landed, head first, on a big rock and cracked his skull wide open. Only a few of the charging monks noticed. These dragged him to the back of Mordred's men where Lupis, who had been excused from taking active part in the combat, was nervously watching the proceedings. Seeing his master dying, Lupis administered the Last Rites. Soon afterwards however he was surprised to see the Archbishop open his beady eyes and try to speak. Lupis put his ear to the old man's mouth.

'F....f.....fuck the Pelagians!' the Archbishop whispered.

Lupis frowned. 'Fuck, Your Grace?'

'A....a....an old Gnostic word.'

'Meaning?'

But to Lupis's chagrin the old man departed without explaining!

The battle-charge however carried relentlessly on, the mad monks waving their rusty swords and brandishing their blunt axes and clubs for Jesus and for Rome, to the ever rising roar of 'Hallelujah!' It was Romulus who now tried to guide them from his horse, but with little success.

Arthur's men were unsteadied at first by the battle-cry, but by the time the stampeding monks crossed the dip in the plateau they had regained their characteristic composure. The auxiliaries then sprang into action. Fanning neatly out into a long line, in perfect symmetry they rapidly covered exactly fifty paces. Then stopping suddenly, about half of them crouched behind their big, body-sized, barrel-shaped shields, forming a wall of solid bronze.

The monks tried heroically to hack their way through this, but were firmly held by the men behind the wall. Hundreds were killed instantly or severely wounded, and the rest soon ran back bleeding, many dropping on the way. The bronze wall followed at a distance, only stopping when the monks had all but melted back like brown mud into the black mass of Hengist's and Mordred's waiting and anxiously watching men.

At a given signal from Hengist, his men then made their move. Better armed than the monks, many with iron helmets, long sharp swords and strong wooden shields, they split into smaller groups and attempted to come at the wall of bronze from different angles. They began with no less bravery than the monks but had not gone far when a great shower of arrows poured down on them like hail! Scores of Hengist's men fell. Then another shower came. And another. It was only in the fourth shower that they realized what was happening. During the advance of the roaring monks the bowmen in the woods had crept up the Hill silently and unseen to do their valuable work. Some of Mordred's men then turned and chased them down the Hill. By now however the wall of bronze had bent into a neat curve while the tightly formed phalanxes of the Knights' men fanned out behind it. They then poured through carefully made gaps in the wall, decimating the disarrayed chargers and forcing them back.

It was Arthur's custom not to engage in hand-to-hand combat unless necessary. He and Lancelot were thus watching all these developments from a vantage point behind their own lines to the right of the main action.

'Mordred is wasting his time chasing the bowmen,' Arthur said to Lancelot.

'Aye, Sire,' Lancelot replied, 'and wasting his men too. For as soon as they get anywhere near the woods they'll be all taken out.'

'Many of the monks have already run into the woods,' Arthur observed.

'Yes, poor bastards. They would've been better off staying with the others.'

'Without that old bishop on the white horse they have no idea what to do, I suppose. That one who has taken over looks even older, and he's totally lost. Is he an old Roman General, d'you think?'

'Probably,' Lancelot replied. He pointed, 'But look how well our Gawain is doing.'

'Ah yes. I see. He's almost behind Mordred's main gang now. Excellent!'

The woodsmen now emerged in droves and attacked from every possible direction. The enemy was soon totally surrounded and in complete disarray. Arthur drew the

Sword of Light and held it out triumphantly towards the battlefield.

'Methinks,' he said to Lancelot, 'that this unpleasant business will be over by sunset.'

Gripped by a sudden urge to make a significant gesture of thanks to Jesus he added, 'I'm going to my tent for a little while. Stay here.'

Lancelot nodded.

On the battlefield Hengist soon got an arrow through his right thigh, tumbled ignominiously from his horse and was quickly dispatched to the other world by one of Arthur's men. After witnessing this from a distance Mordred pulled his mount away from the fighting altogether. In desperation he watched his men being thrashed like weeds as Arthur's army ploughed through them in intense hand-to-hand combat. He was about to quit the battlefield altogether when he heard an eerie, hollow voice: 'No, don't.'

He looked anxiously around at the sprawling mass of dead or dying bodies. The rain poured relentlessly down, yet in the gloom he soon spotted a strange, elongated shadow snaking its way through the bodies towards him. It stopped near the feet of his big stallion, its grotesque form oozing like black liquid from the blood-stained mud. Mordred's mount snorted and kicked at it.

After steading his mount Mordred tentatively asked, 'Sorath?'

'Who else?' the Shadow returned. 'The battle may be lost my friend, but the war must go on.'

'What the hell does that mean?' Mordred angrily retorted.

'You can still be King of the Britons!'

'How?'

'If you go to Arthur's tent you can kill him.'

Mordred grinned. 'He's in his tent right now?'

'Yes, praying I believe, ha, ha! You'll never have a better chance of ridding yourself of him for good. You can then high-tail it out of here and take your time regrouping. Just think about that.'

'But he has the Sword of Light!'

'I know. But move quickly and you can get him in the back before he draws. Come! I will show you.'

The Shadow slithered away towards the quiet eastern slope of the Hill and Mordred followed. Then after quickly skirting the Hill it stopped again.

'Do you see that big colourful tent up ahead there?' the Shadow asked.

'Yes,' Mordred replied.

'That's Arthur's. Your chance of a lifetime.'

Mordred dismounted quickly, tethered his horse to a nearby thorn and drew his sword.

He approached the tent surreptitiously from the side. A few paces from it however, Arthur suddenly emerged forcing Mordred to duck behind the tent. As Arthur went to mount his horse he spotted Mordred's and immediately drew his Sword. Cautiously he approached the tent again. Suddenly Mordred lunged at him from behind the tent brandishing his sword. For a few moments their swords clashed and clanged noisily. But a well-aimed strike by Arthur soon sent Mordred's weapon spinning away like a kitchen knife! Mordred ran to retrieve it. Arthur pursued. But he had only taken a few steps when to his astonishment he became stuck to the ground! Looking down he saw the grotesque Shadow oozing about his feet! 'So you thought you were invincible,' it said, 'ha, ha!'

Licking his leathery lips, his one eye bulging, Mordred

came forward again, gleefully slashing the air with his sword. He got behind Arthur, struck him viciously on his hand with his sword and the Sword of Light fell to the ground. Contemptuously, Mordred kicked it away.

'Do it quickly!' the Shadow commanded.

'I see you have friends in low places,' Arthur said with fatal humour.

Tauntingly, Mordred ran his sword all over Arthur's body.

'The head,' the Shadow cried, 'it must be cut off. Quickly! Do it!'

'B....better obey him,' Arthur said, trembling.

But Mordred took his time! He wanted to savour this moment. He thrust his sword into Arthur's side and Arthur stumbled to the ground. Greedily Mordred watched the blood flow. But by now the Shadow was gyrating crazily.

'There is no time to lose!' it roared.

Startled by the strength of the voice Mordred put his boot on Arthur's chest and raised his sword high.

'Jesus,' Arthur said softly, resigning his spirit.

As he said this however, he saw a light. It came from behind Mordred's head. At first he thought it was the sun. But as Mordred's sword reached its full height and was about to come down, it became clear to Arthur that the light was not from the sun. It actually came from a brilliantly shining white Spear that was travelling rapidly through the air, directly towards them!

Mordred's sword came down, but an instant before it made contact with Arthur's neck the Spear struck Mordred in the back! It went straight through his heart! Blood spurted from him in high black jets as the Shadow disappeared into him. He slumped forward and fell dead in a heap beside Arthur.

'Jesus,' Arthur kept repeating. 'Jesus. Jesus.'

He felt he was floating. *Perhaps it's all a dream!* he thought. Suddenly he saw a white figure approach, carrying a staff.

'Jesus,' Arthur whispered again as the man drew closer.

The man looked down compassionately on him.

'You must be Arthur of the Britons,' he said.

'I....I am,' Arthur said with difficulty, 'and...and you must be Jesus.'

The man smiled and shook his head.

'No,' he said, 'I am Patrick.'

Over the past few days the spirit Dove had been guiding Patrick! He had just arrived at the bottom of the Hill and was told by the Dove to fire the Spear. It took off magically from his hand at great speed and Patrick immediately ascended the Hill.

'Ah, so,' Arthur said, 'Pat....Patrick. Yes. I......I've heard m....much about you.'

Patrick jabbed his staff at Mordred. 'And this must be the Evil Beast.'

'That.......that's Mordred,' Arthur said.

'Indeed.'

Lancelot galloped up suddenly and dismounted. His grim satisfaction at the unexpected sight of Mordred's corpse dissipated once he saw the state of Arthur.

'What happened here?' he demanded of Patrick. 'Are you responsible?'

'I am,' Patrick replied, 'but it's a long story. First we must get your lord's wounds attended to, for I fear the one in his side is very serious.'

The blood oozed from Arthur's side.

'Is it painful?' Lancelot asked.

'V....very,' Arthur weakly replied.

'Get your doctor,' Patrick said. 'When the wounds are dressed and he is back in his tent I'll tell you everything.'

Lancelot galloped away to the battlefield where the battle was almost over. He quickly located Mark, the army doctor, who though busy with his relatively few casualties immediately left them and came with his equipment to Arthur. After stemming Arthur's bleeding, with Lancelot's help he carefully positioned Arthur on a stretcher. Lancelot then placed the Sword of Light alongside him. They were about to carry him into the tent when Patrick said, 'Wait!'

He pulled the Spear from Mordred's back and after cleaning it with grass laid it beside the Sword. Then they carried Arthur away.

'The wound in the side is very serious,' the doctor quietly informed Lancelot outside Arthur's tent after he had dressed the wounds, 'but, thank the gods, he won't die. Now, I must get back to the battlefield, but I'll return as soon as I can.'

Although Arthur could hardly speak he remained fully conscious.

'Now f....friend, you m...must tell us your mir... .miraculous st.....story,' he said to Patrick when Lancelot re-entered the tent.

And so Patrick told them all that had recently happened and also the long story of how the Spear was so intimately connected with Jesus and the great mystery of the Grail. Arthur smiled throughout. When the story was finished, with great difficulty he gestured to Lancelot to come closer. Lancelot put his ear to his mouth.

'This m....man will make a g....good Christian of you,' he whispered.

But Lancelot wept. Never before did he feel such guilt.

CHAPTER THIRTY-ONE

'I AM JESUS!'

'The ancient Greeks,' Pelagius said, 'believed that their gods drank ambrosia, the ethereal elixir of life. And this precisely is what the Grail contains. For, many times Jesus said, "I Am the Life". He gives his godlike, magical *Self* to all who believe in him.'

Pelagius was talking to Patrick. They were in the Grail Temple standing in front of the Tabernacle. Although Patrick fully intended to soon return the sacred Spear to Morganna as he promised, after leaving Britannia he had come first to the Temple, for now at last, his task with the Spear successfully accomplished, he hoped he would be able to see the Grail.

'I believe in Jesus!' Patrick emphatically declared.

'Oh, of that there is no question, Brother,' the Saint replied. 'But belief has many levels. In order to *see* the Grail, belief must be imbued with gnosis, *knowledge*. You must really *know* Jesus, not just in your head, but in your *heart*. It's the eye of the heart that sees the Grail. That's what I mean.'

'I think I know Jesus in my heart too,' Patrick hopefully returned.

'Well, only *you* can tell that.'

'You said, Brother, if I successfully performed my task with the Spear I would see the Grail.'

'Oh, come now! I don't think I was *so* prescriptive. Anyway, I am not the one who decides such secret things. You think far too highly of me, Brother!'

'Who decides then?'

Pelagius pointed to the little white Dove who was perched above the golden door of the Tabernacle.

'Her,' he said. 'The Spirit decides.'

Patrick contemplated the lovely little shining Dove, then in a sudden burst of holiness he resolutely declared, 'If I see the Grail, I'll conquer the whole of Hibernia for Jesus! Ask her. Tell her that.'

'Ah, but look, Brother,' Pelagius quickly returned, 'I think she hears you.'

The Dove spread her wings, flew down in front of the Tabernacle and with her yellow beak tapped three times on its golden door. Immediately it began to open, and a light, brighter than the sun poured from the interior. When the door was fully open and the Dove had flown back to her perch above it, Pelagius whispered, 'I think you should go in.'

Patrick gave his staff to the Saint, joined his hands prayerfully, and after taking a long deep breath slowly entered the Tabernacle. The door closed silently behind him. He was very nervous. At first all he saw was light, an infinite sea of pure, white, penetrating light, but he was not dazzled. He seemed to be floating. He felt almost unbearably light. After a while a yellow point began to crystallize in the distance before him. It expanded slowly and pulsated like a living organism. New colours began to interweave the yellow, iridescent and wonderfully pure colours. Eventually all the colours formed into a very distinct shape: a fabulously beautiful Chalice! When this began to move slowly towards Patrick he sensed the presence of an immense but invisible Being. The Chalice eventually stopped directly in front of Patrick's face and tilted slightly. Instinctively he put his lips to it and drank. No words could describe what he felt then. One thought alone consumed all others: *This is how a god feels.*

After this the Chalice withdrew slowly and eventually dissolved back into the pure white light. Not of his own volition then, but as if the invisible Being was gently guiding him, Patrick turned and walked out of the Tabernacle. The door closed silently behind him.

Pelagius was beaming and holding a bright red rose. 'You're a new man,' he said handing Patrick the rose.

'I feel like Jesus,' Patrick said distractedly as he took the rose.

'You are a Christ!' Pelagius declared.

'What's this?' Patrick asked looking at the rose.

'It's a symbol of you now having a share in the subtle body of Jesus the Christ. Congratulations, Brother. You're a Grail Initiate!'

'This might take a bit of getting used to,' Patrick said. 'I feel weak.'

'Here,' Pelagius said handing Patrick his staff, 'strike the ground firmly with it.'

Patrick struck the ground with his staff.

'How's that?' Pelagius asked.

Patrick shook his head.

'Again,' Pelagius urged.

Patrick struck the ground again. After the third strike he said, 'I think I feel stronger now.'

'Good,' the Saint said. 'Your mission to the Hibernians is about to enter a great new phase.'

'Tell me more, Brother.'

'While you were in the Tabernacle I had a tremendous flash of inspiration as to how we're actually going to defeat the insidious snake-worshippers, and, if it comes to it the Catholics too!'

'I'm all ears.'

The Saint took two chairs from the wall and they sat down.

'You probably don't know this,' Pelagius said, 'but the Catholics have recently introduced a powerful new public ritual in Gaul which they call the Mass. They are gaining a lot of followers through it. It's a ritual derived from the Last Supper Jesus had with his Apostles where, with our Grail, he performed the miracle of turning bread and wine into his body and blood.'

'Oh yes, I've read about that in the gospel!' Patrick declared. 'Surely it's the most powerful mystery in the whole world!'

'Indeed. It is the key to all mysteries.'

'So what's your great inspiration?'

'I propose to inaugurate the Grail Mass!'

'Aha!'

'With *you* as the first celebrant!'

'Oh! And what about you?'

'It can't be me! My presence here in Hibernia, like this Temple, *must* remain a secret. The Grail has too many enemies. However, the Grail Mass will be a public event.'

'You are not making sense, Brother! How the devil can the Grail remain a secret when there is a public Grail Mass?'

'Well, firstly, we don't have to publicly call it the *Grail* Mass, do we?'

'The Gaelic Mass then!'

'Why not!'

'And secondly?'

'As you have just found out, how the Grail is seen is not in my or any mortal's hands. We must allow the Angels to determine how the Quest is ultimately to be achieved. So, because we cannot use the actual Grail in the Mass we must make a replica of it.'

'Aha! And do you mean of crystal?'

'Not necessarily. It could be of precious metal.'

Patrick sat back and thought. After a while he said, 'There is a young silversmith working in my community in Dal Riada who makes very beautiful things for Jesus.'

'Then have him make a most beautiful Grail Chalice for Jesus!'

'I will indeed, first thing I get back.'

'And my inspiration is also that we should have the first Grail Mass on the holy island of Avallliona.'

'I see. But....but....Morganna. What about her?'

'Oh, I think when you tell Morganna of Jesus's deep connection with her Spear and how it actually saved her dear brother's life she won't object.'

'Indeed.'

'And when you further tell her that the sacred apple tree of Avalliona grew from the staff of one Josephus of Aramathea, a personal friend of Jesus, she might even become a Christian!'

Patrick smiled. 'But there's also the Druids to think about. If we are going to use the Grail Mass to propagate faith and belief in Jesus all over Hibernia, their approval will be needed, won't it? MacSaggart is already vehemently opposed to us.'

The Saint shook his head. 'Whatever about MacSaggart, when the Druids in general hear of Jesus's connection with their Spear, it can only enhance their ancient Hibernian mysteries. They'll come round to us, don't fear.'

'What about Merlin! He might be a problem.'

'No. I don't think so. His day is nearly done.'

'My mind is boggling,' Patrick said.

'For Jesus, I hope. What are you thinking?'

'If we can get the Sword of Light to Avalliona for the Mass, the *Four Treasures of Hibernia* will be present, albeit one of them a replica.'

'Excellent idea! Jesus, after all, is now the Lord of the Elements, the Spirits of which are channelled through these magic talismans.'

Patrick sniffed the rose. Suddenly he started prancing about like an April fool!

'I suspect,' the Saint said in his customary calm, 'that you are receiving some good inspiration about the Grail Mass.'

Patrick stopped. 'I am surely. What would you say to the first Grail Mass also being a wedding feast, like Cana?'

Pelagius frowned. Then brightening he said, 'Well, basically I like the idea. But what, pray, have you in mind? I hope you're not thinking of getting married yourself!'

Patrick laughed. 'Oh no, no. God forbid! My appetite has always been for one body only, the body of Our Lord, an appetite which this day has increased a thousand fold. No, Brother; but there is in my congregation in Dal Riada a beautiful boy and girl who are deeply in love, and I can think of nothing more perfect than that their knot be tied at this first Grail Mass.'

'Sounds absolutely splendid!' the Saint said. 'We will make it the centrepiece of the entire event, the sacrament of consummation, eh? But now, dear Brother, to business. We have to work out the details of our new ritual. I feel it will enhance your Christ power enormously. In fact I truly believe that through this sacred feast you, Patrick, will go down in history, not just as Father of your beautiful Culdee children, but as the Father of all Hibernia, nay perhaps of the whole of Christian civilization. Come, let us go to my house.'

CHAPTER THIRTY-TWO

THE GRAIL MASS

There was an apiary attached to the Grail Temple, and the candles used in various Temple rituals were made from the wax produced by its bees, a remarkably slow-burning wax. After blessing one of these candles the Saint lit it from the Grail Flame, put it in a sturdy lantern and gave it to Patrick. It was just before he left for Avalliona with the Spear of Initiation.

'This Flame,' Pelagius said, 'cannot go out provided you pray fervently before it every day. You may make copies of it, as many as you need for your growing mission. I will send you more candles as you require them. But I must warn you: be careful. This Flame will attract all sorts of men *and* spirits, including demons and murderers. And you and your followers will need to *love* them all. That's the hardest part! But love is the only thing that will overcome the growing darkness, and unite all the Children of the Light in the one true God.'

Thanking the Saint profusely for his gifts, his guidance and his blessings, Patrick left the Temple then and, directed as always by the shining white Dove, made his way first to Dunseverick. He stayed there overnight in the castle and next day King Fergus put one of his finest ferrymen at his disposal, so that Patrick was able immediately to make the crossing to Avalliona.

As Pelagius confidently predicted, Morganna was deeply impressed by all the new and wonderful things she learnt from Patrick about the holy Spear.

He told her these things in the Temple of the Virgins while standing in front of its big black marble altar on which the Spear had just been replaced. However, when a little later Patrick spoke of his deep desire to inaugurate on Avalliona a new ritual dedicated to the mystery and memory of Jesus which he wanted to call the Grail Mass, Morganna hesitated.

'And what, may I ask, is the Grail?' she said.

In reply Patrick held up the lantern with the Grail Flame. He took out the candle.

'Here,' he said, 'just try to blow this out.'

Puzzled, Morganna puffed at the Flame, but to no avail.

'Harder,' Patrick said.

Morganna then took a long deep breath and blew again. But no matter how hard she tried, the Flame would not go out.

'Even if you stamp on it,' Patrick said, 'it won't go out.'

Morganna cupped her hands around the Flame.

'And it has a most curious sensation,' she said, 'cold and hot in perfect balance. Is this the Grail?'

'No,' Patrick replied, 'only a wonderful sign of it. But before I continue I would very much like your permission to place it on the Lia Fail.'

'If you wish,' Morganna said and they went down the steps to the Lia Fail which was in its usual spot on the floor directly in front of the altar. Patrick placed the candle reverently on the flat white Stone and stood back. Immediately the whole Temple shook! Morganna's hands flew to her mouth but Patrick closed his eyes and a deep, soothing voice resounded throughout the Temple. It spoke just one word: 'Y-E-S.'

When all became quiet again Patrick opened his eyes, smiled, and put his hand on Morganna's shoulder.

'I think,' he said reassuringly, 'the Stone approves of the Grail.'

'Oh, please tell me what the Grail is!' Morganna pleaded.

Patrick then told her the whole story of Josephus and the Grail. She listened with growing awe and wonder, and when he went on to tell her the origin of her sacred apple tree he knew he had won her completely.

'Patrick,' she said, 'you are the most enlightening man I've ever met. I have puzzled over very many things in my life, but most especially that tree.'

'Perhaps you will call it the "Jesus Tree" from now on. Jesus said, "I am the Tree of Life." '

Morganna smiled. 'I shall certainly consider it. And you may have your Grail Mass here. Shall my Virgins help you?'

'Oh yes, of course High Priestess. I'm sure they will be most useful.'

When Patrick returned to his community the following day he got to work like never before. He first revealed his plans to Benedictus who was overjoyed. Then in a very special gathering of all the Culdees he carefully instructed them regarding the crucial importance for the future of Christianity of what was about to happen in Avalliona. He also sent a message to Arthur telling him how he prayed daily for his recovery. But he also informed him of his plans for the new Jesus ritual and of his fervent hope that the Druids' famous Sword might play a part in its inauguration. If the Sword of Light was present, Patrick said, it would undoubtedly enhance the white magic power of Jesus in Hibernia, and Britannia too.

Patrick also had many long and deep conversations with King Fergus who warmed ever more to the one he now called King Jesus. So fired indeed by Jesus did Fergus become that he actually dismissed MacSaggart as his chief Druid! No other king in Hibernia had ever dared do such a thing! The Druids from time immemorial appointed the king's chief Druid, and he was expected to take the Druid's advice on all matters before making *any* decisions. But becoming increasingly irritated with MacSaggart's opposition to Patrick's work, in the heat of an argument one day with MacSaggart while Patrick was actually present, the King looked at Patrick and suddenly said, 'And *you* are now my chief Druid.'

Patrick was astounded but pleased. Predictably, MacSaggart objected vehemently. He began to quote from memory long tracts from ancient law books which, he claimed, indisputably invested a Druid with a power and authority greater than a king. Fergus listened, patiently at first, but became increasingly impatient with MacSaggart's obscurity and eventually cut him short. 'I can't fathom any further what you are saying,' he declared. 'You've lost me completely. I am sticking to my decision. From now on I am only going to listen to Patrick and quotes from his little book.'

Seething to his depths, MacSaggart slunk away.

So emboldened did Fergus become through this courageous act that he decided soon afterwards to take advantage of an ancient but little used privilege he possessed as King to convene a concave of all the Druids of Dal Riada. Moreover, he insisted that he himself preside. The dismissal of MacSaggart was by the time of the gathering common knowledge, so that the atmosphere at it was very tense. Fergus first informed the Druids that while he would continue to respect their privilege, power and knowledge, nowadays he considered Patrick his chief adviser in all matters specifically to do with religion in Dal Riada. This was greeted with loud gasps, boos and hisses. A long debate ensued in which many of the Druids, young and old, voiced their forebodings and dealt ominous admonitions to the King. Fergus however, remained undaunted and eventually halted the debate, insisting that Patrick himself be heard.

Having by now spent many years in Hibernia, Patrick had by this time gained much knowledge of the Druids, of their ancient, peculiar habits and difficult manners. He stood before them now therefore not only with knowledge and authority but also with confidence. After a few diplomatic pleasantries he began to talk in general terms about their famous *Treasures.* He knew that this was a subject not only dear to their hearts, but also the constant focus of their long meditations, and the very touchstone of their well-known magical prowess. He prophesied that their missing Sword would one day be returned to them and the tactic helped ease the tension. And when Patrick went on to tell them how their Spear of Initiation had, quite unknown to them, become intimately connected with the Mystery of Jesus they began to see both Patrick himself and his God in a new light. For here was meat indeed to fatten their already rich mysteries and give a new impetus to their ancient ways of spiritual initiation.

Although Patrick said very little at this gathering of the Chalice of Rebirth, it was in this roundabout yet courageous way King Fergus achieved for Patrick the intended outcome: the Druids would not object to the celebration of the special ritual feast in memory of Jesus.

Immediately afterwards Patrick decided on midsummer's day for the Mass's inauguration.

The weather turned warm and dry as the day approached. In the fields, ditches and hedges around the Culdee settlement, wild roses, meadowsweet and bright yellow gorse were richly blooming and all day long gentle breezes carried their delicious scents into the community. The Culdees themselves were busy preparing for the wedding. Benedictus naturally was excused this labour, which meant that he spent these long days doing little except deeply inhaling the air like heavenly incense.

About halfway along the narrow cliff path that linked Dunseverick castle to the Culdee community there was a soft mossy bank where walkers often sat to rest on their journey. A few days before the ceremony Benedictus arranged to meet Isolde there in the evening. When he arrived the sun had just set. He found Isolde sitting on her hunkers, chin on her knees. She had a sprig of apple-blossom in her hair and wore a green summer dress with a dark woollen shawl over her shoulders. She was gazing out dreamily over the glassy calm water.

She looked up and smiled when she saw Benedictus. He kissed her tenderly on the forehead and sat down. For a long time they said nothing. Dusk descended. Then a crescent moon rose slowly in the east, and for a while sailed like a celestial boat of light along the dark horizon. Soon afterwards magnificent Venus rose and followed the moon as she climbed ever higher the celestial stairway. One by one other stars came out.

Benedictus lay back, and with knitted fingers under his head said dreamily, 'The Druids call that up there the floor of heaven.'

Isolde smiled and lay her head on his breast.

'And what does Father Patrick say?' she asked.

'About what?' Benedictus asked, stroking her hair.

'About us.......and the stars.'

'He says that the Druids say we all come from the stars.'

'And what do you say?'

'And what do I say, about what Patrick says, about what the Druids say, about what Jesus says, about....about....?'

Benedictus grabbed her playfully and turned her over.

'I can't wait,' he said fingering her soft lips.

'You'll have to,' she teased, biting his finger.

'Father Patrick says so?'

'Yes.' She sat up. Squinting at the sea she asked, 'Can you see Avalliona from here?'

'Sometimes,' Benedictus replied, 'and the Druids say that if you listen carefully you can hear the music of the stars.'

'Music only makes me sad,' she said with a sigh.

Benedictus laughed, pulled her down and kissed her. Once again he was transported to the warmest, sweetest place he ever knew.

'I love you, Benny,' she said softly, 'but I have to go.'

'Why?' he asked.

'The castle gates are closing soon.'

'To hell with the gates!' he said and kissed her again.

But when his kisses became more passionate she began to resist him and he let her go.

The next day a courier arrived in the community, all the

way from Camelot. He carried with him a carefully wrapped, securely tied bundle and immediately sought out Patrick. When Patrick saw the bundle he was elated. It was the Sword of Light! The courier also delivered a written message in which Arthur wished Patrick every success in his mission but also expressing the hope that because of the Sword's powerful ability to inspire strength and moral courage in his Knights, it might be returned to him soon.

Thanking the courier profusely and assuring him that Arthur's wishes would be fully met, Patrick sent the courier on his way.

Never was Patrick so excited! The weather remained fine and settled, and the following morning the Culdees, like a great flock of white sea-birds, set out for Avalliona in a flotilla of coracles from the little jetty near Dunseverick castle. King Fergus put one of his longboats and its crew at the disposal of Patrick, who together with Benedictus, Isolde, and various supplies went at the head of the flotilla. The King himself, who was to be the most important guest at the event, would arrive on midsummer's morning itself, weather permitting, in his own big, canopied sailboat, together with his family and harpist.

Because the weather held up so nicely Patrick wanted to have the Mass in the open air. Morganna however was reticent about this, primarily she said because the Lia Fail had, in her memory, never been outside the Temple. But Patrick, arguing that the gods were obviously blessing the very special event with such a lovely sun (and it would be unwise to ignore them!), eventually persuaded her. Straightaway then he ordered that the big block of black marble that was the altar of the Temple of the Virgins be moved outside. This, with great excitement and much sweat, was soon done by a group of enthusiastic young Culdees. Patrick directed them to a flat piece of raised ground behind the sacred grove from where the blue ocean could be clearly seen.

All of the small population of the island was invited to the Mass. They were told to come early. On midsummer morning the white sun rose majestically in a cloudless sky. People of all ages came, and a few specially appointed Culdees, acting under Patrick's instructions, kept them well back from the altar. They stood around in little groups, sat on the grass or on rocks, chatting, wondering what was about to happen. When eventually the red sails of the King's boat were spotted out at sea the Culdees ordered the people into a standing column vertical to the altar with an aisle in the middle. Soon afterwards the rest of the white-cowled Culdees came in procession and stood in a horizontal line directly in front of the altar, facing it. This meant that the whole arrangement took the form of a cross.

All then stood in silence, respectfully awaiting the King.

When he eventually arrived with his family and his harpist at the little jetty of Avalliona they were escorted with due courtesy by two appointed Culdees to special seats near the altar. Morganna then appeared. Ceremoniously attired in a long robe of scarlet silk she carried the Lia Fail on a bright yellow cushion. Behind her were two of her blue-veiled Virgins carrying horizontally on their bare outstretched arms, the Spear of Initiation and the shining Sword of Light. Behind them the rest of the Virgins, all veiled, walked in silent procession.

When Morganna reached the big black altar she reverently placed the white Stone in the centre of it. Then after putting the cushion on the grass she took the Spear and the Sword from the Virgins and placed them either side of the Stone. All of the Virgins then arranged themselves semi-circularly, creating a blue halo behind the altar with Morganna at the centre.

Patrick then arrived. He had on a bright new white cowl girded by a blue cord that was knitted for him by the Virgins and presented to him earlier in the morning, in honour of the special occasion. He carried his staff in one hand and the Grail Flame in the other. He walked very slowly. Behind him came Ignatius, lovingly holding the little green-bound Grail book of John. Behind him were two more Culdees side by side. One carried the chalice which had been specially made for the Mass by Oisean, the silversmith of the community. It was beautifully crafted from finest silver with rubies, emeralds and diamonds, donated from the King's private collection, inset in a filigree rim below the lip. Around its middle, in three equidistant places, was elaborately engraved the words, 'I Am.' It was filled with golden apple juice specially pressed for the occasion by the Virgins from the apples of their sacred tree. The other Culdee behind Ignatius carried reverently in his outstretched palms a tiny loaf of white bread which also had been baked by the Virgins.

Upon arriving at the altar Patrick went behind it to face the congregation. Ignatius joined him. Patrick then handed his staff to Ignatius and carefully placed the candle in the centre of the Lia Fail. The Flame jumped up! Never did it shine so brightly! Patrick then took the book from Ignatius and placed it beside the Flame. Ignatius rested the staff on the cushion on the grass and joined the line of Culdees facing the altar.

The two Culdees behind Ignatius then approached Patrick who took the chalice and the bread from them and also placed them on the Lia Fail. When these Culdees had also joined their colleagues Patrick looked up to heaven, closed his eyes and prayed silently for a while. Then he opened the book and read aloud its first few lines.

'In the beginning was the Word, and the Word was with God, and the Word was a god.'

He then took the Sword in his right hand and raised it high. The crowd gasped. The sun was so powerfully reflected in the Sword that many people had to look away.

Patrick declared: 'Behold the Light of the World.'

After a few moments he replaced the Sword and lifted the Spear. This elegantly beautiful object was met with a sublime silence. He held it over the chalice and prayed. Soon a little drop of ruby red liquid appeared on the Spear's golden tip and fell into the full chalice. Patrick wondered how many people witnessed the beautiful little miracle!

After replacing the Spear he took the bread in his hand, raised it and said aloud, 'In this bread, O Lord, let there live all the travail and suffering of the world, for love of which you died.'

He replaced the bread, lifted the chalice and continued, 'And into this chalice let there be poured all the crushed fruits of the earth this day.'

He then replaced the chalice and looking up to heaven raised his hands, crying, 'Accept, O gracious Lord, this universal host which the whole of creation, moved by love for you, presents to you at this new dawn.'

He then broke the bread, ate most of it and drank most of the juice.

Soon afterwards mysterious aeolian sounds were heard wafting through the morning air. People looked around and whispered that the fairies were coming! But it was Fergus's harpist who had begun to play.

The soft sea breezes carried the music enchantingly towards Benedictus and Isolde as they emerged from the sacred grove. Hand in hand, smiling shyly, but secretly ecstatic, they walked slowly up the aisle toward the altar. Benedictus had on a long brown woollen trews, tucked into new, black, leather ankle-boots and a pale green linen tunic. Isolde wore a long white cotton dress of simple design which she made herself. She also had a little wreath of summer flowers in her hair that was made by her servant colleagues in the castle where she had worked since childhood.

When Isolde and Benedictus arrived at the altar Patrick blessed them and said, 'Will you be faithful to one another always?'

In unison they replied, 'We will, Father.'

Then he broke the small piece of leftover bread and gave it to each of them. When they had eaten it he gave them the chalice and they finished the juice.

'In the eyes of the Lord Jesus,' Patrick said, 'I now pronounce you married for life. Keep your promise to the Lord.'

'Thank you, Father,' Benedictus said. 'We will.'

'You may kiss the bride,' Patrick said.

As Benedictus and Isolde made their way back down the aisle, many of the Culdees laughed and some of the Virgins cried, but all of the crowd applauded.

AUTHOR'S AFTERWORD

As the Saint had predicted, the enactment and continued celebration of the Grail Mass greatly enhanced Patrick's Christ power. He became almost like the original Apostles after their divine Master's Resurrection and Ascension into the higher worlds. A life-force took hold of him that actually became visible to many people as a soft halo of light radiating from his head.

This tremendous life-giving force however needed to be brought under the control of Patrick's ever-strengthening will. It demanded direction and focus. And the Naasenes provided it.

From his very first encounter with these devilish worshippers of Lucifer, Patrick hated them with a vengeance. And the more he heard of their progress in subsequent years the greater his hatred became. Filled with his new Christ power he set himself the task of absolutely ridding the whole of Hibernia of them.

His initial step was to confront their ringleaders, Palladius and Vivian. Protected by the blessing of King Fergus, with twelve specially chosen companions he set off south. The exotic couple quickly learnt however, that they were being pursued by a powerful northern 'Druid' who was determined to put an end to their cult, and they did their best to avoid him. But their best was not enough! Patrick eventually caught up with them.

He dealt with Palladius first. A great 'biblical style' contest took place between the two mages. Inevitably, Palladius's little white wand was no match for Patrick's powerful staff. Against this arch serpent-worshipper the staff of Christ proved omnipotent. Vivian hid from it like a terrified wildcat! But he raised it against her too. And with a series of powerful passes and prayers he banished the blasphemous couple from the land without further ado.

Vivian ran back to Britannia, her impishly seductive charms dissolving with every step. She quickly became haggard and witch-like. But she made an honest effort to honour her pledge to Merlin (to tell him what she learnt about the Naasenes in Hibernia), and sought him out. When however she got to his hut in the Forest of Elfham she found it derelict and abandoned. The skeleton of Merlin's donkey was the only trace of him she found. In conversations with peasants beyond the Forest she heard only garbled stories of him. Although some thought Merlin had died, others said he had been sucked by some powerful spirit into a stone somewhere in distant Cambria, where he still 'lived' awaiting a propitious time to 'return'.

Palladius made his way slowly back East. In Alexandria he got involved in a sect who unashamedly worshipped Satan and thereby sacrificed his saving link with Jesus forever. He went mad in the end.

Palladius and Vivian had of course set up 'congregations' all over the south of the island, and Patrick did not rest until he cleansed the land of every trace of these. He diligently sought out each Naasene enclave and dealt with it boldly and bravely. His technique was to go covertly with one or two companions to their gatherings, and at an appropriate moment interrupt their blasphemous rituals. Then after strenuously denouncing their leaders he would raise his staff against them uttering long and powerful incantations.

Miracles occurred! If, for instance, the group failed to disperse, Patrick would sometimes strike its officiating priest dumb with his staff. Very stubborn ones he even struck dead! Most of the ordinary congregation usually ran for their lives, thinking Patrick some kind of new and fiercely powerful Druid. But some stayed in order to learn more.

Patrick's reputation quickly grew. People flocked to see and hear him. Many of them he touched on the forehead with his staff saying, 'Receive Holy Spirit.' In this way hundreds of Christian congregations, and scores of Culdee life-communities, all modelled on the first 'cowshed' one in Dal Riada, sprang up throughout Hibernia.

Arthur's wound never healed. Nevertheless soon after the Battle of Badon he was crowned King of the Britons. The ceremony was performed by Morganna in Avalliona in the traditional manner of the Dal Riada kings, that is, while Arthur stood on the Lia Fail. He reigned for many years as a wounded but much loved King, his dream of Logres at long last realized. Arthur's reign actually inaugurated a 'golden era' in Britannia, a time of peace and prosperity that was never afterwards equalled.

Overcome with guilt at the sight of Arthur's wound at the Battle of Badon, Lancelot ended his affair with Guinevere. He tried to assuage his guilt by taking up the Grail Quest. It was said he travelled all over Hibernia, where he eventually died, without however, finding the Grail.

After the Battle of Badon, Guinevere dedicated herself entirely to Arthur's care. But she never told him the truth about Galahad. When Arthur himself died he was buried in Avalliona. At the time Galahad was an extraordinarily handsome young man. Only then did Guinevere tell him the truth of his parentage. He received it stoutly and vowed to follow in his father's footsteps.

Soon after Arthur's death the Round Table dispersed. Many of the Knights then, like Lancelot, went on the Grail Quest, but only Galahad found it.

Inspired both by Camelot and the teachings of Pelagius, in different parts of Britannia monastic-type communities were set up for men and women. Guinevere joined one of these where she became a very dedicated and pious follower of Jesus.

Before he died Arthur renamed the Sword of Light 'Excalibur' in memory of Guinevere. He derived the name from the Gallic word 'escalberc', referring to the Sword's scabbard, for which Guinevere had embroidered a most exquisite sheath. The Sword was returned to Hibernia when Arthur died where the Druids, who by that time were mostly Christians, sometimes allowed it to be used together with the Lia Fail and the sacred Spear in the Grail-inspired Gaelic Mass.

In time the Culdees and the Druids became indistinguishable. The Culdees adopted the half-moon tonsure of the Druids and the Druids adopted the white cowls of the Culdees. New Christian schools were established all over the island in which the two groups combined and shared their knowledge. A distinct Gaelic/Christian culture emerged from the old pagan order. New festivals were inaugurated for the general public.

The true story of the Grail was of course initially only imparted by Patrick to specially chosen followers, usually ex-Druids, twelve of whom always accompanied him as his closest disciple. The Grail knowledge was preserved by word of mouth and handed down in an initiatory fashion through Patrick's apostolically appointed successors. Inevitably however, bits of the story seeped out. For instance, it was well known that Lancelot had once been in Hibernia seeking the mysterious object. It was also said that a Mystery Temple existed somewhere in Hibernia but was underground. In later times it was said that the ethereal object of Lancelot's Quest was guarded by the 'Angel of Avalliona'.

These stories however, merely reflected the truth that after the inauguration of the Gaelic Mass Patrick himself was never again able to find the Temple or speak to the Saint 'in the flesh.' Nonetheless Pelagius's 'Angel' came regularly to him in dreams and continued to inspire and instruct him in the mysterious ways of the Grail.

In the decades after Patrick died, a Gaelic or so-called Celtic Church grew up in Hibernia utterly different in character to, and totally separate from, the Roman Catholic Church which even by the time of Patrick, had declined into a very worldly institution, concerned far more with material gain and temporal power than the promotion of Christian spirituality.

In Gaul, where the Franks proved the most powerful of the invading barbarian tribes, Arianism was widespread and actually posed a threat to the very survival of the Roman Church. Rome counteracted this by supporting the obscure Frankish dynasty founded by Merovee. The kings of this dynasty claimed a bloodline dating back to a boy child of Mary Magdalene. This was the woman who in the gospels kissed the feet of Jesus, washed them with her tears, and dried them with her long red hair; and the dynasty in question became known as the long-haired Merovingians. More astonishingly, they claimed that Jesus was the father of Mary's child, the birth however occurring long before Jesus's utter transfiguration by John the Baptist in the river Jordan.

Of course, the clerical establishment in Rome found this claim both astonishing and blasphemous. But not all of it by any means! In fact, in collusion with highly placed Roman clerics a secret movement was inaugurated in which the alleged bloodline of the Merovingians was used in a kind of occult propaganda promoting them as having a 'divine right' to rule over *all* Frankish tribes. And the propaganda worked! For, after the conversion of the powerful Clovis to Catholicism, Arianism was soon rooted out, the Merovingians thereafter were all Roman Catholics, and the foundation was thus laid for the inquisitional Holy Roman Empire of the Middle Ages. This conversion of the Merovingians was also the beginning of the so-called 'Divine Right of Kings', a doctrine which merely encouraged greed and caused widespread poverty, misery and bloodshed in later centuries.

Patrick and the Holy Grail

The 'Peace of Arthur' eventually ended in Britannia with the arrival there *en masse* of the 'barbarian' Angles, Saxons and other tribes from northern Europe. These new tribes fought the Britons, conquered them, and set up kingdoms of their own. And they kept their gods despite the presence of the black-cross Catholics who, like worms in old wood, never went entirely away, even during Arthur's time. They tried, of course, to Christianize the tribes, but failed. Dimly aware of the power of the new Godman, these tribes in fact only became fully or properly Christianized through the 'barbarian' Gaelic Church which by this time was radiating with irresistible force and magic power out from Hibernia in the west, but had its epicentre in ancient and sacred Avalliona in the north. (The little island was later to become known simply as Iona in memory of John: Ioannes is Latin for John.)

Rome however was not at all impressed with this success of the Gaelic Church! Far from it! For around the same time, especially with the rise of the Merovingians in Gaul, it was beginning in earnest to flex its imperial muscles and sense its great potential for temporal power. Fashioned on the Empire of old, it was utterly determined to create a truly universal Church, with one law, one doctrine and most importantly of all, one Emperor: the Pope of Rome. They wanted, in short, to create nothing less than a Holy Roman Empire, and they did eventually.

In the meantime however, the worst fears of old Germanus of Auxerre were coming true! For in the 6th century the Gaelic Church was proving a virtually irresistible spiritual force and actually became a distinct and very viable threat to all that Catholic Rome stood for. The Gaels had in fact after the time of Patrick spawned a veritable host of Christ-Initiates - saints, scholars and martyrs, all cosmically inspired by their angelic masters and mad to spread the 'good news' of Jesus far and wide. With Hibernia itself fully Christianized, these saints and scholars formed themselves into astrological groups of twelve and set out from their Culdee communities in all possible directions. They were driven by just one powerful thought: to bring the true, holy and magic spirit of their Master Jesus to all who cared to listen. Little armies of them took to the high seas in tiny coracles and they preached wherever they landed, not only to the Picts of Caledonia, to the Angles, Saxons and Jutes in Britannia, but also to the corrupt and murderous Merovingian 'Christians' of Gaul. Some of them even got as far as Russia.

The Roman Catholic Church both feared and hated this alternative Church! They could never fathom its free, inward and essentially esoteric nature. Anyway, was it not all inspired by Pelagius? And had he not long ago been condemned a heretic at a legitimately convened Catholic Council? And if he was a heretic, then surely his Church was heretical too! And as for the Holy Grail, all that was nothing but a cartload of superstitious Hibernian bull!

It all had to be stopped, and soon! For time was running out. Islam was a fast-growing force in the East. Never was there a greater need for Rome to be united and strong.

At the tail-end of the 6th century a dynamic Pope made a very decisive move. He dispatched from Rome a high-powered delegation to Britannia led by a bishop with a name guaranteed to make the Pelagians take notice: Augustine. This Augustine was charged to bring all the far western savages into doctrinal line once and for all! The Anglo-Saxons however resisted them again as they had before. They much preferred their by now well established Gaelic brand of Christianity, and they wanted to keep it.

But Rome never gave up! Slowly but surely, via the Merovingians, it wormed its way into the Anglo-Saxon courts. Then in the middle of the 7th century the die was finally cast. Rome convened a great Council in Northumbrian Whitby where the heretical nature of the Gaelic Church was to be once and for all established and written into the ever-swelling Codes and Canons of Roman Catholic Law.

Although the free, peace-loving Gaelic Church remained a force in Christianity for a long time afterwards, this Council of Whitby actually sounded its death knell. But the conspiratorial background of the Council's staging, and what its consequences were for the future of Western civilization is another story.

environmentally friendly book printed and bound in England by www.printondemand-worldwide.com

ok is made of chain-of-custody materials; FSC materials for the cover and PEFC materials for the text pag